ROUGHNECKS

The character William Zachary Harper first appeared in the book *Bermuda Shorts* by James J. Patterson.

ROUGHNECKS

James J. Patterson
and
Quinn O'Connell, Jr.

Alan Squire Publishing
Bethesda, Maryland

Roughnecks is published by Alan Squire Publishing, an imprint of the Santa Fe Writers Project.

Library of Congress Cataloging-in-Publication Data

Patterson, James J.
  Roughnecks / James J. Patterson and Quinn O'Connell, Jr. — First edition.
     pages cm
  ISBN 978-0-9848329-6-5 (paperback)
  1. Oil industry workers—Fiction. 2. Self-realization—Fiction. 3. Oil well drilling—Fiction. I. O'Connell, Jr., Quinn. II. Title.
  PS3616.A8773
  [R68 2014]
  813'.6—dc23
                    2014007779

ISBN: 978-0-9848329-6-5

Jacket design by Randy Stanard, Dewitt Designs, www.dewittdesigns.com.

Cover photograph by Patty Hankins.

Illustrations by Jack Brougham.

Copy editing and interior design by Nita Congress and Steve Caporaletti.

Printing consultation by Steven Waxman.

Printed by RR Donnelley.

First Edition
Ordo Vagorum

For Jon Husted and Ron Kidd

The people of the earth, the family of man,
wanted to put up something proud to look at,
a tower from the flat land of earth,
on up through the ceiling into the top of the sky.

      — Carl Sandburg, *The People, Yes*

When a man wants to lose himself, he loses himself,
that's all there is to it...

      — Clare Morgan, *A Book for All and None*

You get to know men, not by looking at them, but by
having been one of them.

      — Theodore Roosevelt, *Ranch Life and the Hunting Trail*

CONTENTS

THE WILLISTON BASIN
1979

PRELUDE

IT WAS NIGHT TOWER ON Bomac 34, The Widowmaker. Rain crashed down through the black Montana sky. It crashed down through the blazing lights on the tower in dizzying waves that hammered the floor of the rig and made that iron sing out in a monotonous harmonic blast. Added to the constant high-pitched scream of the big twin diesel engines, it became an earsplitting roar. And the rain crashed down on the men who were trippin' 'er out.

In spite of the rain, that driller had the engines in high-high and like human cogs in a machine, the boys were just gettin' it! He eased up on the brake handle and the next joint leapt up from the center of the floor. After thirty feet of pipe had gone straight up, there passed another joint and another thirty feet. Then came another. The fourth joint surfaced and glided to a stop just outside the mouth of the hole. Instantly the worm, the motorman, and the chainhand were there with the slips and had them in place a bare fraction of a second after the pipe had come to a halt. They knew their jobs and they knew how to ration the tremendous energies required to make it through the night. And they were looking hard into seven more hours before the tower was over.

The worm and the chainhand grabbed their tongs and swung them into place. The chainhand's back was to the driller as he faced the worm with the pipe standing between them, chain tongs taking the bottom male, worm tongs taking the top female joint, and that chainhand yelled into the booming night, "Take a bite!" as the two men slammed their monstrous tongs against hard iron making them latch and grip firm. They owed it to themselves not to miss a trick so each checked the other's latch facing him. No sooner than that the driller hit the cathead, sucking in the worm tong's chain, and suddenly, four thousand pounds of torque broke the joint like the stubborn lid on a jar of peanut butter. The chainhand removed the tongs from the bottom joint, leaving the top ones on to steady the pipe. The driller kicked in the rotary table, turning the joint in the hole to the left, and the two sections separated. Swiftly, the chainhand removed the worm tongs as the driller eased up on the brake handle raising that pipe a mere three inches, and it was free, dangling in the derrick, fearsome and unpredictable, ninety feet tall, weighing fifteen hundred pounds. The chainhand then pushed the awesome stand away from his body, out over the rotary table where the motorman's cautious arm could corral it, and in those precious seconds when he would have leverage, manhandle it further toward its appropriate resting place. The driller slowly let it down as the motorman guided it, sliding down his shoulder and thigh, cradling it into position, until the clang on the derrick floor signaled it had hit home.

Up in the crow's nest, ninety feet above the floor of the rig, one hundred and fifty feet above the earth, unsheltered from the pounding fury of the wind and the rain, the derrickhand stood face to face with the giant elevators that still held the pipe in the driller's control. When the pipe was set to rest on the floor, he looped his rope around the top of it, unlashed the elevators, and yanked the pipe into an upright position so that it nestled in the fingers at the top of the rack where pipe stood in columns ten and eleven strong. The elevators then made their swift descent and were received by the chainhand's upreaching arms. He pulled the backside toward him to prevent it from banging down on the top of the joint and steadied it so the motorman could grab it by the horns and guide it down past the pinhead. The chainhand pushed and the motorman pulled up and together they scissored it shut with a crash and a latch. They pulled away the slips and up shot another ninety feet of pipe.

This process was repeated again, and again, and again, as the night wore on and the rain came down. Another joint was broken. Mud, sediment, and chemicals spewed from the break into the motorman's face and he cursed violently. He stood back from the rotary table and coughed and spat and wiped his eyes. In a frozen moment, that driller, chainhand, and worm held their positions, waiting for the motorman to recover and regain his place. He threw a fierce malignant stare up through the lights on the tower, through a million silver needles raging. His flesh crawled under oozing muddy rags. A chill rippled through him, draining his energy like a shorted-out fuse drains a powerful battery, leaving him disgusted, pitiful, and sick with malice. Voices broke in, "Let's go! Let's go! Let's go!" then washed away. He was standing there invisible and alone, and everywhere he looked he saw cold pitiless iron. It loomed above him. The rain stank of it. It showed in the stares of his coworkers, who regarded him, he was certain, as nothing more than a human appendage of this same iron beast, just as he regarded them.

Before time resumed, before he took his first step, they knew. Their groans and curses and insults were just a distant nagging echo that he answered with his own vicious self-satisfied sneer. But his defiance was hollow. His final triumph reduced to a simple statement, a confession that only God and the universe could hear, and, luckily for him, neither cared. As he moved toward the stairs that led to the bottom doghouse, to an escape he told himself was liberation, he said, "Fuck this."

WHEN THEY WERE OUT OF the hole and had 'er on bank, the driller waved the derrickhand down from the diving board and signaled the worm and that chainhand to follow him into the top doghouse. He walked slowly over to a bucket, fished out a rag, and wiped some of the rain and the sweat and the mud from his face. He then opened the knowledge box, found a pack of Marlboros, lit up, then offered them around. The worm, a big heavy kid, took one gladly. The driller studied the worm as the worm's chubby fingers fumbled with the cigarette lighter. He had only been in the patch three weeks and probably wasn't going to make it. Time would tell.

"Jon," the driller said to his chainhand, "get downstairs and break out a new bit, a J-33. Dress 'er up and get 'er ready." The chainhand had only been waiting to be told. He stepped out into the deluge calmly as though it were a warm spring day. "Fifer," the driller's fierce hazel eyes refocused on the worm, "clean out that junk sub and hose down the floor." The worm looked sadly at his half-finished cigarette and tossed it away as he stepped outside. Then the driller stepped heavily toward the top doghouse door. He was going to find his motorman.

THE IRON DOOR TO THE bottom doghouse blew open as if shot by a cannon. The motorman came awake on the bench where he lay to see the driller stomping furiously toward him.

"What the hell's the matter with you!" the driller shouted and kicked the motorman off the bench, landing him in a slimy sprawl across the floor.

"I decided to sack 'em up. Head 'em back to town with the boys after tower," he said, pulling himself to his feet in an attempt to face the driller man to man. The driller would have none of it.

"Like hell you will!" he thundered, and the two men gripped each other and slammed into the lockers. "You're not sleepin' down here while the rest of us pull a round trip, you lazy shit! You sack 'em up and head 'em back to town now!" From location it was ten miles of dirt and another ten miles of gravel just to the main highway. The motorman had no car.

The young motorman struggled to free his fists, but the driller had the better of him and drove him hard into the lockers two more times. "Now you listen here, you son of a bitch. If you can't get 'er, you can't stay! You're run offa this location, son. So pack up yer gear and get the fuck on down the road!"

As the driller relaxed his grip, the motorman took advantage and sent a fist toward his face, but the blow glanced harmlessly off his cheek, over his ear, and into thin air behind his head. At this, the driller responded with unexpected ferocity. He bashed his hard hat down into the young man's face, slicing the soft soggy skin of his cheek, nose, and forehead while pinning his neck and shoulder to the wall. Faster still, he delivered six or seven lightning strikes to his tender solar plexus before grabbing him by the shoulders and heaving him bodily across the narrow room, where he landed in a crumpled heap on the floor, gasping for air and smearing blood.

The driller picked up his hard hat and waited a moment to see if there was any fight left in his motorman before issuing his final verdict. "You sack 'em up now! And you head 'em out now!"

THE FULMINATING ROAR OF A late summer storm and the black night still loomed over the Williston Basin like a defiant warrior's shroud. But the sparks of the many Sioux council fires had long been extinguished. The buffalo wallows that held the rain could not be found. The white man's iron horse that had thundered across the open palm of the Great Spirit had also faded and was gone. Another had taken its place. They were after the rich black blood of the sacred earth. Had just pulled fifty-eight hundred feet of pipe and were preparing to run 'er back in. The driller stepped back onto the floor and moved directly to his station. The worm, the derrickhand, and the chainhand looked at the old man with concern and then eyed each other, the mud on their faces unable to conceal the knowing looks that every roughneck understands. And the rain, and the night, and the tower continued.

Always be aware. Look out for danger at every turn. Don't lean up against anything and don't touch anything. Keep your ears tuned for strange noises and remember, it's better to run than to wait around to see what's happening.

Rickety outdoor steps had led Zachary Harper to his cousin O'Mally's apartment atop a two-story wood frame building that was badly in need of a paint job. They listened to music, drank some whiskey, and talked about drilling for oil. On that dark last night in Grand Forks, North Dakota, O'Mally's advice had seemed cryptic to Harper's inexperienced mind, like some ancient creed for survival in the unknown, and yet Zachary Harper had left still grasping for the tools needed to prevent unexpected circumstances from finding him unready.

Look out!

HIS COUSIN'S VOICE BROUGHT ZACHARY Harper awake all at once. Immediately his stomach began to churn and boil as he realized where he was and why. His joints were stiff and sore. He had slept under his Jeep, hazarding the elements for the luxury of stretching his legs, and now found himself wedged between the sodden earth and the grimy underneath, and Jesus, it had rained.

Zachary Harper rolled slowly out from under his Jeep and stood up, squinting across the wide multicolored landscape of the Theodore Roosevelt National Park. Erosion had overtaken the deposition of this strange land between one and four million years ago. What the Indians had come to call *mako sica* had been translated in reverse by the French to *mauvais terres*, what people now called Badlands. He did a hundred sit-ups and fifty push-ups, not only to get the blood flowing and free his muscles but to quell the anxiety and fear that nagged his every waking moment—*Am I strong enough?*

He made two peanut butter and jelly sandwiches from a loaf of bread and family-sized jars that he kept within reach in the back of his outfit with his gear. He watched as the ascendant early morning sun went to work on the moist terrain around him, and he slugged down a long drought of mineral water from a plastic jug. He smoked a cigarette and cleared his head.

The name was Brewster Blackwell. It was all he had to go on.

Zachary Harper wheeled his dirt-brown, dirt-covered, black rag-top CJ7 left out onto Highway 85 and pushed in a tape, "Old man take a look at my life/I'm a lot like you," he sang at the top of his lungs. It was ten a.m. when he down-shifted into Watford City, North Dakota, unaware this had been an oil town since the mid-fifties, that the first production well ever drilled in this region was just northeast of town. There were a lot of other things he didn't know. He didn't know where he was going to find a job, but the forty dollars in crumpled reserve notes tucked into his Levi's pocket told him it better be soon.

About half a block past the Sagebrush Bar on Main Street, he parked the Jeep and checked himself in the rearview mirror. He flattened down his heavy mustache with the palm of his hand, adjusted his wire rim glasses, and pulled his yellow baseball cap down tightly over his brow. In the crown of the hat was a black patch with yellow lettering: "Trans-Alaska Pipeline Project." At twenty-seven years old, he was already half gray, but fully aware that simply looking older didn't necessarily make one look more experienced.

The Sagebrush was crowded. Not unusual for ten in the morning. Some looked up to see the stranger enter, but most did not. He walked down the lane behind the backs of the men sitting at the bar, his expression blank, matter-of-fact, and avoided eye contact with those sitting in the booths that lined the opposite wall. He found an unoccupied stool at the end of the bar. Spending any portion of his remaining funds on liquor was a major sacrifice, but that was the way it had to be if he was going to find work, and he ordered up a draft. He smoked. On a shelf above the bar resting on a shot glass was an old baseball covered with faded autographs and next to that four trophies. Tacked to the wall nearby was an old faded piece of paper with tiny ballpoint lettering only a sober man could read, "We reserve the right to refuse service to anyone at any time." The man seated next to him was drinking whiskey and staring straight ahead. Sometimes the man's eyes would follow the barkeep as he shuffled back and forth behind the bar.

When Zak was about halfway through his beer, he got the barkeep's attention and asked, "Do you know where I can find a man named Brewster Blackwell? I hear he may need a hand."

"Yeah. Generally, he's either here or at the City Bar. Or you could find him at home. You just head south a few blocks on Main here, take a right at that Badlands Exxon, and at the end of the second block there on the right you'll see a pink house. That's Brewster's. If you pass a drive-in ice cream stand, you've gone too far."

BREWSTER BLACKWELL OPENED THE DOOR after the first knock. The whites of his eyes were murky and brown behind dark brown iris disks. His mostly gray hair was tousled and his face looked haggard under a two-day growth. Zak could smell whiskey on him. Over the man's shoulder and through the door he could see a bottle of Lord Calvert and a coffee cup sitting on the kitchen table. Brewster Blackwell gave Zachary Harper a curious look up and down.

"I'm a cousin of Calico O'Mally's," Zachary introduced himself. "I understand you and he worked together up on the North Slopes."

"Oh sure," Blackwell said thoughtfully. He stepped outside and pulled the door closed behind him. Zak could hear the sound of dishes and female voices coming from inside. "Calico was a good hand. Threw chain. What'd he ever do with all that money he was savin', start a whorehouse?" Brewster smiled, revealing a row of broken, discolored teeth.

"No, no," Harper laughed, "he's gone back to school. Taking business."

"Shit," Brewster leaned slightly to the left and spat, "well whaddeya know." He took the offered cigarette and broke off the filter before lighting up. "He was a sharp one. Wild as a hare though. Tell'm that when he gets tired of all them books he can come back to the patch and throw chain for me anytime."

Zachary Harper took a pull on his cigarette, looked off into the distance, and came to the point. "He said that you might be able to point me in the right direction to findin' a job out here. I'd sure appreciate your help. I'm pretty broke."

"Hmm," Blackwell took slow steps toward Zak's Jeep, making note of the South Dakota plates as he looked it over. "You're new in the patch, where from?"

"A little town called Wall down in South Dakota. Been farmin' the last few years, decided to try something else."

"Wall," Brewster rubbed his chin, then threw a sly glance back toward the house as though thinking of something else, "that's where they have that big drugstore, ain't it?"

"Wall Drug, yeah, I worked there when I was a kid."

"Uh huh," Blackwell was still preoccupied. "Bought a flying jackalope there, used to keep it in the doghouse. Look," he shifted gears, "let's take your outfit." He trotted over to the Jeep and yanked open the door.

"Um, don't you want to tell your people where you're headin'?" Zak asked as he hurried to catch up.

"Shit," Blackwell grunted happily as they settled inside. Zak noticed the quizzical look Blackwell gave him as he buckled up.

"I've actually fallen out of this thing on a sharp curve," Zak said in self-defense. "Landed real hard on my ass."

"Let's go."

Zak fired 'er up and backed out onto the street while the man filled him in. "I'm lettin' my girlfriend and her three daughters stay with me for a while. Hell. I've slept with all but the youngest. Three of them have kids of their own. They've got enough to keep 'em busy without concentratin' on where I am all the time." Brewster looked around the Jeep as he spoke. At his feet was a paper bag full of cassette tapes. In the back, the bench seat had been removed, and in the three-and-a-half-foot square hollow that remained were a sleeping bag, a pillow, a high-intensity battery-powered lamp, a copy of *The People's Almanac*, a cardboard box filled with foodstuffs, and a water jug. Pressed against the back of the Jeep was a duffel bag; on top of that, a laundry bag filled with dirty laundry. Brewster looked at Zachary Harper, "You livin' in this thing?"

They drove to the Sagebrush, found seats at the bar, and Blackwell introduced Zak to Andrew, the barkeep. He was an older fella, slightly bent at the shoulders, wearing a dirty plaid cotton shirt, dungarees, and work boots. They drank hot toddies.

A couple more bucks. Everyone seemed to know "Blackie," and as they chatted Zachary didn't feel quite as strange as he had a short while ago. Halfway through his drink, Blackwell began to come around. He had twisted off the night before and had been on a drunk ever since. He didn't seem too concerned about anything, except that he needed a lift back out to location so he could pick up his gear. His outfit was down but not to worry. Sooner or later someone from the crew would be in and they'd give him a ride. When Harper offered, Blackwell turned him down but after they had gone around it a couple of times they bought a six-pack for the trip.

It was one of those clear blustery afternoons in the northland, and they rode with the window flaps down. They drove south on 85, and the highway was filled with oil patch traffic. Every car and pickup was carrying crews of roughnecks to or from location. There were water haulers and fuel haulers. Gin trucks. Getter boys. Here and there were the green and white, eighteen-wheeled Black Hills Trucking flatbeds; rigs on the move.

Brewster Blackwell liked to talk freely about his days in the oil fields, and he and Zak chatted continuously during the forty-mile drive down to Westburn 54. Brewster had started out, years ago, racing mule teams, at one time even owned one, and a prize-winner too. He became a roughneck in the 1950s and had broken out in the Dakotas. Had moved on to Montana, Wyoming, had worked offshore in Texas and the Alaskan slopes. He was fifty-four years old and looked at least ten years older than that.

Eventually they passed Fairfield by about four miles where they turned west into some rugged terrain. Zachary Harper followed the tire tracks and deep grooves that rig traffic had carved around blind corners and tall stone walls, trying eagerly to anticipate potential oncoming traffic. Blackie held onto the roll bar above his head as they bumped and swayed and rocked over pit holes and rubble rock, when all of a sudden the tall iron tower of that Westburn rig loomed up out of nowhere from behind a short butte in the near distance. The tower stretched a hundred and fifty feet into the air like some yawning dinosaur, unconcerned about this little flea buzzing circuitously toward it, as though it had been caught in the act, indeed, turning ever downward toward conjunction with the slick byproduct of life on earth, that had lain fermenting for millions of years, thousands of feet below this very spot.

Zachary Harper had seen rigs before on his way West, but this would be the first time he had ever stepped foot on location and all his senses were alert and tinged with anticipation. He followed Brewster up into the top doghouse, and that toolpusher was there with his daylights crew. The atmosphere was tense, as the boys had had to pull a double when Brewster and his crew failed to show, and Zak just stood around not wishing to engage anyone while Brewster emptied his locker and collected his gear. At last, the toolpusher broke the silence.

"I guess yer not drillin' for us anymore, eh Blackie?"

"Nope. Decided to twist off."

"You workin'?"

"Nope."

And that was that.

BACK IN THE JEEP, BLACKIE fussed while popping the last of the beers. A weight had obviously lifted from his shoulders.

"I was just having a bitch of a time putting together a crew that was worth a shit on that rig. No goddamned experience. My car's on its last fuckin' legs anyway. Turn here, we'll head east to Killdeer for a drink. Y' know Zak? That cousin of yours would sometimes have some of that marijuana he'd roll up and we'd have a smoke. Got'ny?" Zak was only mildly astonished at the request, but he broke out a reefer just the same, and after their drink in Killdeer they headed north and then west back to Watford City.

Blackie went home to sleep, and Zachary Harper went to the City Park where he lay out on the grass for a little shut-eye under the huge sky.

THAT EVENING ZAK WENT TO the Sagebrush where he found Blackie getting loaded for the third time that day. They chatted for a bit until Blackie pointed out two women who were sitting at the far end of the bar. The big one was Blackie's girlfriend Alicia. All two hundred pounds of her. The other was an Indian friend of hers named Minnehaha, but her friends called her Minnie. This was on account of her high squeaky voice and the way her ears stuck out from her slick black hair. Minnie was fortyish but it was impossible to guess her age because of the huge black and purple shiner over her left eye and the seven or eight stitches that tracked across her nose. At five feet tall, she weighed in at a respectable hundred and forty pounds, most of which was in her round protruding belly. To Zak's chagrin, she immediately picked up on his unsalted presence and didn't take her eyes off him as Blackie called them over, made introductions, and not soon enough to suit Zak, gave the invisible signal for them to retreat back to their end of the bar. This all made Zak uneasy as hell which wasn't lost on Blackie, who was by now pleasantly high and ready to start a little mischief.

"Well, whaddeya know?" Blackie drawled in some sort of long-lost dialect. His arms were folded over his belly and his eyes were gleaming like he'd just caught the local pastor climbing into the sack with the mayor's wife. "Minnie seems to have taken a real shine to you, son," he smiled at the look of incredulity spreading like a brushfire across Zachary Harper's face. "Now just a second, Zak, don't be so quick to judge. I've had 'er and she ain't that bad. Now donchoo worry, kiddo, ol' Blackie'll set you up," and he clapped a heavy, brotherly palm on Zak's shoulder as he hoisted himself off his stool and took a step toward the other end of the bar.

"Blackie, Jesus, hold up!" Zak pleaded in a strained whisper. "Christ Almighty! Look, I don't have time for foolin' around. I'm practically broke. I've been sleeping outside for weeks. I've got to find a driller who'll give me some work or I'm sunk! Now don't get me wrong, but you're supposed to be my buddy, supposed to be helpin' me find a job. Jesus H. Blackie, you're not doin' me any favors settin' me up with the likes of that!"

Blackie's eyebrows shot up and a strange smile came over his face as he eased back down onto his stool. "What's wrong kid? Don't you think she's purdy?"

Zak heaved a sigh of relief and took a long drink of scotch. "You were serious, weren't ya? You were about to go over there and get me in serious trouble."

Brewster Blackwell rubbed his salt-and-pepper chin and peered strangely into Zachary Harper's deep blue eyes. "I might or might not've gone over there. But you'd a got yerself into trouble, besides," he brightened and held two fingers up for the barkeep, "look down there, she likes you."

Zak stole a furtive glance down the bar and sure enough, Minnie was staring back, no left front tooth.

"Good God, Blackie, what happened to that poor woman's face?"

"Well, since you asked, that little squaw is married to one of the biggest bucks around. He came in here the other night and smacked her around but good."

"What for?"

"Cheatin'."

BLACKIE WAS ONE OF THE last great storytellers and the subject inevitably came back again and again to roughneckin'. He talked about his years in Alaska as a heavy equipment operator and a driller. "I shit you not, it would take sixty or seventy big airplanes, *big* airplanes, loaded right up, to move in just one rig and all the paraphernalia needed to drill a hole. We were goin' down sixteen, maybe eighteen thousand feet on some ob'm. The company provided room and board up there of course. Not like out here where it's every man for his goddamn self." Blackie chortled and shook his head as he took another drink. For an instant he peered into a deep and textured distance before returning to focus on the admiring and inquisitive gaze of Zachary Harper.

"Alaska was a good time for me," he went on, "twelve hours on, twelve hours off. Six weeks on, two off. For days off I'd head on down to Anchorage and hit all the bars and whorehouses. Two weeks of that and I was ready to head 'em back to work. I swear, hard work's the only thing's kept me alive all these years." With his earnings he had bought a bar down in New Town, North Dakota. "I bought it because it was the only bar I had ever been thrown out of. I'm just sentimental I guess. Anyway, before my divorce, my wife would run it for me. I gave it all to her when I left. The bar. My Alaska savings. Shit Zak, I ain't no fuckin' bartender, I'm a roughneck."

You wouldn't think Blackie's coarse and battered hands capable of anything gentle until you saw him pick up a shot of whiskey and his eyes flash refulgently with happy fire. The West had known such men very well. But to hear Blackie tell it, that was back before the last of the cowboys had been chained and shackled and covered over indefinitely by heavy industry, unions, and orthodox corporate uniformity. As Blackie ambled on, Zak shuddered to think of the choices he had been making in his own life and wondered if he would ever be so reconciled with his decisions and their consequences.

"Take this bunch here," Blackie jerked a thumb at the other end of the bar. "Before I came along, Alicia and her people just had nowhere to go. No work. No place to stay. They'd been goin' into the Teddy Roosevelt Hotel and just stayin' with anyone who'd take 'em in for the night. Eventually got run right out of town.

Now that's a fine somethin' for three mothers and their babes, eh? Where they gonna go in country like this?"

Zak grinned.

"That's right," Blackie laughed, "my place." He polished off his whiskey and ordered another round. Blackie insisted that Zak put his money away, and Zak was again reminded of his own jobless predicament and, in a brief flash of melancholy, wondered where does anyone go in country like this, but Blackie's voice brought him around quickly. As the night wore on and the liquor took over, Blackie unstacked the years; years that had left their marks around his eyes and carved a wry and pensive smile across his mouth. The effort in and of itself was revivifying and carried them away to strange, cold, dangerous locales.

"It was somewhere in Wyoming. A night tower in the middle of winter. We'd been turning to the right all night and it was just snowin' to beat hell. At quittin' time there was no sign of relief. We'd have to double. The bit only had about twelve hours on 'er so we just kept turnin' to the right all mornin' and jeez, that snow just kept fallin' like a bitch. Eight hours later there was still no relief. We started taking turns sleeping, still turnin' to the right. After twenty-four hours, we were so cold and hungry I decided to just pick the bit off bottom and circulate to maintain the hole. That toolpusher and the company hand each had plenty of heat and a large supply of frozen food and canned goods, but with an entire crew stuck out there it didn't last long. By the end of that first week we were out of everything and gettin' pretty scared; didn't know which we'd do first, freeze to death or starve. Then one mornin' we had just about given up when we heard a noise outside and saw this big ol' cow fightin' its way through the snow toward the rig. By God, we dug out one of the pickup trucks, got a gun, milked, shot, and butchered that son of a bitch right then and there! Best damn steak any of us had ever tasted. It was two and half weeks we were stranded out there before help actually arrived. Shit, we coulda held out two weeks more! They brought with 'em emergency life support, the whole damn bit, sure as hell we'd all be dead, or close to it. When they got there we was all playin' baseball in the top doghouse with a crumpled-up pop can and a crowbar. I swear, when they pulled up ol' driller Purvis was standin' on the catwalk lookin' down on'm as they piled out of their outfits and he hollers down to'm, says, 'Didja bring any beer?' Goddamn," Blackie laughed and wheezed and coughed cigarette smoke. "Never did find out who owned that cow. We talked about buyin' whoever it was a new one but nobody ever got around to it."

That night Zachary Harper unrolled his sleeping bag on the grassy lawn of the Watford City Park. Before he fell asleep he lay on his back and wondered how long he could hold out. He peered into the brilliant distance of the Milky Way and, before dozing off, enjoyed the thought that its light had traveled thirty thousand years to illuminate his slumbers.

AT TEN THE NEXT MORNING he was back at the Sagebrush. Blackie was there already and the place was jumpin'. Roughnecks, Indians, cowboys, farmers, welders, truck drivers, and the like were coming and going. Many seemed to know old Blackie. When they said hello they'd give Zak a nod, not knowing if he was a seasoned hand or just a worm; they don't ask too many questions about a man. To the ones Blackie thought worth asking he would say, "Look, if you're shorthanded, Zak here is a good friend of a fella I worked with up in Alaska. He's never worked on the rigs before but I know he'd make you a good hand," but there was nothing.

It was late in the afternoon when Zak returned to the Sagebrush. He had spent the intervening hours at the City Park, exercising and reading from *The People's Almanac*. Now, even more than a job, he was in search of a bath. He had been sleeping outdoors and working out for God knows how long and was becoming uncomfortable to say the least. Andrew suggested the Sather Dam.

"Pass Blackie's on the road to Williston there, oh, I'd say about fifteen miles, and there'll be a sign pointing south. Another two miles and there'll be these two giant golf balls sittin' on tees on the side of a big ol' hill. There's yer dam."

Zak pulled a discreet distance off the highway and parked close to the water's edge. Sure enough, two giant golf ball–like objects ten stories high sat in the middle of a hillside. Microwave receivers? Satellite antennas? Nuclear missile trackers? Later, back in town, he would make small talk by asking what in the world they were. Nobody had ever given them a minute's thought.

He rummaged through his gear for a fresh JCPenney long johns top, Levi's, and a bar of soap. After a quick look in all directions, he stripped and tiptoed across the mudbank to the water. Though it was a warm sunny blue day, the wind rolled unimpeded across the low-lying hills and buffeted him with short crisp gusts that sent ripples across the water's surface and raised goosebumps across his flesh. The water was thick and muddy close to the shore, so he walked out till it was near his knees, tossed a bar of Ivory out into the lake, then dived in and swam hard after it out to the clear, cold, blue center. The shock gave him a pleasing jolt of adrenaline and he shouted each time he came up for air. He dove down deep to where the water turned really dark and really cold. He splashed and tumbled about like a slippery young otter. Then for a while he lingered, his toes reaching downward, feet pedaling, arms swirling, snorting like a platypus, his nose and eyes above the water, taking in the deep cobalt blue of the reflected sky, the green hills, the brown and gray jutting cliffs, feeling the cold water swirl about his naked body. He would hold his breath and sink down, completely immersed, weightless, letting his entire body go limp, numb, then float to the surface and lay on his back and watch the clouds. The soap drifted away

and he chased after it. The tension in his limbs and back lifted from him. For the first time in weeks, he relaxed and didn't think.

A shudder through his bones told him when it was time to get out, and he chucked the soap back onto shore and swam back through the mud, laughing and shivering as he wiped the mud off with his dirty clothes before getting dressed. The stink was gone at last and that alone made him feel fresh and crisp like a brand-new one-hundred-dollar bill.

He tossed his open sleeping bag across the hood of the Jeep and made himself a comfortable perch from which to watch the sunset. He lit a reefer. His mind wandered. He thought about his little corner of the earth turning away from the sun. The sudden prismatic refraction of diurnal sunlight altered the colors around him, making the water a richer, colder blue, making the mineral hues of the craggy rock cliffs across the way more radiant. The green on the hillside changed from a grass color to a more royal shade. So did his mood respond with a plunging and soaring sense of renewed excitement. He had crossed the fabled Mississippi twice on his journey West. Deer, Minnesota, had barely passed out of sight in his rearview mirror when he came upon the frail and unassuming first turnings of the mighty river. He had stood upon the bank and thrown a handful of soil over his left shoulder swearing, "I'll never be an easterner again," and continued on.

He had been riding all day since then with the doors stashed behind the tire rack at the back of the Jeep. He had tied a red kerchief around his head and taken off his shirt. "Ha-ha!" he laughed loud. He was gone! Deep country! Outta there! "Oooh hoo! Mmmhmmm! Heyhee-ah, hiyee-ah!" he sang in an off-key hoot. He could suddenly see her pretty face, up close, smell the feral and unmeasured richness of her skin, her breath, as she leaned in for a kiss. These colors that emboldened the scene about him were her colors too, her skin, her hair, her eyes. She had interrupted his long ride between his old life and the one he now sought. Standing in the middle of the road wearing a hard hat with a great red flag in her hand as the giant Caterpillars swung and ambled to and fro behind her, she had welcomed him to the new world. What kind of terrible Eden lay beyond he had no idea.

She smiled as she waved him through.

A mile or so down the road he pulled over, studied his map, then doubled back along different roads. She spoke into a walkie-talkie and dropped her flag as he approached. She smiled accusingly as she strode toward him and asked, "Are you lost, mister?"

"Completely. Want to get lost together?"

"No." Her face and the small patch of tummy that showed under the knot in her workshirt were covered in road grime. A thick leather belt rode her hips over her pants which bunched up at the shins where big muddy workboots were laced only halfway. "But I'll probably be at Canyon's later for a beer."

He raced to the next town and asked around about a place called Canyon's, got cleaned up at the local hotel, and was on his second beer when she appeared over his shoulder as he played pinball. She wore a man's dress shirt over a navy-colored leotard, fresh jeans, and motorcycle boots. She took the machine next to his and played hard. They started out talking about road construction but she soon changed the subject.

"The guys who run the bar are friends of mine, so I can feel free to come in here and let my hair down." To make her point, she pulled the clip at the back of her head and in two or three shakes her hair fell in a breathtaking crimson splash that tumbled over one shoulder and then down in all directions, turning to face him as she did so and finishing off the gesture with her most dazzling look. He simply hadn't realized that she was so pretty. She knew it, and her little surprise delighted her. He stopped playing and just let his ball go through.

They sat at a table in the middle of the room as the bar filled with people. She was studying anthropology. She loved working outside. She loved all the talk and she especially loved the crazy antics of the men she had been working with on the construction crew all summer. Yes, a few were in love with her. Of course, some had to be beaten off with a stick, who, by the way, were as appetizing as frogs in a bowl of milk. Yes, there had been one or two who had attracted her attention over the course of those months. And there was a guy from school who came looking for her and was just appalled at what he had found her doing. Understand though, he is young and doesn't know. As a matter of fact, since taking a few semesters' worth of courses she was learning to see her world with a kind of detachment. She didn't need to travel halfway around the globe to study human behavior or sociological conditions and all that makes us human. She could get a pretty good start with the terrain right around here. Not that she didn't want to travel. She wanted to go everywhere.

She kept Zak wildly entertained. Whereas some people use the word "can't" in every other sentence, or the word "hate" when referring to the countless things that conspire to ruin their day, the word that most liberally flowed from her thin country lips was "love." She loved this and she loved that, and what she didn't love she was just crazy about! Her perspective was as intoxicating as the whiskeys they had switched to when they sat down. Zak could tell also that she loved inventing herself for his amusement.

Zachary Harper didn't realize that his eagerness to listen had charm as well. She appreciated the many crude things he didn't do or say. She accepted the fact that he was traveling West to get a job on an oil rig. She didn't pry or challenge or insist he play the same games with her that she played with him. She had decided to make it easy for him.

Sometime after dark, she finished her drink and, laying both palms down on the table, said, "Look, I'm parked out back. Why don't you let me take you for a ride around town and you can check out the sights?"

"Sounds terrific, what are you drivin'?"

She flared, instantly detesting the idea that he thought what she was driving should matter. He stopped to think. Of course, it stood to reason that if her passions were so easily incited in one direction, they could as easily be unleashed in the other.

"Just curious," he smiled, "you know, guys like cars."

"It's a beautiful old Cadillac," she said with matronly pride. "You can sit in the back."

"Do I have to sit in the back?"

"You do if you want the best view. Wait out by the front door and I'll pick you up."

A moment later he was standing in the doorway of the bar staring up and down the empty street. All was dark and quiet. So quiet he could hear the breeze coming from far across the field opposite. So dark that the two streetlamps at either end of the block only made a small dome of light that was surrounded on all sides but one with pitch darkness. He put his hands in his pockets and took a deep satisfying breath. How completely cool. He didn't even know where the hell he was and he didn't care. *Life is good*, he thought. He listened for the low rumblin' purr of that old Cadillac engine to break the silence. After a few nervous moments out from the alley someone on a bicycle glided around the corner making only the sound of slender rubber tires on the grainy cement road. She skidded to a stop right at his feet, her cheeks rosy and her breath coming hard.

"Well?" she said, her eyes gleaming.

"Well, got me."

"You ride on the seat."

He sat as she pedaled standing up with his hands on her hips. She had been right about the view, her perfectly round derriere bobbed up and down right in front of his nose. To be polite, he leaned far to the right and left but there was no escaping it. Beautiful! She pedaled like a demon and his legs stuck out with the heels of his boots just an inch from the ground. They rode through small-town streets, past the IGA and the Woolworth's, past the gloomy old bank that stood at the center of town, through the quiet neighborhoods where all streets led to the main road and the Legion Hall, and beyond that to the railroad terminal at the outskirts of town. They bumped hard over the tracks to where naked kernels of corn lay in huge piles, three stories high. His legs were wobbly as he stood on firm ground.

"Where are we?" he asked.

She let the bike fall carelessly when she stood down.

"Home," she answered and turned her head in the wind until her hair whipped his face. She stood there waiting, staring at him defiantly until he caught on. When he moved forward to kiss her, she met him halfway and kissed him hard and long. Her mouth was wet and her skin was cold. Her thin lips gripped his, forcing open his jaw. The taste of whiskey was soon exhausted and replaced with the sweet overpowering aroma of her breathing. A second later she pulled away and dashed up the nearest mountain of corn.

As he scrambled over the top after her, she grabbed him and pulled him into the depression she had made. The lights atop the grain elevators cast moonlight blue shadows. Clothes came off. A jacket under her ass. A shirt behind her head. Feet dug in.

"The farmers say that sometimes the corn opens up and swallows a person whole. That there's no way to dig them out before they suffocate," she breathed, bit into his ear, and gripped him hard with her strong, wet cunt. Their pelvises locked. A dewy estrual film coated them. Filled his mouth and nostrils. She led him and turned him this way and that. She took control, then abdicated, then surrendered completely, to see what he had learned, only to incite new rebellions that caught him off guard and helpless. They fought as they fucked. She taught him how to fuck her proper, knowing that, being a man, he would not know how otherwise. When she came, she bit into his neck. She cried and she screamed and clawed his buttocks and back as her orgasm wracked her strong young body and sent tremors all through his limbs. When he came he left her and rose up on his knees and finished into the air, into the night.

"I love that," she said quietly and pulled him back to her. They exhausted themselves and the night that held them. At dawn they made love.

That morning she watched from her kitchen window as he staggered down the side of the corn mountain and dusted off his clothes, scattering handfuls of kernels. He scratched his head. He looked around. She allowed him a moment of bewilderment before hollering and waving from her back porch.

Later, over coffee, he gazed out the window and laughed out loud.

"What's so funny?" she wanted to know.

"Oh nothin', I was just wondering where that pile of corn is going to end up. The Soviet Union, Africa, Asia."

"More'n likely in the belly of some hog or cow. Or that Jeep of yours."

He was staring out the window at that huge pile of precious manna. His face then darkened and he asked, "What if I had climbed down the other side? You wouldn't have seen me." A hard little corn pellet fell from his collar and landed with a plop in his coffee cup. He scooped it out with a spoon.

"That's nothing," she said, ignoring his question, "you should have seen where I found some of those this morning."

She studied his face. Her hair was not lustrous or bouncy as it had been the night before but weighted down and darkened with human oils and ultra-fine corn powder. It framed her face in shadow, hiding it from the sunlight.

"I have a bad feeling about you."

"What do you mean?"

"It's a bad feeling because I believe you are a good man. That I've somehow come upon you in the act of becoming lost. I don't believe there are very many good men left in the world. I have a sense that I may be the last person to ever know you. That would be a shame."

They sat in silence.

"I have to leave for Morris today," she said as she handed him a bowl of melon squares. "School starts next week and I'm already a day or two late in getting out of here. But before you go I have a little present for you. Wait here."

She left the room, was gone for some minutes, and while Zak was waiting he took a look around. The kitchen cutlery was stacked in a box, ready for her departure. Through a doorway there was a small living room. Beyond that he could see into the bedroom. The bed was stripped and the bed clothes were piled in a heap. There was laundry ready to go and a couple of suitcases standing by. In the center of the living room stood a pile of things packed and ready. A stereo, a box of books, a beanbag chair, and a curious wooden box about knee high with a pleasant feminine face crudely carved in the lid. He lifted the lid and inside was another box. He lifted it. No. It was a small table. Under the table was a large brass chalice and beside it a long pointed knife in its sheath. Cloths of different sizes and textures were folded neatly, and resting upon these there was a wooden bowl with a lid. The bowl was filled with small rocks, and on top of these were small bundles of aromatic leaves, herbs. A large leather-bound book and a large stack of letters in their opened envelopes were tucked neatly inside as well. The name of the addressee was Jackie something. He suddenly got the notion that he was violating a very private space and felt a little ashamed.

Just then, she called out from the bathroom for him to bring his breakfast in and join her. She had drawn a hot bath and lit several candles around the small bathroom. He sat on the closed toilet seat and fed her melon pieces as he watched her bathe her perfect body by candlelight. He remembered thinking that the tips of her breasts looked like plump wrinkled apricots. The water darkened her long auburn hair and her brilliant green eyes shimmered as he sat there in silence breathing the steamy air, listening to the water and watching it run rivers and streams over valleys and through crevices.

"Would you like to whack off?" she asked invitingly.

He thought about it, smiled, and shook his head no.

She handed him the sponge.

"When I'm an old man and have forgotten everything else," he laughed, "I'll remember this."

"I think so," she said.

THE STARS EMERGED FROM THE deepening blue sky over the Sather Dam one at a time, then in clusters. He lit a cigarette. He imagined her going through long registration lines, hustling from building to building, attempting to reason with condescending administrators. Somehow he thought she would look ludicrous and out of place in a dormitory, like a tree in a flower pot.

He suddenly felt stupid and sad. Remembering her he realized she hadn't been at all forthcoming about who she was or where she was from or what her plans were other than her very general impressions of things and her current circumstances. Fine. She had taken the encounter for what it was and that was clearly the way he was supposed to take it as well. He was a big boy, he could do that. However, the proximity of his thoughts of her made him suddenly very lonesome.

They had something in common though. Perhaps that she was older than her years. Something about what she chose to reveal to him of herself. Something about him accepting that, whatever it was. More stars made themselves visible at the top of the sky. Somewhere out there, right this minute, she was probably getting the old gang together. He tried to imagine her with other people her age. How she might act, talk, the things she would say. He tried to imagine college boys trying to solve the riddle of her sensuality. How she would have to hide herself and masquerade to just be understood by them superficially. Still, it wasn't difficult to imagine her getting excited about—pizza.

Zachary Harper laughed out loud and tossed his cigarette away. He could still laugh, thank God. Days, weeks, months ago he would have "fallen" in love with her. Allowed that misperception of desire, lust, and ego to tangle into an unrealistic obsession to pursue and "possess" her. But now he was capable of possessing nothing. Those ambitions had evaporated. In another era they might have gone on from there to build their lives together, using their differences to keep their relationship new. In another life she might have been content with that. In this life they were both looking for something very different, though neither could say just exactly what that was. He held her gently in his memory, his arms instinctfully reaching around him to each opposite shoulder, and she soothed his frightened and insecure thoughts.

It was getting cold.

Zak did a few exercises, then drove back to town, stopping at the Badlands Exxon for a shave in the men's room before heading on to the Sagebrush. Nothing was happening. Rather than spend a precious dollar, he made it back to the monument grounds, which were deserted and virtually his, did a few more exercises and slept hard.

IN THE MORNING HE HIT the Sagebrush and the City Bar. He was developing a keener eye in selecting which fellas to approach for work and which to avoid. The final outcome was in the hands of fate, or the gods, or whatever, and this morning, rather than waste away in the bars, he decided to go back out to Teddy's Park where he had found a source of inner peace and strength, where he could at least relax. On a bluff overlooking the Missouri River thousands of feet below, he found an old lookout shelter made entirely of stone by men employed by Franklin Roosevelt's National Recovery Act. He climbed up onto one wall, legs dangling, and ate a peanut butter and jelly sandwich. As he sat there, he lifted his arms and closed his eyes and released his senses to the currents of air and energy that flowed through the great chasm of rock and greenery that reached for miles down and back again. He could taste grass, and water, and trees, and then an unfamiliar stink. He opened his eyes. A thrilling bolt of energy shot through him. His nose moved with the breezes that brushed past his face, and then he found it again.

Buffalo.

Nothing else could smell like that, except maybe an elephant. He looked all around expecting to see one nearby; nothing. He grabbed his stuff and walked back up the hill to the Jeep, keeping his eyes, ears, and nose on the alert. Across the road the grassy prairie stretched on out of sight, yet he could see no sign of anything. But the smell was strong.

Just then a three-quarter-ton Ford four-wheel with a camper on the back came winding through the park kicking up dust. *Unusual for anyone to come out this far*, Zak thought. As it got closer, Zak could see three men sitting in the cab. One he recognized as Blackie but the other two were strangers. When they pulled up, Blackie introduced the driver as Vic Earlman, a buddy who had worked with O'Mally and him. Vic was a big man but the other fella, Danny Waller, was huge. As Danny climbed into the back to make room for Zak up front, Zak asked about the buffalo.

"They're all over the park here, it's a preserve, and yeah, you can smell'm for miles, that is unless Danny's nearby. Hey wasn't Purvis tryin' to raise beefalo once upon a time?"

"Yeah," Vic picked up where Blackie left off, "'cept those damn things're meaner'n shit. I remember one got mad at him and charged through his fence like it wasn't there. Barbed wire was snappin', posts were flyin', they're supposed to be better for ya than regular beef but I doubt anybody could raise'm. They can get it in their head that they want the grass that's over yonder and they're on their way."

Blackie handed Zak a beer.

Vic thought he had a lead on a Westburn rig down around the south entrance of the park that might need hands but there was a catch.

"The boys down on that Westburn rig are either gonna be happy as hell to see us or some kinda pissed off," Vic thought out loud.

"How so?" Blackie asked.

"Well, I'm not sure if they've been pullin' a lot of doubles or if there's a madman on that brake handle the toolpusher's tryin' to run off."

"An entire crew driftin' is a bit unusual, but not unheard of," Blackie gave Zak a quick translation. "But if he wants to run that crew off, well, this'll be that toolpusher's lucky day."

Danny meanwhile had pushed open the sliding glass panel between front and back and was leaning into the cab listening. He was a North Dakota farm boy who occasionally dropped down into the patch to earn some extra cash and raise some hell. He was ready. He jammed his hard hat down onto his head and roared, "Get it! Get it! Get it!" The other three just grinned and shook their heads.

When Zak and the boys arrived at Westburn 54, Vic drove directly up to that toolpusher's shack. Vic knocked once and entered, leaving the rest standing in the doorway, and said, "I'm Vic Earlman, I can drill, and I've got a crew here ready to go to work right now if you need us."

It turned out that the pusher could have used a couple of fellas but that wasn't the deal Vic was looking for, so he thanked him very much and they headed back for the bars in Watford. "False alarm," Vic muttered as he climbed back into the cab. Zak figured that if Vic or Blackie had thought it wise they would have offered his services, but they didn't, so he kept quiet.

After a few drinks, Vic gave Zak a ride back out to the Theodore Roosevelt National Park. He felt sure Zak would land a job in a day or two. One way or another. Vic was a dark-haired sensible-looking quiet type cut from that increasingly rare North Dakota stock blessed with a liberal dose of common sense and decent humanity backed by the force of his convictions. The type of man who wins the respect of his fellows first, their admiration then coming quite naturally. Another farm boy turned rough-neck just a shade older than he looked and he looked about thirty-seven. He was still in his prime. Experienced enough to know all the ropes but not weather-beaten like Blackie. Young enough to still have some high hopes for the future but not lost or bewil-dered like Danny seemed to be.

"We might work together, Zak, we might not," Vic said. "The thing you've got to do is find yourself an experienced driller. You don't want to just go workin' for anybody. Especially when you're breakin' out. You're liable to get hurt. You see, there's an awful lot of fellas out there with no experience, and a lot more who just plain don't belong. It's not like the old days when my daddy was in the patch, for example. Or when Blackie started out, for that matter. Back then a roughneckin' job was hard to come by. Just about the only thing in this part of the country that paid worth a shit. Today there's a hundred and fifty rigs here in the Williston Basin, maybe more, and they'll hire just about anybody as long as they can get a decent day's work out of'm. So you'll find a whole lot of fellas out there nowadays with an 'I don't give a shit' atti-tude toward their fellow crew members. I'll tell you, Zak, you can lose an arm, a leg, or get your ass killed that way. Happens every day. More often than you might think. There's a lot of tricks to this business, and though nobody's gonna babysit you, you can still find someone who'll teach you what they've learned along the way."

WHEN VIC DROPPED HIM OFF, Zak climbed into his outfit and made a couple more sandwiches. His conversation with Vic had been reassuring but had left him with a sharp tinge of dread. "Without experience," and "don't belong," kept bouncing off the walls of his brain and he thought long on the two categories. As the sun went down, he concluded that he wasn't there to take advantage, that if conscientiousness was going to be a factor he would certainly be able to make the grade. But the questions remained. They rose to the surface of his thoughts and all other considerations paled in comparison, his unease returning to lift him entirely into a state of suspended animation. Perhaps it was at the park where he was able to deal with them most directly, in privacy, where he could drop all pretensions and ask himself honestly, *Am I strong enough? Am I ready?*

II

ndrew's counterpart at the City Bar was Eileen. She had an indifferent smile for strangers and for her regulars she had knowing eyes that sparkled as if seeking the jest in every potential encounter. A lot of shenanigans had passed for sport there at the City Bar during her reign of humor, though she understood as well as anyone that the deadly serious aspects of life in the patch must be dealt with straight on. She was in her late twenties, a big heavy woman by anyone's standards, but carried the extra weight with a light, airborne charm and performed her job with alacrity and dispatch. Half the older men in town were in love with her. "A sweet lady," they said behind her back. Her brother Terry was a roustabout down in Texas. On those special days when a postcard would arrive from Big Lake or Orzona, she would keep it close by and show it to each and every roughneck regular who dropped in. During those periods when Terry was out of touch, they would ask about him with concern. When things at the City Bar were slow she would bury her nose in a gothic romance, and when they weren't she would immerse herself in one of the many little dramas that unfolded there at the bar, four days a week, seven a.m. till three o'clock in the afternoon. If ever she could help in some small way she would.

This morning she was all smiles. For once, Sid had stocked the coolers before closing, so she didn't have that little catfight to look forward to when he came in, hopefully on time, that afternoon. She hummed a tune, improvising a melody as she glided down the bar picking up bits of debris—cigarette wrappers, a crumpled napkin, an ashtray to be emptied. This morning, part of making sure that her store was in order meant keeping an eye open for Zachary Harper.

Neither Blackie nor Vic had been at the Sagebrush that morning. When Zak entered the City Bar, his face fell. They weren't there either. Nevertheless, he had a good word for Eileen who waited for him to reach for his coffee before tossing in a shot of rye. "Don't worry, this one's on me." Her eyes were twinkling, her shoulders danced, and her huge rippling bosom came to rest for just a second as she leaned over the bar toward him. "There was a fella in here last night and he was shorthanded," she said excitedly, and her eyes grew wider still as Zak snapped to attention. It was a hot tip and they both knew it. Her look of caution and her walls-have-ears glances to the right and left brought him back to earth quickly. She picked up his coffee cup and beckoned him to follow her to the pay phone at the end of the bar where one could sit at the last stool and place a call. With a wink she reached between her breasts, making a grand gesture, thumb and forefinger pinched together, fat little pinky extended, and handed him a waitress check with a name and number. She flipped him a quarter. He dialed the number. No answer. "Jesse's been in the business for many a year. They say he's a hell of a driller. He's got to show up somewhere sometime 'cause he's home on days off." She refilled Zak's cup with coffee while she talked and paced behind the bar like a nervous stage mom. Eventually she counseled that he take a walk up to the Sagebrush and "keep tryin' that number!"

The Sagebrush was as dead as it had been earlier, and Andrew was glad for a little company. He grabbed a handful of nuts and tipped an ounce or two into a clean glass.

"So, you know Jesse Lancaster too?"

"No, I've never met him, but I hear he's shorthanded." Zak wondered if it was wise to be spreading it around that a driller had work but he couldn't contain himself and figured what the hell, he wanted to know something about the man.

"He's one of Eileen's regulars, but he's in here now and then. He's been around long enough, I can tell you that much. If I'm not mistaken he goes back to the old days down in Gillette."

They talked for a while longer, but Zak was anxious to get back to a phone and anyway, there was little Andrew could add. Zak left the Sagebrush and tried the phone at the City Park. Nothing. He had found a driller who was shorthanded and, what's more, there were two reliable sources saying he was experienced: Zak's only prerequisite. As he hung up the phone, Zak began to fear that the man would hire someone else before he could find him. He spent a frustrating day roaming between the City Bar and the Sagebrush and a restless night on the floor of the City Park.

First stop next morning was the Sagebrush, and Blackie was already half tight. Once aware of Zak's mission they set off in sleuthlike fashion for the City Bar. There at a table by himself in the back of the bar was Jesse Lancaster. Stone drunk. He was not at all what Zak had imagined. He was small, with a dark complexion and a growling, sinister, menacing scowl upon his face. His left cheek was bruised and swollen. When the two men sat down, he barely acknowledged them. He was fading in and out, one minute all business, the next distant and mechanical. When

Blackie mentioned that they had heard he was shorthanded, he came around a bit and belted down another shot of whiskey. They slowly got it out of him that he had been on a drunk for two days and it was obvious that he was drinking to kill pain, not time, so they were careful with their words.

Astonishingly, the man put things back in focus. He was heading back out to location the following day and he had to find a hand by then. He asked Zak if he had any experience and Zak was right up front and said no. He then asked Zak what he had been doing up until now and Zak replied that he was from South Dakota and had been working on a farm all his life. He also wanted to know how Zak and Blackie came to know one another. The fact that Blackie had worked with Zak's cousin was important to him. At last there was a moment of silence and uncertainty and Zak, groping to state his case, said simply, "All I can really promise you is that I won't cause you any trouble. I've got a real strong back. I'm willing to give you a hundred and fifty percent and I need the money in a real bad way."

Jesse Lancaster turned his full attention on Zachary Harper. He studied Zak with cold, blank eyes, examined him like he was checking out a piece of equipment he might be in need of. He looked at Zak's hands, his shoulders, his boots. And for a long uncomfortable moment, he looked Zachary Harper in the eye. He then returned to that strange distance he had been staring into when the men sat down. At last, he leaned forward on his elbows and took another hit of whiskey.

"I'll break you out," he said. "You'll be breaking out on Bomac 34. It's good iron. No major steps. The pumps are fair. It's one hundred and fifty miles west of here in Montana outside of a small town called Scobey. Fourteen miles south of the Saskatchewan border. It's a son of a bitch to get back into. When you get to Scobey you drive down Main Street, pass the grain elevators on the left, over the railroad tracks, take your first left.

Head out maybe five miles till you come to four buttes. They'll be on your right. When you hit those four buttes take a left. That'll be gravel road. Now there'll be some points where the road will curve around and split, but don't get confused. Just stay on that main part of the road for a good twenty miles. You'll come up over this hill and there in the distance you'll see the rig. It's a hundred and fifty feet of iron standing straight up and staring you in the face. We're workin' evening towers now so be there by three p.m. If you need a ride I'll be headin' out in the mornin'. I've got a small camper on location that I'm willin' to share until you get fixed."

Zak was slowly going into shock. He had finally done it. In a little over twenty-four hours, he was going to be standing on the floor of an oil rig, ready or not, to go to work, and this drunken, brooding character was going to be in charge. He wanted to leave that day while Lancaster's sketchy directions were still fresh in his mind. If there were going to be any problems, he wanted time to think his way out of them. He didn't say yes or no to the offer of hospitality, but thanked him sincerely for the job and promised not to let him down. Blackie stopped to chat with Eileen as they were leaving and, while they visited, Zak noticed that Jesse, all alone at the back of the bar, had drained his glass and was just staring vacantly.

The bone in the brown paper bag Eileen had given Blackie was for Duke, Blackie's dog. Duke lived in the backyard at Blackie's house, fastened to the earth by a chain that weighed the poor creature down so that his head hovered off the ground at about a third his natural height. Zak loosened the chain, then unhooked it altogether. As it clanged to the ground, Duke stuck out his tongue in a happy pant.

"Sure, go ahead," Blackie laughed, "he ain't goin' nowhere."

Inside the house they had one last drink together. The bottle of Lord Calvert was nearly empty. A fresh one waited on the kitchen counter. Blackie estimated it would be a week or more before he'd feel like goin' drillin' again. When Zak turned to say goodbye, he was trembling. Blackie cut him short with a wave of his hand, "You'll be back." And momentarily stunned, it occurred to Zak that the possibility of returning had simply not occurred to him.

Outside, ol' Duke walked around to the side of the house and was sitting erect with his nose pointed into a gentle breeze that played with his big floppy ears. He took a keen interest in the passing stranger who paused briefly to pat him on the nose. Duke could smell the familiar odors of whiskey, sweat, and cigarettes but there was a new and intriguing aroma—peanut butter. Duke licked his chops. Zak climbed into his Jeep and fired 'er up. Carbon monoxide stung Duke's tender eyes and nose. His sensitive ears twitched at the loud whuw, whuw, whuw of the engine, and for some minutes after the Jeep had backed out of the driveway and disappeared from view, Duke continued to listen until the rumble of the Jeep slowly faded away.

ZAK DROVE OUT TO THE Theodore Roosevelt National Park for one last visit. He made lunch and watched the afternoon roll by, soaking up the last grains of energy this ancient place could give him. In one direction, the prairie stretched as far as the eye could see. In the other, the Little Missouri had carved an enormous chasm miles across that stretched into the far distances revealing the fragile nature of the terrain beneath the endless rolling grassland. The slump rock and rugged pillars of subcontinental collapse contained for him now an element of mockery. As the sun began to crest the horizon, he made ready to head west for Scobey, Montana, and Bomac 34.

Zak's Jeep thundered down the empty highway. Streams of tar, where the road had been patched, streaked diagonally across his path like thick black snakes. To his right and left, the landscape churned under wild brush that hugged the earth like buffalo fur. Sometimes the land would level a bit and for as far as the eye could see in the fading golden twilight, tall lush grass rippled like the ocean in long, undulant, luxurious waves.

At Williston, he turned west onto Highway 2, and the night came on fast and the wind picked up from the northwest blowing harder and harder across the treeless sloping plains. At Culberston he turned north again following the rolling and fractious Highway 16 into a wind now becoming fierce that beat against the canvas walls of the Jeep and drowned out everything but Zak's thoughts which were timorous and wandering. Instead of the veteran master hand, the confident and wise old campaigner, Jesse Lancaster had seemed seedy, broken, and decrepit. An angry shadow. Moribund, perditious, and used up.

Yet he came highly recommended by the folks back in Watford. On the other hand, they had never claimed he was any kind of hero or champion. Only that he had been at it for a long time. That had to count for something. Anyway. Turning down work at this stage of the game was simply out of the question.

Between Medicine Lake and Plentiwood the wind became ferocious; it heaved against the sides of the Jeep and ripped the canvas top partially away from its fastenings along the rim of the windshield, slashing Zak's face, cutting his ear, and knocking off his glasses. The Jeep swerved and bounded off the road. Zak bounced violently in his seat as he fought to regain control of the vehicle with one hand, holding the canvas away from his face with the other. He slowed to a stop, got out, and wrestled with the wind, scraping the knuckles on his right hand and tearing a hunk of flesh from the left, until the canvas was securely fastened to the windshield once again. Back in the Jeep he lingered for a few moments, long enough to smoke a cigarette and calm down. He dabbed his minor wounds with an old dirty T-shirt. He smoked another cigarette and waited long enough to watch the burning horizon cool and fade to blackness. And in a moment of fathomless grief, he realized that at this point in his journey, he couldn't turn back even if he wanted to. So he shoved on.

When he reached Plentiwood, he turned west once more onto Highway 5 and after passing Redwood and Flaxville finally peaked the eastern slope that overlooks Scobey, Montana. He rolled into town, coming to a stop at what looked like the town's only intersection at Highway 5 and Main Street. On his right was a hardware store. The sign said "Closed." Across from that and directly in front of him was a newspaper building. A drugstore stood on the far left corner and across the street from that was the Ponderosa Bar and Café.

"There's got to be a park in this town someplace," he thought aloud while looking to his right and left. He considered heading back down the highway to find some old dirt road to pull off of for the night but hesitated. He didn't want to wake up staring at a shotgun. He turned north up Main Street. As the loud low rumble of the Jeep bounced off the storefront facades and echoed down the concrete boulevard, he suddenly felt conspicuous in the extreme.

Scobey was a much different town from Watford City. There was more color. It was quieter. The sign at the edge of town had read "Population, 1280." Main Street was barely two blocks long. At the edge of town, past the grain elevators and the railroad tracks Lancaster had mentioned in his directions, he found the rodeo and fairgrounds.

The place looked deserted, but to make sure, Zak drove once around the dirt perimeter by the high white-washed wooden fence that surrounded the grassy field. Perfect for a fair, rodeo, cattle show, or demolition derby, at one end a broken-down back-stop, but no real baseball diamond. He decided to drive out to the center of the park and shut 'er down. Silence. When he hit the lights, total darkness swallowed him and carried him into its dizzying, weightless space. Tingling shards of fear pushed him from the Jeep and he staggered on the grass where he was greeted by a chill wind that wrapped him and pulled him another step deeper into the night. A storm was coming. He could feel the air turn warm with moisture. The wind was with him and through him. It blew through the bleachers at the far side of the park. It rolled over the wooden fence and gently rocked the abandoned hot dog stand whose warped awkward wooden frame thumped the hard ground with a dull dead sound.

He sat down on the grass. He stood up. He figured he'd do some exercises to occupy his body and so occupy his mind, but only caught himself pacing around in a confused little square. He groped his way to the top of the bleachers and sat down. He dug his fists deep into his jacket pockets. The wind tried to take his baseball cap, so he pulled it down tight. Over the far wall of the park, he could see a lone streetlamp throw a dim dirty yellow light against the broad gray shadowy walls of the grain elevators a block or so down Main Street.

"What the fuck am I doing here!" he shouted at the alien night. But the wind picked the words from his lips and scattered the sounds, mingling them with a blustering commotion that was confusing and surreal, and Zachary Harper was momentarily stunned at the insignificance of his complaint. Suddenly, every premise upon which he had based his actions over the previous few months seemed irrational and absurd. He doubted his ability to make simple judgments. How could he then trust himself to handle what was coming? Something very dangerous and very real. Strangers. Heavy machinery. Incomprehensible commands and impatient unpardonable necessity. He rocked back and forth. Electrical bolts of panic shot through him, lancing him keenly, randomly, in the groin, in the stomach, in the chest. He was hot. He was pouring sweat. He was shivering. The empty blackness made him dizzy. He was falling. He gripped the bench with all his might. He wasn't falling. His mouth hung open, and a long strand of drool ran from his lower lip and landed on his thigh making a dark, warm, oily circle on his jeans. His mind, abhorring the vacuum before his eyes and in his heart, filled the blank space before him with a vulgar display of faces and events; filled his ears with familiar yet receding voices; gouged his remaining senses with tastes and smells that were at once familiar and irretrievable. It was an obscene collage that taunted his self-confidence and made him feel small, helpless, stupid, wrong, and pitifully alone.

He groped and stumbled back down the bleachers, barking his shins and scraping his knuckles.

He walked stiffly across the grass to the entrance of the park. Up the street in a stark circle of light, a pay phone stood on a stem next to the streetlamp. He jogged up the road, his boots crunch crunch crunching the gravel and asphalt as he went, while digging frantically into his jeans for as much change as he could find. He jammed the coins through the slot. There was the familiar hiss of the long-distance connection.

A familiar ring.

A second wave of panic shot through him. His sweat turned cold and a nasty shuddering rattled up his spine. His breath rasped audibly in his chest. At the other end of the line, he could feel his old life, so far away a moment ago, drawing near. It had been withering, dangling, drifting away, but it was not yet out of reach. All he had to do was hang on and he could bring it back; it didn't have to disappear.

Or he could let it go.

The memory of that life and its attendant details threatened him with their familiarity. If he let go of that string, those details would soon change; circumstances would alter themselves to conform with the reality of his absence. The numbers—phone numbers, street numbers, numbers of people, numbers of dollars, numbers of friends, encounters, possibilities, built one upon the other—would simply fall out of significance or meaningful array. But something back there, something nameless, had been slowly and methodically devouring what he had come to identify within himself as his soul, he was sure of it now. It had not followed him here and it couldn't follow him here—uninvited.

No, that thing he had no name for was going to starve from inattention and neglect. Out here in the empty distance. In the Phantom Zone. And the closer it came to death, the more his own eyes opened. The more his eyes opened, the more he knew that to survive he had to move. Move and keep moving until he felt the beast release its hold on him once and for all, until he could feel another force, pull him somewhere else—pulling him here, where he could move toward a life of real and acceptable consequence. If he didn't find it, something or someone else would, and he would be returned to the service of the creature at the other end of this long string. He wouldn't get another chance. He would be enslaved.

He slammed the phone back down.

And as he exhaled, his muscles relaxed, and the night, for that one instant, grew calm and sweet.

The wind changed direction. A fat wet raindrop smacked his cheek and rolled down the canvas front of his down vest. He stood there staring at the phone for a long moment, as at a vanishing shore. The light bulb overhead snapped and buzzed. The night flooded into his awareness; the pebbles underfoot and the great black prairie beyond his physical reach were somehow joined. He wanted to rise up and spread out in all directions. He shook his head, retrieved his coins, and walked back to his Jeep.

By the time he reached it, the rain was falling straight down in a heavy shower. With the coming of the storm the wind had died out completely. He climbed into the back of the Jeep, took off his boots, replaced the vest with a dry, warm, hooded sweatshirt, and fished around for his flashlight. He propped himself up against the duffel bag and read from *The People's Almanac* to the dim light of his fading batteries. A while later he curled up and pulled the sleeping bag over him. It stormed all night, and as the rain hammered the canvas roof of the Jeep, his anxiety wrenched and twisted him through a tumultuous and unrequited sleep.

THE NEXT DAY, THE FIRST of September, was sunny, clear, and beautiful. The air had a delicious taste that teased the palette. Zak walked down Main Street and stopped in at a little café for a roll and some coffee. He had hoped to run into some other Bomac crew members, but it was no dice. There wasn't a roughneck in the joint. The place was a local hotspot all right, but it was crowded with ranchers, farmers, townfolk, and old-timers. There were old-fashioned wooden cabinets filled with fresh pies and cakes behind closed glass doors. A fly strip hung in a corner behind the counter. When Zak queried a heavyset man in bib overalls and a hat as to the possible whereabouts of that Bomac rig, the man had never even heard of it. If fact, neither he nor any of his buddies knew of any rigs in the area at all. Zak was baffled until he realized that Scobey didn't look like an oil town in any respect. He wondered if his was the first drilling site to setup in the area, if there would soon be many more to follow. He thought of the insane twenty-four-hour-a-day hustle and bustle of Watford City and wondered if this pleasant little community had any notion of the tempest that was poised to strike.

In the men's room mirror, he could see the scabbed-over scar from where the canvas ragtop had sliced his temple, the scabs on his knuckles too may have been the reason behind the funny looks he was getting from the patrons of the café. He cleaned it up, using a little antiseptic ointment from his shaving kit. Not only was he a stranger, but he looked like he'd been in a fight the night before.

There was time to spare before work so he decided to take a trial run out to the rig and back. Lancaster's directions were easy enough, and the four buttes where he was supposed to make his left actually had a little town named after them: Four Buttes. After a bumpy ten miles, the gravel road turned to dirt, a detail Lancaster had failed to mention, though bifurcated and puzzling it definitely was.

At last he came up over a hill and there in the distance stood Bomac 34.

"It's good iron."

The landscape all around was rugged, woolly, and strange. It was as though a giant had taken the earth by its edges and given it a tremendous shake. The oil rig stood on top of a hill that was no larger or smaller than the endless random field of hills that rose and fell like a massive still-life ocean. He was maybe three miles off, but the vantage point was a good one, so he shut down the

Jeep, rolled himself a reefer, and tried to still the butterflies in his stomach. He would get his chance to see it close up soon enough. For now he was content to just sit and listen to the mild metallic roar of the rig in operation. After a while he turned around and drove back to town, walked the streets, and had a cup of coffee in each of the three cafés that Scobey had to offer. At a quarter till two, he left for work. This time for real.

He arrived on location about half an hour early. None of his other crew members had arrived and, not knowing what was customary, he got out and leaned against the front of the Jeep, trying to discern the responsibilities of the men still on duty.

A line was coming off the tower with a chain attached pulling yet another cable. Zak could see a man in a clean shirt standing up on the platform apparently orchestrating things; from Blackie's description, he must be the toolpusher.

The other men must all be roughnecks.

Two men were standing on the ground having a devil of a time trying to spool out new cable from a giant roll. Zak's eyes traced the white painted girders upward until they came to rest upon a big man climbing quickly down out of the tower. He had a full black beard and bare muscular arms and was covered in grease from head to toe. The big man stopped for a minute to survey the scene below and when he saw Zak, he raised one fist in the air and let out a ferocious roar. He jumped the last few feet to the platform, bounced down a catwalk, and heaved himself down a steep flight of stairs that were next to a big metal ramp, then he ran to the aid of the men on the ground. All the way he was screaming and attacking his job like a maniac. Once he was down on the ground, things started to happen fast and it was clear that, crazy as he might seem, he was an essential piece of the puzzle. But what in hell were they really doing? Zak had absolutely no idea.

A Mercury Marquis pulled up, and Jesse Lancaster, another man, and a woman got out and walked directly to a small trailer

parked nearby. Next, a '76 blue Olds four-door pulled up and parked next to the Jeep. The newcomer remained inside, lit a cigarette, and waited. He was about twenty-four years old with Nordic features, a full beard, and blond hair that fell past his shoulders. He took no outward notice of Zak but sat there smoking, cool and serious, as he watched the goings-on.

Zak was standing there trying to discern which door on the rig would lead to the bottom doghouse where the lockers were kept, when Jesse and the other man emerged from the trailer and started walking toward the rig. Just then the fella in the Olds got out, opened his trunk, and fished out a duffel bag and hard hat. *This is it!* Zak thought, and hurried to collect his own gear from the back of the Jeep.

The men were solemn as they walked toward the rig. He was eager to get on with it. He wanted to shout to them that he was here and ready to go. Wanted to know all their names and assure them that a little patience on their part would be well rewarded in the form of hard work, loyalty, and whatever else was necessary. Jesse climbed the stairs to the top doghouse by himself. Zak followed the other two through a ground-level door where the men went to their lockers and began taking off their clothes. Zak moved to the back of the long narrow room and took a locker that was a bit removed from the others.

There in the doghouse there were no expensive suits, jewelry, or fancy pedigrees, sheepskins, or titles to interfere with one's assessment of a man, and though the others kept to themselves, Zak was acutely aware of being sized up on one level and one level only—how tough and how strong he was. The other two were all muscle. The man who had driven up with Jesse was short, stocky, and bow-legged with arms as big as tree trunks. He was completely covered with hair and looked like a small ape with a smooth quiet face, alert blue eyes, and straight unkempt reddish-brown hair that hung at random lengths past his ears and halfway to his shoulders. The Scandinavian was about a hundred and eighty-five pounds with hands like human vise-grips. The look on his face was pure cynicism. His pursed lips, pinched eyelids, and the short gusts of wind from his lungs as he pulled on his overalls told everyone in the room that he wasn't pleased. There was no conversation, but the way he avoided eye contact, the crisp opening and closing of his locker, and the all-business manner in which he went about his preparations said it all. As far as Zak was concerned, other than his own comparatively poor musculature, they knew he had very little to offer. He was a new hand and not only that, he was a worm. Also, he could tell that there was something else fueling the tension in the air, which made Zak even more self-conscious, uneasy, and sure he was the cause of it.

ZAK FOLLOWED THE OTHERS UP to the top doghouse. That toolpusher was there with Jesse and the driller from that daylights crew. Their conversation stopped when the three roughnecks entered and that daylights driller, a comical-looking Louis L'Amour type of character with a full brown bushy beard and wild blue eyes, gave them each a sardonic "Hello? How are you today?" that elicited only grunts in reply. Whatever their private little joke was, Zak didn't think it was too damned funny. He then spotted a door at the other end of the doghouse that could only lead to the floor of the rig, and he was suddenly possessed with an overpowering need to see it, study it, even if it was just for a few seconds, before it was time to go to work. As he stepped to the door, his ears caught a fragment of conversation over his shoulder.

"Can one of your boys pull a double?" he thought he heard the toolpusher say to that daylights driller.

"Oh hell, George, we can get 'er," Jesse broke in.

Zak stepped out onto the floor but was desperately trying to sort out what was going on back inside. Jesse was trying to reassure the toolpusher that they could do the job. Were they thinking of pulling him and making a member of the previous crew work another tower? Could he possibly have come this far with just five bucks left in his pocket to be turned away? He felt dizzy and sick. He stepped boldly back into the doghouse and when he got the chance he decided he'd argue his case.

"I don't know, George, we've pulled three doubles this week already, I kinda hate to ask," that other driller was saying in a low, serious voice.

"George," Jesse stayed cool, "it's not like we ain't never worked shorthanded before. We can get 'er. We'll start out slow and work up to speed. I don't see any problem." That toolpusher breathed a sigh and folded his hands over his chest and looked straight at Zak.

"Well, what about 'er mister, you ready?"

"Yes sir," Zak said as firmly as he could without showing disrespect. His voice echoed through the top doghouse. He heard the Scandinavian mutter something underneath his breath behind him and turned just in time to see his two crew members step out onto the floor together. As Zak followed them out, it slowly started to dawn on him that four roughnecks work on a crew and they were still short one man. The ominous look on that toolpusher's face took on a new meaning. Whatever task lay before them they would have to tackle it shorthanded with a worm breakin' out. No wonder everyone was so concerned. Right now it was clear that every man on that rig, except one, knew exactly what they were preparing to do. Suddenly Zak wished he could go down to that bottom doghouse himself and ask those daylights crew members if one of them wouldn't mind working an extra shift to help out. Instead, he took a deep breath and followed the others back outside.

As soon as his foot touched the iron platform, his eyes locked onto the center of the floor. There was a round turntable and, standing up through a hole in the center of it, was a pipe firmly in the grip of another very large and heavy-looking device with cables coming off it. These cables stretched up and up into the tower. As he stood there taking it all in, he noticed another device that looked like a giant horseshoe just hanging there suspended by cable from about forty feet above. The cable looped around a shiv and back down to a counterweight—a cylindrical container filled with rocks and debris running up and down on vertical tracks. On the opposite side of the hole several feet away was another horseshoe set up in the same manner. Virtually everything was made of iron.

The Small Ape and the Scandinavian were standing close by, and Zak's first inclination was to turn to one of them and say something like, "Hey, look, I'm a little worried, why don't you watch me through this one," but that was clearly not the thing to do, and he had no idea whether these guys were going to be allies, indifferent, or if they would enjoy watching him fall on his face. He had no idea what type of men they were. All he really had to go on was what he knew of driller Jesse, who, when he hired him, was as drunk as one man can possibly be.

For an awkward moment everyone waited. Up in the derrick that maniac derrickhand from the last crew was climbing down toward them. Every few feet he would stop, let go of the ladder with one hand, wave his free arm deliriously in the air, and scream something unintelligible. He was clearly having a lot of fun at the expense of Zak's crew. The boys on Jesse's crew failed to see the humor. When he reached the floor, he and the Small Ape had a friendly word before that Small Ape began his ninety-foot climb to his station in the sky. It was then that driller Jesse stepped out of the top doghouse.

"Go stand over there!" he shouted while pointing over Zak's shoulder to the opposite corner of the floor. "And one thing you don't ever do is step on that rotary table." The turntable in the center of the floor was directly between Zak and his newly appointed corner where he could see rows and rows of pipe standing three joints strong, reaching all the way up to the derrickhand's station. When Zak arrived at the desired spot, he noticed that Jesse had moved to a corner directly opposite where the driller control station was. Jesse held up his hand for Zak not to move, and the driller walked over to him and had to scream his instructions directly into Zak's ear to be heard over the massive idling engines located just behind Zak's head.

"In a few minutes we're going to be pulling this pipe out of the hole! These are your tongs," and he laid his palm for a second on one of the huge iron horseshoes. "You're going to be putting your tongs onto that top joint. That man there is going to be putting his onto that bottom joint. Once you put 'em on the pipe you push 'em back and make 'em bite. Now, when we've disconnected the pipe, you're going to push it back and rack it here," he then walked diagonally away to where the iron floor ended and a wooden floor began, where, in neat columns, stood the ninety-foot sections of pipe. He pointed with his foot to the exact spot where he wanted that next one to go.

Although Zak understood what the man had said, he still did not know how a person was supposed to negotiate ninety feet of iron and push it twenty feet. He had hoped for more of an explanation. Maybe get taken through the motions. But it was becoming clear that Jesse intended to watch and see how Zak handled it. Returning to Zak's side, Jesse pointed to a big iron V-shaped device that completely encircled the pipe in the hole. "Those things sitting in the hole," Jesse said, "are your slips. They hold the weight of the entire drill string when she isn't moving up or down, and you and Jon are going to be picking them up every time and putting them back."

As Jesse walked back to his station, Zak tested the feel of his tongs. Even though there was leverage, suspended as they were, they still must have weighed more than two hundred pounds and were going to require a massive effort to move, let alone manipu-late. Jesse was now standing at a long lever that was sticking up at forty-five degrees from the floor, and he rested his hand on it quite naturally as he watched the Small Ape finish his climb up the tower. Once in place, he waved down to Jesse who then gave the high sign that everything was ready. He looked at the Scandinavian, and he looked over at Zachary Harper, and a little grin appeared on his leathery old face.

Jesse switched on a couple of throttles, and an air condenser somewhere kicked in with a tremendous hiss. He pushed down on the long lever with his right hand, his right foot ready on a floor accelerator while his left hand grabbed a clutch that was jutting out from a control panel in front of him. Putting that clutch in low-low, he eased up on that brake handle while simul-taneously stepping down on the accelerator. The engines revved. Air pressure somewhere gave three short bursts and an enor-mous iron clamp, already attached to the pipe in the hole, began lifting it straight up. As this was happening, the Scandinavian, Zak saw, was struggling with the slip, and Zak realized he had already fucked up! He had just been told that before anything could happen those slips had to be moved! Rushing to the Scandinavian's aid, he grabbed onto a spare handle and together they yanked the slips up. They were heavy, a hundred pounds or more, and the third handle on the device suggested they might come to sorely miss that third crew member before very long.

The pipe shot out of the hole. One joint passed. Two joints passed. As the third joint glided by, the Scandinavian grabbed those slips again, and this time Zak was right with him, and after the next joint was through they set the slip around the pipe. It was no time for timidity. When the Scandinavian moved for his tongs, Zak mimicked his every move. They felt heavy and strange, though considering their bulk, not as awkward as they looked. Jon threw his against that bottom joint, and Zak threw his against the top with a clang. The latch on the back was plain to see and he pushed back hard, making them bite the pipe and hold firm. Just then, from alarmingly close by, Zak could hear the clanking sound of chain being coiled up and he looked down just in time to see a heavy chain about to tighten around his ankle. He jumped back. The chain led from his tongs to a huge drawworks that was slowly sucking it in, making it tighter and tighter. Winding, winding, it pulled itself off the floor until there was no slack left. Again the air sounds barked as the driller applied more pressure and the joint broke violently, moving the tongs a good four or five inches. Jon then removed his tongs and when Zak moved to take his, Jesse screamed "Leave those top ones bite!" As he spoke, the rotary table spun madly, turning the pipe in the hole to the left, thus unscrewing the two sections of pipe. Jesse picked up on that brake handle a bit and kicked in the motor ever so slightly, and the ninety-foot triple section lifted three inches. Zak looked over to Jesse for guidance as his other floorhand unlatched the worm tongs, and Jesse yelled again, "Push on that son of a bitch!" his motorman gave the dangling pipe a mighty shove and as it swung out past the rotary table, Zak scampered in behind it, placing his shoulder against it, and with all his strength kept it going toward the spot on the floor Jesse had marked with his boot. The top of the pipe remained at center derrick as he pushed against its natural tendency to swing back the other way. As the pipe neared its appointed spot it began to descend the two and a half feet to the floor and, at the last second, Jesse let 'er down with a bang, and Zak hopped instinctively out of the way. Up in the tower that Small Ape slipped a rope around the top of the pipe and released the elevators, transferring the stand from Jesse's control to his own, and yanked back on the rope until the pipe was upright again and clanged into line with the other stands that nestled between the fingers of the rack. Zak could see how easy it would be to have a finger, a hand, or a foot get in the way of this process, and for a disturbing moment he shuddered to himself and said aloud, "I can't believe this is how it's done!"

Going back to his station, Zak looked up in time to see the big red clamp that had been used to haul the pipe out of the hole descending swiftly from high up in the derrick. *Here's another part of the process that'll need doing every time,* he thought. Already he knew he must work the slips and the tongs, and rack the pipe, which was a bitch. Now he thought, "What am I supposed to do with this thing?" Motorman reached up with both arms and, as soon as the elevators were at his fingertips, he grasped the two horns that were toward him, and, as it continued its descent, directed it to the pinhead at the top of the pipe that was sitting in the hole. Zak then moved to his assistance, and together they slammed it into place with a scissoring motion below that six-and-a-half-inch pinhead around the four-and-a-half-inch pipe.

The whole procedure then began again. Zak and the Scandinavian, his only other floorhand, bent down to remove the slips. The motors revved. Up came the pipe. One, two, three. When the third joint had passed and the top of the fourth was out of the hole, they threw in their slips, grabbed their tongs, and banged them onto the pipe, top and bottom, and separated the ninety-foot stand from the rest of the drill string still nestled in the slips. Every step required a maximum physical effort. It was then that Zak began to get an inkling of how tough the work really was going to be. What he didn't know was how many times they were supposed to do this. Just pushing the pipe over to bank was about the most strenuous thing he had ever done. On top of that, no one had bothered to explain what it was they were trying to accomplish. What was the overall goal? It would have meant the world to him to hear someone say, "We're going to have to do this for fifteen minutes," or "We'll need to pull twenty of these things," but he wasn't about to ask any questions. There was no time and no one could hear a thing anyway. Besides, it was a time for action!

He concentrated hard on his duties, on going through the motions as quickly and efficiently as he could. He put out as much as he could each and every time. When he pulled up on that slip, he pulled his share and more. When he heard his motorman holler, "Take a bite!" he hit those tongs as hard as he could, figuring at this stage it was the only way he knew to survive, to earn his wages, and to gain the respect of his crew members. He was constantly surprised by the action and play of the pipe as he pushed it to bank. Each time it would fight that angle a little differently.

When the sixth or seventh joint was broken, gallons of warm mud and sediment spewed from the seam catching both Zak and his partner full in the face. The Scandinavian wasn't fazed in the least but Zak was so startled he jumped back. When the next joint was about to break, the Scandinavian picked up an iron rod from somewhere and tapped the pipe and said, "It's a wet one." Jesse then picked up a denim jacket that was lying on the floor and tossed it over, and the floorhand tied it around the connection. When the joint was broken, the mud came spewing out but not in their faces. Zak was incredulous. "What happens when they run out of denim jackets?" After about fifteen or twenty stands, that Scandinavian gave Zak a quizzical crazy kind of twisted smile when they bent to move the slips. What that smile meant was open to interpretation but Zak felt no hostility, and before long they were taking turns pushing those stands over to bank. Later, Zak realized that smile, and his floorhand's gesture, was Zak's first really encouraging moment in the patch.

On they went, one stand after another. For hours they continued this grueling process without a single break in the action. If anything, the more he got the hang of it, the faster things went. And things were to go faster still. Zak, who was secretly weary after the first few stands, was beginning to feel that driller Jesse was pushing too hard, maybe on purpose. The pace was frightening and though Zak tried to wear a bold face, he could not conceal his fear. As soon as those slips were off the pipe, those engines would roar and up would come the joints. They'd throw the slips right back in and leap for their tongs. By now, he was completely covered in mud from head to toe. The floor was slick with it, making the footing treacherous. At one point driller Jesse hit the drawworks, sucking in that chain, and the tongs, having been hastily applied, came whipping off at incredible speed, snapping their powerful jaws in front of Zak's face before they ricocheted off some iron and came flying back to smack him in the chest, knocking him hard to the floor. Luckily he was unhurt, but the experience scared him silly. He had very nearly had his face torn off; he could have been cut in half or crushed against iron.

He looked in horror over at Jesse as though that driller had been untrue to him. As if to say, "I've been giving you the best I have! How could you let something like this happen?!" The blank looks on the faces of the driller and motorman were inscrutable as they waited for Zak to haul himself up and resume his position. When he grabbed his tongs once more and hit the pipe he could see driller Jesse give him a nod then motion with a look and a gesture, and Zak knew to check the motorman's tong latch as the motorman checked Zak's, and the work went on. All the while Zak was thinking something like this should not be possible. This must be really out of the ordinary, a freak accident, highly unusual, but as he gathered his wits it slowly sunk in that it could happen at any time. He could see how, if the tongs were strung up in the derrick just a little bit crooked or if they were attached to the pipe improperly as he had done or if there was a faulty latch, just as any crooked wrench won't bite completely, one of these monsters could come loose and fly off. The thought was horrendous. He attacked his job with renewed concentration and remained on the alert for any other unforeseen hazards, his cousin O'Mally's words repeating themselves over and over in his mind like a mantra, "Always be aware."

SEVENTY STANDS LATER—THAT'S SIXTY-THREE hundred feet of pipe, at 16.6 pounds per foot, or four hundred ninety-eight pounds per joint, or approximately fifteen hundred pounds per stand, give or take a little mud, or one hundred and five thousand pounds of iron—Jesse brought the operation to a temporary halt. Zak dared not think that the job might be done. He didn't want to know how exhausted he was, afraid that if he relaxed for just a second it would be the end of him. The Scandinavian walked to another part of the floor and started tackling pipe twice as big as what they had been working with. Zak looked with wonder from him to the pipe that was sticking so innocently out of the hole and tried to imagine what could possibly be next.

"Zak!" Jesse barked. "Get over there, we've got to change those tong heads." Zak could see where Jesse was pointing, and when he reached the spot he stood there helplessly looking around and hoping that something would just jump out at him without killing him, but he still didn't understand and so Jesse instructed further. "Those new tong heads! Grab 'em!" Zak picked up two pieces of iron that were lying nearby and brought them over to his tongs, beginning to get the idea that these attachments were to fit the claw of the tong thus enlarging the grip. Meanwhile, the Scandinavian was maneuvering several more large iron attachments into place around the hole where they would be handy. Jesse came off the brake handle and helped Zak adjust both tongs to a larger bite. It was becoming increasingly clear that whatever they were about to do was going to be much more difficult, and Zak vowed to himself that he would at least go down trying. Even bigger slips were brought out. In a way, this had been kind of a break, a rest, but it didn't last long and soon Jesse was back at that brake handle. Once again pipe was coming out of the hole.

After the first joint was out, Zak could see what all the preparation had been for. The next two joints were twice the diameter and twice as heavy as the regular pipe. Unlike the regular pipe, however, this new stuff was straight, that is, untapered at the ends. Without the pinhead to work with, an extra iron collar or adaptor, four feet long with a six-and-a-half-inch pinhead, had to be screwed on tight, just atop the slip, to compensate. The supertongs were applied, and Jesse made the break using a lot more torque than usual. Off came the tongs in the usual sequence and it took both men, using all their might, to counteract the stand's natural pendulation and push it over to bank. Jesse watched their slow and painful progress waiting for a good spot to let 'er drop. It would have to lean against the derrick itself as there was no room left up in the fingers.

When the elevators came down again, Zak could see that there was nothing at the top of the pipe for them to grip, and Jon called out to him, "Hey! Help me with this collar sub." Together they picked up on one of the new attachments and placed it carefully on top of the pipe. "We gotta tighten 'er," Jon said, and the two men grabbed their tongs. "Put yours on bottom." Once it was tight they stood on their toes to catch the elevators by the horns and slammed it onto that collar sub. Jesse revved his engines, the boys removed the slips, and thirty, sixty, ninety feet of collars shot up out of the hole. They threw the slips back in and broke the joint with their tongs once more and then grunted and heaved to get the stand, more than twice as heavy as the usual stuff, over to bank.

Jesse wasn't letting it down fast enough, and it began to overpower them as they struggled to get it over to where the driller wanted it. When he realized that the men were having trouble, he intentionally set 'er down in the wrong spot and motioned to that derrickhand not to let 'er go. Jon looked anxiously over at Zak and warned between breaths, "Look out now. He's gonna pick up on 'er again and we're just gonna have to try and hold 'er and then ease 'er back to where we started. We don't want 'er to dance. If she does, someone's gonna get hammered." When Jesse picked up on it, the pressure was so intense the two men staggered. They eased it back to a perpendicular position and began the grueling process all over again. Five stands were placed, in more or less the same fashion, each one weighing four thousand pounds, leaning each against the derrick.

When at last the odd joint was out, there on the end was the drill bit. This was a grisly-looking device comprised of three circular cones all covered with big sharp iron teeth that fit together so the cones would roll against each other evenly. Amidst these cones were three ominous-looking nozzles dripping with mud. This thing looked like it could chew its way to China if needs be. As soon as that bit was through the floor, Jesse yelled, "Grab the cover!" and Jon nodded toward a big iron bucket which Zak hurried to pick up with both hands. He could see the impression of those bit cones in the bottom of it as he placed the bucket in the hole and that last stand, bit on bottom, was set down into this cover.

The next trick was to get the bit off the pipe. This was accomplished by placing the tongs on the pipe, or collar, to just hold it in place while the rotary table turned just enough to make the break. When they had the last few feet of pipe disassembled and the bit resting in the cover, Jesse ordered Zak down to that bottom doghouse to fetch an "F-3, it's a Smith bit." Zak found it among a half-dozen boxes piled neatly on the floor, and when Zak went to lift it he nearly stumbled and fell. It weighed one hundred twenty-five pounds at least. All his mind and body anguished in the sweet agony of exhaustion as he lugged it out the door and up the long narrow stairway to the drilling floor. Each step tormented his calves, thighs, hips, back, shoulders, and arms. He delivered the bit to the top doghouse where Jesse tore into it, inserting three nozzlelike devices into their appropriate slots. He then excused the men to get a bite to eat, but told them to hurry as he would need them again soon.

ZACHARY HARPER WALKED NUMBLY OUT of the top doghouse and down to his Jeep where he plopped himself down in the front seat. He was so exhausted and emotionally drained that for a few long moments all he could do was sit and stare blankly, in a state of torpor and lassitude, across the raw rolling landscape. It was nearly dark. He wasn't sure whether or not he had the energy to make a peanut butter and jelly sandwich and he wasn't looking forward to eating one anyway. It was all he had been living on for weeks. The idea of going back up there with an empty stomach, however, seemed suicidal.

With his pocket knife, he made two sandwiches. The sun was dropping rapidly from the sky, as though it too were weary. Even the scant vegetation all around seemed to be reaching westward in one last heliotropic spasm of farewell, and Zachary Harper wondered, becoming angry in his delirium, why no trees grew in this strange country, why the land seemed to roll and pitch in so dizzy a fashion. Why nothing stood in challenge to that ubiquitous sky. Nothing except the mean iron tower of Bomac 34.

He woofed absently at his food. His mind, like the countryside all around, was in a tectonic frenzy. Of all the information he had so erudiciously compiled over the years since college, nothing jived with these new sensations of fear, awareness, incredulity. He shook his head violently, much like a night driver shakes his head to fight off sleep, and took a long swig of water. The water ran through him and, for an instant, restored some of his withering sensibilities, cooled his burning insides. The sun disappeared and the lamps on the tower came on, gently highlighting the last remaining hint of bloodstone that the wounded star, his wounded star, had spilled upon this sighing, intractable land.

JESSE LANCASTER WALKED DOWN TO the bottom doghouse to collect his crew as Zak was finishing his second sandwich. He hopped from the Jeep and jogged over to the door arriving just as the other two roughnecks were leaving. Jesse had already given instructions as to what he wanted done next and rather than go through it all again with a worm who wouldn't understand a thing he was saying anyway, waved him off, saying, "Follow Marty and Jon, see if you can't give them a hand." As he trotted after them, Zak figured that was as close as he would get to an introduction.

Zak had yet to see the entire rig and, as he hurried to catch up, he observed a veritable lake of mud that formed a giant pool around behind the rig. The mud bore a strong resemblance to the muck that covered Jon and he from head to toe. When they reached the back of the rig, they stopped at the first of two iron shacks. From these shacks on the ground stretching up to the two big engines on the drilling platform were a pair of huge drive belts. In each shack was a giant pump and, like the engines up on the floor, one was in constant use while the other remained idling, ready if needed to serve as a backup. Zak didn't understand what part these pumps played in the operation but was at least glad to begin assembling the basic pieces of the puzzle.

Marty, the Small Ape, turned on the light and walked around the number one pump, which was screaming so loud it pierced the ears with its high-pitched wail. Jon and Marty didn't seem to notice. Marty took off his hard hat, scratched his greasy, sweaty head, and sized up the situation. He had been up in the derrick all day and so avoided the mudbath that Zak and Jon had been subjected to. Zak was not at all envious. At this stage of the game the thought of having to wrestle big iron all day while perched a hundred and fifty feet in the air was beyond him.

"Whatcher name," Marty hollered. He was all business. Zak stumbled for just a second before he realized what Marty was asking for.

"Zak!"

"Well, Zak, we're gonna need a sledgehammer an'a couple of tirty-six-inch pipe wrenches from up dere inna doghouse." Marty's eyes, set close to his sharp long nose, darted to and fro as he sorted out the situation. Marty's speaking voice, or more accurately, his shouting voice, was pitched an octave or two higher than his looks would suggest and he spoke with an accent that was foreign, no, alien enough to be of his own invention. His attention turned from Zak to the monstrous pump engine set screaming at his side.

"Okay, anything else?"

"Nope, just hurry back, dis's gonna take a while."

Zak ran up, retrieved these, and while returning he heard the number one pump shut down.

In the number one pump house, Marty and Jon had assembled an odd assortment of items. Among these was a four-by-four piece of lumber about three feet in length and a couple of close-ended nonadjustable wrenches made to fit the bolts on the pump cover. These iron bolts were four inches in diameter and big enough to weigh a couple of pounds on their own. Marty held the wrench while Jon pounded away with the sledgehammer, and one by one the bolts came off. When they had removed the first four or five, Zak, still trying to make a good impression on his first day, offered to spell one of the guys, and Jon stepped clear and gave him the hammer. He attacked the wrench with a ferocious volley of blows, wanting, more than anything else, to prove that he was okay, that he could get it. He didn't see the quizzical looks that Marty and Jon exchanged while he swung that hammer.

Another couple of hours grated away as the three men broke backs dismantling that pump. Inside the pump the big rubber swab at one end of the giant piston was hailed out and cracked. It was at the end of a polished steel rod that moved back and forth creating suction. They put the four-by-four between the sledgehammer and the rod and banged away, each taking turns when the other's arms and back were too weary to continue. Eventually the steel rod came free and they pulled it out. They brought their prize up to the drilling floor and they attacked that swab with sledgehammers and wrenches, but it wouldn't budge from the end of the rod. Zak was convinced they were making more work for themselves than was necessary and tried to be diplomatic.

"Isn't there some set procedure for getting these things changed?"

"Nope," they both answered back in unison. Marty turned to Jon and said, "We need an Indian trick," and Jesse was summoned from the doghouse.

He stepped out onto the floor smiling all the while and dealing out the shit, "What's wrong boys? Can't ya git 'er?" and commenced firing orders. "Get them iron rods from over there!" and "Drive them rods underneath!" then "Leverage that son of a bitch!" until finally, "C'mon Harper, you'd better be able to hit harder than that fer Christ's sake!" When they had hammered the new swab onto the end of the rod, the three roughnecks marched it back down to the shack.

"Dohn let ol' Jess scare ya," Marty offered obligingly on their way back to the pump house. Zak could hear him breathing through his long thin nose. "What he yoozly considers d'easy way is often harder dan what most people would consider unbearable." Jon and Marty peeled off a couple of stories of legendary proportions that Zak was only partially able to understand. The language of the patch was still new to him and Marty's peculiar dialect turned his ear sideways. He was thinking of the unbearable pace at which they had tripped out the pipe earlier that evening and how, with another hand and a bit of experience, they could have been pushed harder still.

Once the swab rod was back in place, they had to ram it back up the cylinder by using the four-by-four on one end and the sledgehammer on the other. From there it was back up to the platform to put things away and hose down the floor. Shortly thereafter relief arrived. The time was 11:15 p.m. The tower was over.

JON, MARTY, AND ZAK SILENTLY changed their clothes in the bottom doghouse. Zak was moving a bit slower than the other two, taking his time putting on his clothes on top of all that mud. *A shower on location wouldn't be a bad idea*, he thought. Marty was dressed in a flash and gone. Jon finished next and walked slowly out without saying a word. It was strange. They had worked side by side all day, with more intimacy, perhaps, than men who work in an office might achieve in twenty years, and not a word passed between them when it was over. Still, he liked the Scandinavian with the giant paws. He was gutsy and quiet. Not out to prove anything. To Zak, who had been on the verge of hysteria for some time, that was reassuring. Zak had yet to take the measure of the Small Ape, Marty, who was a little unnerving at first encounter with his peculiar posture and strange unearthly ways, but there was one thing about the man that Zak was sure of: there hadn't been a single complaint, from the floor up, all day.

When fully dressed, Zak sat on the bench there in the bottom doghouse and ruminated quietly for a few long minutes before pushing on. So many questions had been answered. More remained, but it occurred to him, as he sat there with his weary muscles hanging off his aching bones in much the same way as his clothes, reeking of diesel, mud, and sweat clung to his skin, that if the spirits were right, and if he was careful, he might really make it in the patch. This awareness sent a euphoric rush through his entire system, gave him the strength to stand up, close his locker, and move toward the door. He paused and looked around. After all, he had survived the first day, hadn't he? He laughed inside. Sure it was tough, and though it was difficult to imagine how, there was no doubt it could get a lot tougher. In all that exertion, with life and limb hanging in the balance, he had released energy that had been pent up inside him for years. Immured between layer upon layer of misconception and self-deceit. What he had heretofore regarded as his active life, he now saw as passive, acquiescent, compliant, stultifying, submissive, and lifeless. The interdependencies of the world from which he had so willfully ejected—all its relationships, its manufactured and self-inflicted anxieties, its trumped-up rewards, and its false conciliations—were no match for the look Jon had given him when Zak had checked the other man's tong latch, as a natural precaution, after his near miss, to prevent another fly-off. Jon had known, and that look informed Zak that they both knew he got it.

Back East they exacted something of him that only now was he dimly able to perceive. What was it? As of yet he couldn't say. But somewhere deep inside he had known, had felt the loss. And one day he just turned his back and walked away, from everything. Now, the experiences of the day had been like two drops of pure water on a truly desiccated system, causing a small echo, like radar, that reached out to trace the unknown perimeters of a void within himself. He could see that void now preparing itself to contain the pure and as yet unadulterated creature he was about to become. From this day forward, he would be a completely reconstructed creature. Now, for the first time, he had a real idea of the forces he would have to engage in order to give that creature sustenance, shape, definition, and purpose. His former self would become the empty hollow, a shell, then dust, then vapor. "They'll never take from me again," he said under his breath as he moved toward for the door. "Shit," he laughed out loud, "they'd have to find me first."

He laughed again as he opened the bottom doghouse door and realized how goddamned glad he was to still be alive and unharmed.

Outside it was a whole new world. That night tower crew was up on the platform trippin' 'er back in. He could hear their movements. He could hear the roar of the giant engines. He could see the kelly moving up and down with the drill string attached. The beast shining brightly against the blackness of the universe. These were his first real impressions of this new world. *Back East a man can die a thousand false deaths a day*, he thought; here on location you can only die once, as the deity of life commands. *If you can't get 'er, you can't stay.*

The sight of his Jeep as he ambled over to it was comforting. Suddenly, Jon appeared at his side.

"Zak, you got a place to sleep tonight?" his tone was neighborly but by no means familiar.

"I thought I'd try the rodeo grounds," Zak said.

"Where? Back in Scobey?"

"Yeah," Zak tossed his gear into the back of the Jeep.

"Is that where you slept last night?"

"And the night before that," Zak was matter-of-fact.

Jon smiled from beneath his bushy blond beard and a momentary flash in his deep blue eyes suggested that he considered sleeping in the rodeo grounds altogether weird. "Well look, that chainhand who didn't show up today shares a room with me back at the Pioneer. Why don't you follow me back and take his bed for the night? There's a shower you can use."

"Sure, but what if that other fella comes back?"

"We'll kick his ass for not showin' up today," Jon laughed as he walked over to the Olds. "He can sleep in the rodeo grounds."

As they fired up their outfits and swerved away from location, Jon in the lead—their headlights penetrating the black veil beyond the glaring bright circle of lights on tower—Zak pushed in a tape. Danny Gatton's *Redneck Jazz*.

"Hiyaaah!" he shouted. This was too good to be true.

He was reminded of the urban suspicion of the kindness of strangers. The threat of contact. The instinctual revulsion, or at least mistrust, of uncoerced generosity. Zak remembered he had only five dollars left in the whole world. More like four dollars and change. A year ago it would have made him blanch to even think of being exposed to such a decrepit state of affairs, indeed, it was his worst fear. He wondered if all bourgeois fears were so unfounded. He knew that Jon's offer was more of a practical gesture than anything else, but still, he felt he must be doing something right. And he laughed, shouted, shrieked, and rocked as the two vehicles bounced, swerved, and rolled, up and down and around and over, one after another, through the dust, dirt, gravel, and asphalt, and the great big prairie night.

IV

like throwin' chain," Jon stated flatly as the two men sipped whiskey at the Pioneer Hotel bar. "I mean, that's what I'm good at."

"But you're workin' motors now," Zak said. Jon ended every sentence as though it were his last and Zak wasn't about to let him stop talking if he could help it.

"Yeah, well, for now I've got the most experience on the floor, except for Jesse, of course. Motors is one job you've just got to know what you're doin'. Freddy Fifer, the fella who didn't show today, he's just breakin' out too. He started a couple of weeks ago. Before this latest switch, Freddy, bein' new, was workin' worm's corner, where you are now." Jon arranged the ashtray, salt shaker, and a cigarette butt, transforming the table top into an oil rig platform; he completed the lopsided diamond with a tap of his finger, "I was chainhand and Lenny was on motors before he got run off."

"Lenny?"

Jon scratched under his chin, plucked a few flakes of pale brown mud from under his beard, and ground them to powder between his thumb and forefinger, raising a small fine pyramid on the dark Formica surface. He seemed to be making up his mind whether or not to continue with the gory details. When he reached a decision, he placed his big hands on the table as though holding a box between his beefy palms. Inside the box, as if by some strange geomancy, he had placed this Lenny character.

"Lenny's Jesse's kid," he began haltingly. "You should know this in case he shows up again, which isn't very likely after all the shit he pulled. I'm not sure what caused the final problem but we were all glad to see him go, even if it meant I had to give up bein' chainhand for a while and go back to motors. Lenny couldn't handle motorman's responsibilities. He was a real bad apple, that Lenny was. A shame too 'cause Jesse'd been awful proud of that kid when he was first breakin' out. When he put his mind to it he could do anything. On an oil rig that is. I've seen him throw chain. Would've made a good derrickhand too. That's where he belonged, come to think of it, up on that diving board where we wouldn't have to see his face or listen to his shit. But Jesse wanted him where he could keep an eye on him and besides, Marty just won't work anything but derricks. Anyway, derrickhand has to know all about the mud and Lenny's too impatient to learn anything that doesn't just come naturally. He's only nineteen. When he was seventeen I understand his toolpusher wanted him to go drillin'. Hell of a compliment for someone so young. So, naturally, after that, Lenny really got his ass up on his back and figured he was too good for worm's corner. Hell, I'd work worm's corner if Jesse asked, I wouldn't mind, it's a roughneckin' job, after all. He and Jesse always kept it their little secret that Lenny was Jesse's son. Hell, that toolpusher on Bomac doesn't even know it."

Jon paused to take a sip and simmer down. It was clear that talking made him uncomfortable and discussing Lenny was irritating. Zak decided to stay quiet and just let Jon get as much of it off his chest as he wanted. But Zak got ready for a possible explosion.

"You don't know him yet but Jesse'd give you the shirt off his back if you were in need," Jon's attitude softened. "You see, Zak, Jesse broke each one of us out in the patch. Something else you should know. He's got a keen eye for who can get 'er and who can't. That's the only reason we ever put up with that fucker of a son of his. I've been out here in the patch for two years now and I've never worked for another driller, either has Marty and he's been here a year longer'n I have. Who knows? If things go well with you and Fifer, Jesse will have broken out the whole damn crew! But that Lenny just didn't give a shit. About anything. Never pulled his own weight. Jesse was tryin' so hard to make that kid a success that he'd be out on the floor takin' care of motorman's duties while Lenny'd be out fuckin' off somewhere. Then Jesse'd try and smooth it over with the rest of us and that would just make matters worse 'cause we'd hate t'see Jesse getting used like that. We knew what Jesse was goin' through so Marty and I decided among ourselves to let the Lenny thing slide. Hell, we owed the man that much. Besides, sooner or later, well, things would either work out or they wouldn't, you know how it is. But I'll tell you something else, when we heard Lenny had taken a swing at the old man the night Jesse run him off we figured all bets were come due. He's lucky we didn't find out about it's all I can say."

Jon poked the table top with an iron finger and the glasses and ashtray bounced. His eyes flared as his anger returned. "Lenny. He'd go from one to another of us lookin' for trouble and if he couldn't find it he'd sulk and bitch until, sure enough, everybody'd be at each other's throats. Lenny didn't want to be no fuckin' roughneck. I guess his old man should've known that."

"Maybe he did," Zak jumped in, "but maybe Jesse felt it was time for Lenny to learn a trade, maybe the only trade Jesse knows.

Hell, most parents these days can't even give their kids that much. They send their kids to school and expect them to learn one there."

"There, or the military," Jon's voice trailed off. For an instant Zak felt he had helped reconcile some of Jon's contradictory emotions. But Jon gave his head a little shake as he mulled it over. Clearly, some of life's contradictions are irreconcilable.

There was only one other customer at the Pioneer Hotel bar, an older fellow sitting quietly by himself. The room was dark but for an eerie glow backlighting the bottles behind the bar and a faint glimmer from electric wall lamps, which were supposed to resemble candles but were bent, awkward, and tacky-looking. Jon got up from the booth to have a chat with the lady barkeep. Zak, meanwhile, was so exhausted that he had slipped into an airy limbo where body and soul seem to float. He was held together only by a powerful curiosity that suspended his discomfort and fear, clarified his thoughts, and routed the confusion that had overwhelmed him the night before. In this condition he was quite prepared to go on as long as was necessary.

"So tell me, Zak, where're you from?" Jon returned with two more drinks, eager to change the subject.

"South Dakota. A little town called Wall, about fifty miles east of the Black Hills, on the border of the Badlands National Monument."

"You sound like a tour guide," Jon said without a trace of inflection. For an instant Zak shriveled, not sure if Jon was joking or challenging his veracity, or both.

"I was farmin' mostly," Zak said quietly between sips.

Jon eyed Zak curiously for a painful second. "I'm from *North* Dakota," he said coldly, circling for some point of intersection, "but I was through Rapid City a number of times when I was in the Air Force."

"Yeah, well, that's not far from there. Y'know, I was pretty shocked to see that pipe actually get bigger when we got near the end there," Zak steered back to the safety of the rig like a beginner swims for the side of the pool when his toes no longer touch bottom.

Jon sat back in the booth and ran his hands through his thick blond hair, pushing it back away from his face. His hard hat had kept the mud from reaching just below the hairline, leaving a margin of white skin as though some cosmic thespians had come along and painted on this roughneck face, and Jon, one minute the quiet motorman, the next minute the rakish interlocutor, stepped outside the scene to help Zak with the crucial lowdown. "That bigger, heavier pipe is to give a little more weight and stability to the bit so when it comes up against a harder formation it'll hopefully keep drillin' downward instead of goin' around it. But we've never really had any problems turnin' to the right or trippin' in or out. On the Widowmaker, the problem is with the juice."

"The what?"

"The electricity."

"No, I mean what did you call the rig just now?"

Jon shook his head, his blue eyes flashed as he raised his hands in mock terror. "The Widowmaker!" Now, wearing that painted-on mud-gray face, he looked like the roughneck host of a late-night TV horror show. Zak laughed, any tension he thought was there had disappeared. "I shouldn't be callin' it that, really," Jon was suddenly contrite. "It makes Jesse mad as hell when he hears one of his crew callin' it that. He says, 'It ain't no fuckin' Widowmaker when I'm on that brake handle!' and he's right. Not that those other Bomac drillers are at fault, mind you, but Jesse's never even had one man hurt in the patch. Not bad after thirty years, eh?"

"Not bad," Zak agreed. "Go on."

"Electricity can be the most hazardous part of the job. It's generated right there on location, obviously, and, what with the rig bein' solid iron and water everywhere—mud, scrubbin', hosin' it down all the time, the rain and snow and ice. Now, not on Jesse's crew, mind you, but a couple of other crews have had problems with motormen who weren't knowledgeable, and this particular electrical system is a little quirky. A couple of guys have gotten zapped."

"You mean killed?"

"Yeah."

"Goddamn."

"That's why motorman's job has got to go to the man with the most experience 'cause it's his responsibility to keep those motors runnin' clean and he's got to know how to handle the juice. The coincidence is that the two fellas who died were married and we don't get many marrieds here in the Basin. Marty's married. He and Cynthia live with Jesse on location when we're workin'." Jon stopped for a second. He looked embarrassed by what he was about to say. "Cynthia," Jon laughed, apologetically, then, after searching for words that weren't there, said nothing. Zak thought of Jesse, Marty, and his wife, Cynthia, all crammed into that small trailer and remembered Jesse's offer to put him up. From then on he put the possibility out of his mind completely. Then another question he hadn't had the nerve to ask anyone else came to him.

"Jon?"

"Yeah?"

"Just how many ways are there for a man to get killed on an oil rig anyway?"

"The obvious answer would be one, I guess, but the truth is they're finding new ones all the time. But hey, at least you get to die young, and in perfect health," he smiled. "No wasting away in some beat-down home, or VA hospital, where no one gives a shit about you after watching everyone you ever loved go down first, eh?"

THE WIDE WOODEN STAIRCASE AT the Pioneer Hotel creaked loudly as the two men made their way up to the second floor. The Pioneer was an old hotel, built in the 1920s. Though the floorboards sagged with age, Zak could see where the banisters had been carefully repaired over the years. Upon closer inspection it seemed that everywhere he looked a carpenter's careful handiwork was in evidence, each repair masterfully painted over and incorporated into the worn and easy character of the place. Drywall new and old, floorboards replaced, generations of electric, phone, gas, all running in logical and illogical patterns, as each era of existence left its mark, told its story, if one knew where to look, how to read. Zak felt woozy as he climbed the stair, light-headed and worried he might fall. In his exhaustion, his perceptions wandered in and out of the surreal. He grabbed the railing. He could feel the whole of the structure merely by touching the railing as he steadied himself, moving slowly up the stair, listening, breathing the musty air, filled with the corporeal elements of wood, mineral, and cloth. The smoky vapors of humans in their passing and the traces of themselves they left behind. He wondered if living outside had made him a stranger to human dwellings.

Now he felt that, by touching the walls, he was actually shaking the hands of craftsmen long gone who had placed this humble structure in his path, that he had been placed in the lap of that thing for which we are forever searching, yet which is all around us, like the rolling hills, endless prairie, and bottomless sky, would that we had more than mere instinct to detect its presence, to give it a name, to communicate with it directly. He didn't feel at home. He didn't even know if he belonged. He was a stranger in this house. In his fatigue he imagined that old building rising above and below him, holding him, bending, creaking and yielding to him. *It is all right to be old*, Zak thought, if he could grow old like this old building. He then laughed and stumbled down the hallway after his crewmate.

The corridors were long and narrow and Zak ricocheted off each wall in slow motion like a slow-moving pinball. They entered Jon and Fifer's room through a slender doorway onto an uncarpeted floor. There was a sink, two modest beds, and on the left an open closet space.

The water pressure in the shower at the end of the hall was weak. With his big toe Zak stirred the brown muddy pool that rolled off his body to keep it running down the drain. When Jon returned from his shower, he found Zak in his sleeping bag on the floor between the two beds fast asleep. For a moment Jon looked at Zachary Harper, twitching in his sleep there on the floor, and at the extra empty bed, before turning off the light.

SUNLIGHT. BRIGHT MORNING SUNLIGHT FLOODED the room through pale white curtains that did not stretch completely across the imperfect glass of the hotel room window. Zak snapped awake the instant Jon stirred. Usually a sound sleeper, Zak had acquired during the past months an extra sense for detecting small noises. As he lay there staring at the cracked plaster ceiling, he thought it might be nice to quietly shift his sleeping bag up onto the extra bed, seeing as how it was morning and Fifer was unlikely to return to use it now. And then it hit him.

"Ah!"

What he had done was attempt to lift his head. Every square centimeter of muscle in his body had twisted in the night like a rubber band, been dipped in gasoline, and burst into flame with the slightest movement.

"Uhnnn!" He heard himself groan as he tried to relax. His head fell two inches and hit the floor with a thud. His face stretched into a silent, painful grimace. His eyes darted back and forth as he frantically tried to assess the damage, figure out what was wrong. His bones were wrapped with barbed wire to which his shredded muscles clung angrily. Between his muscles and his skin was a layer of coarse sandpaper. He shouldn't move. He was prepared to lie there for weeks if need be. He couldn't lie there for weeks. His bladder was bursting, he needed to pee.

Jon rolled over and continued sleeping. Zak winced again with pain. The tops of his feet, his arches, shins, calves, thighs and buttocks, his back, shoulders and arms, even his armpits, his neck, were all noisily complaining, shrieking, rioting, threatening his bastille with grappling hooks and torches. Every body part was connected to every other body part with dull rusted pins. A movement in one sent an angry chain reaction to all the others. A torturous, clamorous grapevine of bad news. The cacophony inside his brain was deafening. Outside his skull the room was quiet but for Jon's heavy breathing.

He started to laugh. His ears were ringing so loud he could barely hear himself think. How could he possibly put in another day of exertion when he couldn't get off the floor? He planned each movement carefully ahead of time. First, he flung himself forward and sat up. His muscles screamed. He screamed. He climbed up to his knees and grabbed the post at the foot of the vacant bed. His fingers hurt so bad he could barely make a clutching fist around it. He drooled and this made him laugh some more. His injured self could hear his uninjured self laughing insanely. His okay half reminded his injured half of the hours he had spent exercising all those weeks out in the parks, "you dumb shit!" he belched as he spoke and laughed some more. This gave him the hiccups. They were now in genuine hysterics. Both of them! Laughing, drooling, and hiccupping. The more they laughed the more they hurt. Their tummy muscles burned, ached, and threatened to cramp up and the thought of going into a full body charley horse made them laugh harder still.

"Uh," he stood up, "mmm," he took a step, "fuck!" he took another, his palm slapped the wall, "whoa," his hip hit the table's edge. He sputtered, spat, hiccupped, blustered, and laughed and groped his way toward the door. Tears streamed down his bright red whiskery cheeks. Jon awoke and sat up on his elbows, squinting, in time to see Zachary Harper giggling, snorting, and hee-hawing from the room in his underwear, stumbling from the room like some loopy, addle-brained, meandering lunatic.

A SHORT WHILE LATER ZAK found Jon downstairs at the café and eased himself into the chair opposite. The waitress arrived with OJ and coffee for two. Jon's way of saying he was buying. An old-timer with a serious limp entered the café carrying a stack of newspapers, the *Billings Gazette*. Suddenly, Zak was overcome by a burning sense of nostalgia and curiosity.

"Interested in the paper?" he asked his partner.

"Nope."

Zak tapped on the table impatiently. He lit a cigarette. He got up and tried to mask his stiff movements in a posture of nonchalance, digging into his pocket for loose change. At least he could spring for the paper. He went to the counter and picked one up. He scanned the headlines. Jon scanned the profile of Zachary Harper who, as far as Jon was concerned, was absorbed in a ludicrous review of a world that didn't concern either of them. Zachary Harper read aloud.

"A New Glitter Beckons From the Hills. While there isn't exactly a 'gold rush' in Montana, and no new deposits have been discovered, there was a twenty to thirty percent jump in activity around existing sites when the price of gold started up five years ago…" Zak was about to make some remark as to whether or not Jon had ever done any prospecting, might even have suggested it would be a worthwhile way to spend their next days off but, upon seeing Jon's look, decided to keep his newsy ruminations to himself. They continued on in silence.

Spacecraft Spots New Moon, Ring: Mountainview, California (Associated Press). Trailblazing Pioneer II survived two perilous crossings through debris making up the rings around the giant planet Saturn on Saturday, then delighted scientists with evidence of a previously unsuspected ring and a possible new moon…

Firewood Scarce, Costly. The price of firewood has jumped thirty-five dollars a cord and figure you're going to run out anyway come February 1.

Attack Suspect Surrenders After Victim Swims for Life...

Post Office May Make a Profit...

New Nightmare Haunts Uganda...

Lawyers Pan Judicial Picks...

The food arrived. The Great American Heart Attack Breakfast. Two cheese omelets, home fries with each (genuine red-skinned potatoes chopped with onions and peppers piled high in the corner of the grill), sides of sausages, toast, and griddle cakes. The two men attacked their plates like a couple of hungry coyotes. Eventually they settled down to a more humane pace and it was then that Zak was able to devote at least a part of his attention to the problems of the day. "I've got to find a place to stay," he thought out loud as he speared a sausage with a fork already spilling over with omelet and potatoes, then plunged the whole ensemble into a pool of ketchup.

"What're you thinking of doin'?" Jon asked as he momentarily came up for air to tear open a tub of orange marmalade.

"I'd like to pitch a tent somewhere. See if I can't stake out a plot of land," Zak conjectured as he moved triumphantly on to the flapjacks. Jon's blue eyes grew wide.

"Oh yeah? Where?"

"I don't know," Zak's fork marched through the triple stack. He doused the spongy cakes in more syrup. The food was restoring Zak's faculties. It was the first hot meal he had had in weeks. Spying a bottle of steak sauce on the next table he leaned way over to fetch it, without thinking, and his ribs, arm, and back screamed as he attempted to stretch them, so bad he just kind of stayed in that position, with one arm resting across the next table, with a knee jutting out into the aisle between them. Jon got up calmly, took the bottle of steak sauce, and displayed it elegantly over his right forearm.

"Excuse me sir, is this what you're looking for?"

Zak painfully regained his chair, amused by Jon's Bistro de Pioneer haughtiness, but not enough to laugh, and took the bottle and poured its contents over his toast and the remainder of his omelette. He took a deep breath and resumed his meal. His eyes scanned the sunny street but his vision roamed the rolling plains surrounding Bomac 34. "Maybe that farmer or rancher or whatever he is who leases out the land Bomac's on would let me stake out a spot." He looked at Jon for some sign as to the plausibility of this notion and interpreted Jon's lack of response to be affirmative. "I can see it all now," he rested his forearms on the edge of the table, a fork in one hand, his knife in the other. His jaw muscles worked. "Yeah." He nodded his head as though he and his guardian angel were deep in discussion. "Not a bad idea." He loaded up another forkful. They held up their coffee cups for the waitress who had dutifully returned with a fresh pot. "It would be close to location. I can't afford another tank of gas."

Jon listened intently.

"Once I get down to where I think I have just enough gas left for one more ride into town I'll leave the Jeep at the tent and then just walk to and from work. Yeah, I think I'll cruise out there after breakfast and see if I can get his permission."

"I'll ride out there with ya," Jon said and went back to concentrating on his food. If it were him he would simply bum the money, stay in the hotel, and pay everyone back on payday. A roughneck asking permission. This was something he'd have to see with his own eyes.

Zak's cheeks bulged with food. He smiled anyway.

IN THE JEEP, ZAK PUSHED in a tape, *The Rosslyn Mountain Boys*, and they smoked a reefer on their way out of town. When they reached the four buttes, they turned down the gravel road toward location until three miles from the drilling site, they swerved into the rancher's private drive. Dogs came barking from all directions. The ranch house was lifeless, so they pressed on to the barn which turned out to be the epicenter of canine activity. Two golden labs galloped out to meet them, sniffing the air and barking. From somewhere out of sight other dogs barked back. Zak climbed down from the Jeep and held a fist to each dogs's nose for a sniff. From under a tractor nearby came a tall skinny ranch hand, and from inside the barn came the old dog himself. He was tall, heavyset, and severe.

Zak stuck out his hand and said, "Howdy," casual and friendlylike. The old rancher looked from Zak's face down to his outstretched hand, as though he wondered what in the world Zak expected him to do. At last he got the idea and placed his hand in Zak's. When Zak gripped the old man's hand the old-timer did not return the hand clasp and the dry, limp, leathery palm felt cold and unfriendly, sending a chill up Zak's spine.

"You a lawyer?" the old man asked.

"No sir, my name is Zachary Harper and I'm workin' on this Bomac rig over here on your property. I just hired on with them and I was wondering if you would be kind enough to let me pitch a tent somewhere not too far from the rig."

"Kind enough," the old fella said in a shamelessly mocking tone while turning to his ranch hand, then returning to Zak's open gaze said, "You boys are used to takin' whatever you want." He pulled a pipe from his overalls and lit up. A dank, sweet, blue cloud hovered for an instant and then dissipated.

"If you'd rather I didn't, I'll understand," Zak said and took a step backward.

"So, what're you fixin' t'do in this tent of yers?"

Zak laughed nervously, "Stay in it till I get paid and can afford to put a roof over my head." He looked at Jon for support but Jon wore a blank face.

"Well, makes no difference," the man said. "Where you want to go, young fella, is just down this road a piece," he pointed with the stem of his pipe down the private drive that continued on past his ranch, "until you come to a crick. Follow that crick a little ways and you're going to come smack up against a great purple outhouse with a moon on the door. I built it myself when I was a kid. There's a bend in the crick right there that's been my favorite fishing hole long as I can remember, and that's a long time. See for yourself. Drop a line in there some morning and you'll catch yourself some breakfast. Ain't nothin' better. That's the spot to pitch yer tent."

Zak then made the mistake of offering him some money from his future pay and all the farmer did was spit.

"Pitch yer tent, then get back up on that rig over yonder and find me some oil, and when yer done, punch another hole and find me some more. And by the way, that's the loudest fuckin' thing I ever heard, and she never quits." He turned to walk away. "I've gotten used to it. Don't think the animals ever will."

AS ZAK AND JON BOUNCED down the dirt road that led to the creek, Zak let out a loud hoot.

They pulled up next to the outhouse and jumped from the Jeep like a couple of fearless skydivers.

"Yup! I think these accommodations should suit you to a T, Mr. Harper!" Jon laughed and kicked a stone into the creek. "The plumbing works, you've got running water." He lifted his nose and breathed in the cool breezes that wafted down the canyon carved by the creek between the hills. "Hell, the Pioneer doesn't have central air conditioning!" He turned to see Zak lying on his back in the grass holding a freshly lit cigarette between his teeth, staring pensively up into space. "How's that mattress?" Jon inquired, caught up in the housewarming spirit of the event.

"A bit on the firm side, good for the back though, why don't you try the sofa?"

"We can't be sitting on our ass! This is moving day. Now let's see this tent of yours?"

Zak dragged thoughtfully on his cigarette, his brow wrinkled, lifting the bill of his cap and his bent wire frames made him look cockeyed. "A tent would be nice."

Jon decided to sit down after all. "I thought you said you had a tent."

"Nope. I said I'd like to pitch a tent out here, didn't say I had one."

"Y'know, I'm beginnin' to worry about you. Been out in the patch just one day." Jon shook his head and reached for a Marlboro. Zak smoked a Vantage.

"Oh hell," Zak explained, "the nights are cool, the days are warm, the weather's still good. I'll be all right."

"All right. Sure. Until a coyote comes along and takes a bite out of your ass while you sleep. I don't mind tellin' ya, you've got a strange way of doin' things, mister."

"I'm a worm, ain't I?"

"Yup," Jon laughed, "that you are."

THEY STILL HAD A COUPLE of hours to kill before they were due back on location and so they palled around Scobey doing errands. Jon gave Zak the cook's tour. They stopped in at the grocery where Zak unabashedly spent the last of his funds on big jars of peanut butter and jelly, a half-dozen loaves of whole wheat, several packs of smokes, and four rolls of toilet paper. Jon picked up a loaf of white bread, some lunch meats, a jar of mayonnaise, a jar of whole dills, and a six-pack of Pepsi.

Jon took Zak to the coin laundry where Zak refilled his plastic water jugs from a tap at the sink. They drove out to the rodeo grounds and sat on the bleachers and ate sandwiches in silence.

"No sense in taking two vehicles," Jon said as they were leaving for work. "You can stay in the hotel again tonight if you want."

They parked Zak's Jeep behind the old hotel and threw their gear and groceries into the back of Jon's Oldsmobile and were off. Jon peeled off the highway at those four buttes and drove like a madman. His tires were bald. His shocks were gone. They rumbled and rolled down the winding dirt and gravel roads that led to location like they were on the Mad Mouse's Wild Ride. Zak hung on for dear life, lifting himself off his seat before each crash landing as they launched and hurled themselves over every rise. *What the heck, he thought, a wreck might have been preferable compared to what might be waiting for them on location.* They were facing another day shorthanded and the thought of repeating the trial and strain of the previous day's effort was quickly becoming more than he could stand.

When the hundred-and-fifty-foot tower of Bomac 34 crested the horizon, Zak felt compelled to speak up.

"What do you think they'll have us doin' today?"

"A man never knows in the oil field."

Well shit! Zak thought. Given what we did yesterday a guy should have some idea what the next few days will be like. He didn't appreciate Jon's complacent attitude but Jon just wasn't very talkative and, as they drove on, the car continued to pitch and swerve with the crazy dirt road. Zak sat back in his seat and tried to calm himself. *Wait and see,* he thought. Jon waited for every new turn in a road he had traveled many times; Zak would wait and take what was coming when they reached Bomac 34.

They arrived on location at twenty minutes to three. Jon parked the car a short ways from the rig. When the dust had settled, he took a quick look around before concluding, "Shit." No Fifer. Zak pulled the handle on the door and made a move to step out, but Jon didn't budge. He just flipped on the radio and dug into his shirt pocket for a smoke.

"Eight hours is what they pay me for and eight hours is what they get," his Zippo clanked open and a burst of flame was followed by a gust of sweet blue smoke that hit the windshield and rolled back into Jon's squinting eyes, "not eight hours and twenty minutes." Zak pulled the door closed as though he agreed but, frankly, he was itching to get changed and just sort of buck himself up for the long day's work ahead. Instead they sat and smoked and listened to the radio. Had he been on his own he would have been in there and dressed, ready to go. There was no pipe standing in the derrick. A large, red, six-wheeled flatbed truck was parked next to the catwalk. Zachary Harper spent the remaining minutes before work resisting the urge to ask stupid questions.

At five minutes to the hour Jon got out of the car, and at exactly the same instant the trailer door opened across the way and out stepped Jesse and Marty.

In the bottom doghouse the three men were just closing their lockers before going up to the floor when the door opened and in waltzed Freddy Fifer. He was six foot one, two hundred thirty pounds, mostly fat. He wore old cowboy boots, Levi's, and a Western shirt that stretched over his bouncing belly. He had short messy black hair, a round pudgy face, and small friendly brown eyes behind thick black-framed glasses that squished against the doughy clay of his face.

"Well, I may be late but at least I made it!" he announced, throwing his big arms open wide in a gleeful gesture of reunion.

All right! Zak wanted to shout. Marty and Jon barely looked up.

"Well, well," Marty said as he waddled past Freddy on his way out the door, "look what de cat dwragged in."

Jon was on his way out as well and as he turned from his locker said sweetly, "Hi honey!" then gave Freddy a loud smack! on his fat right arm that must have stung like hell. "You're a lucky son of a bitch you decided to show up today." He paused for a meaningful second before calling him, "chainhand," and stepped through the door.

Freddy's ruddy cheeks bunched up like overripe crab apples and his fat little mouth formed a silent O as he gave his arm a rub where Jon had let him have it. He huffed and hustled down the lane of lockers, sat down on the bench, and began changing his clothes. Zak could tell by the man's concentrated effort that he was moving as fast as he could—slow as molasses. As Zak started for the door, Freddy realized he had forgotten his manners, stood up in Zak's path, held up his drawers with one hand, and stuck out his other hand for Zachary Harper.

"Hi, I'm Freddy. So you're the new worm?"

"Zak Harper."

"Glad to know yuh." Freddy's eyes were like his handshake, weak, friendly, eager, kind, and a little afraid.

"You ever bin chainhand before?" Freddy asked as he huffed off his cowboy boots.

"Nope."

"Ah, that's too bad." Freddy sounded genuinely disappointed.

As Zak skipped stairs up to the top doghouse, he wondered if facing his first day as chainhand caused Freddy the same feelings of apprehension and anguish that Zak had felt just the day before. All he really knew was that they were going to have a full crew, for better or worse, to combat whatever problem was going to be thrown at them that afternoon and things didn't hurt so bad after that.

Up on the floor Zak was relieved to see there was really very little going on. A "Test Situation," someone called it. They weren't turning to the right, that is, they weren't drilling. Everything was stationary. The motors were running as always and their constant high-pitched scream ripped the air. Jon, in his new capacity as motorman, immediately set out to run a check. He checked the water levels, temperatures, the oil, and made sure they were getting plenty of number one diesel fuel. The first motors he checked were the giant twin Superior diesel engines up on the floor pulling the drawworks.

"We need oil," Jon said, and the two of them went down to the ground and fetched four five-gallon buckets of oil and carried them back up the stairs. "Those old seals on these engines leak about fifteen or twenty gallons of oil a day, so I check on'm at least once every tower."

From there he went down to the light plant which was next to the mud shack. The light plant was powered by two generators, and so he checked both of those motors. When that was done, he continued around behind the mud shack and the mud tank to where the desilter was located. The desilter was run by a Jimmy Motor, another of Jon's responsibilities. From there it was around to the other end of the mud tanks to the desander, and he gave its motor the once over.

Meanwhile, back up on the floor, that toolpusher, Jesse, and a six-foot-five-inch, two-hundred-sixty-pound giant of a man were standing at the doghouse door going over some figures. When Fifer arrived, ready to go to work at last, no one even looked up. Zak, who had been trying to blend into the walls, approached Freddy and said, "Look, I'm just going to kind of follow you around if you don't mind."

Freddy shook his head. "Don't mind at all. C'mon, we'll Zurt up!" He then broke out a couple of grease guns and handed one to Zak. From there they proceeded at a leisurely pace to roam randomly over the rig, hitting various spots with grease. As they stopped here and there, Zak noticed some rather nasty bruises, cuts, and scrapes all about Freddy's fingers, forearms, and shins. "Worm bites," Freddy explained.

"How'd you ever learn where all these Zurt spots are?" Zak wanted to know after they had hit about twenty.

"Hell, nobody ever showed me. I just make the rounds whenever things are slow and every now and then I come across another one." Freddy was a likable fellow and his approach to life was obviously much like the way he located his Zurt spots. It occurred to Zak that Freddy could answer a lot of questions, that together they might make learning the ropes a little easier.

The big fella up there in the top doghouse with Jesse and the toolpusher was, according to Freddy, "The Man From Halliburton."

"Don't know his name," Freddy volunteered as he hit the Zurt gun and a shot of grease went splat! all over a joint. "Halliburton runs the drill-stem tests. No telling how long we'll sit on this one." Forever would be fine with Freddy. "Sometimes they only run a few hours, sometimes more than a day. Depends on what the big boys want it to say. That's his truck down there, the red one."

Back in the top doghouse, they found Jon leaning quietly against a locker by himself smoking a cigarette and listening to Jesse, that toolpusher, and The Man From Halliburton continue with their strategy session. When Freddy and Zak walked in, however, invisibility was impossible and the three roughnecks eyed each other as if to say, "This is not the place to be." Without a word, they followed Jon out the door. Zak was about to ask Jon what he should be doing when Freddy grabbed his arm and said, "C'mon Zak, let's start scrubbin'!"

Not having the slightest idea what he was agreeing to, Zak followed Freddy as he waddled and huffed his way around the rig. They picked up a couple of plastic five-gallon buckets that the dope for the pipe comes in, threw in some water, a little soap, then added some diesel fuel for cutting grease. They grabbed a couple of wire brushes and started scrubbing the pump house. *Unreal*, Zak thought. When in doubt just start scrubbing the rig. Zak set himself to scrubbing that pump house. Every now and then, Freddy would look up as he lazily scrubbed away to see Zak applying all the elbow grease he could possibly muster. And Freddy Fifer did not know what to make of Zachary Harper.

WHEN THEY WERE ABOUT HALFWAY done scrubbing that pump house, they looked up to see Jesse urgently waving them up to the floor. As if on cue, Marty came tearing out of the mud shack and Jon was already taking double steps up the stairs to the floor.

This apparently was the moment everyone had been waiting for. Once they were topside, Jesse gave the command to "Prepare the floor!" and Zak followed Jon and Fifer through the motions of readying the collar subs that they had used to yank the larger pipe through the hole near the end of the trip the day before. Next, the tongs were greased up with new dyes put in them. While this was going on, Marty was steadily climbing upward to his station, ninety feet above the rest of the crew.

Jon, Fifer, and Zak changed the tong heads and as they did, it dawned on Zak that they were preparing to trip that son of a bitch out of the hole exactly as they had the day before. His thoughts became frantic as they made ready for another grueling combat session with that iron. My God! Is it going to be like this every day? Jon seemed to have a quiet smirk on his face, and Freddy Fifer was already sweating profusely. At least Freddy represented another pair of hands and that had to account for something.

That day and into the evening they tripped more than seventy stands out of the hole, plus another six stands of heavy collar. With three men working those slips and four hands to push those stands over to bank, it had taken a lot longer to reach the exhaustion level that had come so early on the day before. Still, the work was feverish and grueling. He was surprised to see that there was no bit on bottom when that last collar was finally through the hole. Instead, there were pipes. All different shapes and sizes neatly packed together which stood sixty feet high in the derrick once completely out of the hole. These were the testing tools. The Man From Halliburton, who had been standing next to driller Jesse throughout the entire trip, now stepped in with authority. The next step was to disconnect these pipes and that Halliburton man took Jesse and his crew through their paces. To Jesse he screamed over the din of the engines and the hiss of the drawworks, "All right, pick up on 'er another half foot!" and then to Jon and the boys, "Throw in your slip! Okay, now hurry and change yer dyes! Your tong heads!" To do that, a reducer was needed because the pipe they were now dealing with was smaller and of varying shapes. "Take your bite here!" he showed Jesse where he wanted that next pipe separated. After all twenty-five pipes had been dismantled and laid down on the floor, Jesse disappeared into the top doghouse putting his crew at that Halliburton man's disposal. Zak hired out to give him a hand down on the truck while the others stayed up on the floor and lowered his pipes to them.

When that Halliburton man climbed up onto the back of the flatbed and stood there like a colossus, his mighty arms folded, and Zak bounced up after him, and for several minutes they watched Marty climb slowly down from the tower.

"How long've you been with Halliburton?" Zak wanted to know.

"A few years," the man spoke with an easy voice that was almost a drawl. He reached into his shirt pocket for a Pall Mall, tapped it against his wristwatch, dried his lips with his sleeve, and lit up.

"They a good outfit to be with?"

"Sure," he looked at Zak, sizing him up for a second, then leaned over the side of the truck and spat. "They believe in starting a man from the ground up. That's my experience with 'em anyway. Y'know," he gestured up at the floor, "this life gets awful tough on a guy after a certain point. I went out roughnecking for ten long years. Hard years, boy, I'll tell you the truth." He obviously thought that Zak might now, or sometime in the near future, be in the same boat. "I thought sure as hell I was going to burn myself out here in the patch. That's no lie. Jesus," he spat once more, clearing the edge of the truck by several feet. "I was drinkin' too. But there's some pretty smart fellas out here hidin' out under all that mud. Some guys know when the time is right to make a change. Others are content to keep doin' the same old shit forever."

"So you've been with them for a while?"

"I guess. It feels like I'm just gettin' started though. Halliburton gave me a break. Started me out loggin'. Put me in the logging division, I should say. Then it's a matter of going out and running your drill-stem tests," he ticked off the successive stages of his career thus far on his long fingers, "and then becoming a district manager. That's the job I'm up for now. From there it's into the home office where you can start workin' your way up the ladder. A few more years out in the field and I'll be just right for it. I'll have all the experience a man could possibly need, that's for sure. I figure that in five or six more years I'll be makin' a hundred thousand a year or thereabouts. Their benefits are real good."

He had an almost serene composure, as though nothing that could happen at the next instant would surprise him in the least. As though this hell-raising son of a bitch had emerged at the other end of his scuffling days miraculously unhurt, indeed, better for it, master of his own fate, to the point where he actually knows what the hell he's doing, knows what he wants. Perfectly content to close one chapter and begin the next. Unlike Blackie or Jesse, who would go down roughneckin'. The Man From Halliburton stood there on the back of that truck with his big hands resting on his hips watching Jon attach cable to a boom line that ran up through the derrick from the drawworks on the floor, around a shiv, and then back down again. "Halliburton also has a cement subsidiary that, I believe, is the largest manufacturer and supplier in the world. That's what they tell me anyway. After I've done with this I wouldn't mind jumpin' over to that side of the company. Hell, it'd be something different." For The Man From

Halliburton all things were possible. Tomorrow wasn't such a mystery.

Just then Jon called down to the two men there on the truck and tossed his line over the side. On their end was six feet of chain and a hook. The boys up top wrapped the chain once or twice around the end of a pipe, inserted the hook through the chain, then let it swing overboard while Marty, at the brake handle, let 'er down. Once the pipe had sunk below floor level, the critical part of the operation rested with Jon as it was then his job to monitor the progress of the pipe and relay that information to Marty. The idling diesel motors made verbal communication impossible, so Jon used hand signals as to whether Marty should hold it, raise it, lower it, squeeze it, set 'er down, or just go easy.

Down on the truck that Halliburton man had a firm hold on the line Jon had tossed down to him and was thus able to guide the pipe toward him and Zak as it made its perilous descent down the thirty feet from the floor to the truck. Once there, they leveraged it into position using its own weight to guide it into the proper spot among the other pipes there on the truck. One after another. Things went smoothly until that last pipe was on its way down. When it was still several feet above their heads and descending rapidly, Marty misread Jon's signal to go easy and thought he meant to let 'er down. Zak saw the line above the pipe go slack and he reacted instantly, pushing off the pipe as it came crashing down, flinging himself completely off the truck as far as he could to get clear. He was tumbling through midair not knowing if the pipe was following right behind him, going to fall on him anyway, or if at that very instant that Halliburton man was taking the full impact of it back up on that flatbed.

Zak hit the ground with a ferocious thump and rolled and rolled until he was under the catwalk with the clanging of falling pipe resounding horribly in his ears. When things had settled down and he knew he was all right, he jumped to his feet and saw The Man From Halliburton sprawled across the pipes on the truck. The pipe that had come loose was leaning against the truck with its free end jammed deep into the earth just inches from where Zak had hit the ground and rolled.

That Halliburton man got up slowly. He was dazed but okay. That pipe had hit the truck right in front of him and when Zak had pushed off he had done likewise hoping to influence its fall away from himself and his roughneck helper, accomplishing this within inches of disaster. Zak, ignorant of what had caused the accident, thought there might be casualties up on the floor and so dashed up the stairs expecting to see that the boom line had snapped, that the drawworks had stalled—carnage, bloodshed, anything. He found Jon, Marty, and Freddy standing there looking stupidly from one to another with pale expressions of embarrassment and relief on their faces. Zachary Harper looked from one to the other and his stomach churned and his knees got weak and a horrible warm clammy sweat suddenly flushed up under his clothes. He felt light-headed and thought he was going to puke. Just then The Man From Halliburton tapped him on the shoulder and, with a motion of his head, ordered Zak back down the stairs.

Oddly, his voice was calm. "Hey you sons of bitches. You damned near killed us. We'll lay down this pipe. We're not in any big fucking hurry."

He shook his head with disgust and after a ridiculous silence followed Zak back down the stairs. It took them several minutes to dig the fallen pipe out of the ground. Up on the truck the pipes that had rolled when all hell broke loose needed to be rearranged. Zak helped him finish loading up and he was gone.

Nobody really had very much to say as they cleaned up the floor and hosed it down. Jesse then excused them for a bite to eat. It was the first break they had taken all day and the tower was nearly over.

Zak fetched his groceries from the back of Jon's car. He was shaken and a bit dazed. Jon quietly took his things and retired to the bottom doghouse, leaving Zak outside to eat alone. Awash in the glaring light of the high-intensity lamps on tower, Zak sat on the hood of the Olds and quickly made two peanut butter and jelly sandwiches. Already, the events of earlier that day seemed like they had occurred months ago. To a different person even. He didn't know what to think. He didn't even know if he should think. Everyone had said they were sorry. There was nothing more to be done. The fact that, at this moment, he or that Halliburton man could be writhing in agony, maimed, or dead, didn't seem important. He wasn't. They weren't. And that was that.

He bit hungrily into his sandwich and looked up at the tall shimmering tower. The constant screaming idle of the engines assailed his ears. *That thing really is a beast,* he thought. A dangerous, caterwauling, demanding, grotesque, mindless thing. And in a perverse moment of schizophrenic glee, with hard iron side by side the fragile humans who worked its cold hard machinery, he thought it all so beautiful. That he wasn't dead or injured: beautiful. That those hideous things could just as easily have occurred and didn't; that, even if they had, this thing would still be standing there, under these same stars, making this same hideous noise; that he or someone else would have been the only thing missing or changed: beautiful. Beautiful by nature of the simple terrifying clarity of it all. He felt as though he had inadvertently slipped through a hole in his consciousness and was able to perceive, in glimpses, a world, a universe, much much larger than himself, with him in it, or without him.

A chill wracked his spine. Doubts crept back. Two close calls in as many days. The simple law of averages told him that if this shit kept up, sooner or later something hideous and irrevocable was going to happen. Yesterday's mishap with the tongs was the result of his own inexperience. Fine. He could work to better himself. But today's episode was so much broader in scope that all his perceptions were changed, brought into a new, compelling focus. Whether it was his mental error or that of another made no difference. They were all in deadly peril. Blackie had told him story after story. O'Mally had armed him with a code for survival. Vic had warned him against heartless indifference. But that iron told the ugly, undeniable, beautiful truth. It flew at him from thirty feet above his head. Its ferocious jaws swung around and snapped inches from his heart. Heart? Experience? Marty and Jon held those in abundance and still their efforts were wanting. So what's the answer? Zachary Harper felt that if he didn't find it fast his trip to the oil patch would be short lived. "Always be aware." Always.

I'm a dead man, thought Zachary Harper. Then he laughed— a mean little disgusted harumph.

It was a mild night. The sun, which had thrown a reddish-orange hue upon a thick layer of strato-cumulous clouds reaching halfway to the naked horizon, was now gone, leaving the stars to peep through in spots as through an old diaphanous blanket which had survived the years but not without sacrifice to the hungry moths of summer. Zachary Harper drank from the jug of laundromat tap water and continued his musings, his eyes fixed upon the tower. Again, he had the disorienting sense of a past self, receding, ever more distant, like some old bell buoy that bobs suspended, its broken, eldritch toll marking the end of land astern. From that past, words that had always lacked definition or relevance suddenly came unstuck and floated in the forward hull of his consciousness. On the forbidden planet of his previous incarnation the word "Trust" had been demoted to a mere utilitarian device, a fiduciary expedient. To risk job and reputation on something as intangible as "Faith" was the trademark of a fool, a harbinger of failure. And "Confidence" was never fully assured until someone's gonads were placed as collateral in hand, ready for squeezing.

Here, these ephemeral concepts were to be basic elements of survival. Tangible, as visible as the tools and iron pieces that fit together in this puzzling cold construction. And God, it felt good. But trusting in the faith that Jon and Marty were pros who knew what they were doing was simply not going to get it. If he were detached, even for a moment, as he had let himself be during his brief interview with The Man From Halliburton, and blindly allowed others to shoulder their moment-to-moment responsibilities without being attuned to their every move, then he truly was at the mercy of fate. And fate doesn't give a shit. Fate is waiting to touch you with its brutal heavy hand, or to caress you with the benevolent gifts and the rewards of life. Here he was not risking mere professional ruin, which, at one time, had eclipsed even his fear of death, but he was putting at risk his time on this earth, and above all, his chance to pose and answer questions, basic questions that we all tend to avoid, tell ourselves are pointless. Who am I, why am I here, what is to be done?

Marty emerged from the top doghouse where he and Jesse had been having a chat over a bite to eat and, after a brief stop in the bottom doghouse to shake Jon loose, the two roughnecks ambled over to where Zak was gulping down the last of his sandwiches. There was a problem with the number one pump and it was up to them to investigate. Before they could get it checked out, relief arrived and the tower was over.

JON, MARTY, FREDDY, AND ZAK changed clothes in the bottom doghouse. Jon and Freddy wanted Marty to follow them into town for a drink but Marty thought he'd wait and see what Cynthia felt like doing. They'd either see him in town or they wouldn't. When Marty had gone and the others were ready to push on, Freddy laid a chubby palm on Zak's shoulder. "Look, Zak, you're more'n welcome to share our room tonight if you want."

No hard feelings. "Thanks."

"Yeah, at least you'll be able to get a shower," Jon added, passing the peace pipe. Drenched in mud, grease, and sweat at the end of those eight hours, it was unbearable to think that he wasn't going to get a shower right away. Jon then turned a friendly growl on Freddy, "And this worthless bag of shit still owes us for working shorthanded yesterday," and threatened to smack him on the arm again. This time Freddy hopped back and put up his dukes, laughing nervously. Jon moved in like he was going to take a poke at him but at the last second relented and just walked past him toward his Oldsmobile. Freddy flinched anyway.

Freddy Fifer tried to follow Jon and Zak back to town but the way Jon was driving Mario Andretti would have had trouble keeping up. Looking back from time to time to check Freddy's progress, it looked for all the world to Zak as if Freddy had gotten off the tricky dirt path and was just driving aimlessly over the open fields, feeling his way. His headlights would disappear and reappear on the distant horizon, and Zak settled down and trusted that God or somebody would intervene and help steer the poor bugger back to the main road. Jon certainly wasn't going to.

Back at the Pioneer, Jon and Zak had already ordered their drinks at the bar and claimed a booth when they heard the heavy metallic lobby door slam as Fifer entered, neglecting to stay with the big door long enough to ease it shut. "Goddamn thing," he muttered in embarrassment. An old-timer looked up irritably from the lobby couch where he sat watching an ancient black-and-white television set. Fifer couldn't tell whether the old man disliked being interrupted from his show, or if he disliked being interrupted by the dirty, smelling likes of one Freddy Fifer. These roughnecks did have a rather disquieting look and attitude about them. But what of it? They were paying guests, they had a right.

Freddy flashed a big muddy "Hi fellas!" type grin at his two buddies and squeezed himself, all noise and bustle, into the booth next to Jon. Zak laughed as they grabbed their drinks to keep them from spilling. Jon threw Freddy a hopeless look and waited for Freddy to get comfortable before speaking.

"Now, fat boy, get your ass up and get yourself a drink. What, do you expect Mary Ellen to drop everything and walk all the way over here just to wait on you?" And with a sideways wink at Zak, "While you're at it, you can pay for these here. Hell, you may as well make it another round." Freddy obliged immediately, disattaching himself from the booth with as much ruckus as he had sitting down.

"Don't worry fellas, tonight the drinks are on me!" he announced happily as he headed for the bar. This was the part of roughneckin' Freddy liked best.

"Look," Jon directed Zak's attention to the seat of Freddy's sagging blue jeans as he shuffled away. Jon shook his head pitifully.

The Pioneer Hotel bar was a dark and cozy little space with entrances both from the street and the hotel lobby. There was a jukebox, a shuffleboard, and in behind the tables and booths, a pool table. Four men were seated at the bar, locals, all of them over the age of sixty. Two wore cowboy hats and boots. One wore work pants and a work shirt. The other had dressed for the occasion in an aqua-blue polyester jacket. A couple of other fellas from that Bomac daylights crew were at the far end of the bar, one of whom was the wild-looking derrickhand Zak had spotted the day before.

Now a fella doesn't ask too many questions about a man's past, but when Freddy arrived back at the booth and had got himself settled he couldn't see anything wrong with striking up a conversation about the present.

"So, tell me Zak, how do you like roughneckin' so far?"

"It's too early to say. I'll tell you one thing I do know, you guys earn your money!" All three of them laughed and Zak looked from one to the other and leaned forward in a confidential manner. "Speaking of earning money, this being broke isn't any goddamned joke either. How often do we get paid?"

"Every other Friday," Freddy piped up before Jon could answer. "We got paid last Friday night so we won't get paid again till the Friday after next."

Zak's face fell. It was only Sunday night! How was he going to get by for two weeks without a dime? He had food to last awhile but gas for the Jeep was looming in the near future as a major problem.

Freddy dug into his pockets. Zak and Jon watched as a mound of Freddy's worldly possessions began to form there on the table. Fifties, tens, hundreds, ones, fives piled up, popping out of every pocket, along with a Swiss Army knife, strips of paper, receipts, backs of match packs, coins danced and fell to the floor or twirled madly, lint. A handkerchief, no, it was a pair of underwear. A quick scolding from Jon and the underwear disappeared. With this pile in front of him, he then proceeded to pluck out the debris. Phone numbers got stuffed into a shirt pocket. Change was scooped off the table into a chubby palm. Then he began to separate the bills. Jon watched this procedure incredulously as Freddy put the hundreds and fifties in one stack, flattened them out, and then did the same with the tens, fives, and ones. About nine hundred dollars. He counted through the hundreds and fifties and placed them in his left pocket, the rest he jammed into his right. When he was done a fifty remained. He pushed it over to Zak.

"Now goddamnit Zak, a man's got to have at least a hundred bucks on him these days or he can't survive," Freddy tapped a fat finger on the bill. "Isn't that right, Jonny boy?"

Jon's eyebrows shot up as he looked from the bill to Freddy Fifer. "You're not only fat, slow, and ugly, you're a dumb son of a bitch who can't count. Give the man another fifty bucks!" But Jon was already reaching for his wallet where, in neat, crisp, brand-new bills he found a fifty and laid it atop the one Freddy had left for Zachary Harper. Freddy was doubtless carrying everything he owned, Jon probably had an account somewhere.

"Look, are you guys sure you can spare it?" Zak stammered self-consciously. "It's a long time till payday and…"

"Shit, catch us in a couple of weeks," Freddy waved him off. He was feeling expansive and ready to dispense a little philosophy while this mood of brotherhood and benevolence lingered. "Y'know, I figure that with a car and a thousand bucks a guy can pretty well start his life all over again, anywhere, anytime, anyhow. Some gas, some whiskey, keep the outfit in shape, get to the next rig or the next job, whatever it might be. Everything a guy needs to get out of one jam and into another!" He and Zak laughed, Jon shook his head.

"Christ, Zak," Jon had heard enough. "Isn't it great to know somebody's got it figured out?"

"No, seriously," Freddy pleaded. "Simplicity, is what I mean. As long as a fella can keep his life simple, you know, without tying up whatever resources he has in a lot of unnecessary shit, he can stay mobile, I think mobility is key."

"Here's to simplicity and mobility!" Zak offered a toast.

Jon was then reminded of another reason for giving Freddy shit. "Say, fat boy, where were you tonight when we were trying to fix that pump?" He threw an elbow into Freddy's lard-covered ribs for emphasis.

Freddy's cherubic jowls fell jiggling and his eyes were wide and fearful. "I was up in the doghouse talking to Jesse about throwing chain."

"Yeah? What did he say?"

"He went over the basic moves with me, took me out on the floor."

Zak wished he had been there. He knew that throwing a chain was somehow involved in the process of putting pipe back into the hole, and if it was at all as tough, and it had to be, as pulling pipe out of the hole, any type of demonstration beforehand would be welcome.

"Tell you the truth," Freddy went on sincerely, "Jesse said that I ought to talk to you about it. Said that you were the best hand he ever broke out in the patch, that nobody threw chain better or faster'n you."

Freddy was a manchild, overweight and out of shape and therefore not at all assured of his functions. And Jon, surprised to find himself holding the lifeline of Jesse's words of praise, dropped for a moment his tone of derision and sarcasm and threw him a rope.

"Well, you're lucky we didn't have to pull a round trip today. You sure don't want to have to throw chain for the first time after pulling sixty-five hundred feet of pipe."

Round trip? Zak asked himself. It could only mean tripping the pipe out of the hole and then turning around and running it right back in again. All during one tower! He was right, things could get worse.

"I guess the best way for you to start, if you're lucky, would be during a drillin' tower. When you're just sittin' there turning to the right you only have to throw it once every so often when it's time to make another connection. You don't have to move so fast." Freddy now had something to wish for. Jon turned to Zak and explained further, "When you're trippin' in, or fast holin' after riggin' up, it can be murder to have an inexperienced chain-hand workin' the floor with you. You are makin' those connections every few minutes and when that chainhand misses his throw, you've then got to tighten those pipes with your tongs instead and that means takin' a bite and torquin' it, takin' a bite and torquin' it, takin' a bite and torquin' it, and Jesus, it just kills your arms. It also slows you way the hell down and you lose your work rhythm, which is another pain in the ass. You don't want to have to go through that more'n once. On the other hand, if you're quick to learn, you can get in an awful lot of chain throwin' in a short period. Depends on the individual."

"Yeah, well this individual would like to take as much time as possible!" Freddy had already heard enough. He changed the subject. He had heard that Zak was a farmer, which reminded him of a story. "Back in high school we renovated a tractor once," Freddy said. Jon rolled his eyes and took a sip from his rye and Coke. He would have said something but nothing sharp enough came to mind; besides, Freddy was now atop a steep hill and ready to roll. "I took Mechanical Engineering. An old tractor had been donated to the school. Somebody's uncle had been out plowing a field when his induction papers came to go fight World War II, or was it Korea, hmmm. Well, he just parked it right there where he was when he got the news, went off to fight, got killed, and that ol' tractor sat there ever since 'cause nobody had the heart to move it. Think about it. Year in and year out, that tractor sat there, weeds and shit growing all up and through it, with them still workin' the field, planting soy or wheat, and that old tractor just sittin' there in the middle of it all like a gravestone. Like one night, that guy's ghost was gonna come back, fire 'er up, and finish plowin' that field like he hadn't never missed a beat! It was all froze up and rusted to hell.

"We had a devil of a time gettin' parts for it, went combin' through junkyards and old barns. We just had to invent or reengineer a lot of stuff. By the end of the year we had that old thing runnin' like a top. I'll bet they're still usin' 'er too. Y'know? I had more fun in that ol' shop class than I had the whole damn time I went to school. I used to tell my guidance counselor that they should let some guys just go to shop, y'know, turn that part of the school into kind of a shop college. A lot of guys, y'know, just aren't much good at all the other shit they teach, might as well be doin' something useful, doncha think? He thought I was just shittin' him but I was serious."

Freddy shook his head, "What can ya do when you live in a shoe?" He saw that their drinks were empty and went to the bar for another round. When he returned his thoughts, had skipped ahead a few years. "Seismographin', now there's an enjoyable job. I had a bunch of goin' nowhere jobs when I got out of high school then I took a job seismographin'." Freddy had picked up on Jon's didactic tone and was overjoyed to have another worm to share his experiences with. Jon was a good listener and Zak was eager. Freddy had a green light.

"You see, there's a stage, just before they decide where they're going to set up a rig, where they do their geological surveys. They set off dynamite and other explosives in order to get readings on what's below the surface by measuring the sound waves that bounce back. I drove a thumper truck, which is a little different as we didn't use any explosives, which was fine with me! The thumper truck hammers the ground and a recording truck nearby takes the readings. But all the time, y'see, I'm watching those roughnecks living from hole to hole, making that good money, doin' what they please, and I'm sayin' to myself, 'That's what I ought to be doin.' It took me a while to get up the nerve. I'm damn glad to be breakin' out with Jesse Lancaster, he's just about the best. I only wish things didn't have to move so fast. I'm not exactly ready to start thrown' chain right away."

"Shit, you'll do all right once you get started," Jon said. It was the one bit of encouragement Freddy had been looking for all night. Freddy's next remark seemed curiously personal.

"Anyway, I'm twenty-one years old, still real young, and there's plenty of the world that I haven't seen yet, y'know?"

"Yeah, well, take my word for it," Jon said under his breath, "there's plenty of the world you don't need to see. This here might just be as good as it gets."

"Here, here," Zak agreed.

They proceeded from that point to get completely drunk. When the bar closed they staggered up the stairs, took showers, and, for the second night in a row, Zachary Harper unrolled his sleeping bag on the cold tile floor in Jon and Fifer's room. He was drunk. He was glad to be alive. He still ached all over but no longer cared. That these were good guys with big hearts was easy to see. They weren't going to willfully do him any harm, and he felt lucky to have drawn them as crew members. He stretched out on the floor and relaxed like he hadn't done in months. As he went to sleep, he could hear himself laughing at Jon and Freddy who continued to give each other a hard time as they climbed into their beds in the dark.

"Hope yer a sound sleeper, Zak," Freddy warned, "ol' Jonny there saws logs like a pioneer."

"Yeah," Jon continued Zak's initiation, "and if you wake up with a sore arsehole in the mornin' don't go blamin' me."

And Zachary Harper set the incident with The Man From Halliburton aside from his thoughts.

THE NEXT MORNING ZAK GROANED as he staggered to the bathroom, stiff, sore, and hung over. The three of them clomped downstairs for breakfast and although Zak offered, Freddy insisted he was still in their debt and so he picked up the check. Jon and Fifer poked fun and bitched at each other all through the meal, occasionally turning their attention to Zak, "You should've seen this son of a bitch yesterday mornin'," Jon said, wagging a stick of bacon in Zak's direction. "He was hurtin' so bad I didn't think he was gonna make it."

"Yeah? My first day trippin' nearly killed me," Freddy commiserated.

"Oh man," Jon laughed. "Freddy was cryin' and groanin' like he'd just had his appendix out. Christ you were somethin'."

"He's right, man, I never hurt all over so bad in my life."

"Not only that, you nearly killed the rest of us! Every other stand was gettin' away from you. Shit, fat boy, iron was flyin' around that derrick like there was a war goin' on. I swear, every time he'd push 'em over, we'd all have to run for cover." Jon laughed and raised his hands over his face like he saw one coming right that instant.

"That's not true, Zak, a couple got away from me, not every other one. I'd've been okay if that fuckin' Lenny would've helped."

"Lenny!" Jon scowled. "Remember he stood there with that one stand just dancin' like crazy, like he didn't care whether it hit him or not. He kind of sneered at it like it was an asshole or somethin'!"

"That Lenny was scarier'n any piece of iron."

"Oh yeah, remember at one point during that trip he walked over and said something to you? Jesse and I thought he was going to kill you. What did he say?"

"I don't know, I couldn't hear him." This got a laugh from Jon, who was clearly more amused by the prospect of a confrontation with Lenny than Freddy had been.

"Say Zak," Jon changed the subject but threw Freddy a wink to keep his attention, "Freddy's got a tent out in the back of his outfit he says you're welcome to if you're still in need, right Fred?"

"Oh yeah, it's almost new. I've only used it once or twice."

"Well sure, thanks."

Jon and Freddy exchanged quick "I told you so" glances back and forth. Zak couldn't tell which one had bet against him. Now that he had a few bucks in his pocket, it must have seemed a sure thing that he would take a room.

They hit a few spots in town and goofed off for a while before returning to the Pioneer for a couple of beers. They eventually bought a six-pack for the trip out location road.

They set up the tent a safe distance upwind from the outhouse and as they headed for work, Zak looked forward to the night when he would have a private place to go, to think, to adjust, to be himself.

ZACHARY HARPER'S THIRD DAY AS a worm hand on Bomac 34 was also the third day of September. It was gusty and cool. Comparatively speaking, it was an easy day. Freddy's wish was granted: It was a drillin' tower. They were turnin' to the right. The kelly, a huge steel device suspended in the derrick and attached to the topmost joint of drill pipe, turned with the pipe as the rotary table down on the floor turned, and the entire drill stem, thousands of feet long, spun swiftly and smoothly.

When Zak and the boys were dressed and ready, Freddy took Zak around and showed him worm's responsibilities. He was to visually monitor that kelly's slow descent through the derrick as it followed the pipe turning down into the hole, and record every ten feet of progress by taking a sample. Zak followed Freddy up a steep staircase at the side of the rig to a slender perforated iron walkway just a few feet below floor level. "Derrickhand mixes the mud down in the hopper," Freddy screamed in Zak's ear and pointed through a gap in the winterizing wall to a shack down on the ground. "The mud then runs through that hose up into the kelly and flows down through the pipe all the way to the drill bit where three high-pressure nozzles force the debris back up to the surface outside the pipe along the sides of the hole. It comes back through that return line and into this shale-shaker!" Freddy slapped his palm against a square iron device that stood about waist high beside him. "We'll come back to this in a second." They moved down a couple of steps to a smaller box. "This is the desander," and on another couple of steps down the line was the "desilter." Then he pointed to a lake of mud next to the rig, "It eventually ends up there in the reserve pit."

They made their way to the end of the catwalk alongside the giant whirring belts that stretched from the big twin diesel engines up on the floor down to the pump houses on the ground. These pump houses were nestled among a line of iron shacks, and Freddy, seeing Zak was still confused, started with the one on the far end. "That one's the light plant that powers all the lights on the rig. The next one down is the hopper where derrick-hand mixes his mud. After that, you have your mud shacks and it's from there that the number one pump draws the mud it sends down the hole. The number two pump is used for the mud mixer in the hopper; keeping the viscosity level just right is tricky. You'll have to get Marty to explain it, all I know is that the hole gets priority at all times, as far as these motors are concerned, and that number two pump has to be ready to fill in if number one goes down. So we keep number two runnin' constantly, if only at a low idle."

With the extent of his knowledge now exhausted, Freddy turned and Zak followed him back the way they came. Freddy negotiated that slender catwalk with surprising agility. They were still twenty or twenty-five feet above the ground and Zak found himself hurrying, looking down, and constantly reaching for something to hang onto as he tried to keep up. Back at that shale-shaker, Zak took his first sample as Freddy supervised. He scooped out a couple of mounds of muck from the shale-shaker into an old-fashioned prospecting type of wire net pan. He shook out the mud, rinsed it, shook it some more, rinsed it again, and then took a handful of whatever was left and put it into a small sack. This he stored in a rack behind the main motors up on the floor for future reference. Freddy reminded him to keep alert to how many feet per minute they were drilling, which would be contingent upon how deep they were and how many hours were on the bit. These factors would change from one drillin' tower to the next. Freddy was very patient and very concerned that Zak get every detail down pat. A friendly contrast to the lack of instruction during those first two grueling days of tripping.

Collecting those samples was to be Zak's primary responsibility and, when he wasn't doing that he figured, unless he was told otherwise, he'd scrub. And did he scrub! He did more scrubbing than anyone else on that rig had ever seen! He didn't realize it, but he made a lot of friends that day. Jesse, as it turned out, was glad to have found a hand who wasn't going to be dead weight, and a scrubbin' crew makes that driller look good. Marty was happy because Zak scrubbed both pump houses, inside and out, they being derrickhand's responsibility. But it was Jon who, throughout the course of the day, kept a cocked eye on Zak's scrubbing madness. At one point, Jon actually climbed a ladder to join Zak on the pump house roof.

"You silly bastard!" he smiled. "You don't have to do all this scrubbin'!"

"I know, but I want to make a good impression with driller Jesse, and, to tell you the truth, I ache so goddamn much that this is kinda helpin' to work my joints free." Getting up that morning had been at least as tough as the two preceding and coupled with the aftereffects of eight or ten scotch and waters he was in dire need of an ameliorative. He liked to drink as much as the next guy, but he wondered how men like Blackie and Jesse did it.

"You can get used to damn near anything," he could almost hear Blackie saying.

That third day also brought another new wrinkle. Every couple of hours, when the kelly reached a low point in the derrick, everybody dropped what they were doing and dashed up to the floor to connect another joint of pipe to the drill stem. Freddy had been dreading this moment for days, weeks, all his life, and it was clear to everyone as they took the floor that first time that Freddy was just nervous as hell. He would have to throw chain. Even though Zak was relieved that the pressure to perform was no longer centered on him, he felt for poor Freddy, whose diffident looks from hand to hand would have inspired compassion

in all but the most stone-hearted wretch. Just as they were about to begin, Jon held up his hand for Jesse to wait. He walked over to Freddy and spoke something into Freddy's ear. Freddy nodded his head with the shameless air of a man who has been granted a temporary reprieve and the two roughnecks changed places. Jesse smiled and shook his head. As Jon took chainhand's position for a quickie demonstration, the sigh of relief all around was damn near audible. Zak was glad to see it done correctly if for no other reason than he wanted to be ready for anything when Freddy did eventually take hold of that chain and prepare to give it a throw.

In a hole next to the rotary table, the mousehole, sat the next joint of pipe to be connected to the drill stem. After they had thrown in their slips, Jon slammed his tongs onto the bottom joint and they unlatched the kelly from the joint in the hole. The three floorhands had to then push the huge steel kelly over to the pipe in the mousehole and make it up. From there Jesse hit the drawworks and hoisted the assembly out of the mousehole. "Dope it up!" Jon hollered as they shouldered the pipe into position. He motioned with his head to a bucket nearby and Zak, ever ready, ran to it, not really understanding what was needed. The bucket was full of some greasy goop and a brush, and he immediately slopped the pinhead with it as Jesse let down the pipe. Jon and Fifer then guided the male pinhead down into the female box end of the pipe waiting in the hole. At this point Jon picked up the free end of a long Y-shaped chain, one end of which was attached to the chain tongs, the other end wound around the make-up cathead on the engine. Then with one arm, Jon adroitly flipped the chain, and with a ferocious crack! it leapt upward from the bottom joint to the top one wrapping neatly in whip-like fashion four times just above the pinhead. Jon stepped closer, still holding his end of the chain tight, and with the flat of his gloved right hand, he deftly guided those wraps so they wouldn't lose their grip as Jesse hit the cathead, violently sucking in that chain, thus spinning the top pipe madly for only an instant until it was tightly screwed down into the bottom one. Chain tongs then went onto the top joint, worm tongs to the bottom to tighten it one last little bit, and the connection was made. *An astonishing procedure*, thought Zachary Harper. It had been accomplished so smoothly and so fast that he feared poor Freddy's anxiety would only increase.

Next, Zak was instructed to scoot down to the ground, attach the boom line to another thirty-foot pipe lying in the rack, and follow it up the beaver slide to the floor where they would place it in the mousehole for the next connection. As soon as they started up that beaver slide, however, the pipe began heaving danger-ously from side to side, and Zak corralled it between his legs to calm it down, bruising his ankles, shins, and legs in the process, giving him some worm bites of his own. He didn't want to think of it coming free altogether.

When they had done, Jon put a brotherly arm around Freddy's shoulder and gave him one last piece of advice as the three men left the floor, "Remember, whatever you do, don't let go of that chain after you throw it or you'll loose your wraps, and worse, when Jesse hits that cathead, it'll whip around like crazy and you'll scare the piss out of poor old Harper."

A couple of hours later, they were back up on the floor for another connection and Freddy made his first throw. The chain did not leap into position making tight wraps as it had for Jon but hopped feebly to the top joint wrapping twice tightly and once loosely, and Jesse was careful not to spin the cathead as violently as usual. The tongs also needed to be applied one additional time for good measure, but the connection was made and Freddy hadn't fucked up after all; that was the main thing.

THE DUST RAISED BY JON'S Oldsmobile as he and Freddy rocketed away from location had long settled when Zak finally wheeled his

Jeep around and rumbled down rig road headed for home. He was taking his time. He felt strange, disoriented. He pulled off down that rancher's private drive and his headlights threw a bright moving bubble of light across the big dark house and barn. The prairie trail looked so different at night. Several times he slowed to a crawl and basically just guessed if he was still on the right path. At last he came to the outhouse by the creek. Four trees, forming a windbreak there, silhouetted eerily against the starry night. He tossed his sleeping bag into the tent, and, without premeditation, stripped naked and walked down to the water. He stood with arms outstretched. He closed his eyes, breathed slowly and deeply, and listened as spirited gusts of wind swept the clanging, banging, screaming, clattering noises of the day from his head, stirred the restless lonely trees abruptly while playful, prankish, zephyrean fingers teased his taut and weary skin, stroking him with a long cool hypnotic caress, raising goosebumps. His scrotum and nipples tightened. Hanks of hair lifted from his neck and brow. He stepped into the chill creek water, ten inches deep at its rushing center, sat down, lay back against the smooth rocks, and burrowed his buttocks into the sand. He completely relaxed beneath the brilliant cold stars. As his body grew accustomed to the cold clear water rushing over him, he breathed in through his nose and out through his mouth. He urinated. He emptied his mind as well as his bladder into the jetting stream of the dark merciful night. After several moments, his body said enough, and he sat up, using handfuls of creek sand to grind away the grime from his day's work. He emerged without shivering, dried off, and wrapped himself in a woolen blanket from the back of his Jeep, rolled a reefer, and sat down on the grass overlooking the gully that wound and stretched away between the swollen mounds of earth that rose up like buffalo humps beyond the creek.

He leaned back on his elbows and faced the sky, all the while keeping company with the long, black tree limbs that gently waved across his field of vision. The wind washed over him with an erratic rhythm, in waves that made him tingle, as though the tempest itself had been made capricious at having found him and his unlikely trees, waiting there in the midst of all this bleak and desolate nothingness. It rewarded him with sound, a distant elegiac echo. Its singing but a small part of this chorus that filled his ears and excited his heart. What was it? A bird? Some desperate or lonely animal? That echo accented other sounds, the movement and energy was all about him invisible, yet very present. His senses were lured by all. There was no longer the phony separation between his senses, his intellect, and his spirit. He had felt the cleansing undeniable stream as it coursed its velvet smoothness over his body, over the submissive eroding earth. He could hear the snorting intake of air and water by some animal a few hundred feet away, as though he were growing some new kind of eyes, eyes that needed only the suggestion of light.

Suddenly, he understood the strange feeling he had had on the way home but couldn't then verbalize. It was *calm*. That day's tower had presented no immediate life-and-death situations, and he was becoming comfortable with his new persona forming. Indeed, he was changing. He could not lament the death of his old self, for it had died too long ago. He had been carrying around a stinking corpse while believing the lie that life is death. That the putrid odor of his decaying soul was somehow sweet and narcotic. Whenever *this urge to change course had commenced in him before, it had caused him fear, anger, and at those times he had lashed out viciously to pro*tect himself, his status. The suggestion, or threat, that he was but as yet unformed, insubstantial, only half a man, and the tricks he had been taught to convince himself it was not so, now all lay exposed as the merest fakery and conceit. He was now many miles down a different road. Although he might look back, that which he had left was, as of this minute, completely out of sight.

An animal down the creek a ways thumped off slowly when he had drunk his fill. Zak wondered what it might have been. He was completely unconcerned for his safety, as he had nothing that the creature might want. He felt everything that moved or also felt and was a part of this vast scene that seemed vibrant, electric, and teeming with life. The season was changing. He could feel the subtle differences in the air, in the ebb and flow of the currents and chemicals around him. The moon and the stars that shone on the water in the creek and across the coarse, rolling, grassy surface of the land caused a reflection, not so much from the rippling liquid surface but from the entire illuminated depth of field. The currents swept through him like a natural coagulant that fused him to the surrounding scene. The gentle shiver that ran through his rib cage tied him to the quivering moment, impelling him to voice a medicine song in answer to it. Not a mantra that would engrain it to his being—for they were strangely separate—but a response, an articulation of another kind that states the willful elements in common and those too that set him apart. We are all here, we are all temporary, yet we are forever; we will all willingly perish to give this great difference meaning, so that some other thing may rise from this loneliness and, too, succeed in becoming. He thought none of these things in words, but he felt them and knew them at once.

He thought about two kinds of death. One that is good, that makes way for new things—like he was a new thing—and the other, the death caused by selfishness. When selfishness kills it stands in the way and nothing new becomes. *Wasted. How appropriate*, he thought, that the vernacular of his time had adopted that word for selfish death for murder. It seemed evil to have that profound understanding and not change. To compel the truth to lie. To compel anything to reflect and then become its own hideous contradiction. He understood, too, that there are other forms of death that he was as yet unaware of. He tried to find a tone that would state his case harmoniously to all that was placed around him. That would differentiate him and yet declare his solidarity. At first it was just a sound that came from deep within his belly and up into his chest. When he found a tone that didn't drown out this sense of life and place he held in his ears, his mouth opened, and his throat and lips fluttered with the very vibration of it. After you have journeyed out into the universe and have perceived that it exists, you must bring that perception back with you and it must blend with that little universe in which you have chosen to spawn. The water in the creek, the wind, the trees, the rolling plains of grass were singing. His mouth formed words that no human ever sang or spoke, though he was not the first to find such words, for they have always been on the tips of tongues.

V

The last time Zak saw Calico O'Mally they spent a day together in Grand Forks, North Dakota, getting the Jeep in shape. They checked the belts and hoses, changed the plugs, removed the catalytic converter, and put on new heavy-duty shocks. Then they moved on to the interior, and Calico helped Zak unbolt and remove the bench seat from the back. "This'll make me a great living room sofa," Calico laughed, and, indeed, when they had done, they lugged it up the stairs to his apartment, mounted it to some cinderblocks, draped an Indian blanket over the entire setup, and placed a lamp overlooking one shoulder. "My homework couch!" it was duly commissioned.

"And you have a place to stow your gear, hell, you can even sleep in there," Calico said, referring to the neat square hole in the back of the Jeep where the seat had been. On the floor in the front, O'Mally found Zak's book box filled with cassette tapes and assorted reading matter. Calico picked through the cassette tapes, throwing the good ones in a paper sack—Dylan,

Neil Young, Jerry Garcia, Johnny Winter—and threw the rest, including books—the Viking Portables by Nietzsche and Ralph Waldo Emerson—all in the trash. "If any roughnecks see you readin' and listenin' to any of this shit they'll think you're strange for sure," he warned. These were replaced with David Allan Coe, Waylon & Willie, Johnny Cash, and Steve Goodman.

As night had fallen, they moved back upstairs and Zak opened a fresh bottle of Dewar's scotch.

"That Jeep is ready for anything," they agreed.

They sat on a rug in the center of the room and toasted Zak's adventure long into the night. At one point Calico dug through a closet and found a couple of duffel bags where he kept his rig gear. Out came two hard hats, one barely used, both a dark red, one with little or no markings, the other completely plastered over with stickers from the various companies he had hired out with. "You don't want this one," Calico said of the latter, "you're a worm and you'd better not act like you're anything different. Besides, this is as close to a trophy of my roughneckin' days as I'm gonna get." He placed the hat prominently on a shelf and gave Zak the naked red hard hat, a pair of baggy rumpled-up overalls, gloves, and a never-worn yellow baseball cap with a Trans-Alaska Pipeline Project patch in the crown. They talked seriously about drilling for oil, Zak hanging on every word. Most of which he didn't understand. Of course, there were some things he could understand. Things he was willing to risk an awful lot to get a taste of.

They talked about college, and Zak was startled to hear Calico say he was scared. He was scared of being the oldest guy in class. He was scared of taking a subordinate role to teachers he may not respect. "Jesus Zak, I'm used to smackin' a wiseacre across the mouth. What if one of them cunts says somethin' and I haul off and hit 'im before I know what I'm doin'?" He was scared of how smart the other students were. He was scared of books. He was scared of college girls. "Shit Zak, up there on the slopes, well,

I've been payin' for it for so long I don't know if I remember how to *talk* a girl into it, y'know?"

"Just let the women take care of that, you won't have to say much," Zak laughed. "You're older, been around, more mature, that'll mean a lot. As for the books, all I can say is, read'm. If you're vague on the meaning of a word, look it up. Even if you're looking up two or more a page and it's slowing you down to a crawl. Don't take for granted that you know what the author is trying to say. Stick with it and the pace'll soon pick up. In a month you'll be in the same boat with everyone else. But you gotta hit'm hard and let everything else take a backseat. You're a hard worker. You'll be fine."

At last, they fell asleep there in the living room, each resting his head against one of Calico's duffel bags as the stereo played a side of *Tonight the North Star Band* over and over.

The next morning, as they were saying their goodbyes, Calico produced one more item fished from the depths of his roughneckin' years. A beat-up copy of *The People's Almanac*.

"Here, if you need to read somethin' you can read this, it's perfect for roughneckin'. It's got a little of everything. Nothing in it is so long you can't get something out of it during one good dump. And brother, that's about all the time you're gonna have for readin'. Besides, when them good ol' farm boys see you reading something with the word almanac in it, they'll figure you're all right.

"Oh, and by the way," Calico added as Zak fired up the Jeep and prepared to head West, "it's not called a *tower*, but a *tour*."

"Tour?"

"Yeah, like tour of duty, 'cept the way all these good old boys speak, different accents from all over, different variations of roughneck-redneck-ese, it comes out sounding like *tower*. And fuck, tower makes more sense really, but you should know, officially, it's a tour, they're interchangeable."

"Tour, got it."

"And Zak, don't call me unless it's an emergency, okay?" and then smiled warmly as Zak put 'er in gear. "Hey wait! Look, I want you to take this," he said and dropped to one knee, rolled up his pant leg, and began to unbuckle a leather strap that wrapped around his shin. A moment later he handed Zak a beautiful leather scabbard from which Zak pulled a hand-made bowie knife with an elk-bone-and-aluminum handle. The name "Ruana" was etched into the blade at the base. "Be careful with that. It saved my life countless times. I don't figure I'll be needin' too much life-saving in business school. You just take good care of it and it'll take good care of you."

"Hey buddy," Zak said as the two clasped hands.

"Keep yer wits about you. Just remember what I said. Don't take any chances. You'll be livin' from paycheck to paycheck out there. Hand to mouth. But you won't owe nobody nothin' and you can come and go when you please. If you think somebody's got their ass up on their back you look'm right in the eye, keep your mouth shut, and wait for them to make the first move. If you think you're in a bad situation—if that driller rides your ass too hard, or somebody says somethin' you don't like—you just twist off. Don't think nothin' of it neither. No need to explain nothin' to nobody. You just walk off that floor, get your gear, hit that Jeep, and head 'em down the road. Come back a day or two later and pick up your check. It's called bein' free, Zak. And there ain't nothin' like it on God's green earth. If I need you I'll send a note to Watford City, care of General Delivery. Drop by the post office every now and then and check and see if there's something there."

"Will do."

As Zak roared away, Calico let out a war whoop and raised his fists in the air. Zak stuck his fist out the window, and watched as his cousin got smaller and smaller in his sideview mirror.

AFTER A QUICK COUPLE OF breakfast sandwiches, some exercises, and his morning constitutional there in the big purple outhouse, Zak dragged the duffel bag Calico had given him out of the Jeep and fashioned a sofa-type backrest. He pulled off his shirt, doused his broad hairy chest with baby oil, and sat down to read in the glorious morning sun. With his jug of water beside him he flipped open *The People's Almanac*. Calico had been right, as usual. In the intervening weeks Zak learned that on August 5th, 1914, the first traffic light in the United States was installed at Euclid Avenue and 105th Street, Cleveland, Ohio. That same year there were seventy-five thousand people killed on the job and another seven hundred thousand injured. He read about French auto driver Louis Chevrolet, and he learned about the many countries with populations smaller than the city of Baltimore. He read how, at the turn of the first millennium, devout Christians believed the world would end on that date and so traveled to Palestine to be on hand for the blessed event. Disappointed, they returned to Europe and told of their abuse at the hands of the Muslim Turks who reigned in the Holy Land. A crusade was begun to force them out. He read about Father Gourier who fed his guests overrich food, until it killed them. This morning, as he thumbed through the big fat paperback, he landed in the middle of a biography of George Washington and was just about to keep going until his eyes fell upon the subtitle, "Psychohistory," and he paused, reminded of Asimov's *Foundation*.

> Mary Washington, hardly the perfect American mother depicted in schoolboy biographies, was a bad-tempered shrew who largely succeeded in her efforts to make George's young life miserable. All of her children got away from her as soon as they could, and George was no exception. As her son advanced in the world, she openly resented his success, claiming that he thoughtlessly neglected her. She refused to participate in any ceremony

honoring him (including his inauguration as president) and deprecated his achievements. Emerging from this background, it is not surprising that Washington fell head over heels for a succession of young ladies, in hopes of winning the love and admiration he had been denied at home. Frustrated in love, and particularly for his hopeless passion for Sally Fairfax, Washington was similarly disappointed in the early stages of his military career. His father had died when George was a boy, and it was only natural that the shy, socially insecure youth should turn to warfare as a means of establishing his own manhood. But his first combat experience, when he was twenty-two, was an ill-managed fiasco for which young Colonel Washington was held personally responsible. It may be assumed that all these personal disasters contributed to the celebrated patience and perseverance that were among Washington's most notable features in later life. He had learned that the only way to cope successfully with his environment was to gain rigid command of his own passionate nature.

"Georgie Porgie puddin' 'n pie, kiss the girls and make them cry," Zak could remember his own mother saying every time the first president's name was mentioned. It was strangely comforting that the father of his country had not been appreciated and couldn't stand the bullshit at home. Zak wondered if a deeper precedent hadn't been set. Although Washington had swung the ax that separated the blossom from its contemptuous root, had George, a fatherless son, been the one to cleave the continental gap between generations as well? Was the transfer of power between generations the most violent struggle of all? Zak remembered the struggle his and other families suffered over the politics surrounding Vietnam. He considered Jesse Lancaster, mentor to Jon, Marty, Freddy, and himself, who could not inspire the same respect, admiration, or motivation in his own son. Was this a contemporary dilemma? Or was a more universal syndrome at play? Obsolescence is inevitable. Wisdom is scarce. Youth is invincible, and therefore blind.

Chief Red Jacket of the Iroquois Indians called Washington the "town destroyer." Washington didn't free his slaves until after both he and Martha were dead.

And what had Zachary Harper learned when he felt the call to step out into the world and take his place? That everywhere he was met with confusing signals. If he were to find a place for himself, must he wrest his space from someone else? Couldn't he just create a new space altogether? When he first attempted to summon the warrior within himself he found to his horror that his kindred spirits were in full retreat, the battlefield overrun, spoiled, used up. And those who would be his mentors and teachers were all in opposition. Wherever and to whomever he turned, he had found a wasteland. He made up his mind, in secret, that his only alternative was to seek an alternative and to do that one must go a-yondering. On the next page under the heading, "Little Known Facts," his eyes fell upon this paragraph:

> One of the most mysteriously misleading facts of the Washington Legend is the story of the pious general kneeling in prayer in the snow at Valley Forge. Not only is there no evidence to support this tale, but Washington was notorious in his parish church for his refusal to kneel at any of the customary moments in the Episcopal service. As his minister declared disapprovingly after the President's death, "Washington was a deist." Although Martha was a devout churchwoman, George never shared her

enthusiasm. On communion Sundays he always walked out before taking the Eucharist, leaving Martha to participate in the service alone.

Zachary Harper had known men who dignified their docile, manageable capitulation and housebroken idolatry, in the language of deference, homage, and prostration. Men to whom grovelling was a way of life, who zealously defended their chosen space for kneeling, and who designated kneeling space for others. Refusing to kneel never occurred to them. Zachary's eyes left the page and scanned the rolling tumultuous landscape. *We will all humble ourselves before something, and, if we do not make that choice, it will be made for us.* Where had he heard that? He flashed for an instant on the screaming, gleaming tower of Bomac 34. To some, these issues matter little, if at all. Others are aware of the trade-offs they make and choose to live happily behind the bars of their own rationalizations, comforted by the sound of the cattle-driver's yips. He flashed again on faces, names, acquaintances, and placed them all on that narrow steep stairway leading up, like a gallows, to that oil rig platform.

At the bottom of the page was this quote from George himself:

> How pitiful in the eyes of reason is that false ambi-
> tion which desolates the world with fire and sword for
> the purposes of conquest and fame, when compared
> to the milder virtues of making our neighbors
> and our fellow men as happy as their frail conditions
> and perishable natures permit them to be. 1794.

I guess he ought to know, thought Zachary Harper.

ZAK TOOK THE REST OF the day easy. He snoozed on and off in the warmth and privacy of Freddy Fifer's tent. He waded in the creek and tossed a dozen or more softball-sized rocks up onto the shore and made himself a small fire circle. When he was done, he scanned the naked horizon and laughed at himself. "What is there here to burn?" He rolled into town and purchased some canned goods, an opener, potatoes, corn, a big pot, a smaller one with a long handle, some coffee, assorted necessities, a bag of charcoal, and a small shovel. At one of the local cafés he was able to beg a chipped coffee cup, a cracked plate, a bowl, some bent silverware. They even threw in an old skillet and a couple of pots for good measure. On his way to and from town he stopped from time to time to chase down a tumbleweed, or to pick up some boards that had fallen from the back of a pickup. By the time he left for work, the back of the Jeep was filling with burnable matter.

That fourth day on location was simply another drilling tower and in the course of eight hours they made four connections exactly as they had done the day before. Fifer's chain throwing had not improved, or gotten any worse. Those wraps still limped to the top of the joint, but got there nonetheless. The rest of the time was taken up with scrubbing, group chores, and individual projects. The nucleus of the crew, Jon, Marty, and Jesse, got along so smoothly that the atmosphere in that top doghouse was positively homey. When he told the others about his difficulty finding firewood, it immediately became a group project to search the rig for suitable stuff to burn. Jesse came up with some thick planks that had been used during nipple-up. Marty, Jon, and Freddy each contributed to the effort, and by the end of the day there was a pile of junk sitting beside Zak's Jeep.

Meanwhile, Zak was still self-conscious about having virtually no experience soldering or tearing down motors and pumps. He knew he could scrub, however, and when he wasn't up on the floor giving it his all he scrubbed his heart out. He assiduously marked the downward progress of the kelly, something he would later do by sheer instinct, and took his samples dutifully.

Also, he made it his business to keep abreast of what the other crew members were up to, and whenever they went on a mission involving basic maintenance, he would drop whatever he was doing, if at all possible, to observe, assist, and pick up pointers. Apparently, certain guys who had hired on in the past had been colossal assholes and yet, in some cases, had ended up working with them for quite some time. In contrast, he could tell by how at ease everyone seemed with him that, for the time being at least, they were glad he was on their team. He was also feeling comfortable enough to start asking questions. Jon and Marty were really the only ones to ask, as Fifer hadn't been at this kind of work much longer than Zak had and Jesse, well, Zak just didn't want to bother him.

That evening Zak was scrubbing the catwalk leading to the shale-shaker when Jon called up to him.

"Hey Zak. We need you for a minute, okay?" Zak bounded down the stairs and followed Jon at a gallop toward the hopper where Marty was dumping big sacks of mud powder, which he tore open with a wicked-looking knife, into the mixing machine which was the hopper itself. Marty seemed all in a fluster. He had fallen behind and that toolpusher would be back before you know it to see if that viscosity level was up to where he wanted it. As soon as he had done with the last sack, they dashed around back to a long row of mud sacks stacked up about chest high along the wall. They each grabbed one, "Hurry de fuck up wid deez here!" Marty hollered and scurried back to the front door of the shack. The sacks weighed a hundred pounds or more and each man's legs wobbled as he hurried with his load. Marty carried his inside, Zak and Jon dropped theirs at the door and ran back to fetch two more. When they were a dozen or more ahead of Marty's feverish pace, Jon and Zak paused, leaning against the mud sacks at the back of the shack to catch their breath. They lit up.

"Y'know, you seem to be a pretty strong fella," Jon said.

"I'm about average, I guess I'm as strong as some, others are stronger. These bags could come in smaller units," he laughed, mildly curious as to what Jon might be getting at.

"Yeah," Jon chuckled, "well, they're heavy. That's for sure. But you're pretty strong all right, for your size and all, there's no doubt about that. Tell you what, let's see you raise one of these sacks over your head, like this." Jon clenched his cigarette between his lips and, straining under the weight, heaved one of the sacks up over his head, raising veins in his neck and arms, squinting from the smoke drifting into his eyes. Zak began to raise his bag but turned and looked up. There on the roof of the shack was Marty holding his long knife, ready to tear it open over Zak's head.

"Got damn it Jonny! You tipped'm off!"

"I didn't!"

Zak left them there barking and cursing. A short time later from his perch up by the shale-shaker, Zak spied Freddy Fifer passing by the bottom of the stairs, covered in mud powder from head to toe, looking for all the world like some roughneck ghost wearing black-framed glasses.

"Two worms on one crew," Jesse laughed strolling up to peer over the side of the rig to see Marty and Jon duck into the mud shack down below like a couple of marauding Apaches. "I ought to make 'em pay for them mud sacks."

IT WAS ABOUT ELEVEN FIFTEEN p.m. when Zak arrived back at the campsite. He washed his hands and face in the creek, brushed his teeth, and slept soundly in the warmth of his bag in the tent.

The next morning he awoke feeling truly rested and fresh after two relatively easy towers, and this would be the last work day before days off. He made a fire that he started with a jar of number one diesel fuel and the junk he brought from location the night before and boiled creek water in both pots. In the smaller

one he tossed some coffee grounds, in the larger one some potatoes. He opened a can of beans'n franks and set it at the fire's
edge. When the potatoes had softened up a bit, he dumped out
the water and poured in the beans, a piece of beef jerky, a couple
of raw eggs; he then nipped the leafy end off a tomato and tossed
it in whole. He opened a bottle of Lea & Perrins Worcestershire
sauce and shook it vigorously at the concoction.

Later, as he sat by the creek, reading *The People's Almanac*
and taking the day easy, Jon and Fifer came rolling up in Jon's
Oldsmobile.

"Roughneck stew!" Fifer laughed as he took a whiff. He
scooped some out with a tin can and the three of them ate and
drank.

"Y'know," Freddy said through a mouth stuffed with stew,
"some people might think yer nuts to stay out here like this, but I
think it's cool as shit."

Jon shook his head. He was carefully sipping the coffee from
a Styrofoam cup he'd found on the floor of his car, trying to leave
as many grounds as possible in the bottom of it. "I'll bet it's cool,
you come out here tonight and take a bath in that creek, fat boy.
That's gotta be cold, Zak."

"It is."

ZAK AND THE BOYS ARRIVED for work that day at about two thirty
in the afternoon. When Jon and Fifer pulled up alongside the
Jeep, Jon got out of his car and slammed the door shut, clearly, all
pissed off.

"What's the matter?" Zak hurried over, thinking maybe Jon
and Freddy had gotten in a fight during the short ride from camp
and maybe he could help set things straight.

"Black leg," Jon scowled as he tromped toward the doghouse.

"Black leg?" It sounded like a pirate's nickname, or some
tropical disease.

"The pipe in the derrick," Freddy said, hustling along after. "You call that black leg. Looks like we're gonna have to finish trippin' that son of a bitch out." Zak stopped and stared up at the tower. He had noticed the pipe standing in the derrick when he pulled up but had made no mental note of it. Over the course of the last few days he had accustomed himself to not taking anything for granted. They changed clothes and Jon led the other two roughnecks up to the top doghouse. Sure enough, that daylights crew was pulling pipe out of the hole. Marty was already climbing the tower and Jon, Zak, and Fifer melted out onto the floor and replaced their daylights counterparts in midswing.

Rory, that daylights driller, hollered "Whooee!" at how smoothly Jesse's hands gave relief. Rory stayed with that brake handle as Jesse had yet to arrive, and for a half-dozen stands the boys worked with a foreign driller. When Jesse stepped out onto the floor he was all smiles. The whole process came to a stop when Marty reached the derrickhand's station. That daylights derrickhand, the wild-looking one, turned over his safety belt and began his long climb down. Marty, when he was ready, waved down to Jesse, who took hold of that brake handle and they were off! They were looking at pulling the rest of the pipe out of the hole, changing the bit, then running all of that pipe right back in again.

Now that the crew members all knew one another a little better, the work didn't seem nearly as strained as it had those first two trips. Even Jon seemed to lighten up. Before too many stands, they were up to speed, yanking those stands out of the hole at a ferocious clip. "Hey old-timer!" Jon goaded Jesse on. "You sure are slow! Is this as fast as you can get 'er!" and when those joints broke and the mud flew into their faces, Jess would throw his head back and laugh like hell. Occasionally Freddy would slack up when they were pulling on those slips and Jon would scold, "Goddamn it fat boy! Pull on those sons ah bitches! Pull on 'em!"

And when they'd take a bite with their tongs he'd scream, "Make 'em bite! Make 'em bite!"

When they were at last out of the hole and had broken out a new bit, Jesse said, "All right, hurry up and grab a bite to eat," and he wasn't kidding. Before Zak had finished making his second sandwich, they were called back up to the floor. He was shoving the last big bites into his mouth as he took his station.

Zak's new function as they tripped it back in was to stab pipe. This wasn't entirely new to him as he had stabbed pipe when making connections the last two days but it was much more intense as these stands were ninety feet high instead of the smaller thirty-foot joints used during connections. Just trying to steady the ninety-foot stand with only his shoulder as it hung there in the derrick was tough enough. Next he had to coordinate with driller Jesse, who lowered the stand down over the hole at the exact moment Zak stabbed the six-and-a-half-inch-diameter pinhead straight down into the six-and-a-half-inch pipe. If Zak missed, Jesse had to pick that stand up again for a second try and Jesse yelled, "Harper! What do I have to do, put hair on it for ya!?"

By the end of the day Zak's shoulder was absolutely raw and any and all movement was extremely painful. In spite of this, Zak was having an easy time of it compared to poor Freddy. He had been terribly anxious over his first real bout with the chain and for good reason. Already exhausted from tripping out, he was looking at throwing it maybe ninety times if all went well. It didn't. By the middle of the trip back in he was huffing and puffing and his arms were like rubber. When his agony, futility, and despair reached unmistakable proportions, Jon, in a Simonian gesture, suggested they change places, saying, "Here, let me take over for a while, maybe you can get some pointers from me." Each and every time Jon threw that chain it was just perfect. That pipe would make up just fine. Those wraps would leap from bottom to top. The drawworks would hiss and screech, and that mighty chain would spin that top section down into the bottom one clean and clear. The pace picked up measurably. Down, down, down those joints disappeared through the floor of the rig. The rows of stands waiting in the derrick emptied one after another. Jon and Freddy changed back, and though Freddy attempted to emulate Jon's fast breezy style it wasn't long before the pace slowed once again to accommodate Freddy's jerky, unsure way. And in Freddy's face you could see disappointment, self-ridicule, and shame with every feeble attempt giving birth to an even more feeble try.

Zak had gotten into the habit of continually asking himself, "Where's my danger?" In this instance, his danger was clearly Freddy Fifer. That chain was thrown immediately after Zak stabbed pipe and his face was always just a little too close to that stand for comfort. He could see all too clearly that if Freddy were to lose the tail end of that chain as Jesse was sucking it in, Zak's face would be right in the path of that lethal flying coil and this conjured gruesome, horrific images. It was a long, long day. Relief seemed to show, magically, just as they touched bottom.

Exhausted as he was, Zak trotted down the stairs to the bottom doghouse knowing he had just made it through his first whole week of work. It was one of the most spectacular achievements of his life. He wanted to shout, dance, celebrate, tell the world! Freddy, on the other hand, was morose as he sat on the bench in front of his locker wearing the woeful expression of a man breaking into pieces. Zak's euphoria dissipated as soon as he set eyes on him. Zak patted Freddy on the back as he walked past him to his locker.

"I'm twistin' off. I can't get 'er," Freddy blurted out forlornly.

"No!" Zak said with an incredulous whisper.

"I'm serious, I let you guys down up there. I suck at this. I'm headin' back out to the farm." He lifted his hard hat off with both hands and pitched it into his locker.

Just then Marty and Jon bounded into the doghouse happy as pups. As far as they were concerned, work was already far behind them. When they saw the blubbering lump of goo named Freddy Fifer sitting there on the bench, they stopped in their tracks. It was Jon who broke the silence.

"Hey lightnin', hurry up'n change, we're gonna go get drunk!"

Freddy slowly unbuttoned his shirt, staring straight ahead.

"He's thinkin' of twistin' off," Zak informed the others.

"What for?" Marty looked genuinely startled. Freddy said nothing.

"C'mon, Fred, snap out of it," Jon scolded, unwilling to surrender his jovial mood so easily. "Tomorrow you'll be so hung over this'll all seem like a bad dream. You think too much, that's all." But Freddy was inconsolable.

Marty meanwhile sidled up to Zak and asked, "Whadz iss problem?" Then he stepped over to Freddy and pumped him once in the shoulder, "Hey, kit? Do ya tink I care if id takes all fuh-kin' day t'throw some pipe ina holer? You tink we got some-blace bedder to be? Who fuh-kin' cares, man?"

"Really, Fred, it's just no big deal, hey, you can only get better!" Jon tried to lighten the load but the buddy-buddy stuff clearly wasn't working, and having tried that, they all stood there stupidly and watched poor Freddy plummet beyond their reach. There followed an agonizing moment of silence before the others moved toward their lockers.

A moment later the bottom doghouse door opened up and in walked Jesse Lancaster. This was the first time Zak had seen the driller, or any figure of authority, venture into the roughnecks' lair. He assumed that traditionally this was taboo. But Jesse had a sixth sense about his crew and he walked right over without looking at anyone and sat on the bench next to Freddy. He waited a moment, then laid a palm down on Freddy's knee. The others backed off.

"You did a hell of a job out there today, Fifer. We're all proud of you."

Freddy darted a stupefied glance at his driller. He wanted to state his case to the contrary. Say he was sorry, but that he was twistin'. The words filled his mouth, but he was unable to speak. He was ashamed of how his quivering voice would sound ringing in the ears of these men he respected so much, wanted to be like.

"That was one hell of a tower we just finished," Jesse went on.

"Sure was," someone said.

The craggy, time-worn timbre of Jesse's voice showed the effects of a thousand similar towers. "We got 'er done. We can be damn proud of the work we put in. Each of us." He waited a few seconds for silence to once again fill the room. "There's no reason for you to think that you didn't put out and contribute one hundred percent and carry your share today Freddy, because everyone in this doghouse knows that you did. We're all men in this room, and each and every one of us did a man's worth of work today." Jesse Lancaster lifted his hand from Fifer's knee, rose to his feet, and walked out of the bottom doghouse, shutting the door softly behind him.

Freddy leaned forward and reached into his locker as the others resumed changing their clothes. Out of respect, everyone avoided his liquid eyes until they were out under the bright burning lights of Bomac 34.

VI

Main Street, Scobey, Montana, was quiet on this calm, cool September night, except for three roughnecks whose footfalls on the hard pavement echoed off the storefronts and up into the cool black sky. As they crossed the street from the Pioneer Hotel to Simone's Bar, one roughneck, with a big blond beard, sauntered confidently; one wore octagonal-shaped glasses with bent wire rims, a yellow baseball cap, and moved swiftly, almost invisibly; and the third, who lagged just behind the others, was fat.

Jesse, Marty, and Cynthia were already seated at the far end of the bar when the rest of Jesse's crew walked in. The bar was crowded, smoky, and loud with the murmurs of men and women in conversation.

Jesse and Marty were talking in low voices, drinking rye. Marty had combed his sandy hair back and it now hung evenly in a Buster Brown cut halfway down the back of his neck. Marty had a long, full Roman nose that at first glance made his flaming green eyes seem too close together, a look which made him appear very, very alert.

Cynthia was sipping languidly on a 7Up while staring pleasantly at the rows of bottles on thick glass shelves in a big oak cabinet behind the bar. She was a harmless lump, without poise or posture, and wore a wisp of a smile on a face that was a bit too round, framed by greasy hair that clung dull and flat against her skull. Most people would call her simple. She greeted the newcomers with a nervous smile and watched with alarm as they took up seats in a crude semicircle all around her. When the one in the yellow baseball cap offered to buy the next round and boldly asked her what she wanted, she became totally flustered and her face turned bright red until Marty came to the rescue explaining, "She don' drink nuttin' 'cept sebbin-up." When the men turned away from her and resumed their conversation about oil rigs and the like, she was, once again, able to relax, sip her drink, and return to thoughts that had occupied her before these others had arrived to disturb her. She sighed. In one corner of the mantelpiece behind the bar sat a big fat smiling Buddha, carved from rich red cherry wood, with a sign that hung around his neck which read, "Be Proud of Your Belly!" In its lap was a dusty old beer bottle.

Jesse was glad the others had dropped in; he had news.

"That company hand thinks we've gone down far enough," Jesse announced with a concurring finality to his voice. "We'll probably tear down next week."

Marty and Jon nodded, unfazed.

Freddy, ciphering quickly that a week or two could conceivably pass without him having to throw chain again, shouted, "All right!"

Zak, on the other hand, experienced a momentary flash of panic. What did it mean? Was it over this fast? Would he have to get another job?

"So where're we goin' next?" Freddy wanted to know.

Jesse looked thoughtful as he considered his chubby young chainhand. "I'm not exactly sure yet, but I think the next location will be south of town."

"Well, a lot's got to happen before we worry about that," Jon said. "Tearing down's a bitch and a half, full of hazards and complications."

"Tink dat new fella sout ah town'll have an outhouse for ya, Zak?" Marty snickered and wheezed causing chuckles all around, indicating that Zak's living preferences had become a bit of an in-joke with the crew. They all turned to him, grinning with anticipation to see how he handled a poke in the ribs.

"I sure hope so, a bear can't take a shit in the woods around here."

"Yeah!" Cynthia blurted out unexpectedly. "No woods!"

After another round, the little group broke up. Jesse, Marty, and Cynthia were bound for Watford City where Marty and Cynthia had a cozy little house and Jesse lived with his wife June on the other side of town. Zak and the boys decided to remain at Sam's and, as the others filed out, an image of Marty's Cynthia imposed itself, hauntingly on Zak's mind. He had been struck by how little notice had been paid her by her husband and his friends. They would offer her an eye as they talked, but there was never any attempt to bring her into the conversation, nor did she make any effort at all to carve out any sort of space or notice. The only consideration she received was an endless supply of 7Up to sip, and once, during a lull in the conversation, Marty turned on her alarmingly, making a whooshing sound with his mouth and cheeks yelling, "Wild geese in flight!" and proceeded to pummel her fat arm with a crisp and powerful series of blows that went on way too long, causing her to wince and squeal, her mouth a wild little circle. Zak expected her to be angry but instead, when it was over, she melted under his massive arm and looked adoringly up at him, willing to endure a little whimsical cruelty in return for a little genuine affection. Out of politeness, Zak had thought a couple of times to talk with her but there had been no way to do it naturally. To pay her any undue attention would clearly have been out of line.

The three remaining roughnecks ordered drinks and moved over to a table along the opposite wall.

The plan had been to hit each of the six bars Scobey had to offer but now, in the cozy bosom of Simone's bar, drinks in hand, nothing seemed to matter but that they blow off a little steam on their way to getting completely drunk.

Zak looked around the old saloon. The walls and ceiling were made of tin, just like the great cowboy bars of old, stamped in squares beautifully embossed with coats of arms and fleurs de lis. Among the locals, farmers, and ranchers, here and there were tables of local women, older, to whom the rough-hewn world of the men all around them was comprehensible, manageable, familiar. Hard work showed in the women's knotted fingers, in the way they held their cigarettes, in the worry lines around their mouths and the smile lines around their eyes. Some had been to Sophie's Beauty Shop that morning for this, their one night out a week. Some wore bright solid colors with matching plastic earrings and bracelets. They watched the goings-on, made note of who was present and who wasn't, and laughed quietly at the spectacle before them.

The walls were jammed with pictures. Charles Russell prints depicting scenes from the Old West. A cowboy turning to shoot his six-gun from the back of a swift black stallion. Cattlemen sitting around a campfire playing cards, eyeing one another suspiciously. Paintings by local artists of awkward landscapes, barns, and prairie life. Booze ads of yesteryear. The room was much longer than it was wide and light just seemed to get absorbed in its cavernlike depths. Zak noticed a painting in the back of the room on one of his many trips to the john depicting an Indian warrior triumphantly holding a freshly taken scalp up to the heavens with his mouth fixed open in a triumphant screaming rage. A wicked-looking knife in his other fist dripped blood. Another picture showed a high waterfall that spilled over a rocky cliff descending in a fine spray that morphed into stars in outer space. There was a picture of a beautiful young woman riding naked, sidesaddle, on a goat, holding a golden chalice up to the sky and smiling at a cloudy wind goddess who was attempting to sip from the cup. In one corner near the beaded curtain that led to the very back of the room was a tall sculpture made from elk antlers. A female manne-quin, dressed in buckskin, was imprisoned within.

Zak looked at his watch and he gulped at his drink.

"There's no rush," Jon said.

"Simone doesn't exactly keep regular hours," Freddy laughed.

"Is that her behind the bar?"

"No," Jon answered, "that's Lillian, Simone's sister. And that fella there is Hal, Lillian's husband. You'll know Sam when you see her."

"Yeah," Freddy jumped in like he was about to tell Zak the craziest thing he ever heard. "Simone is Sam. Sam is Simone. They're one and the same person! But you can't call her Sam until she asks you to."

"That's right, and she ain't asked you yet, now has she?" Jon scolded.

"Nope," Freddy smiled, embarrassed, then frowned. "Has she asked you?"

Jon was silent as Zak rubbernecked around the room, trying to guess who and where she might be.

The two roughnecks looked toward the bar, then said in unison, "Ain't here."

Jon, pointed with his cigarette in the direction of the bar. "See those candles on either side of that mirror?" Zak zeroed

in on two ornate brass candleholders with fat white candles on either corner of the mantle. "When those are lit she's here, when they ain't…"

"Is she really so mysterious?"

"Fuck no. She might make tinhorns like fat boy here a bit uneasy, but she's got her own kind of class, her own style, that's for sure. She'll cash checks for a whole crew if they give her a little warning. Heck, even if they don't most times. See that safe over yonder? That's the real McCoy, I'll tell ya." At the front of the room under a window sat a huge black old-timey safe with a giant combination knob and a big brass handle. "You know, we could be at the head of another big oil boom. Sure, we're the only rig around these parts right now, but you never know. Simone seems to be the only person around who's aware of the possibilities. Some towns just love all the cash that oil patch traffic brings but resent having to lift a finger to accommodate us. I mean, we're goin' strong twenty-four hours a day, seven days a week, and when a town closes up at five p.m. and doesn't open again till morning, or if the local hotel won't check anybody in till three p.m., those evenin' and nighttime crews just get left out. Now Sam here will stay open late even though she's supposed to close. She'll open again early, or her sister will, just for that mornin' crew if she thinks she's needed. As far as stayin' open goes, the marshal doesn't come through that often, and he doesn't care. He knows she's got it under control."

"Hell," Freddy tossed in his two cents, "when a man's on days off with a couple thousand bucks in his pocket, he can get real generous if he's got somewhere t'go. So, y'know, it doesn't make sense to piss us off. They do it right down in Watford, boy."

"Christ, nobody better go'n piss you off, eh fat boy?" Jon made a fist and pulled it back aimed at Freddy's fat arm, Freddy flinched, the blow never came. Just then Freddy's fat face went limp as he took notice of something over Zak's shoulder. In Zak's right ear he could hear the clattering of bracelets and the rustle of clothing. His senses filled with perfume that made him a little dizzy. A warm hand rested on his shoulder.

"Well, gentlemen, I see you've found a replacement for poor Lenny at long last. Will Jesse be joining us later?" A deep sonorous accent, was it French? sounded behind Zak's ear.

"No ma'am, he's come'n gone," Jon answered.

"Oh, that's a shame. Tell him I am sorry I missed him."

Zak turned and rose to his feet. Simone was taller than he, fiftyish, wore a long robelike gown of purple and blue held together by a ropelike weave that hoisted her big, milky-white bust upward. Her hair was jet black and carelessly piled on top of her head, falling down here and there in lazy ringlets. Her makeup was heavy, dark around her eyes but shading off into a bluish gray around the eyelids. She had those painted-on movie-star lips that look nothing like her real ones. Big silver rings in the shapes of serpents, charms, and strange twisting designs adorned every finger. Zak thought she was beautiful. Over her shoulder Zak could see Hal, behind the bar, lighting candles with a long brass lighter, the same kind Zak used to light the candles with in church when he was serving mass as an altar boy, with a flint on one end, a snuffer on the other.

"Simone, it's a pleasure," he said. Her hand landed gently in his for a long squeeze rather than a shake. Her skin was warm and soft. Slippery even. "Jon was just telling us what a friend you've been to the roughnecks here in town. My name's Zak Harper."

"Well Zak, we're hoping there's a lot more where you came from." She glanced over her shoulder to the bar where Hal caught the look and began pouring shots. "You're from back East."

A bolt of electricity hit Zak in the spine. He looked quickly at the table; Jon and Freddy eyed one another. "Well," Zak explained, "I'm from all over."

"So am I," Simone smiled. "Gentlemen, I want you to enjoy yourselves tonight," she said as Lillian arrived with three shots of whiskey. "We'll stay open late. Zak, you must come by some afternoon when it's not so crowded and tell me about being from all over. I want to hear everything. We'll get out the map if we have to. Sound like fun?"

"Simone, you can consider me a regular."

"Then you'll have to call me Sam," she smiled and glided away, touching customers on the shoulder as she went, leaning over here and there for a kiss on the cheek. Across the room the wild-looking derrickhand from the daylights crew followed her menacingly with his eyes as she passed through the beaded curtain at the back of the room, and Zak didn't see her again that night.

"Whoa!" Zak said as he drifted down into his chair. Jon laughed loudly. Freddy looked relieved. The Irish whiskey went down smooth and the pace of their drinking picked up in earnest.

Long after the rest of the town had gone completely dark, the three roughnecks left Simone's, each turned silent by the sheer emptiness of the world into which they stepped, made all the emptier by the unfathomable distance of the universe that looked down upon them from above. Back at the Pioneer, they took turns in the shower and later, when Zak stretched out on the cold tile floor in Jon and Fifer's room, he wished he was back in the warmth, privacy, and comfort of his tent by the creek. In fact, he was seriously considering getting up and driving back out there the very instant that he fell into a spinning lonesome sleep.

VII

The next morning Zak was awake early and crept silently from the room, leaving his friends to sleep off the previous night's dipsomania undisturbed.

He had a light breakfast downstairs at the café and watched the gray early morning brighten through the large picture window that looked out upon a side street. He missed his *People's Almanac* but settled for the *Billings Gazette.* The lead story on the front page was about opening day of public school. A story in the *Gazette* the day before regarding the availability of school lunches for all students had omitted the fact that some grade-schoolers were required to bring their own. The editor extended his apologies to any pupil who went hungry because of the error. Another story reported that an illness that infected two dozen residents of Powell, Wyoming, that July and August was not hepatitis after all. The true nature of the illness was still unknown. Wyoming Department of Health and Social Services officials said they would make no further attempt to answer questions about the disease. A fifty-one-year-old father of fourteen was sentenced to ten-month work release for killing a thirty-one-year-old man in a bar. Yugoslavian president Tito was warning against foreign interference in his country and criticized what he called "imperialist forces" for their lip service to human rights in seeming contradiction with their support for white minority regimes in South Africa. National Rifle Association members who had enjoyed the exclusive rights to buy surplus guns from the U.S. Department of Defense at cost since 1905 were now losing that privilege. It was said that to sell guns only to the NRA was discriminatory and amounted to a federal subsidy for the NRA. Japan was mourning the death of Lan Lan, a pregnant giant panda who died of kidney failure taking her infant with her. It would have been the first born outside of mainland China.

Also on that front page it was reported that fifty different companies were seeking exploring rights for steam and hot water over three hundred thousand acres bordering on the Yellowstone National Park, calling it the Island Park Geothermal Area, for the purposes of generating electricity.

Zak munched on a piece of white toast lathered with butter and grape jelly and sipped his coffee.

Not exactly the *Washington Post.* Zak smiled and looked out the window. He would have loved a good internal policy debate, perhaps an update on the alternative energy movement. His brow wrinkled. The current price of a barrel of oil would surely be more important to the good people of North Dakota, Montana, and Wyoming than some fucking bear dropping dead in Japan. After all, nobody's coming all the way out here to drill for oil at three dollars a barrel, but twenty? Twenty-five? Thirty? It's a fucking gold rush! Is anyone paying attention here? Would Paul Volcker, President Carter's Federal Reserve appointment, keep raising interest rates until money became so expensive there wasn't a cent to be borrowed by anyone? Would raising those rates really put a dent in the runaway inflation that Zak felt was the real legacy of Vietnam? Once financial institutions became accustomed to charging high rates of interest, would they ever be satisfied with less? But how high could interest rates go before the entire economy choked to death? Twelve percent? Eighteen percent? Twenty? Everyone at the bank where he once worked had condescendingly said, "Never happen."

Zachary Harper had a sixth sense that told him when experts start using the word "never," sell all your shit and head for the hills.

It suddenly occurred to him that he had no idea when the Federal Reserve was scheduled to meet next, and that made him smile too. Because, he told himself, he didn't give a shit either.

He was glad he had spent the night in town. He was clean. He was fed. And he needed to get his laundry done.

WITH HIS STREET CLOTHES IN a duffel bag and his work clothes in a potato sack, he set out for the laundromat across the street from Sam's. Anyone upon entering that establishment as Zak got his loads under way would have known immediately that here was an oil field worker, or, more specifically, a roughneck. The street clothes consisted entirely of outdoor wear while the work clothes were entirely encrusted with mud. The reek of oil, diesel fuel, and grease filled the room. As he fished them out of the sack, huge chips flaked off, leaving a pile on the floor and a trail to the machines. The washer and dryer smelled of that diesel after the first wash, so he put them through a second time.

As his clothes tumbled, on and on Zak sat down with his F.W. Woolworth's Daily Aide which he used as a diary. It had been weeks since he had opened the little brown hard-backed book, and he had a lot of catching up to do. He reached into his empty shirt pocket for a cigarette, and finding none, dashed out to the Jeep where he kept a fresh pack under the beanbag ashtray that sat next to the gearshift. It occurred to him that he had smoked very few cigarettes the last several days. The reason was simple. He needed his wind. *This would be a good time to quit*, he thought. He left the package unopened in his pocket. Zak flipped open his Daily Aide and pondered over the events of the last two weeks. Rather than attempt to render them chronologically, he decided it would be best to begin with the here and now and work his way backwards as memory came to him.

Just as he was putting Bic pen to paper, the back door to the laundromat pushed open and a tall, slender, elderly man shuffled into the room. He wore a Goodwill-type sport coat and slacks that were so old, tattered, and so heavily stained it seemed they could never have been new. He looked like a city bum from one of those black-and-white depression era buddy can you spare a dime newsreels. The old man glided past a row of dryers then slipped into the men's room. Zak couldn't remember seeing any guys like him in the small towns that dotted his journey west. He figured that small towns generally weren't big enough to support them. No places to hide. Not enough quality refuse. Worse, everyone in these small burgs knows *who* and everyone knows *why*.

Zak turned to his diary with a heavy sigh of relief. He was no longer so completely on his own. He tried to imagine Calico sitting next to him; to hear his cousin talking his oil field talk filtered through Zak's new experiences, taking it all in stride like it was no big deal, just another week in the patch. He recalled the numerous times he had listened to Calico spin yarn upon yarn about his oil field adventures and it all seemed so archaic. Hard to grasp and appreciate fully. He would like to hear them all again. It might have been just another week in the patch, but it was a pretty big week in the life of Zachary Harper.

The old guy had been in the john for quite a while. Just as Zak was considering tapping on the door to see if the old buzzard was still alive, the bathroom door opened and out stepped a new man. He had shaved, combed his hair, and cleaned himself up considerably. His efforts revealed an intelligent face. He had a full head of white hair, parted high on the left side with a lock that turned over his forehead and fell into his right eye. The hair that had overrun his collar in back added a kind of worldliness to his look. This was a hard man to gauge. In his day he might have been physically big and powerful, just as he could always have been the way he was now: tall, lanky, and spry. As the old gent drew closer, Zak could see that his eyes were a brilliant violet, the whites clean and unmuddied. Zak, determined to satisfy his curiosity, he held up a hand as the stranger attempted to move past him for the front door. He clearly didn't appreciate being summoned in this manner.

"How ya doin' today?"

"How ya doin' today?" the old man answered, mimicking Zak perfectly. It was a creepy thing to do and Zak instantly regretted having said anything as the old man stopped to look him up and down, eyeing him the way a coyote might some possibly edible creature.

"Not bad."

"Not bad," said the old man as though he had never heard it put quite that way before. Zak, going under the assumption that when in doubt optimism can sometimes be an effective diversion, smiled and pointed out the window.

"Looks like we're going to have another beautiful day today," he said cheerfully.

"They're all beautiful," said the old-timer with a for-all-you-know bite to his voice. Still, the old man turned to look out the big window as though following some parade of phantoms moving down the empty boulevard. His brow wrinkled.

"But you may be right, this one might be particularly beautiful."

Zak reached into his shirt pocket for his cigs, tore the pack open, and gave it a shake, "Smoke?"

"Nope, I sure don't, but I'll take one just the same if you don't mind," he placed it behind his ear. Zak lit up. The old-timer then took the cigarette from behind his ear, and putting it to his lips, said, "Got a light?"

"I thought you said you didn't smoke?"

"I don't, but what the heck. You've never lived without trying right?" Zak offered him a light the way you might offer a horse a lump of sugar, to lure it close, to see it, smell it, try to understand it, without necessarily being aware that the horse may have the same reason for taking it. Before touching the tip of the cigarette to the flame, the old-timer paused, taking a good long look at Zak and then he dipped the dry end of the weed into the flame. His hands were old, the skin cracked here and there, but showed no signs of a lifetime of hard physical labor like the other men, in town, young and old. On the contrary, his fingers were long and had a delicate touch. The old man threw his head back and drank in the smoke luxuriously, as though he had been smoking, and enjoying it, all his life.

"Want to sit down?"

The old fellow pinched his pant legs above the knee and sat down a couple of chairs away. He made a show of crossing his legs and getting completely comfortable, indulging in a moment of relaxation as though he really had someplace else to be, taking another long pull on his cigarette, holding it in, aiming his lips at a point in the ceiling, and letting it out slow.

"So, you're a roughneck," the old man ascertained correctly, eyeing the mud on the floor. "But you didn't get those premature gray hairs on the floor of no oil rig."

"How do you know?"

"I bin around, I know a lot of things."

"My name is Zak Harper."

The old man took a long second before lifting his hand and placing it in Zak's. The handshake was weak and noncommittal and the old-timer waited patiently for Zak to relax his grip before taking his hand back. Zak again reminded himself to quit shaking hands so much.

"I'm Corey," he paused to see if the name rang a bell. "Corey Nightingale."

"I'm glad to know you, Corey."

"And I'm glad to know you. Some of the folks in town who don't know any better call me Crazy Corey. Ever hear that name?"

"No."

"Some others call me Moony, 'cause they say I'm Moon Mad," he said with what Zak thought was either a touch of pride, or irony, or mirth, maybe all three. Zak waited a few beats, making sure to exhibit no outward signs positive or negative.

"I like it here in Scobey," Zak said, hoping to bring them to more familiar ground. "I came up here a week or so ago from down in Watford City."

"Oh I know. You're the one's here to replace that kid who got run off."

"Yeah, that's me," Zak chortled. He was struck slightly dumb. It seemed as though everyone he met these days knew all about him. Like it had been in the news or something. *Flash! Zak Harper arrives in Scobey! New Bomac Worm Survives First Week on Widowmaker! Lives Outside! Builds Fire! Eats Weird Food!* "Well, this neck of the woods is a bit more relaxed. I've been real lucky to date. I don't have much money and that rancher who leases the land our rig is on was nice enough to let me pitch a tent right on his old fishing hole."

"Yeah?" Corey scratched his freshly shaved chin and took another pull on his cigarette. "Well, it's got to beat sleepin' out in the park," he said spitting smoke through a soft chuckle. "There's an old hot dog stand in that park, in case you ever need to get in out of the rain. By the way, who'd you talk to over there?"

"Over where, oh, you mean the rancher? I guess I talked to the man himself."

Corey nodded his head. His shrewd look told Zak that every name and every place in this region was going to be very well known to him.

"Oh, I see. So you spoke with Mr. Coster himself, did you?"

"I must have."

"Well, I know that fishing hole. It sets next to an old outhouse that old Coster built himself back in the thirties. He and his boy liked to camp out there overnight and just keep fishin' all the next day. He lost that boy somewhere along the line."

"How so?"

"How? How does anyone lose anything? Hmm," Corey scrutinized Zak carefully. "There's a lotta things you don't know, I can tell. Oh, you're a smart one, no doubt, but there's a lotta things you don't know. I'll bet you think ol' Coster stands to make a bundle if you guys strike oil, hmm? Well, he won't make a dime. That's right."

"Why not?"

"Because people are of the opinion that if oil is found on their land that their problems are over, but they're wrong, and when people find out that they're wrong, they get mighty upset. You know that. Have you ever heard of the Burlington Northern Railroad?"

"Should I have?"

"Maybe you should have and maybe you shouldn't. Do you think that just because a man owns the land, what's on the surface, he also owns what's underneath?"

"Well, I would imagine any rancher, landowner, would know the difference between surface rights and mineral rights."

"Never occurred to many a poor rancher and farmer too. I'll tell you what. But mineral rights take precedence over surface rights. Now a hundred years ago or so when the government wanted the big railroads to connect the East with cattle country, they gave the railroads the land to put their tracks on, and the railroads negotiated for so many miles of land on either side of those tracks. So when time came to sell off all the land they owned, they sold the surface but kept the mineral rights. Now if they think there's oil under there, or anything else worth a good Yankee dollar, they just come and get it, like you boys with your rig. Don't get me wrong, ol' Coster gets a pretty penny for his inconvenience, but it don't amount to a thing compared to say, one percent of any oil you might find. See? Now there's something you thought you knew..." The old man sat back with a satisfied grin and stared off as though he could see through the walls of the laundromat to the world outside.

Okay, thought Zak, *maybe this guy is a little nuts.*

"You said he lost his son?"

"Well, yeah, y'see, after ol' Coster realized his boy was gone and wasn't comin' back, he never used that ol' fishin' hole much." Then Corey Nightingale suddenly caught a notion and looked at Zachary Harper with a n*ewly s*uspicious eye. "Y'know, Coster, he's kinda particular about who's usin' that fishin' hole. He musta taken a likin' to you. Yes he sure musta. So I'll give you a tip. You stand at the door of that old outhouse and you look up the hill right in front of you, then you walk up to the top of that hill, you'll find somethin' you didn't know was there, and I'll tell you something else not too many men know."

"Yeah?" Zak didn't know whether to simply humor the old guy until his laundry was done or make real inquiries. What happened to the son? What's at the top of the hill? Wait and see.

"Coster, he's a rich and powerful man," Corey's tone dropped to a hushed type of whisper usually accorded privileged information. "He's got an airplane and he flies it himself. He likes to go to Las Vegas. He'll jump into that plane of his and he'll scoot down there for the weekend. He's got good-looking women that he sees down there. That kind of thing. Yeah, he sure knows how to spend the money on the ladies to get'm to do what he wants.

He flies up here a day or two later and his wife Nancy is never the wiser. Bin doin' that fer years. Bet ya didn't know that?" And Corey sat back again and grinned a self-satisfied grin.

"Well, that all might be true," Zak smiled, giving the stranger the benefit of the doubt. "Of course, I wouldn't know. But Mr. Coster struck me differently."

"That's because you're from back East and you only believe what you see and what you hear, or what you've heard or what you've read from someone who told you you had to believe'm on accounta they should know. But out here things are different. There's a lotta things you don't know."

Zak was suddenly aware of the hot temperature there in the laundromat, the noisy drone of the machines, the echo of his and Corey's voices, loud one minute, hushed and careful the next, the sweet stinging odor of the detergents and bleaches and diesel. The old man's clothes had a stink to them too, masked only slightly by hand soap and Old Spice.

"Well, anyway," Zak tried again, "he's got a good spot out there. It's just right for me, for now. That's why I'm sorry I've got to leave it next week as we're changing locations."

Corey's eyes brightened, "You bottomed out? You bin told where that new location's gonna be yet?"

"I've heard it's somewhere south of town, but no, we haven't been told exactly where."

"Well," Corey sat back, shifted his weight on his chair several times, crossed and recrossed his legs. "There are a lot of powerful men in this town. You wouldn't know it, but I do. I'll tell you something else. I know exactly where that next location is going to be. And yeah, there's probably a man or two down around that country that might let a guy have a spot for a while.

"Now you take Stitch Cronan, for example," Corey rolled on. "Stitch is a big powerful man. Six foot two or better, two hundred fifty pounds 'r more. I suggest you chat with him about a place to stay. Old Stitch had a shack down on a ranch he owns south of Scobey. I lived in that shack once, though that was many years ago. It's a square little place with four rooms. There's three chairs and a sofa. A single bed in the bedroom with the springs busted out on the right side of it. If I remember correctly, that shack might even have electricity."

"When did you stay there?"

"Oh, about twenty, twenty-five years ago. No reason to think it ain't still there. I was workin' for Stitch back then but times change, don't they? Anyway, I'm sure ol' Stitch don't use it much. Maybe during hunting season, y'know?"

"So how do I find this guy?"

"Ah. Hmm, well, Stitch isn't a hard guy to find if you know where to look. He's got a new Dodge '79 pickup. Blue. Randy Hughes has a red TrailBlazer; you might see Stitch riding with Randy from time to time. Sometimes Stitch can be seen riding in a '77 Toronado belonging to Carey O'Niel. Stitch helps her out once a week with chores, odd jobs, and the like. The type of stuff a man might do for a woman. Especially if he was in love with her. Carey O'Niel is a beautiful woman and half the town thinks there's something funny going on with her'n Stitch, but I'm here to tell you it ain't so. She's the widow of one of Stitch's best friends, Skipper O'Niel. Old Skipper got crushed under his wheat combine and that was the end of him. Messy ugly way to go.

"Stitch has a place at the south end of Main here. He's got another spot north of town and a spread south of town where your next location's gonna be. Yes, Stitch Cronan is a very important and powerful man. Loves sports. He announces all the Scobey High School basketball and football games. He's got his own plane too."

Zak thought Corey might be getting his stories mixed up.

"You watch football, doncha Zak?"

"I used to."

"Tell me somethin'. Do you believe that everybody on that field is who they're supposed to be?"

"I never gave it any thought but right now I'd believe just about anything."

"Well, hmmm, there aren't too many people know this. Stitch Cronan, he loves to play football. I mean, he really loves it. He'll jump in that plane of his and he'll fly down to Houston, or L.A., or San Diego. He'll be settin' there on the bench wearing somebody else's name, somebody else's number, but Stitch Cronan, he'll play. Y'know? There's quite a few guys like Stitch Cronan. It happens more'n you'd think. Not too many people know it. I know it. Now you know it too."

Corey began emptying his pockets, searching for something. Before long, on the seat between them, there was a pile of all his worldly possessions. A small tube of toothpaste, a toothbrush, a comb, a couple of old handkerchiefs, a slug of chewing tobacco, and a disposable razor. From an inside pocket he pulled out four small bundles of business cards, each bundle held by a rubber band. As he thumbed through each stack, he paused here and there to give Zak a brief sketch of certain "powerful individuals" from all around the country. This man was from Texas, this one from Chicago, here's one from St. Louis who is wealthy and has this, that, or the other thing. Corey drew up intimate dossiers on each, reciting facts that even their loved ones couldn't know about them. Stories so incredible they were believable. Zak nodded his head all the while encouraging Corey to continue on, until Corey Nightingale realized he was being regarded as a serious man.

By this time they had been talking for more than an hour. Zak's laundry was done. He was leaving it sit. When Corey had finished the walking tour of his pockets, he at last found what he had been looking for in the first place. It was a little ball of tissue paper he kept loose in the lining of his coat. He held his knees together, placed it reverently in his lap, and slowly pulled the paper away until there rested in his cracked and spotted hands a shiny medal with a faded and tattered cloth attached.

"There are few people," Corey let the sentence trail off unfinished. His long thumb and jagged forefinger caressed the little icon. "You know where this is from," Corey said in a near whisper. He was falling away fast.

"No, no I don't," Zak prodded softly. It wasn't a military medal, and, judging from the French words and the Maple Leaf on one side, he assumed it came from Canada.

"I was given this, I earned it, oh, it must have been, hmmm," Corey began again. His eyes turned watery, and searched a far-off terrain. His expression changed from a ponderous, searching, curious, far-off gaze, to one of warm familiar recognition, to a halting fearful sadness. At last, the man folded the old medal back into the sepulcher of tissue and jacket lining, certain he had just recounted the entire story; that the explanation for all that had passed, how he had come to be here, in this way, in this old laundromat, in this faraway and unknown place, had been revealed to, and would live on in the memory of, this unlikely newcomer. He looked at Zachary Harper with trusting naked eyes. "And now you know."

The old-timer returned his things to his pockets. Zak busied himself gathering up his laundry and even swept up the dried mud chips he had scattered across the floor with a broom he found in the back room.

Corey followed him out to the Jeep and when Zak turned to say goodbye, Corey shook his hand enthusiastically, putting his free hand over their hand clasp, lingering in an odd manner that made Zak think he had more to say.

"Look, I sure appreciate the chat, can I get you a cup of coffee?" Zak said, his real intention being to buy the old man breakfast. If Zak was sure that a certain percentage of what

Corey told him was Total Mars, then it also seemed plausible that a certain percentage of what Corey had told him would be totally accurate.

"I don't want any coffee."

"Well, how about the bar, I could get us a beer or something."

"Stitch Cronan likes to drink. But he only drinks on Tuesday afternoons and then he only drinks at Ginger's Bar, down the street there." Corey nodded his head in the direction of the bar. "You get on over there next Tuesday afternoon and you'll find him. You'll know just who he is too. Ask him to let you stake out a spot and don't beat around the bush about it either.

"And another thing," Corey said as Zak climbed into his outfit and fired 'er up. "You're a smart one, no doubt. But here's one last thing you don't know. Just about dawn, you go into that old outhouse by the creek and right there where the first light comes through the moon on the door, you'll see a little something there."

"I will," Zak said.

"See that you do."

"Good day, sir."

As Zak pulled away, Corey turned and crossed the street. In his side mirror, he saw Corey peering into the window of Simone's Bar with his hands cupped over the glass. After a moment the door opened and Sam, wearing a long morning robe with her hair all down, a shocking black against her milk-white face, stepped out onto the sidewalk to invite him in, looking to the right and the left as she did so. The familiarity of their greeting was curious, as was Corey's appreciative bow before he stepped inside. As she closed the door behind them, Simone stopped and took notice of the Jeep. For a moment she seemed to be looking directly into the mirror, making eye contact with Zachary Harper.

THE SUN BALLOONED HUGE AND red on the horizon as all that afternoon Zak lay out on the bumpy lawn beside the creek by his tent. As darkness advanced, Zak knew that the boys would be expecting him back in town, but he couldn't see getting into another all-night boozathon. His alcohol intake of late was beginning to offend his normally abstemious nature and though he felt beholden to Jon and Freddy for including him in their doings and hated to disappoint them, he decided to turn in early just the same. He had to be ready to get back to work the next afternoon and wanted to be in tip-top shape.

That night he was startled by some gruff noises outside his tent. Coyotes looking for food. Zak slept with his hand on the thick leather scabbard of his knife.

Later, that same night he was awakened again and crept outside to investigate. Finding nothing, he sat down by the water, drinking in the peaceful night. The balmy air had turned cool, then chill, and the moon did not impose itself outright on the terrestrial scene. He saw in the sky a swirling flash of color. It faded, to be replaced with tall spectral pillars of light—glittering, crystalline, ghostly towers rising high beyond the distant horizon. Was he mistaken, or could he hear something, a musical resonance, broadcasting itself to the outer cosmos? Zak shook his head to clear his senses and listen. He wondered if the many thoughts cascading through his mind were similar, perhaps even identical, to those that welled in the hearts and emotions of men and beasts a hundred, a thousand, a hundred thousand years ago, as they looked on in wonder at these same northern lights? He wondered if the hint of the unknown had comforted or taunted them with the knowledge that there is always more, so much more. And he could almost hear the old man's voice:

"There's a lotta things you don't know."

VIII

That second week Zak walked the mile and a half to location every day and found that walking was helpful for getting him limbered up and ready for the day's work ahead. It was a tough week, too. Four of those six days were spent tripping pipe. Two of those were the grueling round trips and the tricky and tedious laying-down process associated with drill-stem testing. The big boys down in Texas wanted to be damned sure before they abandoned that hole. Out of four crews working six and eight—that's eight hours a day six days a week—Zak learned that two of those crews had worm drillers. Jesse Lancaster, far and away the most seasoned man on that rig, had more experience than any two guys there. Over drinks at Simone's, he revealed this was his eleventh year on the Widowmaker alone.

"When did you first break out, Jesse?"

"With the Greeks," Jon broke in on the old man.

"Drillin' y'mean? Oh, just about '54. Oh ho ho, it was rough, I didn't want to go drillin'. No no. I got pushed into it. Went out to work one mornin', November, there was just a few snow-flakes flyin' by. This one driller we had, as soon as he seen that he was gone. He was unemployment bound. It was right in the boom y'know. This one toolpusher comes and says 'Jeez, y'know Jesse, I need a relief driller 'cause one of my drillers has twisted off, another got his arm broke.' I said, 'I don't wanna drill.' He says, "Yes y'do.' I says, 'No I don't!' But I helped him out. Then he comes up'n says, 'I got good news and bad news, the good news is I don't need no relief driller no more, the bad news is you're goin' permanent driller.' I said, 'But I don't want t'drill!' and he says, 'Either that or look for a different rig.' Well there weren't many rigs around. 'Aw shit,' I says, 'who told you I could drill?' Same thing happened with this rig here. Eleven years later he still hasn't found another driller."

Each day Jesse would step from his trailer, ready to go to work, and just listen to the thousands of noises all happening simulta-neously, cocking his head like some old prairie dog looking to spot trouble before trouble spotted him. He was able to discern the slightest variation from what he knew should be working out there.

Because of Jesse's experience, and the relative inexperi-ence of his other drillers and crews, that toolpusher came to rely almost exclusively on Jesse's crew to perform the critical tasks as they came up, a situation in which Jesse took great pride. If that toolpusher could postpone a difficult task four more hours until Jesse's crew arrived he'd do it, just making that bit last as long as he could. As a result, Zak and the boys ended up having some of the most horrendous towers imaginable. When the boys would start to flag a bit from the grueling pace, Jesse had a way of jamming the brake handle and popping the clutch, making the entire rig, from ground to crow's nest, shudder and shake! Everyone, no matter what they were doing, would snap to attention instantly, and Jesse would simply smile and raise his eyebrows as if to say, "Well, how about it? Let's get back to 'er!" But they were good, and they were getting better. None of this had gone unnoticed by the other crews. They were beginning to refer to Jesse's crew as the "Golden Boys of Bomac!" and when they sensed trouble coming, in the form of another trip or test, their motto was, "The Golden Boys'll take care of it! The Golden Boys can get 'er!" which was not as irksome as it could have been because it was true. But there were larger issues involved with one crew shouldering the lion's share of the load.

Carl, or "Old Smoky," as the boys called him because of the S-shaped briar that was forever puffing smoke out of his big reddish-brown beard, was worm drilling for the crew that worked daylights, seven a.m. till three p.m. Old Smoky and his crew were all local boys from over in Flaxville, between Scobey and Plentiwood, and drove to and from location in Carl's big blue Blazer with a gun rack in the back large enough to hold all five rifles. They were called "The Cowboy Crew" because they all wore cowboy hats, boots, and kerchiefs, chewed tobacco constantly, and not one of them ever took their boots off for love or money. They'd wear those boots even while working up on the floor instead of the steel-toed Red Wings, which were just standard wear for most roughnecks. Toes are cheap in the patch and that extra few millimeters of steel protection could mean a lot. Jon, who paid extra attention to a man's style and comportment, didn't appreciate wild deviations from what he would consider smart or sincere. He just thought that Cowboy Crew was fucked in the head.

During that third week, Zak also learned how to read the geolograph. This was a square device with a domed lid. Dead center in the geolograph was a twenty-four-hour clock with a needle. Under that needle ran a spool of paper, in the margin of which was scribbled all the pertinent information needed for an accurate description of the well. Ever so slowly that needle scrawled across the surface of the page providing anyone who was interested a detailed account of what was going on out on the floor every minute of every day. It counted how long it took to go down a foot, and Zak had to catch his samples every ten feet. It recorded the elapsed time from when they began a trip to when they had 'er back drilling again. It showed how long every connection took. If he had a moment to spare, either when he arrived on location or sometime during that tower, he'd lift that lid and take a peek at what had been going on over the course of those earlier towers.

It was Frank Kramer, the company hand, who showed Zak the meaning of the cardiogramlike lines inching their way across the paper. When Zak had an extra minute, or when he was on his way somewhere that took him past the machine, he might come upon Frank standing there studying those lines, or find him simply leaning against the machine, having himself a think. More and more, Frank—a serious man, older than Zak and the boys, but a bit younger than toolpusher George Cleaver—seemed to enjoy those little explications, like maybe they were helping him work something out in his mind that had become a major preoccupation.

Zak got so proficient at reading the geolograph that if he was up in that top doghouse a minute or two before the daylights crew came off the floor, he might laugh and say as they came through the door, "Looks like that thirty-seventh stand gave you boys a little trouble!"

After a hard tower of tripping pipe, Jesse and the boys would all gather in the top doghouse for a coffee and a smoke. Jesse would laugh, "Jeez boys tonight we sure had those slips a-crackin' and those tongs a-breakin'!" Freddy was gaining confidence with each throw of the chain, picking up the pace, getting stronger and stronger.

"Is it my imagination, fat boy, or are you losin' weight?" Jon chimed in, teasing but half-serious on one of those occasions.

"Well," Jesse answered for his chainhand, "throwin' that chain'll either make a man out of'm, or kill'm."

Each night and most of every day Zak slept like a mummy all wrapped up in his sleeping bag inside the tent by the outhouse by the creek.

MONDAY EVENING, GEORGE CLEAVER, TOOLPUSHER working for the Bomac Drilling Company rig number thirty-four, had had the providential good sense to pretend he needed some supplies in town and get the hell off location before he killed someone.

"Bourbon," Sam called out to Hal when she saw George enter the bar. Hal, who was tending bar while she got caught up cleaning highball glasses, simply nodded and reached for the Wild Turkey.

A combination of irritating setbacks, incompetence, unavoidable circumstances, and personality clashes had, over the previous weeks, united to put George in a black mood, and it was those notorious black moods that had earned him the nickname "Rusty" behind his back. Frank, the new company hand, was a good man, but goddamn it, anybody with one brain to rub against the other could tell they had been going all out for weeks. With only one driller out of four truly experienced at that brake handle, they were lucky to be on schedule at all.

George looked to his right and left at the old duffers sitting next to him at the bar and that suffocating feeling that had roared up inside him from time to time since he was a kid threatened to explode again. He needed room. Over the years George had come to know the triggers and off switches of his fiery temper very well. He studied that temper like it was a strange and dangerous animal that had come to live in his house. He learned to channel its ferocious energy into his work. Being out on location twenty-four hours a day seven days a week helped. Staying on top of so many men and so many details allowed him to vent in all directions, and things made of iron don't break so easy, he chuckled to himself. If he had to run off a crew, or put down some rebellion up on the floor, all he had to do was act like himself when he was mad. Let's face it, some silly little mess-up you let slide today could happen again tomorrow and blossom into a full-blown disaster. And sometimes, naturally, George didn't have to pretend.

Maybe Frank was right. Maybe they could've gone faster. But for that you need four good crews all up to speed, and where you gonna find four decent crews out here? With so much work happenin' down around Williston and Watford it was a miracle he put together four crews willing to come out this far at all. Or maybe he should run off one of those worm drillers and take that brake handle himself. That would sure take a load off Jesse and his boys and he'd have another top-notch crew to help move things along, but that would be a short-term proposition; what he needed was a long-term solution. Nope, then he'd be too busy to push tools. What to do?

George took a sip and let out a gasp as the sweet fiery elixir burned down the hatch. He watched Sam, dipping glasses two at a time into the hot water, then into the rinse. Her beads and earrings clattered and clacked, her breasts swayed beneath her billowing blouse. Her hair was pulled back, revealing a pale white neck. He wondered if these old farts sitting so stiff and silent at the bar had ever made love to a woman like that? *Hey, you fucks!* he wanted to shout. He wanted to see some spark, some sign of life. He wanted to know if these guys were survivors of the Great Charade, or if they had always been stay-at-home types who had been perversely rewarded for their timidity with the longevity they so coveted all through the years. He knew the answer by the way they avoided eye contact. By the way they tried to ignore the roughnecks when they came to town. The way they snickered at Simone behind her back and sure enough disapproved of her when an opinion was called for. Yeah, he knew the type. The type of asshole he had come to the patch to escape. *Oh fuck you!* he thought. He just wanted to kick all their asses. He took another sip that burned not at all. He shook his head, and gave a deep chesty grunt he couldn't stifle no matter how many shots he hit it with.

Now Jesse Lancaster. There's a driller. Truth be told, it was Jesse and his boys who were gettin' 'er done on this location. That's a fact. What he wouldn't do for three more just like'm. Old Smoky was capable but that friggin' crew of his, what a bunch of nutbuckets they were. And the rest? Shit. Rory, he had to admit, was okay, slow, but okay. He held up a finger and ordered another drink. Sam's was the only bar in town that stocked his brand, so he gratefully drank every drop. She assured him he was the only customer who ever called for it.

That goddamned Frank. Yeah, he's young and all but that's no excuse. It wasn't bad enough that they both had to live side by side on location, but you'd think that he'd a figured out by now how to go about keeping those fuckers down in Texas off their backs long enough to get the fuckin' job done. Sure, the money boys are nervous nellies, but you can't let them rule your roost every goddamned minute. Christ Frank! Don't be such an ass-kisser! Tell them what they want to hear and keep the rest on a need-to-know basis. Yeah, George shook his head again like he had split in two and was listening to his other half, he knew it wasn't as easy as all that.

He thought about Frank, ten years younger than he, broke out in the patch as a roughneck in California. He knew the job but he was also the type that speaks the language of the city boys and bankers pretty good too. George drained his glass. He could see himself in the mirror behind the bar. He had news for his own apparition in the mirror staring back at him. *You ain't never gonna be no company hand.*

His temper flared viciously. He wanted to fling his glass at the row of bottles in front of him. Maybe get the attention of one of these silent sleepy cadavers warming their bloodless arses there at the bar on either side of him. In any event, that Frank had been up his ass for two solid weeks. "Keep 'er drillin', keep 'er drillin', keep 'er drillin'." Frank had been good-natured about it, was aware of all the stress they were under, but how in the hell was he supposed to keep 'er drillin' when he had just one good crew and they were runnin' another goddamned test every time he turned the fuck around? Huh? And don't tell me it's the boys down in Houston, they go along with you, Frank. We've been chewin' up bits right and left what with all the formations we've been goin' through, but every time we get a new bit back on bottom and start turnin' to the right again, out come the friggin' Halliburton boys and another tower, or two, or three, would be lost findin' out what we already knew. We haven't found any goddamned oil yet! Had the hole caved in? No. Had we lost pipe in the hole? No. Lose a bit? No. This ain't Bakersfield, California, where the weather's fine and there's everything you need right at your fingertips. *This is the fucking Overthrust Belt man!* Deal with it! Oh yeah, and here's Frank, standing there by the geolograph, holding up a printout and wondering out loud why we haven't gone down but fifty feet in three friggin' days. George had wanted to grab that skinny fuckin' city boy by his store-bought button-down denim cowboy shirt and just beat the snot out of him.

And George Cleaver laughed quietly, angrily, out loud.

Jesse and Rory he could count on, Carl and Andy he had to watch. Everyone knew that Jesse and his boys were the ones doin' the lion's share of the work. When George tried to apologize for all the extra responsibility he had heaped on them, Lancaster would snort, and spit, and say in that singsong voice he used when accepting a challenge, "Well, the boys are getting a bit blue around the gills but I think they'll give it another go for

ya, George." It was told among the older drillers he knew down in
Watford, who had been out roughneckin' in the old days down in
Gillette, and it was told by the company hands and the other tool
pushers like himself that Jesse had, in his younger days, worked
the floor all by himself. That's something he would have liked to
have seen. And Jesse, more than ten years older than George, was
still up there on that drillin' floor, gettin' it! Jesse could make a cat
laugh the way he'd jerk his shoulders and wiggle his eyebrows and
look all about the room before volunteering to do the impossible.
"Aw shit, George, we can git 'er!"

*At least there wouldn't be a worm driller on that brake handle
when he arrived back on location later,* George thought. He bought a
pint of bourbon from Hal and resigned himself to getting tight and
sleeping it off before that morning crew came on about eleven p.m.

As he ambled out to his pickup, George mulled it all over.
He knew Frank had been a well-respected driller before hiring
out as a company hand. But he had only pushed tools for a short
period before moving up the food chain. Ideally, you'd want that
company hand to be a damn good toolpusher as well. George,
representing Bomac, Frank representing the oil conglomerate,
should be in lock step, but not always. George knew he had
done a marvelous job getting results out here, but those results
just weren't always gonna jive with what Texas wanted to hear.
Everyone looked at the same reports the geologists were making.
Everyone started out on the same page. So how did we get here?
Wherever the fuck "here" is.

He looked up and down the street. The sun was setting. It
was a beautiful fall evening. Then he looked at the dismal street
with its closed shops and sleepy countenance. "This town needs a
whorehouse," he said out loud before climbing into his truck. He
reminded himself to get each of Jesse's boys a case of beer next
time they went on days off.

Of course, he never did.

WHEN GEORGE ARRIVED BACK ON location, Marty and Jon were just coming down the stairs from up on the floor as they saw him pull up. Aware of George's volatile disposition, they watched with mischievous glee as he hobbled out of his pickup, tucked the little brown sack under his arm as he reached for his stuff off the front seat, snarled deliriously at all and sundry, and stagger over to his trailer, slamming the door shut behind him. The boys knew for sure that drilling towers like this one would be few and far between during this nasty little stretch. Jesse had told them all to take it easy. No problem there.

Zak had busied himself all evening with scrubbing the light plant. This was a thankless chore as light plant engines raise such a screaming racket that it's hard to be in there for more than a few minutes without going insane. Regardless, Zak had done his usual thorough job. When he was done, he went looking for the boys to see if they needed a hand with whatever it was they were about. He had fallen into the habit of bugging the fellas for projects, and tonight they were ready for him. After looking nearly everywhere, he at last found Jon and Marty under the rig cleaning up the BOP, or blow-out preventer, that sits atop the hole anticipating disaster.

"Dis big ting has big old rams in it that cut off the flow upward if we hit a gas pocket and it wants to burp up all dat pipe'n mud!" Marty explained.

"Anything I can do?" Zak asked. Marty straightened his ovoid shape and, tilting his muddied hard hat, gave his brow a wipe with his right forearm.

"Yeah," Marty said, half-distracted. Jon, meanwhile, was moving around the huge BOP with a rag and a scrub brush paying them no mind. "You can git ober to dat tool putcher's shack and tell 'im we need d'keys to d'V-doors right now, okay?"

Zak was off at a trot. Not knowing what the V-doors were or, for that matter, the microscopic length of George Cleaver's fuse. Jon and Marty stepped cautiously from under the rig and watched as Zak marched over to the toolpusher's trailer and tapped politely on the door. No answer. He knocked again.

Inside the trailer, the tappety-tap-tap at the door invaded George Cleaver's tumultuous slumber much the same way the company hand's timid little rapping would. A wave of nauseating disgust brought him spinning unpleasantly back to the surface of consciousness.

"Fuck off Frank," he hollered and rolled over.

The door opened. Zachary Harper stepped lightly into the trailer.

He walked quietly to the back, where the toolpusher's shadowy form lay in a heap. Zak was about to make the fatal mistake of reaching out and touching him when Cleaver's voice, cold, hard, and alert, issued from the hulkish adumbration there on the cot in the darkness.

"Did you come in here to wake me up?" He sounded terribly awake.

"Yes sir."

"Then what the hell are you tiptoein' for?" George swung his feet off the cot, and they landed on the floor with a menacing thump. He reached for the pint by his bedstand and took a long, wet pull on it. "This better be fucking good," he snarled and slapped his palms against his chest pockets, looking for his cigs. Thirty-five years of smoking filterless cigarettes added just the right amount of gravel to his voice. Zak took a cautionary step backwards.

Outside, across the square patch of dirt between the row of trailers and the rig, Jon and Marty were standing together, sheepishly awaiting the outcome of Zak's interview. They were getting worried. Uh-oh looks spread across their faces. Things were just too quiet. Zak, after all, was a nice guy. Their consciences were beginning to bother them.

"We lose pipe in the hole?" George asked.

"No."

"The number one engine down?"

"No."

"Anybody get killed?"

"No."

"Then what the hell do you want!"

"I need the keys to the V-doors."

There was a long silence. Zak held out hope that George, once awake, would realize that this was official business and hand over the keys so that Zak could be on his way and let George get back to sleep.

"You son of a bitch."

"Excuse me?" Zak said quietly, confused and utterly blank.

George sprang from the cot and slammed an open palm against Zak's chest, driving him into the wall forcing every square inch of wind from his lungs. George's fist clutched shirt, chest hair, and skin. With his other hand he grabbed Zak by the belt and, lifting poor Zak clean off his feet, carried him hard into the wall behind him, bringing him forward and back again and again with mythological ferocity, a cataract of oaths peeling unintelligibly off George's tongue.

"You!" *slam!* "son!" *slam!* "of!" *slam!* "a!" *slam!* "bitch!" *slam!* Next he dragged Zak to the door, knocking things clanging and clattering on their way and flung him bodily out. Zak hit the ground hard a full five feet from the trailer with George leaping out right after him just a-howling!

Marty and Jon came trotting up and stopped in their tracks when they saw George Cleaver's face. Between them lay Zachary Harper, pawing and squirming in the dirt, fighting for air.

"If you weren't the only crew worth a good goddamn on this rig I'd run yer asses off right this minute!" George bellowed, and in two steps was hovering over the three roughnecks staring right down at Zachary Harper. "I want to know who sent yer ass in t'see me! Who was it? You goddamn," just then, Freddy Fifer, of all people, stepped in from out of nowhere and placed himself squarely between that toolpusher and Jon, Marty, and Zak.

"C-c'm-mon, G-G-George, wha-what's 'ah m-matter? They didn't mean n-nothin?!" No one had ever heard Freddy stutter before and George peered into Freddy's fat worried face as if to ascertain whether or not the roughneck was fakin' it, trying to make a monkey out of him. He wasn't. George stopped.

"George!" Jesse came trotting up. Calm and serious, he pushed the others away. He got right up in George's face and said quietly, "You know I can't have you gettin' tough with my hands, George. Jesus George, you bin drinkin'!"

There was a long silence.

"I'm not gonna say nuttin' 'bout that George, but now I gotta go talk to my crew, and if they wanna twist off, then we'll have to sack'm up."

"Aw shit," George said and went back inside his trailer.

Jon, Freddy, and Marty helped Zak to his feet. He was shaking. While Jon and Marty dusted him off, Freddy found his bent-up spectacles and handed them to the worm.

Jesse looked from Marty to Jon. "You two get back down to that BOP and finish what you started. Then you come up to the top doghouse for a meetin'." Looking at Freddy he said, "Git on over there and see if you can't give them other prick-a-lutes a hand." When Freddy was gone, he turned to Zak. "Are you all right?"

Zak nodded. He didn't think anything was broken, but his wind hadn't entirely returned. He put his hands on his knees and leaned forward. Long strands of saliva escaped his lips and for a long minute they both thought he was going to puke.

"C'mon up to the doghouse with me."

Zak tried to straighten out his glasses as they walked toward the rig. Inside the top doghouse, Jesse poured Zak a half cup of burned coffee, filling the cup the rest of the way from a bottle of Black Velvet he had stashed in his locker. "Don't tell anybody you seen this," he said and poured a shot, straight, into his own cup. Zak took a few sips. He was coming back to earth.

"Yeah," Jesse leaned back against the knowledge box and reached for a cigarette.

"What happened, the boys send you in there?"

"To get the keys to the V-doors. I take it that's a joke."

"Yeah, shit. Them assholes. C'mon out here a sec." The two men polished off their drinks and stepped out onto the brightly lit floor. Zak's chest was becoming mighty sore. Jesse put an arm around Zak's shoulder, turned him around, and pointed to a big empty space at the far end of the floor.

"Y'see Zak, down there you got yer catwalk?"

"Yeah,"

"Okay, then you got yer beaver slide that comes up to the floor here?"

"Right,"

"Well then, you see that big empty space at the end of the floor over top that beaver slide?"

"Yes,"

"Them's yer V-doors, son."

Back in the doghouse Freddy arrived, looking very tense. Jon and Marty followed, looking alternately sheepish and disgusted. Jon got a coffee, Freddy found a stool. After a second they all stared at Jesse.

"Okay, look, no toolpusher's got the right to lay a hand on one of my crew. As far as I can see, Zak's got every reason to twist off." Jesse looked directly at Jon and Marty. "And if he twists, I can't see any reason the rest of us shouldn't either."

"Sure thing," Freddy spoke right up.

"It'd mean headin' back to Watford," Marty was thoughtful, nodding his head. That would be fine with him.

"It'd serve that cocksucker right," Jon said scornfully. "He'll have a hell of a time gettin' another crew to come way the fuck out here."

"The other crews would have to pull a double," Jesse speculated.

"Yeah, an' let dem get somb ob d'fun we bin gettin'!" Marty almost smiled.

Jesse turned to Zak and said, "Are we twistin' off?"

Zak leaned back against a locker, hooked his thumbs in his pockets, and looked down at the floor. "Jesus."

The three other roughnecks all started talking at once. "We should go over there and demand an apology and then decide." "Or maybe we oughta just go over there and beat the shit out of'm." "We could turn that fuckin' trailer of his over on its side before we leave." "He's bin takin' advantage of you Jesse, not just us, y'know."

Jesse held up a hand and said loudly, "That's enough." Turning to Zak, he said, "Now I'm askin' you a question, mister. Are we twistin' off?"

Everybody was primed for Zak to say yes, and right up until he opened his mouth, that's what he intended to say. But as he went to speak he realized it would mean everyone would miss their bottom-hole pay, breaking up the crew, returning to Watford and starting all over again.

"No."

"That's all I want to know."

"I can't see quittin' over a misunderstanding that was largely my fault," Zak was thinking out loud, sorting his way through this mess, but was also willing to go with whatever the group decided. The room was silent. All eyes were on him. "On another night, hell, I might've caught on. It mighta been funny."

"Poor judgment," said Marty.

"All the way around," said Jon.

"Good move, Zak!" Freddy almost cheered.

They nodded their heads and went about their business. As they went out the door, Zak felt a cool breeze through his hair. Shit. No hat. He sighed, walked down the stairs, crossed the wide muddy patch between the rig and where the company hand and the toolpusher had their trailers, and knocked on George Cleaver's door.

After several more knocks, the door opened and a sleepy George Cleaver looked at Zak with disbelief.

"I left my hat in there."

"C'mon in." Inside Zak picked his hat up off the floor. As he stepped to the door, George said, "That shouldn't've happened tonight."

"You're right."

"Jesse's got the best crew on the rig. He says you're workin' out real good too. You twistin'?"

"No."

"Good. Anything else I can do for ya?"

"Not that I can think of."

"Goodnight then."

THE ONLY OTHER DRILLIN' TOWER that week fell on Wednesday, and Zak spent most of the day scrubbing and keeping his eye on that kelly. As it turned down and down, there was a point when he could no longer see it from the ground and soon he could hear the whip-cracking hiss and thunder from the floor and know that Jesse was picking up on 'er. Then it was a matter of dropping everything and running like a madman to assume his position for the next connection. As the evening progressed Zak would, from time to time, drift up to that top doghouse for a cup of coffee and a cigarette and bullshit with the guys. Jesse had them unload a shipment of bits and had some other projects for them, but mostly they were on their own. Just before quitting time, Zak went up to that top doghouse again to see if there were any last chores to be done and found Jon and Jesse having a cup of Black Velvet coffee, chatting about changing location in the next couple of days.

"You can bet ol' Rusty'll have us layin' down pipe tomorrow," Jesse was saying as Zak entered the room.

"Yeah, well, breakin' those joints every thirty feet instead of ninety, plus havin' to run 'em all down that beaver slide one by one's, gonna be a bitch," Jon complained. "Wish we had a laydown machine. Do we get another crew to help out?"

"Shit," Jesse spat into the waste bucket, "we can git 'er."

Something about Jon's cantankerous attitude made Jesse smile. "Hey, y'know? I hear them new Canadian rigs don't need a junk basket when they tear down."

"No?"

"Nope, they open a big hole right there in the floor and the tongs and everything are just lowered down and they'll be right there waitin' when you nipple back up instead of having to raise and lower everything over the side in those old junk baskets."

"Makes sense," Jon said with an irksome harumph, as if it had been legislated somewhere that practical, labor-saving ideas were not to be employed by any rig employing him as a crew member. Suddenly Jon and Jesse looked up as though they had just noticed Zak standing there, and Jon smiled over at Jesse. "Y'know, I kinda like the way ol' Rusty rearranged Harper's glasses. Makes him look just crazier'n shit. What d'ya say," he threw a nod at his driller, "what d'ya think of that new worm? Is he gonna make it?"

Jesse's smile slowly faded and he stared thoughtfully into his coffee cup. He gave it a delicate little shake and watched the swirling liquid for a long moment. When he looked up, he was staring straight at Zachary Harper. The look on Jesse's face was serious as a heart attack.

"Yeah, he'll do all right, he's a hand. But I'll tell you one thing, he ain't never farmed."

IX

Jesse Lancaster had always wanted to go to sea. He had taken a boat up to Alaska from Seattle to Anchorage, had worked for a brief stint offshore up there, but he had never fulfilled his lifelong dream—to stand on the deck of his own seaworthy vessel, in the midst of a long, uncertain voyage, and contemplate the vastness of oceanic space; to inhale the salty vagabond winds. To see with his naked eyes, unobstructed, three hundred and sixty degrees, the curvature of the earth. To glimpse with wonder all manner of unknowable life, sustaining, enduring, perpetuating, undisturbed or merely unconcerned with the human travelers who ride the hazardous unpredictable border of hydrosphere and gaseosphere. Sometimes in early evening or along about dawn, when the prairie breezes came up breathlike over his menial sanguine form, he would stand upon the rig's quarterdeck, gazing across the rolling turbulent landscape of the Williston Basin and imagine the rig an old but hardy steamer bounding over the waves. In a way, the rig was like a ship, self-sufficient, with its own power source and crews, its own mission to perform. He was its captain. He would look up through the girders on the tower and view the huge mountainous clouds rolling overhead, or the movement of the stars as the earth turned beneath them, and for a fleeting moment he could stir within himself the sensation of that movement, and he would hold to his brake handle as though it were the rudder of the world.

That the Williston Basin had been a great lake millions of years ago made profound and perfect sense to Jesse Lancaster. Special drill bits were needed to chew through fossil and shell formations at those depths. Jesse would sometimes pause by the shale-shaker there along the catwalk and reach his hand into the delicious muck and find shells and strange fragments of prehistoric life. He kept the most unusual specimens in a shoebox back in his trailer. The then and the now were somehow connected through him, he could feel it. And that feeling is what kept him going.

Tonight there was something out of sync, something disturbing and wrong. He was restless and uncomfortable, jittery and on edge. The worst of it was that this feeling had come upon him for no apparent reason. The engines sang, the pipe turned to the right, Carl and that Cowboy Crew were going about their duties, and everything was running sweet. Now that the decision had been made to begin rigging down the following day, even George was beginning to behave like a human being again.

But Jesse paced in the top doghouse. He had remained behind after tower this night, when the rest of the boys had gone their separate ways, with the intention of giving Marty and Cynthia a little privacy, but really, he was attempting to remain in a familiar place long enough to give those shadowy forms lurking below the surface of his memory a chance to reveal themselves.

Surprisingly, he found himself staring into the kindly face of Flip Johnson, the first man he had seen die in the patch.

How tough it was back then for young men willing to work! A job so hard to find in this harsh and pitiless territory. You'd take anything! And a roughneckin' job? Men would come from miles away. Leave their families! At every location stood lines of hungry, desperate men waiting for a chance to show what they could do. The man on the rig who fucked up once, or got hurt, was replaced right then and there by the next man in line, and if he couldn't get 'er he couldn't stay. Getting some experience was the hardest part of it all. On Flip Johnson's second day of work he had been told to climb the derrick and replace some cable, had lost his footing, and on the way down he had torn his strong hands into unrecognizable clumps of raw meat and bone pulling on that cable in a futile attempt to break his fall. Another man was called from the line of hopefuls and the work had gone on. There was Pete Cavenaugh, a driller who had gotten his arm caught up in the chain as it sucked into the cathead, tearing the limb completely off in the longest split second Jesse had ever experienced. On the way into town they ran out of gas. Pete bled to death. Eight pints. Doesn't sound like much, does it. Jesse could sit down and drink eight pints of beer without batting an eye.

It's a lot of blood.

When he moved up the ranks and became a driller, suddenly responsible for the lives of his crew, the condition of the rig, the integrity of the hole, he vowed that no one stranger's fortune would be worth the life and limbs of one of his own, and his crews, throughout the long years, had been grateful, loyal, and like family.

Family.

Jesse shook his head, pushing the truly unbearable images back. *Not tonight*, he thought. Besides, the patch had broken many a roughneck's heart. She was a tough mistress. He didn't consider his particular set of heartbreaks and disappointments at all different or special.

He poured himself a drink and pulled up a stool beside the knowledge box where he could watch from the corner of his eye the goings-on out on the floor. Carl was at the brake handle and he was really putting his boys through their paces. They were sloppy and inefficient. Yet they attacked their jobs with such enthusiasm Jesse had to smile. Yeah, they were something. They were all cursing and sweating, dropping things, blaming one another for their own mistakes. In spite of it all, they were getting the job done. He laughed to think that most people in town didn't even know this rig was here. Oh yeah, the bar, restaurant, and hotel crowd knew, but not the rank and file, the early to bed early to rise church-going ma and pa taxpayers. Usually, Jesse took solace in the relative obscurity of his profession, but not tonight.

"No one knows what goes on in the oil field," he said through a sigh. And, fittingly, his words were drowned out by the hiss and roar of the engines and the clang and clank of iron and chain.

Zak, come to think of it, should be throwing chain, thought Jesse Lancaster. The way Zak watches Freddy and roots him on, he seems chompin' at the bit to give 'er a whirl. Freddy's next in line though, the job should rightfully go to him and if the kid succeeds it'll make something out of him he couldn't have accomplished in two lifetimes.

Like Ziggy.

What a funny little guy that Ziggy was. Jesse had been on more than one crew where the current driller was simply voted off that brake handle and Ziggy voted on. Jesse believed it was Ziggy who taught him that smooth-as-silk touch when bringing that pipe out of the hole, how the flow of the moving pipe could increase or decrease with the fluid movements of a well-working crew. Or how to take a little weight off the bit while turning to the right so the entire weight of the drill stem wouldn't force the bit to go anywhere else but down down down. "Seeing downhole," Ziggy called it. He claimed he could close his eyes and see the walls of that hole plain as day by just touching that brake handle. Jesse always chuckled at such a notion. Then he frowned.

"It's just tradin' one form of warfare for another!" Ziggy reasoned lightheartedly when he left the patch to fight in Korea. Well, many a good man hadn't returned from the Williston Basin either.

When Jesse was still a worm, he and his crew arrived at work one evening to find everyone on location dead. They had unexpectedly hit a pocket of H2S. You could almost see it, invisible waves in the air like heat rising off a tarmac. The first whiff you know there's something very wrong. The second whiff drops you. The third whiff you're dead.

Right now Jesse could smell trouble.

He searched his memories for some clue to his present confusion. His stomach turned. These things had made an old man of him, he reckoned. Or were about to. Every day he would look in the mirror and wonder if today was the day his age would suddenly catch up with him. How long would he be able to trust his faculties? How much longer could he get 'er? Tonight he felt as though he had come upon an unexpected crossroads. Over the years wisdom and experience had replaced youth and bravado, and this had been a comfortable thing. Would he find out too late if he was slipping? Most men, even the good ones, had gotten out long before this. The only guy he knew who was older than he and still drilling was old Blackwell. Blackie would say, "Who gives a rat's ass how old you are, Jesse? Drill till you drop son, drill till ya drop!" Yeah, there was a roughneck for you, true blue, tried and true, through and through.

Before dawn he ambled back to his trailer and lay down on his cot. His joints felt different, uncomfortable, strange. Like he was in someone else's body. There were new aches and pains. His ears reached beyond the sound of Marty and Cynthia, both snoring in the back, beyond the incessant harangue of the engines out on the rig, to seek the comforting rhythm of ocean waves lapping pleasantly at the sides of his lonesome trawler. As he began to drift, he spoke softly to old phantoms who came to pay their respects. Dream images loomed perilously in the darkness behind his eyes, like moving stately mountains of floating ice in a near yet incalculable distance.

THE FOLLOWING DAY MARTY WAS not required in the tower, so he was free to assist the men on the floor. It was Zak's first opportunity to observe Marty in action for any length of time and only then did Zak notice the severity of Marty's problem with his walking. To call it a disability would have been wrong. He got around just fine. He didn't walk so much as he bounced along on the sides of his feet with his toes turned in. He moved swiftly and fluidly with premeditation. His body compensated for his awkward gait, trying to let his feet touch ground as little as possible. Indeed, whatever the nature of his peculiar walk it seemed uniquely tailored for climbing girders, hopping down catwalks and up beaver slides, as though he had had his feet broken and realigned for that very purpose.

Their job was to pull over six thousand feet of drill string and lay the individual thirty-foot sections of pipe down on the ground. As the pipe came out of the hole, Jesse would bring it to a stop after every joint instead of every three. The men would throw in their slips, disconnect the pipe with their tongs, and then push the pipe over to the beaver slide where the boom line was attached and the elevators removed. This was the tricky part of the procedure, because the guys would have to steady it with their hands to prevent the pipe from rolling side to side as the boom line was fixed to one end. Then, like Keystone Kops, they would run single file down the long flight of stairs in time to catch the pipe, disconnect the boom line, and lay the pipe down in racks on the ground. From there it was back up the stairs on the double to attach the next joint waiting to be hauled out of the hole. They repeated this action over two hundred times. In just seven hours, the job was done.

George Cleaver was amazed. When all that pipe was down and ready for the roustabout crews to arrive and load it on the flatbeds to be hauled to the next location, George took Jesse aside and said, "Look, just let the boys take it easy for the rest of the tower. Empty out the mud pits and that'll be that. Take a hose to 'em and call it quits."

Then George climbed into his pickup and left to run errands before the next shift came on. He had a lot on his mind. He listed his priorities. Of the four crews he had teaming up over the next couple of days, two of them had worm drillers. The next immediate step would be to tear down that kelly. No small chore. It's a massive chunk of iron, as big as a full-sized car and even heavier. He was sure as hell that Carl didn't have the slightest notion how to do it quickly and properly. After all the work he had thrown at Jesse and his crew these past three weeks, he felt guilty asking them to do any more, especially after the day they had just put in. He didn't have time to supervise up on the floor, however, and that kelly absolutely had to come down. He brought his pickup to a halt, cursed one time, then turned around and beat it back to location.

Zak, Marty, and Jon were down opening the trap doors, letting the mud flow into the reserve pit. Jesse and Freddy were at the top of the stairs having a chat. It had been one hell of a day. They had never performed better as a crew and everyone could feel it. Everyone was up. Jesse hadn't had to rattle that iron once to get their attention. Instead, he'd rattle that big iron as a way of hootin' and hollerin' at the ferocious pace they were able to maintain! Even Freddy had at last found himself. He was Jesse Lancaster's chainhand. Freddy could tell there was no longer the shadow of a doubt in his driller's mind whether or not his new chainhand could get 'er. Jon, normally flip and sarcastic where

Freddy's roughnecking skills were concerned, hadn't chided him once all day about being too slow or too fat.

Jesse threw a soft elbow at Freddy to get his attention and nodded tellingly in the direction of rig road. From the top of the stairs, they could see a considerable distance through the winding lumpy sage-covered humps of earth. The dust had hardly settled from George's truck when there in the distance came those headlights back again, bouncing down the road, kicking up dust in the other direction. Jesse knew what it meant. Freddy had a good idea. They both looked at their watches. *Whatever he wants, we're too tired for this,* Jesse thought wearily.

George came huffing up the stairs wearing his most apologetic face.

"What happened, Georgie boy?" Jesse smiled. "You ferget to kiss us goodbye?"

"I just got to thinkin', Jess, we got that worm driller and his bunch comin' on after you there, and well, I hate to ask you this, but before you finish up, let's disconnect that kelly and give that Cowboy Crew a head start getting it out of the way."

Jesse looked at his watch again, for George's benefit, and finally, after turning it over in his mind, shook his head no.

"I can't ask my boys to do that for you George, hell, we're half-dead as it is. But I'll tell you what I will do. I'll stay up here with you and we can get those cowboys started, and if they can't get 'er, we'll babysit till Rory and them come on in the morning. As loosey goosey as them cowboys are, they're roughnecks after all, and it's roughneck work, and if they can't get 'er, well…" his eyebrows danced.

"I know, I know, you're right," George wrinkled his brow. He looped his giant thumbs through his denim belt loops and pondered.

Meanwhile, Freddy's eyes bulged as he looked up at the big kelly. He whistled, and breathed a sigh of relief.

"All right Jesse, you're right, relief should be here any minute, I'll be in the doghouse," George Cleaver turned and headed for the top doghouse door, and Freddy made for the stairs.

I'm Jesse Lancaster's chainhand, thought Freddy Fifer, *can ya beat it!*

But as George Cleaver reached that doghouse door, he turned and pointed to the pipe sitting in the mousehole. It was the last piece of the drill stem that hadn't yet been sent down the beaver slide.

"Well at least let's get that bit off and packed away. We'll let them cowboys take it from there."

At least? thought Jesse Lancaster, and he walked over to the top of the stair where he could see his chainhand already halfway down. He looked toward the reserve pits but couldn't see Zak, Marty, or Jon anywhere. He figured they'd come running when they heard the motors and saw that kelly moving.

He called Freddy back.

"Sorry Fred, we ain't done yet," Jesse apologized as Freddy huffed and puffed back up the stairs. We gotta hose down the floor, but before we do that George wants us to disconnect that bit. No big deal, we can get 'er."

Freddy looked at the pipe sitting in the mousehole. He and his crewmates had purposely left everything ready for the next crew to twist off that bit, then run that last thirty-foot pipe down the slide.

George wants it done. *Just like a boss*, Freddy thought moving over toward the pipe as Jesse reached his station. Just like a boss to give one last order, not because he had to, but because he could.

He put his shoulder to the pipe and nodded to Jesse, who revved the engine, and ever so gently picked up the kelly. As that pipe, weighted with heavy collar subs and the bit still on bottom, lifted a few inches and began to pendulate toward the center of the floor, Freddy struggled to keep it under control. His boots slipped in the mud on the wet floor and he nearly fell to his knees. He slowed that pipe down just enough so that it only got away from him just over the rotary table, where he hopped comically to the other side and corralled that pipe from behind. Soon he had it stable, hanging above the rotary table, stationary. Jesse then raised the whole ensemble high above their heads.

Jesse waited patiently as Freddy trudged back over to the mousehole. There in the hole rested the bit breaker, a big, heavy iron bucket the inside bottom of which was shaped like the three giant cones the bit would be set into. He looked to the stairs for one of the others, and when he didn't see them, he leaned down, bent at the knees, and yanked that bit holder out of the mousehole, and slipped and slid across the muddy floor to the hole in the rotary table and dropped it in with a bang!

Jesse then lifted up on that brake handle and ever so slowly let 'er down, as Freddy guided the bit down and down, turning the pipe so those cones just set right down in that bucket as pretty as you please.

He then grabbed motorman's tongs, the dyes already changed to the larger pipe size, and he slammed them onto that pipe with a crash and a latch.

What happened next no one would ever be able to say for sure. One thing we do know is that Jesse Lancaster did not see Freddy Fifer's foot touch that rotary table. Was Freddy already slipping on the muddy floor? Were the tongs not set right and did they miss their bite too causing him to slip and fall?

Either way, when Jesse hit that cathead, those tongs broke that joint and Freddy's right arm with a loud and horrible *Crack!* And that rotary table spun, breaking Freddy's left ankle, leg, and knee, *Crack! Crack! Crack!* before tossing him aside in a heap against the drawworks.

Zak was on his way back up to the drilling platform, taking the long way up past the shale-shaker. As he reached the top of the stairs, he glanced up at the floor and didn't understand what was going on. He could see Freddy lying motionless with his head smack up against the drawworks. He saw Jesse frozen in disbelief. He saw George step out of the top doghouse and stop dead in his tracks, staring at Freddy, not understanding what his eyes were telling him. Zak jumped over the railing, ran up the stairs, crawled over a motor, and landed in a crouch at Freddy's side.

"Is it your head?!" Zak screamed to be heard over the engines.

"My leg!" Freddy screamed.

"Try to stay calm!" Zak hollered. Freddy's left leg looked multijointed and was resting there in many impossible directions. There was a patch on his pant leg growing with dark red blood.

"My arm!" Freddy managed between hurried gasps for air.

Zak could see Freddy's right hand wasn't aimed in a proper direction either.

"Uh, uh!" Freddy cried out trying to turn his head to look. He let out a heartwrenching scream. His agony was escalating instant by instant. Sweat was pouring. His eyes grew wild. He opened his mouth and had to take a series of short hysterical pants to get up enough wind to scream again. His tongue stuck out. He was panting again, taking shorter and shorter breaths each time, screaming louder and louder. "Ah! ah! ah! ah! ah! Aaaaaaaah!" until his face was contorted beyond recognition.

Jesse and George landed at Freddy's side, Jesse was shaking. "Freddy! Shit!" He looked at Zak, "In the doghouse, emergency fireblanket!" Zak was off at a gallop. George took off to find Frank.

The fireblanket was in a box on the wall; Zak grabbed a jacket off a hook.

Back out on the floor he placed the rolled-up jacket under Freddy's head. Jesse had him by the shoulders and was having trouble screaming over the engines right on top of them.

"Freddy!" but he couldn't get Freddy's attention.

Jesse and Zak wrapped Freddy's writhing torso in the blanket. Frank and George came running up. Frank had the first-aid kit, and George had some rope and a stack of guns and ammo and girlie magazines for making a splint.

He tossed the keys to his pickup over to Jesse who was staring, ashen faced, at his chainhand. "Jesse! get downstairs and find the stretcher! Then get over to my truck and back 'er up to the bottom of the stairs!" George then turned to Zak while taking a knife out of his jacket pocket. "Zak! Got a knife on ya?"

"Yeah."

"Well get 'er out and let's get this boot off him!"

It would have been hard to believe that Freddy could scream any louder than he already had, but when George and Zak began cutting into that tough leather boot he started hollering louder than ever. Zak looked up.

"Don't pay that shit no mind! Just cut!" George yelled, and Zak began sawing off that boot with a vengeance.

When the two knives started up Freddy's tight blue jean pant leg, Freddy began rolling his head from side to side and thrashing about wildly. He was a big heavy fella and Frank had to kneel at his shoulders and pin him down bodily while that pant leg came off.

"Oh sweet holy God," George gasped when he saw the leg. The fibula was jutting up through the skin just below the knee in splintered shards, and he and Zak were suddenly catching a fine, warm, sticky spray right in their faces. They could taste Freddy's blood. They recoiled backward. Zak frantically wiped his forearm across his mouth and turned away just as his stomach emptied and splashed over the iron floor behind them. George was stunned.

The knee was so badly mangled that the leg moved freely in all directions. When they collected themselves and resumed cutting the pant away and when Zak grabbed the leg to steady it, Zak's hand mistakenly clasped the tibia that was jutting out through the skin at the back of the calf. Dark red muscle bulged through the broken skin like mattress stuffing made from beef steak.

"A tourniquet," George muttered, regained his composure, and then screamed, "we need a tourniquet!"

Zak staggered to his feet, then stumbled off for the top doghouse. Just then Jon and Marty came strolling up onto the floor, "Hey, what's goin' on? Are you all right?" Jon asked, seeing the blood on Zak's face as he passed. Zak just pointed at Freddy and kept moving. A second later Marty was standing over Freddy assessing the situation. His bright eyes were blazing. Marty threw off his hat, loosed his overall straps, ripped off his flannel shirt, and stripped off his long john top. He grabbed up George's knife and swiftly began tearing long strips out of the back of that white shirt.

"Cut dat gotdamn pant leg up to de crotch," Marty ordered. As George set to doing that, Zak arrived back with a whole box of twine.

Marty dropped to his knees and jammed the heel of his big hand to the wound that was spitting blood, grabbing the twine from Zak's hands as he did so and in a second, had cut a long strip that wrapped around the leg just above the knee. Freddy started to scream and thrash his free leg wildly.

"Holt dat!" Marty screamed, and George and Jon both pounced on and secured the good leg. To Jon he screamed, "Go get me a stick about dis long!" and he held his arms up showing the length he wanted.

"Oh my God! Oh fuck! Help! Help! Sweet Jesus, ah! Ah!" Freddy bellowed.

"Freddy!" Frank hollered in exasperation as he struggled with the man's shoulders. "Why don't you do us all a favor and pass out!"

Marty wrapped the twine about Freddy's thigh just above the knee. Zak helped Jesse untie the stretcher behind them as Marty sat back on his heels and looked things over. "Der's a gudt break dere," he pointed to the bone jutting through the flesh. "Dat ankle broke a couple a ways. Dat knee's all fucked up, too! We gotta wrap his upper body in de blanket, dat arm looks broke too."

Jon returned with a sliver of wood about two feet long, and Marty put it under the twine and, when he turned the stick, the twine tightened the spraying spluttering blood dropped to an oozing trickle. "Gudt!" Marty said. He then set about tying bandages around the exposed parts. While he worked around the knee, he saw the kneecap dangling and swiftly placed it back where he thought it should go before wrapping it tightly. Jon returned with a freshly cut plank that was the perfect length, and Marty quickly held a group conference over poor Freddy's writhing bloody form.

"Now, dis gotta happen fast. I'm gonna straighten out dis leg. Den we gonna tie it up. Dis ankle we do twice. You guys put dem magazines all along here and we'll duct tape'm to his leg. Den tape'm up good and tight one more time. Den we hoist 'im onto dat stretcher. Frankie, you gotta sit on his chest. Got it?"

They all nodded.

"Oh shit, oh please, oh God! No, no no!" Freddy screamed.

"Den let's do it!" Marty said.

Frank hopped onto Freddy's chest. Marty, who had scooted down to that ankle, moved it into a normal-looking position, and with both hands pulled down firmly, yanking the entire leg into as straight a position as possible.

"Oh! Uhnnn!" Freddy's groans and murmurings took on an unholy sound.

"Quick, put dat!" Marty indicated the magazines and when they were in place yelled, "tape it!"

Freddy was now screaming in a contorted, unintelligible groaning gurgle.

Frank was muttering constantly, hysterically, tears streaming down his face, "It's okay Freddy, we're going to go as fast as we can, we'll get you through this buddy, hang in there, you're going to be all right pal, quit screaming Freddy, we'll get help, Freddy, please Freddy, quit screaming, Freddy, you'll be okay Freddy," but nobody, especially Freddy, could hear him.

Zak cut lengths of twine and handed these to Jon and George who tied Freddy's legs together.

"We gonna pick 'im up straight, Frank, you hop up and kick dat stretcher underneat. Wait!" He put a hand to Frank's shoulder, keeping him on Freddy's chest. To Frank he yelled, "Whatever happens don't let doze arms get free!"

Marty ran around and crouched next to Freddy's face, took it between his strong bloody hands, and looked Freddy in the eyes. Freddy stopped screaming. Marty had to shout to be heard.

"Freddy! We goin't put you on dat stretcher. It's goin't hert. You gotta stay straight. You can't fight us and fall off. You are really hert. You are gonna make it, but you really are hert."

Freddy nodded.

"M-my glasses!" Freddy screamed.

"Fuck dem," Marty screamed back as he turned away. Zak saw them lying by the rotary table and stuck them in his pocket.

On the count of three, Frank hopped off and Zak, Marty, Jon, and Jesse lifted Freddy a foot off the floor as George slid the stretcher underneath him. With Frank now off his chest, Freddy could really get some wind and his screams resumed full force as they tied him to the stretcher.

"Jesse," George hollered, "get on the phone and start waking people up in town, tell 'em we're leaving location for that clinic and we're gonna need real help."

Marty sent Jon down to the hopper and told him to get five or six mud sacks down to George's pickup truck. On the double!

Zak and George picked up the stretcher with Zak at the head and George at the feet and started moving for the stairs. The stairs were too narrow to allow more than one man down at a time, and worse, the stretcher was too wide to fit between the railings. Two men would have to carry him, chin high, all the way down the thirty-foot flight. George and Zak heaved to lift Freddy up over the railings, then George carefully took the first few steps, backwards down. When Zak hoisted Freddy even higher to compensate for the eighty-degree incline the chainhand's dead weight crunched down on that leg and he thrashed violently, spinning his head around, screaming, his face up full flush against Zak's. Both Zak and George stumbled, nearly losing Freddy over the side.

"Freddy, you silly bastard!" Zak screamed angrily, right into Freddy's ear as soon as they steadied themselves. "If you think it hurts now, wait till I drop your ass down these fuckin' stairs!"

"Listen!" George screamed, "This isn't going to work. We've got to go back up and take him down head first. He's moving too much and he's bleeding like crazy!"

From that point Freddy made a conscious effort to subdue himself, crying softly and whimpering between breaths as they paused at the top of the stairs to retie him to the stretcher.

When at last they reached the bottom of the stairs, they hustled him over to the waiting pickup truck, laid him in the back and Zak jumped in beside him. Marty hopped in and placed those big heavy mud sacks, like sandbags, all along his legs to keep them from moving. George slammed shut the gate. Marty hopped out. They roared out over grass, dirt, and gravel just as fast as George could push it. He had the accelerator pushed to the floor and was manhandling the wheel like a cowboy wrestling with a steer.

Zak was hanging on for dear life and Freddy, tied to that stretcher, bouncing and vibrating around the back of that truck, screaming, "Stop! Oh please Jesus, slow down! Help me God! Aaah! Aaah!"

"Don't you think we should maybe go easy?" Zak screamed through the open back window.

"Go easy?" George hollered back, taking his eyes off the path to look at Zak for emphasis, then swerving violently to find the lost path again. "Look goddamnit! Goin' slow isn't going to make his leg feel any better is it?! The best thing we can do for him is get him to the hospital as quick as possible! That's all I'm trying to do!" And they bounced and they roared and they swerved for forty miles before coming to the main road.

JESSE, JON, AND MARTY HOSED the mud, blood, and puke from the floor and finished dismantling those collar subs and were itching to get started for the clinic when relief showed. Carl and the boys were rapturous at not having to trip, lay down pipe, or even empty the mud tanks.

"You mean you lost another chainhand?" was all someone said.

Marty drove a late-sixties Ford station wagon he named Jezebel. She was green with sheep's wool covering on the front seat. As Marty zoomed off headed for town, Jon was busy hacking his way into Freddy's locker to get his clothes. Most important was his horseshoe belt buckle where he secreted his cash in its false back. As Jon trotted out to his car toting Freddy's things in a ball under his arm, he took a quick look around the grounds for Jesse. The driller's Merc was still parked beside his trailer, but Jesse was nowhere in sight. Jon was worried about the old man and had half a mind to drop Freddy's things in the backseat and go have a look for him.

The Lenny episode had hit Jesse hard, and Jon, Marty, and Freddy had worked shorthanded until days off that week to give Jesse time to find another hand back in Watford. That's when Jesse had hired Zachary Harper. Not that Jon had anything against Zak, as a matter of fact it was rather uncanny how adaptable Harper was, on the floor as well as off, but from then on Jon had had two worms to contend with instead of one. A dangerous proposition under the best of circumstances. And now this.

Jon tossed Freddy's things into the back of his car in a paralytic gesture of despair. He could have kicked himself in the ass. While he had been down at the mud tanks with Zak and Marty, Freddy had been up there doing a job that was clearly meant for two men at least. That poor fat uncoordinated slob had gotten himself all busted up for no good reason. Now they would need another hand, and with so few rigs in the area they would probably have to bring one in from Watford City or hire another worm. Jon lit a cigarette, took another futile glance in all directions for Jesse, then got into his car. Something told him he better get moving. Time was wasting. He wheeled his car around and took off, hell-bent for leather, down rig road.

FROM THE TOP OF A sage-covered hill a hundred yards off, a flicker of light. A small dark man lit a cigarette and watched the rig gleaming bright in the black prairie night. He saw Jon's car peel off into the blackness beyond the rig. He watched the headlights cut beams through the blackness. He heard the engines on the rig. He heard the men on the floor shouting to be heard over those engines. He could hear the engine of Jon's car trailing off into the distance. He could hear the stillness behind all these sounds. He listened to the stillness. He smoked and drank and watched and listened.

NOT HALF A MILE FROM location, Jon's headlights picked up Marty and Jezebel stopped in the middle of the roadway. Marty had the hood up and was flapping his arms over the engine, trying to dissipate a cloud of smoke. Jon fishtailed to a stop, and then lined the front of his car up to Jezebel's back bumper and hit the horn a couple of times. Marty waved and got behind the wheel while Jon pushed him off the roadway.

"Dat gotdamned fuel pump," Marty spat as he climbed into Jon's car, stepping up to his ankles in empty beer cans, sandwich wrappers, and nonrefundable Pepsi bottles. They streaked off once again for the hospital and, as they turned onto the main highway, they passed George's pickup headed back to location and slowed down to see if George would stop and give them the lowdown but he kept on going. And Jon and Marty agreed that it was a crazy night.

FREDDY FIFER WAS LYING ON a table in the emergency room of Daniels County Memorial Healthcare Center. He watched the second hand of the big schoolroom-type clock up on the wall steal inertly along from one second mark to the next. As he watched, the spaces between those marks grew farther and farther apart, wider and wider until the seconds stretched way beyond any preconceived limits of aoristic measure. Time had widened stretched into huge fathomless planes and multisided dimensions. Two large-bore IV drips were going into each arm, one with blood, the other with fluids. The morphine they hit him up with as soon as he arrived had him in a languid, swirling, laconic state. They cut away that splint. He clutched the side of the table he was strapped to with his one working arm and groaned. The second hand moved smoothly, sensuously along, he relaxed his grip, he tried not to listen to the words but concentrated on the calm, low, atonal voice of the doctor as he worked his way up Freddy's leg, cleaning and wiping away clots and dictating to his assistant.

"Open comminuted fracture...pure torsion injury...fibula... the posterior and anterior cruciate ligaments...tibial bone..."

When George realized it was going to be a long haul, he left Zak with Freddy and went back to the rig to ride herd over that crazy Cowboy Crew.

Just outside the emergency room the door to the main lobby burst open, and in came a crowd of people carrying a fourteen-year-old boy. He had been riding his trail bike after dark, taken a spill, and torn up his right leg something awful. Bone was jutting through his trousers and the good people who had found him had been unable to stop the bleeding. They thought he would die, he looked so bad. The room went hush as the doctor calmly and efficiently gave his orders. The emergency room staff had to forcibly push the lad's people, except his parents, out of the room and calm them down so they could work.

When the boy was stable, the doctor went and found Zak in the lobby. "Two compound leg fractures in one night, and a broken arm," he said in amazement. "I'm just a GP, Mr. Harper. But I had some orthopedic and lots of trauma experience in Vietnam. You guys did a good job getting him here. And I'll tell you something. The tourniquet was a good one, but luckily that bumpy ride here loosened it, and though he lost a lot of blood, loosening that tourniquet probably saved his leg, we'll have to see. He didn't bleed out, so that's to be thankful for. Anyway, the arm break was clean, far enough below the elbow and high enough from the wrist. I set it and put a cast on; that should be fine. The knee, the ankle, whoever straightened out his leg, well, got lucky. He's in a bit of shock, understandably. He has some spiral fracture issues going up the thigh. Both these patients need to be transported to Billings for surgery in the morning, and there's an ambulance big enough to carry them on the way here from down in Sydney; should take another hour, then it's a five-hour drive from here." He shook his head and then turned to address the young man's people, who were beside themselves with worry and blame.

In the ER, Freddy Fifer dropped his head back onto the stainless steel table and rejoined the heedless motion of the clock's second hand.

Jon and Marty arrived, still wearing their mud-covered rig clothes, boots, and hard hats. The thin film of dried drilling mud that entirely covered them was bright white in the glare of the clinic's lights. They looked like antediluvian mud soldiers, water world storm troopers, molemen. The people in the lobby quieted and made way for the two roughnecks who pushed their way into the ER and, spying Freddy behind a square patch of curtain, entered his space cautiously. They each squeezed his good left hand and looked into his eyes. Freddy's dopey eyes rolled from one of his buddies to the other. They paced around the table eager, excited and full of positive vocal reinforcement.

"Dat gotdamn Rusty!" Marty hissed, trying not to raise his voice, and jabbed a short grimy finger downward through the air. His hair bounced and his eyes flashed. "De way he's bin pushin' and pushin' de last coupla weeks, sumpdin' like dis was bound t'happin'!"

Fuckin' A! Freddy thought. He prayed that these two wild tigers wouldn't bump the table as they paced back and forth.

Jon's perspective was a little more self-effacing. "Yeah, but you guys should've called me when that bit needed breakin'. Shit, Jesse knows I've done that job dozens of times. No offense Freddy, but you had no business doin' that alone."

Freddy rolled his head to look at Jon and spoke his first coherent sentence since the accident, "No shit."

Everybody finally agreed that it was just one of those things, and Jon, Marty, and Zak quickly held a conference that ended with Jon volunteering to run over to the Pioneer and pick up some beer.

MARY ELLEN SWAYZEE DIDN'T RECOGNIZE Jonathan T. Sandlak when the roughneck entered the Pioneer Hotel and positioned himself at the end of the bar near the outside exit. He normally changed clothes in the bottom doghouse before leaving location, and as he stood there in full roughneck gear watching her talk with one of the old-timers at the end of the bar, it occurred to him that she always dropped what she was doing to take care of him. Now she simply looked up, made a gesture that she recognized him as a customer and that she'd be over soon enough. As he stood there in his roughneck disguise, he looked at her differently, candidly. In this new light she was tough, experienced, and strange. Out of politeness, he normally averted his eyes around women, but for the moment, emboldened by his anonymity, he allowed his eyes to roam over her body. She had a country girl's hips and derriere. Hands that already showed the scars of a life of hard work yet were still young enough to reveal a feminine delicacy. One hand rested on a hip that jutted out under her ordinary waitress skirt. Her breasts were small, but bunched up by her bra like some full, plump, bite-sized fruit in the front of her blouse. Her hair was thick and brown and hard to part. As she listened to the one who held her attention, her eyes wandered back to the waiting roughneck who, in turn, was shamelessly studying her every aspect. He wasn't leering, he was admiring, and she liked it. A bolt of electricity shot through them both. Her head cocked slightly, her eyebrows came together; until at last she said, "Excuse me," and leaving her customer in midsentence, marched toward the end of the bar.

"Is that you in there, Jonny?" She reached for his hard hat and pretended to peek down a hole as she lifted the lid. He had forgotten he still had it on. In his roughneck gear he wasn't at all shy, and this excited her. Though she shifted back to the familiar woman he had known before tonight, there was a new intimacy between them. It was as if she had said, is that you looking at me like that? Is that you no longer hiding the fact that you like me? Figuring out that I like you? What a relief to at last be real with one another.

"So, how's it goin?"

"Slow," she smiled, then jerked her head ever so slightly in the direction of the only other customer at the bar. "Verrry slow,"

"I need a couple of six's of Pabst," he reached under his overalls to get at his jeans pocket for some cash.

"Having a party out at the rig?" her eyes twinkled. She kept her eyes on him as the rest of her turned in the direction of the cooler. They studied each other warmly.

"No. I'm gonna take'm over to the hospital," he shook a cig from the pack and withdrew it the rest of the way with his lips. "Freddy had a bad fall tonight, busted his leg all up, broke his arm." She lit it for him. "Some of us are gonna hang out there till he's in the clear."

"Freddy? Oh no. Oh I'm so sorry. Poor sweet Freddy boy?" She turned from flirtatious to earnest in one easy moment. She straightened and tipped him out a glass of draft before reaching for the cooler lid. He noticed the hair on her forearm was golden in the dim bar light. He hadn't realized that she even knew who Freddy was. And now she was talking as if they were all good friends. He supposed they were. "How bad is it?" she asked.

He leaned on the bar and felt a mountain of pressure lift off his shoulders as he took a long sip of beer. "I haven't seen anything like it since 'Nam. Either has Marty. It's real bad. Thank God Marty had some experience in the field over there." He tilted his hard hat to the back of his head. There was a laugh in his voice. An incredulous, unfunny, little laugh. She thought it was a brave laugh; this accident could have befallen him. It registered that he mentioned the war. She waited for him to say more. He didn't.

"Is there anything I can do?"

"Um, yeah, let's get together sometime soon, okay? You know, sometime when we're both not working."

"I'd like that."

"Yeah, so would I."

She watched as the serious young man in his endearingly ludicrous riparian garb stuffed the bagged-up six-packs under his arm and clomped out the door. Everything ordinary seemed precious and bold. She picked up a rag and wiped up the dried chips of mud from where he had been leaning.

WHEN JON GOT BACK TO the hospital, he and the boys stayed outside, quietly sipped their beers, and waited, while inside the ER, Freddy was getting tucked away on a gurney bed with his leg all trussed up and his arm in a sling, IVs hanging upside down. It wasn't long before a big box-shaped ambulance pulled up at the side entrance. White-clad hospital people quietly and earnestly discussed the logistics of getting two trauma patients inside with all their attendant IVs, and which available attendant would be best for the long ride down to Billings.

The boys stashed their beers and tossed their cigs, then trooped in to wish their broken chainhand good luck. He looked as beaten and forlorn as a man can possibly look. His face sagged in a pale sickly hue. His voice was all but gone. In his right hand he limply held out his x-rays, and Jon took them as Marty and Zak looked over his shoulder.

"Whooooweee!" Marty let go with a low whisper. Circled in yellow crayon were all five breaks, two at the ankle, two in the leg front and back, and the knee. It was Freddy's certificate of valor, a memento of his brief career as a roughneck.

It took a few minutes to get the young lad into the vehicle, and Marty and Jon helped two attendants lift big Freddy's gurney. The three roughnecks stood in silence as the ambulance pulled away, its whirling lights, no siren, throwing an eerie warning through the town as it glided out of sight.

BEFORE THE BOYS TURNED IN that night, Marty worried about Jezebel. "Dem Getter boys'll be haulin' down rig road early an' if Jezebel gets clipped, Cynthia will have my gottdam head!" He was still moving fast. His eyes darted back and forth as he tried to figure his way out of the situation. They decided to sleep for a couple of hours and hit the NAPA dealership for a new fuel pump and then head out and get it installed before all hell broke loose when that rig started to move early next day. So Jon and Zak were both sleeping hard in their beds when Marty, sleeping on the floor between them, woke up and started kicking and bitching at them to get up and get their asses in gear.

They found Tony, the NAPA dealer, eating breakfast at the café next to Sam's. He made the boys sit and wait until he finished a second cup of coffee before heading over to the shop and breaking out a new fuel pump. Marty had been right about one thing: The eighteen-wheel flatbeds of the Getter Trucking Company, the smaller one-armed gin trucks, and pickups were all thundering down rig road kicking up huge clouds of dirt and gravel, just ready to get it!

Luckily, Jezebel had been spared. The trucks hammered out new paths, coming and going on either side of her like water flowing around a rock in midstream, but some had cut it pretty close. Zak and Jon jumped out to get a head start on tearing out that dead fuel pump while Marty went back to the rig to pick up Cynthia.

When Marty and Cynthia arrived, back at the car Jon and Zak could see instantly that she was in a black mood. Her anxieties had been stretched to the limit. Her major complaint was that Marty had thoughtlessly left the car in the road all night, taking an unnecessary risk with their only means of transportation. He tried to point out that the car had not been damaged in spite of his poor judgment, but she was not impressed. Nothing was worth risking getting stuck in Scobey, Montana! Nor was she very happy about spending the whole night pacing back and forth waiting for word about Freddy. Cynthia was not the type to wail and raise a loud harangue, but today she gave Marty and everyone else in earshot both barrels. She raged against their flippant apologies and flagrant disregard for people's feelings. Everyone was stunned. No one could remember seeing her so upset.

It had all started with Jesse. She looked forward to making little snacks for Jesse and Marty when the towers were over and the late show was coming on the little black-and-white TV the boys had rigged with a coat-hanger antenna. But last night Marty hadn't come home from work, and Jesse just stopped in to get something and left without changing his clothes or having a bite to eat. And he simply let it drop that Freddy had been hurt as he walked out the door. She had to go running after him to learn that it was at all serious. It was then she noticed how bad he looked. Worse than when he had run Lenny off. How was she supposed to sit and watch the late show by herself when Jesse thinks he's the one who hurt poor Freddy? Did Jesse hurt Freddy? She didn't think that he would just twist off and head to Watford City. So where was Jesse? And why hadn't anyone gone out to find him?

Marty had no good answers for her. Not coming home and keeping her in the dark were serious offenses requiring immediate apology and a long cooling-off period. The only thing he could do was plead guilty on all counts and throw himself at her mercy. Which was hard to do on rig road, with the sun already up and those trucks kicking up dangerous amounts of dirt and gravel. She climbed in Jon's Oldsmobile and rolled up the windows to keep out the dust and locked the doors to keep out the riffraff. With her arms folded across her chest and a scowl on her fat round face, she refused to speak to or even look at anybody.

While Jon worked under the hood, Marty and Zak lay down on their backs and crawled under the engine. The three men wrenched and banged and cursed that new fuel pump into place as all the while those Getter boys practically zoomed right over top of them. Zak and Marty pulled their legs in close several times to prevent being crushed under the tremendous onrushing wheels. They tied kerchiefs over their mouths to keep from choking on the dust.

After that pump was finally in, it took a feat of diplomatic brilliance to coax Cynthia out of the Olds and into Jezebel. She was intentionally being as obstreperous as possible. They certainly were unworthy of her cooperation and so it was left to Zak, for some reason, to make the pleas that eventually moved her, and even though he was sweet and never ignored her, he was still a man, a roughneck friend of Marty's, a co-conspirator, and not to be trusted. She cracked her window a tad, listened to Zak explain that she had every right to be angry, that it had been a crazy night and day, any way you looked at it, but the job was done, and although she could ride back to location with him and Jon if she wanted, wouldn't she rather ride into town with Marty? Once she did, this madness would end and they could get away from all these trucks. She at last opened the door and marched back to her own car.

When they had her simmered down and sitting quietly, but not calmly, in the front seat, Marty got behind the wheel and, as Zak and Jon looked on from under the hood, Marty hit the starter. Jezebel chugged, whinnied, wheezed, and after a final shudder, died away completely. Marty spat out the window and slapped his palm down on the dash. Cynthia meanwhile was on the verge of panic. It wasn't just the car. She could see the basic support systems of her life coming apart, no less, and as Jon and Zak looked stupidly from one to the other and Marty sat there and cursed, she began to suspect that this mean little comedy was being played out for her benefit. That the car was ruined for good and these jokers were going through the motions to get their pal Marty off the hook. Well it wasn't going to work. She shot Marty a look. Then she got out of the station wagon and returned to the Oldsmobile where she could resume her pout from a safe distance.

But the boys truly were vexed. They scratched their heads and chewed the matter over until at last, thinking of nothing better, they decided to take the new fuel pump out and put it back in, again hoping that in the process they would discover what had gone wrong. Again Zak and Marty lay under the car with the big semis roaring past their legs. Again Marty closed his eyes, crossed his fingers, and turned the ignition. Nothing. There was only one explanation. Willy had sold them a bum pump. Jon and Zak appeared at Marty's window, their kerchiefs still over their noses like a couple of outlaws. What now? Marty rested his big head on the steering wheel just as Cynthia marched back from Jon's car and climbed into the rider's seat with an I told you so click of her tongue. Marty turned his head away from her to face the boys, making a terrible grimace.

"Aiyaiyaiyaiyaiy!" he screamed and flung open the car door. The boys backed off as he pounded to the front of the car. Jon and Zak followed him, yipping like a couple of hounds.

Marty stood before the engine clutching and unclutching his fists. His green eyes darted. His aquiline nose pointed downward to infinity. He paced to the driver's side of the engine, stalking his prey. He stood hovering over the window-washer tray. "Tools!" he shouted.

Jon dashed off to grab the toolbox they had just put away as Marty lifted the window-washer tray out of its holder. He then disconnected the tubing that carried the liquid to the windshield, then rummaged around in the back of his outfit, and came up with a roll of duct tape, an old coffee can, and a hose for siphoning gasoline. Marty stuck the end of the washer tray tubing into the carburetor and secured it there with a piece of tape he tore off the roll with his teeth. After siphoning off enough gas to fill the coffee can, he poured it into the washer tray, holding some out to pour directly into the carb. Then he carefully climbed into the driver's seat, holding the tray out the window with his left hand. Jon then taped down the hood so Marty could see as Marty turned the ignition and fired her up.

Jon and Zak skipped over to the Oldsmobile and prepared to run interference for Marty and Cynthia. They started out slow. Marty was holding the wheel with one hand, the cup full of gas out the window with the other, and as they started to roll, the gas sloshed over the edge of the cup covering Marty's hand and running down his sleeve.

It was then that poor Cynthia lost her grip on the entire situation. She started crying and muttering that they were both going to be burned alive, squashed under the wheels of a Getter truck, out of transportation, out of work. She cried and shrieked and stomped her feet. When her hysterics threatened his driving space, he let go of the wheel and reached his strong right arm over and thwacked her good letting the blow land just wherever it could.

They made it up and over that first hill and coasted down its other side with no problem. On the next little stretch of level ground, Marty kept his feet off the brake and off the gas. The car found its own slow speed regulated by the trickle of gas going into the carb from the washer tray. If they had been on paved road this crazy idea would have worked like a dream, for a little while anyway. He looked over at Cynthia, who was sobbing hysterically, and Marty screamed, "Aiyaiyaiyaiy!" at her, causing her to jump and flinch. Next was a downward slope, no problem there either; he tapped his foot lightly on the brake and coasted.

It was on the following upward slope that the idea fell apart. Unable to use the accelerator to increase the flow of gas, and gravity alone insufficient to draw additional fuel into the engine to compensate for the extra drag, Jezebel crawled to a stop once again in the middle of the road.

Now they were in real trouble.

The big trucks bounding over the hill just ahead of them had no way of knowing there was a broken-down vehicle in their path, and sure enough, as soon as Marty and Cynthia had rolled to a stop, a giant eighteen-wheeler came screaming over the top of the hill and swerved, horns bellowing, missing them nearly, spraying them hard with dirt and pebbles.

Marty's heart leapt up into his throat. Cynthia very nearly swallowed her tongue.

Jon and Zak drove onto the top of the hill, where they got out of the car and started directing traffic away from their two vehicles. Marty got out of the car and climbed the hill to join his two buddies, leaving Cynthia alone in the car screaming her head off. She wasn't leaving the car to get smashed. And he obviously didn't care any more for her than he did for their car, their future, anything! They were doomed!

At the top of the hill Zak and Marty conferred while Jon motioned the trucks over to one side. Zak and Jon would leave Marty to take over from there while the two of them went off to get Zak's Jeep. If, in the meantime, Marty could hail a passing trucker and borrow a towing chain, Zak could pull him back to town. It was a deal. Anything to get off that crazy dirt path and away from those maniac Getter boys and the perpetual cloud of flying rocks and choking dust. Jon and Zak sped off, leaving Marty on the top of that hill, level with the tops of all the other hills, waving his arms at those Getter boys, looking like Mighty Joe Young pushing those big semis this way and that around his poor wounded auto and his terror-stricken wife.

When Zak and Jon returned they found Marty, wearing a big heavy chain around his neck, forming a dust-covered human barrier in front of his car, keeping the trucks on the return side from colliding into the trucks charging up the go side. Wheeling and dealing. Zak slung the Jeep into position, threw his outfit into four-wheel drive as Jon hooked them up and they were off! Jon, loyal comrade that he was, in the lead running interference for their desperate little convoy.

They cannonballed up and down the crazy terrain. In and out of the endless procession of semis, gin trucks, flatbeds, and pickups. Jon was flashing his lights, waving one arm, honking his horn, and screaming, "We're comin' through!"

In the Jeep, Zak bounced in the driver's seat and tried to keep up. The side and back windows of the Jeep's ragtop were of that foggy plastic no human eye can pierce, leaving Zak visibility only through the front windshield and side mirrors, so he couldn't see the real excitement that was taking place behind him.

Zak's big tires were picking up tons of dirt and gravel and spewing it all over Jezebel like machine-gun fire. In seconds, the windshield was so pockmarked visibility was gone. The headlights busted out. The paint all along the hood and the sides was peppered by a million pellets. Marty could only guess when to touch the brake and when to leave off, smashing again and again into the Jeep's invincible back bumpers.

For Cynthia, there was no end to the madness. Those forty miles to the Four Buttes turnoff lasted a screaming, clutching eternity. Every time she came close to Marty pounding him and beseeching him to stop he brushed her away with a strong arm, bloodying her nose and bruising her arms. She was a raving, ranting, very upset person.

It was at just this time, as that main highway was coming into view that the Jeep got a flat.

As soon as they all three rumbled to a stop, Cynthia leaped from the car, her eyes wild, her arms flailing, "Look at it! Look at it! It's ruined! I told you so! I told you not to tow it! Look at all the money this'll cost!"

The windshield was completely pitted. All four headlights and the parking lights were smashed. There were ten thousand pockmarks from one end of the wagon to the other. The grillwork in front was a twisted mess. The body of that automobile was quite obviously ruined. Zak took a step back in horror. Jon, who had gotten out of his car to see what the trouble was, retreated the second he saw it. Cynthia pounded on Marty's chest. Then she ran at Zak and pounded on his chest. The veins in her neck were bulging. Saliva whipped into a white lather at the corners of her mouth. Her normally ruddy cheeks were crimson with rage as she kicked and punched and screamed. Getter boys honked their horns cheering her on as they passed in both directions. Marty, helpless until now, looked at Zak as if to ask, *What should I do?* Zak shrugged. Marty then lifted her up in a big bear hug, shushing her and squeezing her. Her fat belly jiggled under her dirty red T-shirt. Her arms and legs pumped until, at last, she had no more wind to carry on. When he put her down, she crawled sobbing back into the car, determined to protect what little there was left. She cocked her head, and staring into a distance, resumed her argument with some unseen party.

Zak tried to explain to Marty that he hadn't known how bad they were getting it, but Marty shrugged and smiled, "What can ya do?"

Nothing about the car, that's for sure, Zak thought, but he could do something about Cynthia's ravaged feelings. He went over to the car and sat down beside her. Tears were streaming down her face and her lower lip completely overlapped the upper. He knew that there was a tirade going on inside her head and felt that maybe if he gave her a chance to pour some of it out on him it would make her feel better.

At the risk of sounding trite, he said, "I'm awfully sorry about what's happened, Cynthia, I really am. It's just a bad deal. A bad deal all the way around." Her body became stiff and still. She clutched the wool seat covering. Her face relaxed and she stared straight ahead. But she was listening. "It's not our day, that's for sure," Zak pressed on, "no sir, just not our day."

She sniffed a couple of times and ran an awkward hand across her nose. Then bowed her head and rubbed her eyes with her palms and murmured in a little voice, "That's for sure." It wasn't often that she heard compassion, sympathy, and understanding in a male voice, and even though what Zak was saying did nothing to ameliorate the reality of the situation, he could tell by the way she knitted her brow that the thought and the gesture were well taken. As long as someone cared about her distress, there was hope for all of them. Even the thunder of the passing Getter trucks was hushed for that one moment by her last quiet sob as she relaxed her grip on the wool seat covering and her shoulders resumed their familiar slouch. Zak realized, as he witnessed her pure grief-stricken outpouring, that they had all been riding on a collective momentum that had to stop or be stopped somewhere. Rig road on moving day was as good a battlefield as any.

With those Getter trucks still roaring past, the only thing to do was get that tire changed and get out of there in one piece. Marty, Cynthia, and Jezebel were towed to the Cenex station in town, after which Jon and Zak retreated to the hotel, where they threw themselves on their beds and were out cold in seconds.

It was early evening when the two roughnecks stirred, took turns in the shower, and clomped downstairs.

In the hotel lobby, Zak and Jon found some old-timers gathered in stony silence before a big box black-and-white TV where some young men, hands bound behind their backs and blindfolds around their heads, were being slowly pushed through an angry mob, the words "Tehran...Ayatollah...Hostages..." coming from the speaker turned up loud.

"Think we outta nuke'm?" someone asked.

"Quiet," someone else scolded, "I'm trying to hear."

The two roughnecks decided to go elsewhere for an early supper before heading off to work.

IN THE DAYS AFTER FREDDY'S accident, Jesse didn't return. The men began tearing down the rig, all four crews working the same shift. In the middle of this process, days off for Jesse's crew rolled around again. Jon put things this way.

"Look, without Jesse or another crew member, once we spud-in at the new location, well, we'll be shit out of luck, I say we beat it on down to Watford and see what's up."

They flipped a coin. Jon drove.

They arrived in town along about dusk. Zak recognized the place, but in other ways he was seeing it for the first time. He could tell the roughnecks from the local townsfolk at a glance now. He could see clearly how the oil traffic influenced every aspect of the town's daily life. How, unlike Scobey, the town had assimilated the integrated elements, but there was a price.

Although there was very little sign of decay in either town, there was little or no opulence either. The oil business in the field, Zak decided, is rigged for efficiency and speed. It was this total abandonment of any pretense to permanence that probably didn't set right with folks who had intended to put down roots here. Across the region, as the boys made their way south, Zak could see that atop of all the cattle and croplands sat the newly erected steel and aluminum buildings to house the support services needed to facilitate the ever-fluctuating needs of the oil patch. Any aesthetic architectural design was forsaken but for the purposes of efficiency and need. The harsh lines of expedience added a sense of urgency to the ancient landscape. Immediacy by its very nature is a temporary condition. Even though the oil boom with its highs and lows had lasted more than a generation in this area, the underlying notion was that at any second, the oil patch itself might simply pick up and move elsewhere, taking everything with it. This was the unspoken anxiety that got under the skin and carried with it a dull numbing edge. The bottom line was that little Scobey would remain should the oil traffic disappear. Watford City, on the other hand, would more than likely just dry up and blow away.

When at last the two men reached town, it didn't take long to find out that Freddy had a trailer parked in the City Park.

Zak and Jon drove first to a liquor store and bought a bottle of whiskey, then to the park. The park itself had become an overflow station, so to speak, as trailers and RVs had claimed one corner of the place and there was a small roughneck village cropping up, already filling about a quarter of the space. They strolled between the vehicles. Freddy's trailer was smack dab in the middle. "Howdy gents!" they heard a welcome and familiar voice call out from an open window.

Freddy was camped out on a comfy old sofa, the cast on his leg stretching up past the knee, his right arm in a cast with a sling around his neck. He had only been delivered from Billings the night before and so Jon and Zak unpacked his duffel bag, propped him up in front of a television set with the bottle of whiskey conveniently within reach. Then dashed out to the store and got him fixed up with TV dinners, sandwich stuff, and an extra bottle. They opted for whiskey over beer, partly because he wouldn't have to get up for a piss so often and, too, because Freddy's buddies might drink all the beer.

"It's going to be tough leavin' Fred in that ol' trailer, he looks like dog shit," Jon said quietly as he and Zak made their way back with the provisions.

They sat around and had one last drink together, not saying much. As Zak and Jon were walking out the door, Freddy called Zak back into the trailer. "Here," he said, digging into a sack beside the couch where he lay. "I bought this before breaking out, thought it might come in handy, shooting a snake or something." He pulled out a rolled-up chamois and laid it out on his lap. It was a new Colt .45 long barrel, shiny and black. Zak didn't know much about guns but it looked expensive. "It's my favorite gun," Freddy continued as he fished through the bag and came up with a box of bullets.

"Freddy," Zak laughed, "I really appreciate this but I don't…"

"Pick it up and look it over. It's loaded. Remember, there's no safety on these guns, so if you stick it in your pants like Doc Holliday, you *will* blow your balls off! But that's the very same gun that was issued in 1872 by the U.S. Army. It fought the Indian wars, the Mexican War, the Spanish-American War, they called that gun the 'peace maker.' That's the gun that won the West, Zak!"

Zak handled the gun without putting his finger through the trigger loop. "I'll want it back someday, don't forget, but I'm not going huntin' for a spell, that's for sure, but you, the way you like to be outdoors with the coyotes and all, you never know. Oh, and here," Freddy kept digging in his bag and came up with a new coffee pot. "Never got to use this either. It's an old-fashioned percolator. C'mon, take'm both. I might see a snake from time to time when I'm back drivin' thumper trucks, but until then you go ahead."

"Don't worry, Fred." Zak tucked the chamois into his jacket, figuring it was easier to take it than to refuse; he grabbed up the pot as well. "I'll get 'em back to ya by the time you're on your feet again. Thanks." Zak moved toward the door.

"Zak?"

"Yeah?"

"I damn near got the hang of it, didn't I?"

Zak stopped at the door. A cord of emotion tightened around his throat. Freddy's eyes were wet behind his thick glasses now held together with duct tape. Zak smiled warmly and nodded yes.

"You take care of yourself."

Zak stepped outside and took a deep breath before walking to Jon's car.

"What was that all about?" Jon asked. "Is he gonna be okay?"

"Yeah, he's all right, gave me this coffee pot," Zak said solemnly. As they pulled away, he could see the light from the table lamp beside Freddy's couch glow forlornly through the deepening blue dusk. For a second, he thought he saw Freddy's big head bob up, like he had lifted himself for a moment to glimpse his friends drive off.

The gun, wrapped in its leather rag, fit uncomfortably under his arm inside Zachary Harper's canvas vest inside his jacket.

X

When Eileen saw Jon and Zak step heavily into the City Bar, she dropped what she was doing and hurried over to them, her face full of alarm, her voice shaking, somewhere between anger and fear. "What's been going on up there in Scobey?"

Jesse Lancaster had been there since she opened that morning and was now half-sprawled across the bar, stinking drunk and getting worse by the second. No one would come within five feet of him. The energy pouring off him was violent, irrational, and dangerous.

Jesse had to squint to recognize the two roughnecks stepping cautiously toward him. He shrugged his shoulders with a woozy growl and looked away. As they drew closer, he turned on his stool to get as much of his back facing them as possible like an angry gorilla. Jon and Zak eyed each other. They then took stools on either side of the driller.

"Get away from me!" he scowled and pushed his elbows out in each direction to reclaim his space. His mouth hung open. His eyes were fixed on no set target; rather, his senses were all tuned in two directions, anticipating assault from either side or both.

"C'mon, Jesse," Jon said in a voice that was dry, carefully implying nothing. "Why don't we get some food and dry out a little. It's a long drive back to Scobey."

"Scobey?" Jesse spat with atrabilious sarcasm and contempt. "I ain't goin' back to Scobey."

"Now no one's tellin' ya you got to go back to Scobey. God knows you don't haveta if you don't wanta," Jon spoke calmly, slowly. "But if you were to come back up, well, you could ride with us. We'll worry about your car later. It'll be easy. Whaddya say, huh?"

Jesse whirled around to face Jon dead on. The whites of his eyes were reddish brown. His breath was stale but for the whiskey vapors. His teeth were dirty. His clothes stank. For a second, neither Jon nor Zak had a clue what the old man was going to say or do.

"Look goddamnit," Jesse started out slow and calm, attempting to approximate Jon's reasoned tone of voice as nearly as possible but falling into near-violent anger quickly and he was speaking way too loud. "Don't you fuckin' hear too good? I ain't goin' back to Scobey or anyplace else! I'm twistin' off! I'm through. Finished! I've had it! Now the two of yuhs can get the hell away from me and leave me be!" This last he bellowed so the whole room could hear. Men looked up. Some started from their chairs, wondering if now was the time to put an end to this. Zak looked them back into their seats as Jon concentrated on his older driller.

"Jesse, that just don't make sense. You know it don't," Jon's voice dropped down to nearly a whisper. "We're all countin' on ya, Jesse, all of us. Shit, if you quit we're all out of work."

"Listen!" Jesse started in one direction, then the other, not knowing which way to direct his thoughts. He sliced his hand gently through the air for emphasis, and, looking at that hand, it was as though he held it there to keep the madness of his thoughts back just long enough for the meaning in what he was about to say to get through. "You guys don't want me for a driller. No wait! Now hear me through." He was concentrating on keeping as much of the slur from his voice as possible. He didn't want to sound like he felt sorry for himself. He wanted to sound like the same old Jesse giving the boys some constructive advice. "You've got to look at what happened to Freddy." And he brought his hand down for emphasis again. He spoke each word slowly. "Really look at it. How'd you like that should be you, or Zak here, or Marty. Huh?" He looked imploringly from one to another, his hard black eyebrows edging upward under a hanging lock of dirty black hair. "The day I start hurtin' people, that's it. You know it. I know it. If it was you, you'd feel the same goddamn way. So get the fuck away from me and start lookin' for another job."

"Jesse, I know you feel responsible for Fifer. Shit, maybe it is your fault. But you know that sometimes accidents just happen. Nobody's perfect. You know you're still the best driller out there, bar none. We need ya. George needs ya. Shit Jesse, I don't want to work for anyone else."

Jesse waited. When next he spoke, it was like a father to a young son who doesn't understand a grown-up hurt. "I'm not going to hurt people, Jonny. The day I start is my last day. I ain't drillin' anymore. No goddamn more. That's it. I might go back after a while and work the floor. Go back to worm's corner and start over. Sumpthin'. But no more drillin'. A man's got to know when he can't get 'er."

Jon tossed a look over the back of Jesse's shoulders at Zak for some help, finding it hard to keep coming up with positive ideas. Zak took a stab.

"Christ Jesse, I just think you're taking this a bit too hard. I mean, I'm a worm, and, well, I suppose I can sit here and think of a dozen times at least in the past few weeks when I could easily have gotten hurt, but, well, Lady Luck's been with me, that's the only difference I can see. Hell, I think that if you were to ask Freddy himself he'd be the first to say there's no hard feelings."

Jesse listened in silence, then shook his head no.

It was like that time there at the City Bar when Jesse Lancaster and Harper first met. How Jesse would come and go. Drunk out of his mind one minute, crystal sharp the next. He straightened up and looked Zak coldly in the eye.

"Everything you say is true, Zak. Everything. Taking Freddy on was a gamble. There's no doubt about that. And some men might excuse themselves on those grounds. Some men might be damn glad that company hand and that toolpusher were there when it happened to back him up. Glad that he could point the finger at that toolpusher for stretching the normal bounds of propriety by asking us to do a job that might have gone to the next crew. Another man might say, 'Well, these things happen,' but that's not good enough for Jesse Lancaster, son, and I'll tell you something, I don't know where you come from or even if you are who you say you are and I don't care. I've seen the way you come runnin' when it's time to pull your fair share and I've seen you do work that should rightfully been done by some of the others. You're a good hand, Zak. That's why you haven't been hurt. That and because, know it or not, Jonny here, and myself, Marty, and yes, even Freddy, have all been keeping our eye on you. When you know what I know, when you're on top of every minuscule event happening on and around the floor of an oil rig, there isn't a man on that location that you don't know what he's doing every minute. You know how long it's going to take him to do a job and you know if he's going to fuck it up. Yeah, you know that too. You know when and you know why. And mister, you do something about it beforehand. I learned those things early, the hard way, they are a part of my life. That, to me, is what responsibility is all about. Without it, what've I got? There's no pension waiting for me when I get too old. I have no savings to speak of. All I have is a lifetime of respect, self-respect, damn it. The admiration of good men. Nothing more, nothing less. I made great roughnecks, and I mean great ones, out of the most ordinary hands. What driller on that fuckin' Bomac rig would have lasted an hour with Freddy Fifer as his chainhand? Zak, I'm just too damn good not to know when I'm goin' down. I don't believe that in my shoes you wouldn't feel exactly like I do." Jesse was no longer addressing Jon and Zak but was speaking quietly, fluidly, his words barely audible, staring straight ahead, as though explaining himself to God. "I should have known. I've said no to George a thousand times. So why, why, why didn't I get Jon, or Marty? It would have been so natural. To have stayed out on that floor was unthinkable! Worms make mistakes like that. Not me. Not the kind of driller I once was."

Jon and Zak were out of ideas.

"Look, why don't you guys just fuck off," he finished bloodlessly. He was drunk and it looked like he was going to stay drunk for a while. Jon and Zak conferred silently eye to eye. Whichever way Jesse was going, he was going to have to get there by himself. There was no telling what his next move was going to be. At last, Jon's nod toward the door shook Zak loose. They stepped away from the bar.

"Hell, there isn't anything more we can do here," Jon insisted quietly.

Zak wasn't so sure, he was inclined to keep ordering drinks and ride this out with Jesse, like he would ride out a bad trip with a buddy back in school but felt he had to give Jon his due for knowing Jesse better, longer. He couldn't tell if Jon was just impatient or truly felt confident that leaving was the right thing. In any event, they bought a couple of six-packs for the long drive back to Scobey.

Zak was tired. Jon and Zak rode in silence. The monotonous terrain rolled by. Tomorrow they would either start work on Bomac 34's next location or Jesse would fail to show and George would be forced to put together another crew by hiring a new driller. Zak was tired; in his fatigue, a slow dull pang of despair pierced the numbness. The prospect of being out of work again so soon after thinking he had found himself in an ideal situation, especially after his compromise with George, which come to think of it, was beginning to look like a catastrophically bad decision, pushed him down in his seat. His head rested against the door window with a thunk. At least this time around he had a few dollars in his pocket and wasn't a total stranger. Everything was riding on a man who was seriously drunk and hundreds of miles from location.

BACK IN SCOBEY AT THE Pioneer Hotel bar, Zak was on his third Dewar's and water, still mulling all this over while Jon took the first shower upstairs, when someone sat down next to him and said, "It's all yours."

This man had a solid medium build with a square jaw and strong shoulders, long blond hair neatly combed straight back, and penetrating blue eyes. He had the kind of curious good looks a lot of movie stars have. A kind of everyman symmetry to his face but with something extra, something perhaps a little manic, a little on edge, thrown in. His clear pale skin stretched taught across the bones of his face, and when his facial muscles moved, you could see them all working in unison, driven by natural mechanics but fueled by emotion. A face revealing nothing but hinting at everything. It took a whole second for Zak to recognize him.

"Jon!"

"Well, what do you think of the real me?" Jon took a step back, rubbed his face all over with his big hands, and brushed his hair straight back.

"I'm impressed!" Zak looked him up and down. Clean pressed jeans, a clean shirt, and a polished pair of brown two-tone cowboy boots with pointed toes that looked real sharp. His usual brash, impertinent stare was now accompanied by a hitherto invisible cat-who-ate-the-canary grin, and this bold countenance, taken as a whole, could only mean one thing.

"You've got a date!"

Jon opened his mouth in silent hilarity, and his head bobbed as he scooted onto a stool and ordered up a rye and Coke.

"Who is it? A girl back in Watford?"

"Nope."

"No shit. Someone here in Scobey?"

Jon was grinning to himself as well as at Zak as he laid his money down on the bar. He was a little surprised that Zak hadn't picked up on this development from the start. Freddy had figured it out right away. To Jon it seemed so glaringly obvious. Zak took a long, dramatic look around the empty room as though every eligible woman in Scobey, Montana, were present. At last when he saw the strange barkeep, it hit him. He smiled a big smile that pushed his frameless glasses high up on his cheeks. "Mary Ellen," he concluded, drawing out the name in a playful roguish tenor. Jon smiled again and took a long pull on his drink. As he did so, he caught a glimpse of himself in the mirror behind the bar. His cocksure expression, the one that had gotten him in so much trouble back home, in high school, the one that needed hiding in the military, was back. He was at the same time secretly embarrassed by and proud of his own good looks.

Zak patted Jon on the shoulder, wished him luck, assured him he'd steer clear of the hotel room that night and, as they parted company, wanted Jon to "ask her if she's got a sister."

"Will do, partner."

ZAK SHOWERED UP AND BEFORE he left the hotel for his camp-site, he talked the barkeep into slipping into the café and getting him a couple of packets of prewrapped coffee grounds for next morning. He was looking forward to some privacy and some rest. As the Jeep roared into the cool black night, Zak could feel the tension from the past several days, one big long day really, fall from him like dead tree bark. He wanted to retreat into the wilderness. Retreat from the intimate beginnings of Jon and Mary Ellen's courtship. Retreat from the ugly pain that warped Jesse Lancaster and tormented poor Freddy Fifer. Retreat from Marty's crude approach and Cynthia's simple and stunted world view. He wanted to crawl into a hole and cover it over. He wanted to crawl inside his own skin once again and see if there was anything new to be found there. Something, hopefully, more perfectly whole, complete, and comprehensible than what he had left behind on his last visit.

The Jeep was loud. Too loud to bother pushing in a tape. He used the loud drone of the engine and the steady rattling of the ragtop against the wind as a bed beneath his thoughts which were more images than words and ideas. He pulled the hood of his soiled green sweatshirt over his head. He felt like a monk. He could see himself locked away in the isolated confines of some distant monastery. Tucked away in the forested wilderness. Removed from time. Poring over ancient and esoteric dogmas by candle-light. Preserving a daring, unused rationale for a time capsule to be rediscovered by a more intuitive and inquisitive breed of mankind. Living on bread, homemade wine, and the alms of strangers. Then taking his personal quest out into a world where few would recog-nize him. He wanted not only to be alone but to be left alone.

He wondered if the self that he had created and introduced to his new friends was real. He had stripped himself down, emotion-ally and historically, to nothing more than an amalgamation of impulse reactions to the needs of every moment. He had drawn on no personal history to come this far, had not arrived here as the result of a logical progression of events but had willfully altered his course in midstream. He had ripped himself out of time, out of place, and inserted himself here. Set the right plant down in the right soil long enough and it will invariably take root. Other lives were now integrating, inevitably, with his own. He wondered if it was wrong of him to interfere, if by being there he was altering, in one way or another, the lives of all he touched. If he truly didn't belong here, then he was injecting into their lives a dangerous and inappropriate element. If he had not come West then he wouldn't have been there to make the decision not to twist off. No. If he hadn't been a trained creature of compromise, it would never have occurred to him not to twist off. It surely had occurred to everyone else. For a brief moment it occurred to him that he should get back to his campsite just long enough to retrieve his things, Freddy's tent included, and push on down the road. He had some money. He could get another job like Jesse had suggested. Maybe hire on with another rig down around Watford. Hang around just long enough to earn another couple of paychecks, and when he began to learn more than the names of his new crew, figure that was the time to split once again.

At the campsite Zak tore off his boots and climbed into the sleeping bag with his clothes on. He unwrapped Freddy Fifer's fully loaded long barrel Colt .45 and scrutinized it under the light of his flashlight. He wanted desperately to step outside the tent and squeeze off a couple of rounds, for no other reason than to smell the powder and hear the report, to feel the kick. He had never fired a gun this powerful before. There was no doubt that everyone in the farmhouse down the way knew exactly what a gunshot sounded like and would come running with guns of their own. He wrapped it up, placed it under a shirt pointing away from himself, and went right to sleep with one hand still resting on the weapon. He didn't dream.

Along about dawn his anxieties over his now-uncertain job situation woke him, and he emerged from the tent into the mystic blue premorning light, stretched, and set himself to gathering dried grass and whatnot, including debris from the floor of the Jeep, to kindle the fire. The ground was wet on his bare feet. The air was crisp in his lungs. In the Jeep he also found the boards from Freddy's splint and a box full of ripped-up and bloodied guns and girlie magazines, most of which he included in his kindling pile. One photograph, untorn and unsullied, was of a young woman holding her breasts protectively while leaving her sex completely exposed as she stared nervously at him from the page. He tore the picture from the magazine before tossing the latter in the fire. He filled his coffee pot with spring water, dropped in the packet of grounds and, once that was set in the burning pile of junk, retired once more to the tent with the picture from the book.

Her hair, which didn't belong parted at the side, was tossed recklessly over the top of her head as though she had just landed in this position and, as if given the choice of surrendering her breasts or her sex to the approaching viewer, had voluntarily parted her legs. Her breasts were the type men typically drool over. Big and young enough to still have plenty of bounce. Her nipples were puffy and pink and aimed in opposite directions. They looked as though you could sweep them completely off the top of those big billowy mounds with one swipe of the tongue. Coconut cherry marshmallow. She held them guardedly and the more Zak studied her face, the more he saw her as cross, perhaps even jealous of whomever might want to take them from her. She seemed to be saying, *These are mine. These are for me. You won't treat them right. You'll maul them, burn them with your whiskers. You won't take the time to explore them. You think you know what they are, but you don't. How could you? You can have this. This is what you're really after anyway, isn't it?* Between her legs was a slight wisp of golden brown hair that curled tightly directly over

her taut and tucked-in little slit. Hardly what you might consider bush. There was not enough flesh from her buttocks to hide her rectum yet there was just enough there to form a capricious little smile on the blanket where she reclined. Her belly was small and round and unlike most, if not all, the women in these magazines, she looked remarkably defiant, unabused.

Zak closed his eyes and there was Jackie, the girl from corn mountain, lowering herself down onto his lips, her wetness creating an atmosphere of its own, breathing into his nostrils as she stared down between her breasts to see him tasting her, then arching her perfect neck and chin upward with her own release as her hand reached behind her and took hold of him. He moaned loudly, shuddered over and over again and, after a long moment, opened his eyes. All was gone but the sunlit green canvas wall of the tent. The tent smelled of mold. The bright green filtered light washed everything around him. The air was thick. He wiped his hand on a soiled shirt from his laundry pile, buttoned up, and staggered out to get some coffee.

It was a glorious morning. The creek water sang as it lapped, slapped, and tinkled over the rocks echoing off the short canyon walls and the big big sky. Zak gulped down a cup of coffee, then adjourned to the outhouse for his morning constitutional. As he sat there musing over the possible events of the day, he focused on the fact that last night, tonight, and tomorrow could be his last here by the creek and suddenly regretted not having spent every night here. He remembered something Corey Nightingale had said about this place, this time of day, in connection with Coster's lost son. He pulled the outhouse door closed and followed the beam of sunlight that poured through the crescent moon on the door and landed on the wall behind him. Something was there all right. He pulled himself together and then stood up and out of the way to get a closer look.

The wall at that spot was covered with dirt, dust, and grime, and as he lightly rubbed it with his fingers, he was able to reveal some marks in the wood. He withdrew his knife from its shin scabbard and slowly scraped the crud away. There, in neat little burn marks, as though they had been done with the hot coal from a skinny cigar over the course of many mornings such as this, were lines of verse. He opened the door full, to enlist the aid of the sun as perhaps the author had, and then ever so carefully continued his excavation. In a short while, whole long strings of words were visible, snaking in a contiguous chain around the inner wall of the outhouse beginning and ending there above the seat where the dawn's early light formed a brilliant crescent moon. He dashed back to the tent for a piece of paper and a pen, and before long he was sitting by the fire with a fresh cup of coffee and these words:

> In memory of Tommy Coster
> Born in '25, died in '44
> And to sons of old fools everywhere
> Who go marching off to war
>
> There's a scented breeze blow'n
> O'er crops finished grow'n
> Like the farmer's hand sow'n
> Crops that ne'er grew before
>
> Just count the seconds past the lightnin'
> Don't y'find the thunder frightenin'
> If y'do they'll have y'fightin'
> In someone else's war
>
> 'Cause we all got to die sometime
> Say the old men past their prime
> Who won't see the future
> That I'm dyin' for

And there's a scented breeze blow'n
O'er crops finished grow'n
Like a father's hand sow'n crops
That ne'er grew before.

Signed C.N. 8/44

ZAK TUCKED THE PAGE INTO *The People's Almanac*, made a couple of sandwiches, poured himself some more coffee, and took these out to a rock by the creek. As he read and reread the poem over again, his mythical image of Corey Nightingale began to loom very large. "If you stand at the door of that outhouse and look up the hill in front of you, and then walk up to the top of that hill, you'll find somethin' you didn't know was there."

Zak dropped everything and went to stand in the doorway of the outhouse. He stared to the top of a hill that stretched out before him and walked up the hill to the top. From there, he could see in all directions. And all the other hilltops were just as tall as the one he stood upon for as far as the eye could see. In one direction he could see the chimney and part of the roof of Coster's house a mile or so off. The other way he could see the crow's nest of the rig, he could hear the odd clang and clank echoing in the distance. He turned slowly, wondering what it was Corey wanted to draw his attention to. He looked down at the outhouse. His eyes followed the creek as it wound through the hills, disappearing around a bend. As he turned, his boot stepped down on something hard. He looked down, he kicked away the grass. It was a gravestone. As he searched the grounds atop his hill, he found several more. Most of the writing had worn off the crude stones, but over in a clump of sage there were three little headstones jutting up. On the middle one he could make out, "2 Years Old" and on the ones to either side, "3 Years Old" and "4 Years Old," respectively.

"The cost of living out here is high," he said aloud. He sat down in the middle of the little family graveyard, and the monastic impulses that had come upon him the night before returned. He thought of the wandering troubadours, poets, people who shunned the material world because of its distraction from the pure and high-minded, well expressed act or thought. Priests, nuns, saints of all kinds, Peace Corps volunteers, ambulance drivers, firemen. He wondered again about his own monastic impulses of the night before and tried to reconcile them with what had happened in the tent just moments ago. He laughed at himself. What would the priests, poets, and roughneck dreamers of his monastery call themselves or be in worship of? The Sacred Order of Runaway Slaves? The Abbey of the Abyss? The Loyal Brothers and Sisters of the Fertile Crescent Moon? The Society of the Immaculate Holy Pin-Up of Mr. Coster's Creek? The sun climbed steadily lifting and blending the many colors sprinkled across the distances into their purest focus. He removed his shirt. He felt an empathy with the lonesome observer who has renounced everything, perhaps even his own talent, so that nothing might escape him; who does not seek to exploit his God, his self, or his insights farther than the singular comfort of awareness, that reaches for but does not pretend to infinity yet strives to be ready at all times for the encounter that will call or summon his being into motion and response. "There's a scented breeze blow'n..." Tommy Coster's epitaph could have been Zachary Harper's baptismal prayer. That day in the laundromat Zak had tried to package Corey Nightingale. Had tried to put his stories and his kooky stereotype into some comprehensible and dissectible mold. Now he had stumbled across this man's marker, an arrow pointing in opposite directions yet arriving at the same point at the same time. Corey had reached his audience all right. Here, in this sepulcher of unfulfilled dreams and hard realities, Corey had made his statement to the only audience that mattered.

As kids, Zak and his pals had argued over who was better, Elvis or the Beatles. They tallied up record sales as evidence. Who had more number one hits. Who sold more albums. As a businessman, he had listened with nodding acquiescence to lawyers and bankers pat themselves on the back and describe their clever manipulations of the marketplace, their sales and promotional strategies, as an "art form." This or that guy was a "real artist" when it came to closing deals. "I mean it, the way he does his job is a real art!" At the time, Zak thought it a mere conceit but now he found that form of hubris infuriating. The clever huckstering of these clowns shared nothing in common with individuals cursed with real talent, driven to cultivate it at the cost of personal relationships, wealth, and physical well-being. Still, the businessman in him tried to understand both sides.

"All I have is a lifetime of respect," Jesse's voice broke in, "self-respect, damn it. I'm just too damn good not to know when I'm goin' down."

And Zak wondered what had pushed Corey Nightingale over the edge.

XI

Down an old gravel road fifteen miles southeast of Scobey, Montana, over a cattle barrier and through a dilapidated but functional wood and wire picket, left past a row of blue-topped grain storage bins arranged in order of height, then up and over a grade that reached eastward to the sky, was the next location of Bomac 34.

At nine o'clock that morning there was very little happening.

A 'dozer had been out the day before leveling a big square patch where the rig was to be mantled up. It also dug the two swimming pools that would serve as the reserve mud pits. The hole, already begun, consisted of twenty-four-inch tubing set six feet deep in the center of the square.

A gin truck was nearby unloading a couple of Black Hills Trucking flatbeds, and off to one side was a new Chevy Bronco parked next to a big ol' Oldsmobile that had seen better days.

Inside the Bronco, Marty, Cynthia, Jon, and that daylights driller from the last location, Rory, were sipping Cokes and smoking cigarettes—except Cynthia, that is, who didn't smoke, and only drank 7 Up, Sprite, or ginger ale. They were getting each other caught up and wondering out loud whether or not Jesse Lancaster would show for work that day.

"I'll tell you boys one thing," Rory said, sitting in the driver's seat holding his pop can and cigarette in one hand resting on his knee while his other arm dangled over the back of the seat. "We sure missed you guys around here while we were tearing down. That goddamned Cowboy Crew had us all runnin' ragged. I for one have had it. They just don't give a shit how they do anything!"

Jon reacted to this with a chortle as if to say, yeah, what else is new? He didn't like that Cowboy Crew on principle and was more than willing to condemn them on merit.

Rory went on, "I caught a couple of 'em tossin' railin's in the mud tanks," he said casually, as though he felt compelled to check off his list of indictments for the public record even though their crimes were already legend. "Naturally, they were stackin' things just any ol' way an' tearin' things apart just sloppier'n hell."

Marty gave a grunt. He knew, as did they all, that how neatly you packed up the rig had a lot to do with how difficult it would be to nipple-up at the next location. Being derrickhand meant that he was second in the pecking order and because he aspired to go drilling himself someday and because he spent his time with his ass quite literally out on a limb, he took these criticisms and these procedures seriously and hung on Rory's every word.

Now Rory didn't have any notion to go pushing tools, which was the next logical step up the ladder, so to speak. Making the jump from driller to toolpusher was a big step and carried responsibilities a lot of roughnecks just wouldn't naturally want to take on. A driller like Rory with a hardworking crew that didn't cause trouble and kept that bit turning to the right, could, generally speaking, always get that toolpusher's ear should there be a need.

"I told George, I said, 'Now goddamnit, you run them sons a bitches off just the first chance you get,' and he better, else he's gonna find himself alone on this rig with them fuckers, 'cause I swear I'll twist, and if Jesse cuts out, which seems likely, that Cowboy Crew'll be the only ones left…"

"Derr's de Parker Brudders," Marty reminded him of the fourth crew.

"You're right. And they're pretty green. They might put up with more bullshit than most, and they like to stay together. I guess he could go a couple of days with two crews workin' twelve hours…well, it's just a lot of bullshit. If Jesse don't twist off I bet George runs 'em cowboys off today. I sure wouldn't trust them bastards with nothin' important when we nipple up. As it is I'm watchin' 'em like a hawk. Like I got nothing better to do than babysit them cocksuckers. That's the problem workin' out here in the middle of nowhere, not enough hands." And it was understood that he didn't just mean guys who were willing to roughneck, he meant honest to goodness hands, guys who could get 'er.

Rory was a strange but likable bird. He had big bulging eyes that resembled billiard balls. He kept his dark, thin hair cropped so close to his head you could see scalp when he wasn't wearing the green hunting cap that was his signature. He wore that cap even under his hard hat, which made his big ears stick out like some cartoon caricature of a humanoid mouse. His upper lip poked out over big buck teeth. In spite of his comical appearance, strangers always took him seriously—partly because at first glance they thought he was insane, but mostly, because he was all business, always. He lived and breathed the oil field. He dedicated his life to it the way some people get religion. On days off, he could be found poking around location, fiddling with this and tinkering with that or just hanging out watching another driller do his stuff. He didn't hang with the roughnecks much. Some, if they noticed, thought him snobbish. The patch was all he ever talked about though, and everyone noticed that. If a bunch of them were sitting around chewing the fat like they were today, and the subject somehow got changed, he would sit and listen patiently until it was his turn to make a point, and then launch right into some patch-related subject that might be light years from where the rest of the group was going. He wore work clothes exclusively.

"One can only stand so much ob dat guy," Marty would say behind his back. All Jon had to say about Rory was, "Well, he's consistent." Rory's crew generally gave good relief and if he said he could handle a job, he handled it. He wasn't the best man in the patch, but this didn't concern him in the least. In fact, the best of them might not regard Rory as very good at all. If a job came up that was a little too much, he would just sit back, fold his arms over his chest, and say, "Someone else is gonna have to get this one." Just the same, he would be in the oil field as long as there were fields to be in. He was a lifer. Right now, it was the Cowboy Crew that was making that life miserable.

Jon flipped an ash out the window. "Rory, you know our crew is shorthanded. I'll be surprised if Jesse even shows up, which means we may not even *be* a crew. That's number one. Number two, if Jesse *does* come back, it'll be a miracle if he shows up here with a new chainhand. And number three, should George run them cowboys off, workin' this old iron with just three crews means that every day some crew or another is gonna have to double 'cause one crew is always gonna be on days off. I don't know," he paused in that the-world-is-out-to-fuck-with-us way of his, "Maybe we should all twist off and head'm back to Watford."

Rory shrugged and sipped his soda.

Jon was silent.

Cynthia looked alarmed.

Marty grinned. He was counting on his bottom-hole pay from the last location to help offset the cost of the new Bronco.

Cynthia knew this and was frightened to think that her man might suddenly be out of work. Marty always found her terrified reactions amusing. Given a little time, these things usually had their own crazy way of working themselves out. He'd twist off with the others if he had to, but he had to admit he could use the dough. "Wait and see," he offered lightheartedly.

Cynthia frowned and stared off into a gloomy distance afraid to speak, when all at once she gasped and giggled and pointed west where could be seen a dirt-brown ragtop Jeep CJ7 trailing a small convoy of gin trucks and Black Hills flatbeds loaded with gear.

The mood inside the Bronco lightened considerably.

"Hey," Jon said, "did anybody ever tell Zak where this location was? I didn't."

Nobody had.

"How's that new worm workin' out?" Rory asked, ignoring the obvious humor in the fact that Zachary Harper must have left Scobey heading south until he found some rig traffic and simply pulled in along behind.

"Good," Jon chuckled. "He'll be a hand. Never saw anybody hustle so hard when they didn't know what in the hell they were doin'."

"I hear he tells everyone he's a farmer from South Dakota but that he's got an Eastern accent, wouldn't say 'shit' if his mouth was full of it, has soft hands, and never talks about farmin'." Rory gave the stubble on his chin a rub and then concluded, "Jailbird."

Jon laughed some more. "I don't think so."

Marty, on the other hand, was intrigued at the notion. "Y'know, der is sumpdin ob der mastermind about dat guy."

"Shit," Jon shook his head, "You guys're nuts. Zak's a college man. Got it written all over him. Reminds me of a lieutenant I had in the Air Force."

"Don't mean nothin'," Rory said with all due respect. "Isn't he the one who's been stayin' in that tent way out by Coster's place? You gotta figure that anybody who would choose to live by himself, outside all the time, has got to be some kind of loner. You never know about loners. Besides, what's an Eastern college man doin' out here roughneckin' in the middle of nowhere?"

"Maybe he's goin' for a degree," Jon suggested.

"Oh yeah," Marty howled, "dat night he tangled wit Rusty he got tree huntred sixty degrees!" There was laughter all around.

"Here in the patch you can't get a degree till you pass yer drill-stem test," Rory laughed through a kazoo-like film of cigarette phlegm. He washed it down with a sip of pop, then righted himself by taking a pull on his cigarette.

"Yeah," Marty was getting excited, his beady green eyes darted back and forth over his long skinny nose. "An' whad about all dem gray hairs? Bin a while since he was a schoolboy."

"Well what are *we* doin' here?" Cynthia blurted out. "I mean, if this godforsaken place is good enough for the bunch of us, why not some nice college man who just might want to get away and work for himself for a time?"

"Maymbe he's one ob doze serial killers!" Marty bore down on Cynthia's uneasiness. "Maymbe he goes around, where no one knows him, bein' all nice an' shit, then, when ebryone gets likin' 'im he strikes, bam! bam! bam! and chops 'em all up with that big knife he wears on his leg unter his pants!"

"You stop it! You're scaring me!" Cynthia drew back and slapped at her husband with a chubby palm. She held her hands over her ears while Marty gave her a bear hug and everyone laughed. She liked Zak. And although his insaniac towing of Jezebel had demonstrated that he might be just as crazy as the rest of them, it was hard to sit in this new Bronco and feel bad anymore about their old car. Zak could be unyielding, sure, but he could also be understanding. Zak always behaved as though he had no better place to be when sometimes you knew his mind was really somewhere else. Most of all, deep down, she could feel his affection for all of them: Jon, her man, Jesse, as well as herself. That was rare in a world where people come and go like they do in the patch. Where people guard their true feelings with tough talk and rough-edged cynicism or out-and-out belligerence. She always felt nice inside when Zak was around. He always had a smile and a kind word for folks, even strangers. When Marty let go of her, she felt her face redden. She wanted the last word. "Zak ain't no jailbird. He ain't no stuck-up college man either."

WHEN ZACHARY HARPER CAME OVER the ridge and saw the big dark postage stamp the bulldozer had made in the otherwise woolly countryside, he was at once struck by the immensity of the work about to commence here in the Montana hell and gone.

That big square patch was the only symmetrical thing out there, and the logic behind it made it seem like a strange piece of mathematical art. Nowhere else in this landscape was there anything flat, nor were there any angles or straight lines, but there on that manmade plateau was order, cognizance, the notion of a preconceived idea set down in an otherwise chaotic universe. Any sentient being who might happen upon it would get the notion that an idea can become a thing. Zak was driving his Jeep at the end of a train of gin trucks and flatbeds all zeroing in on that square patch with violence and thunder. Like pilgrim workers pledged to the well-being of the piece, they would make it bigger. It was to be their devotion. As they drove through the dirt and the brush they were making a road by the sheer weight and determination of their vehicles, like blood forcing its way through solid muscle until capillaries and arteries form.

Zak spied Jon's Oldsmobile and veered off from the column and headed out overland toward it. As he bounced and hammered through the sage and underbrush, he could see the boys spilling out of another vehicle parked nearby and would have, from any distance, recognized Jon's strong slender build and Marty's unique husky rondure. Another fella, Rory, slipped out of the driver's side and strolled over to a gin truck nearby. Zak scanned the terrain round about, but saw no sign of Jesse Lancaster, neither his Merc nor his trailer.

Zak came bouncing to a stop next to the Oldsmobile, shut his outfit down with a roar, and hopped down. Jon and Marty watched him while leaning against the new Bronco, and they had a word with each other and a laugh at Zak's expense before he was within earshot. Zak reached for his cigs as he drew near and offered them around with his hellos.

"You guys been here long?"

" 'Bout'n hour."

"We were the first ones out," Jon said, then threw a glance at Marty who very nearly winked.

"No word from Jesse?"

"Nope."

Zak began to wonder what he was supposed to be catching on to—why these two dopes were standing there looking stupid and digging their toes in the dirt—when he noticed Cynthia sitting in the cab of the Bronco turning red and about ready to burst. Zak beamed. His eyebrows lifted over his glasses in a comic interrogative, while the rest of his face broadened into his biggest smile.

"Is this thing yours?" Zak asked Marty, whose head was bobbing up and down, causing his Buster Brown haircut to shake forward and back. The three of them let out with whoops and screams, slapped each other's palms in the air and banged body parts together like school kids scoring their first touchdown.

"Well let's see what this baby can do!" Zak screamed, and the three of them clamored into the vehicle just a-hootin' and a-hollerin'!

"You guys are pretty funny," Zak laughed as they bounded over the first rise. This was wide-open range and grazing land not quite as undulating as that of the last location but still oceanic. The sea was just a little calmer in this area.

They bounded over the hilly mounds and bluffs with Marty jerking the wheel this way and that. Cynthia alternately giggled with delight and shrieked with terror in the shotgun seat up front. Zak clung to the backseat and the window sill, arms outstretched, laughing each time his ass left the seat. Jon just smiled.

"Picked 'er up in Williston yesterday," Marty said over his shoulder. "I got to tinkin' dat ol' Bomac'll probably be in dis neck ob de woods for coupla more holes an' wat wid de winter comin' up right around de corner, an' dis bein' pretty harsh territory once dat snow decides to hang around, we figured we ought to be prepared." He looked over to Cynthia who was lost in a daydream and brought his mighty palm down with a slap! on her fat thigh, making her squeal, "Didn't we?"

"Be prepared!" She giggled right on cue.

Jon shot her an Oh Please look. His tolerance of her simple ways apparently had its limits. Cynthia rubbed her thigh and wrinkled her nose.

"Well I think it's just the ticket. Congratulations. Cynthia, have you ever been in a new car before?"

She shook her head no, delighted beyond words.

"How much did you get for Jezebel, if you don't mind me askin'," Zak was a bit nervous seeing as how a person could feel that he was directly responsible for trashing their previous vehicle. Marty and Cynthia seemed to have dealt with all that just fine.

"Nuttin', she's at d'shop. Gonna tow 'er back to d'house in Watford. I'm gonna work on 'er on days off. See if I can't get 'er fixed up."

"Hey that's great, then you'll be a two-car family!" For some reason, that was funny and they all laughed. "Do you drive, Cynthia?" Zak asked innocently enough.

This question startled her more than the slap on the thigh had and immediately Zak wished that he could withdraw it. She blushed deeply and then looked over to Marty for help. Marty, however, always waited an agonizing moment whenever she was on the spot. It was his way of first allowing her a chance to get out of it by herself. It was an unwelcome opportunity. The thoughts came upon her too fast for her to sort through them. There weren't enough words for them all anyway. *And they're waiting for an answer! No! I can't drive! Never! Couldn't! I'd die if I had to! I won't! Things happen so fast when I try to drive! Isn't it great that Marty does all the driving? 'Cause he's my man and he looks after me and he understands that I positively cannot drive! So I don't HAVE to drive!* She stammered and blushed deeper, her eyes darting frantically from Zak to Marty to Jon to Marty and back to Zak. There was no way she could have made such a complicated explanation out loud, especially to men who expect answers that are short and to the point. Just before it would have been cruel to wait any longer, Marty stepped in and said, "She don't drive."

Their joyride took them in aimless directions over grassy fields, hills, and wide-open spaces. Marty demonstrated all the extra features, the four-wheel drive, the heavy-duty thises and thats, the dashboard gadgets, the deluxe sound system, and the like, as Jon passed around some fresh warm beers.

"We figured what de hell's a point in workin' all the time if all you end up doin' is fightin' de got tam elimints. Jonny and I was sayin' dat in dat Jeep've yers yer like an old-time cowboy and his horse. Travelin' round de country. Livin' outside. Sleepin' out on the land at night listenin' to de coyotes. There aren't many places you can't go. Jezebel wadn't goin' nowhere."

"Yeah and the Jeep eliminates many of the hazards of moving about in this kind of terrain. In fact, it turns a major obstacle into something fun. I gotta admit though, there's a lot more room in here for sleeping," Zak laughed. "Wanna trade?"

"I don't know," Jon said. "I kind of think of a car as my reward for all the work and bullshit I put up with. Leather seats, a big engine, a smooth quiet ride. Something nice to take your mind off all this crap. Maybe a new Toronado. Sure a car like that'll take a beating out here, but who cares? When she goes down for the count, pony up and get another one. That's what makes America great, right?"

While Marty and Zak prattled on about the relative differences between choosing a practical vehicle as opposed to a luxurious one, whether having a vehicle that could conquer all the elements a harsh place like the Williston Basin could throw at you wasn't in itself a luxury, Jon's thoughts roamed back to his date with Mary Ellen. When she answered the door of her apartment, she shrieked when she saw Jon all clean of face and dressed in military green slacks and a loud Hawaiian shirt. She normally dressed down when bartending, not wanting to give any of the local men the idea they could start trouble, but tonight she wanted just the opposite effect without affecting too startling a change. She decided on her favorite jeans, the really tight ones with the perfect hole in one knee with threads that stretched across and rhinestones up each leg. She had pretty calves and ankles and liked the way her pants came down to the middle of her shin. She wore medium-high white pumps that she reckoned would still only bring the top of her head to Jon's chin. A white halter top that showed off the tantalizing contour of her breasts with a lace-up front allowing just a peek. Over this, to cool things off and to keep her warm when the sun went down, she threw a baby blue sweater that very nearly matched her eyes. Her hair she parted on the side for a change and clipped it back on one side. She decided on bangs. A touch of gray eye shadow that always gave her eyes that dewy look. As she put on her lipstick, red, it occurred to her that she had never kissed a man with a beard before. She decided upon a thin gold chain with a cross that she considered to be more like an arrow pointing down to where the good stuff was, two plastic bracelets that made a clackety sound when she moved suddenly, dangly brass earrings and a coral ring her mother had given her completed what Jon soon discovered to be a pretty delightful picture.

They drank a beer in her apartment and then left to get some food and take it out to the country and watch the sun go down. He had cleaned the Oldsmobile from top to bottom, but when she stepped inside he was hideously embarrassed. Boot scratches on the dash that he had never noticed before seemed to jump out at her. The carpet was stained and torn under her perfect ankles and those hot white shoes. The lighter was gone, from the time Ogre had drunkenly lit a cig, given the lighter a shake, and then tossed it out the window. He had to pump the brakes every time he slowed the car down making a wheezing sound as he jerked his knee up and down like a spaz. By way of apology, he made nervous jokes about how tough a roughneck was on his ride, and although she clearly didn't care about his car, he began thinking seriously of taking that little trip down to Williston himself.

After a drive out to Four Buttes, they parked the car on high ground and watched the sunset while sharing sips from a bottle of wine. When he first drank after her he could taste lipstick on the bottle's rim and its flavor mingled with the wine. As the sun set in her swimming blue eyes, he tried to concoct a sentence without sounding like a stupid come-on, to tell her how pretty she was and how he hadn't realized, when she interrupted his thoughts to say, "I'm glad you shaved your beard. I didn't realize you were so handsome. Did you shave it off just for me?"

He thought he would just look away and say no, that he was getting tired of it and had meant to cut it off weeks ago. But when he looked at how different she had made herself from the girl he had come to know at the hotel, and when he thought of how much he was enjoying her company, something inside told him that for once in his life he didn't have to bullshit. He canceled that last order and he looked her directly in the eyes and said, "Yes."

"That's so sweet, thank you. You know I liked your beard, but you're much better looking without it. Some men grow beards to hide a weak chin or a scar, or simply because they're shy, but you should never hide such a handsome face."

He meant to just lean over and kiss her for being so nice to him. He had only wanted one taste more of that delicious wet wine and lipstick. But as he began to pull away, she gently touched his shoulder asking him to linger and their mouths opened deeper. As he drew her close, her arms folded around his neck and her mouth slipped entirely into his and then withdrew and his mouth slipped entirely into hers and he withdrew. His big hands felt deliciously rough against her back. He was astonished at how light and pliable she became in his grip, how dizzy it made him just to feel her pressed against his chest. When they parted, his eyebrows lifted and he smiled with surprise. She took a deep breath and linked an arm through his as naturally as though they had been together for years.

"Wow, Jonny, I'll have some more of that, please."

That night when he dropped her off, they kissed again for quite some time in the car in front of her apartment. He cupped a hand over her breast and felt it, its firmness and its shape. He felt her nipple, the size of a quarter, harden in his palm through her halter top. He was embarrassed by his work rough hands and didn't want to push his luck so he didn't go any farther, though she ached for him to. She didn't invite him in and he didn't ask her permission. They made plans to see each other again just as soon as possible.

As Jon sat there in the Bronco reliving every sight and smell from the night before, Zak was thinking about the winter. Until this moment it had seemed a long way off. But now he remembered seeing the local townsfolk scurrying about in the past week or so with loads of firewood, snowmobiles on car-drawn flatbeds being taken in for servicing. He had noticed plows being attached to the front of pickup trucks in people's driveways and garages. Local kids had put down their lacrosse sticks and were playing street hockey. It was coming closer every day.

"Speaking of winter," he said without thinking, "how bad is it going to get?"

"Oh," Marty cocked an eye at the others, "'bout de same as Sout Dakota."

WITHOUT THE TOWER FOR A landmark it was difficult to say over which hill the location was. No one had paid any attention, of course, to the crazy zigzag direction Marty had taken off in when they first headed out. There was nothing manmade for miles around, and so Marty had just opened 'er up. They four-wheeled over one steep rise after another taking each like a dinghy taking the waves out on the open sea, except that now they were in need of a rescue party.

"Does anybody here know exactly where we are?" Zak changed the subject.

"Yahwhooooooo!" Marty bellowed, for at that moment they surprised a bunch of cows grazing on a steep declivity. "Yeeehaw!" he hollered again as the animals scattered in all directions.

"Stop it! Stop it!" Cynthia cried. "You're scaring them!" Marty just howled the more and pulled the vehicle to the outside of the herd and, reaching under the dash, grabbed the CB mike. and flipping a switch on the dash he brought the mike to his lips.

"Moooaaah!" could be heard booming through a concealed loudspeaker outside on the roof.

"Ahhhmooooooo!" he bellowed again. Marty then wheeled the Bronco in a semicircular orbit around the herd, gradually slowing to a much less frenzied pace. In another moment, the cows collected themselves in a fast but easy gallop alongside of them. Cynthia's alarm dissolved into a childlike glee and she rolled her window all the way down, put her hands on the sill, and rested her chin there. Zak found himself sitting there in the back momentarily charmed by the fluidity of her emotions, and tried not to think that if they had hit one of these beasts, they would all be in pretty bad shape right now.

"Okay team, this has been real, but let's get'm back to location and see what's up," Jon said.

"Dat's what I bin tryin' t'do for de past half an hour!"

"I was afraid of that," Zak chimed in.

Marty brought the Bronco to a stop, and they climbed a nearby hill and looked in all directions. The prairie wind whipped their faces and lifted hair from under collars.

"Over dere," Marty pointed, and when they squinted into the distance they could barely make out a cloud of dust.

BACK AT LOCATION, THINGS WERE beginning to heat up in a big way. George was just pulling up with his toolpusher's trailer in tow. Carl and that Cowboy Crew were right behind him. Rory's boys were behind them, including the mammoth derrickhand Zak had observed in action his first day out.

George cursed out loud as he stepped down. "Shit! No Jesse."

George was all bent out of shape, mostly at himself. Having to pamper that Cowboy Crew through every phase of their duties had become a silent irritation and a constant distraction. And now George had neglected to hire a backhoe to dig the drainage ditches that run three-quarters of the way around the rig. So he blamed that Cowboy Crew for his current negligence. Rory was right. He should run them bastards off, but how? Who would replace them? And how was he going to keep a fight from breaking out and his good people from twisting off?

But maybe there was a blessing in all of this after all. George smiled. With an endless procession of semis and gin trucks on their way and due to arrive at any moment, time was of the essence. He yanked a tape measure from his pocket and paced around the imaginary rig, marking with his boot where he wanted those drainage ditches dug. He then assembled his drillers, Carl, Rory, and Marty subbing for Jesse, and told them that every available hand was to grab a shovel and break dirt! That included the Parker Brothers, who arrived on the heels of Rory's men.

The Parker Brothers were the swing crew on Bomac 34 taking the towers of the men on days off. Zak hadn't seen much of these guys and they were largely a mystery to him. Once a week they relieved him and once a week he relieved them. He knew only that they were called the Parker Brothers because that's what they were, brothers. All but one that is, and it was easy to tell the odd man out because he was dark and the rest were fair. One of their crew was a most unlikely roughneck. He was very young with a slight build, a baby face, and large quiet eyes. He stayed back from the others and followed their lead as shovels were passed around and everyone took to digging. As time went on, Zak kept his eye on the kid and noted that he had to dig twice as hard and twice as fast to just keep pace with his older, bigger brothers, and everyone else for that matter, who were making an effort to be sure but not pushing it to the limit the way he had to. To test this theory, Zak decided to try digging just as hard as the small guy was. To use the same amount of energy he appeared to be using, just to see how it felt.

He dug like a madman! He drove his shovel mercilessly into the ground again and again, keeping his eyes down and concentrating on his work. His progress was incredible. He made the walls in his part of the ditch even and smooth. He made the floor level and flat. He charged along, thinking all the while about that young man's lot in life. Having to take things the hard way because he was small. Things that came so much easier to the others. Things they took for granted. He thought of how oblivious the others were to his plight. Perhaps Zak was trying, in his way, to make the statement that you could choose to do something the hard way just-for-doing-its sake. His thoughts rolled over and over. Either way he looked at it there was a stiff, irrefutable problem here. The small guy worked harder than the rest so that they could never say he didn't pull his fair share or that he couldn't get 'er. But if everyone employed the same relative amount of energy the smaller guy did, then he would still be faced with the same problem, getting half as much accomplished as the rest. Working harder than the rest, Zak made more progress than anyone and working as hard as the smaller guy, he made twice as much progress. There was no leveling ideology. Zak began to feel that attempting to match the effort and stamina in that young man with a certain ferocity of his own was rather like trying to find east by going west. But he could try. He could also kill himself, he thought, and stopped for a second to catch his breath and let his heart ease up a bit. When he looked up, he saw that Jon had moved way ahead to give him room. That Jon was looking at him with a strange expression on his face that was somewhere between humor and contempt.

At last Jon stopped and said, "Zak, the canal is in Panama, this is a drainage ditch that we're digging because Rusty is too stupid or too cheap to hire a backhoe!"

Zak looked down the line the other way. Marty had reacted to Zak's quiet explosion of energy with an explosion of his own, figuring that a drainage ditch was as good a place as any to just get it. He paused for a half second and looked up at Zak with a wild half-crazed bedlamite grimace and screamed, "Whadd're ya stoppin' for?!" and flung himself back into digging with a vengeance. Jon shook his head; they were both nuts.

Soon those Getter and Black Hills trucks could be heard in the distance rumbling toward location and, like his Sioux predecessors, Zak wanted to put his ear to the ground and gauge the size of the herd. Maybe he would have been able to tell also that there was a small contingent of gin trucks intermingled with them. As the parade started to arrive, George began pulling roughnecks, one by one, out of the trenches and farmed them out around location until that Cowboy Crew were the only ones left digging.

And George Cleaver smiled.

Zak was one of the first hands selected, and he was hired out to ride as a swamper on a gin truck. This was a modified half-tractor with a derrick and a pulley in the back. Zak considered it a lucky break because he would be out of everybody's way and wouldn't have four different drillers telling him what to do.

It was then that the Getter toolpusher arrived to take command of operations and the assemblage of a massive oil rig was under way.

That Getter toolpusher wasted no time setting everyone in motion. He directed traffic with a CB radio, barking orders to semis and gin trucks alike. Coordinating efforts while at the same time organizing through George and the four drillers at his disposal the teams of men that would be sent from one task to another.

Using the hoists on the gin trucks, two huge wooden mats were lifted from their beds on the semis and set in place on the big square patch of level ground. After the mats were set down there came the subs. Zak was thinking that when in doubt what to call a piece, call it a sub. These subs consisted of two genuinely enormous ironworks to be set parallel to one another on the mats making up two sides of the rig's infrastructure. One faced the mud pits; the other was attached to the top doghouse.

By now the parade was in full swing, as one after another the flatbeds arrived. Semi-orderly commotion, hustle, and bustle that kicked up a cloud of dust rising from the trampled path in a vermicular weave that snaked through the grass country as far as the eye could see.

George, meanwhile, was running from one side of the slowly formatting rig to the other, his tape measure ever present, frantically trying to keep things in their proper geometric perspective, and succeeding admirably. The pump houses had to be assembled on the ground exactly where the belts would stretch down from the engines on the as-yet-imaginary floor overhead. The subs also had to be equidistant from the hole in the center. There could be no mistakes. The catwalks were assembled and the beaver slide unloaded and moved into place. As the afternoon wore on into early evening, the pace remained constant and unremitting. There was only enough time to do the job. No breaks.

All the while that Cowboy Crew kept digging those ditches, and slowly the message began to sink in that if any water needed boiling they'd get hired out to do that too.

It was in the midst of all this frantic activity that the flow of traffic was interrupted for a brief moment by a small trailer being pulled by a Mercury Marquis which separated from the parade pulling discreetly up alongside the toolpusher's trailer on the away side to the rig.

Zak was standing in the back of a gin truck attaching some cable with a hook on the end to a piece of equipment. Marty and Jon were running with those Getter boys. So it was left to Rory, standing atop a recently assembled pump house, to raise the lone cheer when that Mercury door opened and out stepped a sober Jesse Lancaster.

The big white tower arrived right behind him, looking majestic, even on its side, tinged dusky vermillion by the setting sun. The bottom of the drawworks constituted the working floor of the rig. All in all virtually tons and tons of iron.

SINCE EVERYONE WORKED THE SAME shift until they nippled up, Sam's place back in town that night was just jumping with roughnecks and Getter boys as well as her regulars. From their booth near the front, Marty, Cynthia, Jon, and Zak had a good view of the action. After a couple of drinks, Zak seized the opportunity to make a few inquiries regarding the men of Bomac 34, most of whom were still strangers to him. Marty and Jon got into a competition to see who knew the most about as many of them as possible.

Sitting with Rory at a table a few feet away was Billy Knott, Rory's motorman and closest friend. They had worked in the patch together for many a year, most always getting on the same crew and if not, at least with the same rig. With them was their chainhand, "Smoke" Denton. Jon and Marty were careful to point out that Smoke was very finicky about his roughneckin' image. If he couldn't throw chain he'd as soon not roughneck, and preferred instead to hire himself out as a welder or carpenter. Smoke was a sullen, gruff, unshaven character, and Zak sensed that the moniker fit the man's aura and temperament as well as the way he burned up pipe with the throw of his chain. Zak remembered as well that Jon, now a motorman, was reported to be the best chainhand that Jesse had ever seen, which had to account somehow for the strange glimmer in the Scandinavian's eye as he described Denton's peculiarities as to what he would and wouldn't do on the floor of an oil rig. In any event, Smoke Denton was Rory's first choice as chainhand on this or any crew.

An older fella worked worm's corner for Rory, and his last name, the one folks knew him by, was Frye. He was a very private man, and Jon speculated as he pointed him out sitting at the bar chatting with the locals that Frye had been a mystery for so long that everyone had simply given up trying to figure the old boy out. That he had been a driller for many years was common knowledge, and it was just assumed that his aging memory had had something to do with his returning to worm's corner. He wasn't too particular, seemed glad enough just to be working, and was known to be a real solid hand.

"He'll sit and sip beer with you all afternoon," Jon said, stealing a glance at the old man. "He won't say much but he'll listen to everyone else tell their stories, and he'll laugh."

"Yeah and he's real comical when he laughs cuz he ain't got but two teeth!"

"If someone is trying to remember some detail from a story," Jon looked at Marty for a nod of verification, "and Frye was around when it happened, he'll speak up, but he rarely, if ever, comes up with a story of his own. At least not in front of the younger guys."

"Shit, ebbrybody's younger'n Frye," Marty laughed and took a drink.

"I mean, none of us was around when he got started, and he probably thinks that nobody gives a shit about times they've never seen or places they've never been."

"Maybe he's right," Zak wondered aloud.

"That's so sad," Cynthia blurted out. The three men looked at each other and then just exploded with laughter. At first she was offended. Their hilarity was contagious, and she was glad to be having fun whether it was at her expense or whether it was just that at that moment all the troubles of the past few days had suddenly subsided and they could all be happy again.

"Cynthia, you're just priceless," Zak said as things calmed down. "Let me get you another 7Up." The others raised their empty glasses indicating another round was in order.

Zak stood next to Frye as he waited for Sam to get his drinks. Frye just stared straight ahead. Zak could think of reasons for a man to be silent about his past. Perhaps too, like Corey, Frye wasn't showing his medals to just anybody. Zak took a look around the room. The last member of Rory's crew, the wild, bearded derrick-hand was nowhere to be seen. "His name is Ogre," Jon had said with a disparaging shake of his head, as if the name told the whole story.

At another table not too far away were the Parker Brothers. They were from Michigan and had migrated West together, taking odd jobs in small towns until they hit Watford City, North Dakota, and one by one had broken out roughnecking. How they had held together through the trouble times was something that impressed everybody. It made good sense to Marty.

"One good ting 'bout roughnecks. They don't let each udder starve!"

Andy, the oldest, was worm drilling on Bomac 34. He was the only Parker Brother to have worked all positions from worm's corner to derricks, and, if inexperienced with that brake handle, he was at least level-headed and knew what went where and when. This impression, Zak could tell, they were repeating from Jesse verbatim, because what Jesse said was gospel, and their belief in what was true about those Parker Brothers had the feel of dogma. Besides, George had also said that Andy would do all right in time.

Not like Carl, "Old Smoky," who had all the experience a man needed but was still as useless as tits on a bull when it came to whipping a crew into some kind of shape.

Sitting next to Andy was "Chug" Parker, chainhand, and sitting at Andy's other side was young Hale. Paul Kimberly, their motorman, had been sitting with them earlier but had moved to the back room where he was trying to win some money at pool from a couple of local farmhands. Carl and his cowboys were conspicuously absent.

Talk eventually settled on Jesse Lancaster. That he looked beat to shit they all could see, but Jon, and Zak in particular, agreed that the madness they had witnessed a couple of nights earlier was gone from his face, leaving only weariness and fatigue. Cynthia noticed that he hadn't changed clothes since the accident and they all thought without saying it out loud that Freddy's accident was already sinking rapidly into the past.

Jesse had looked different in other ways as well. There was a cleansed, purged difference to the man. An untwisted cathartic ease that made his expressions and movements seem more fluid, lighter on his feet. Zak was no psychologist but somewhere in this concatenation of circumstances, pain and heartache, things seemed to be evening out, hopefully, and for the better. Jesse hadn't had too many words with George or the boys before turning in at the end of the tower. That he was back to drill was clear. There was to be no undue attention paid to the events of the past few days. What was needed now was time. Time for things to settle down. Time for the old routine to reintroduce itself.

After a long silence, Marty sighed. Then he sat back in the booth like Papa Bear. Jon set the new agenda as though with that sigh Marty had called a meeting to order.

"Well, we still haven't got a chainhand," Jon opened the discussion.

Marty had already moved past that, he smacked his lips and looked around the table. "If we're still shorthanded when we spud-in I tink ol' Jesse will ask Zak if he wants to break out throwin' chain."

At that moment the big doors to Simone's Bar blew open with such ferocity that two short, square panes of glass cracked in the windows on either side of the doors.

There, filling the entire doorway, was Rory's derrickhand. He was huge, ferocious, and he was drunk.

"My name is Samson Dowdy!" he bellowed. Anyone who hadn't dropped what they were doing when the doors blew open was paying attention now. "And I'm the toughest man in Daniels County!"

The derrickhand's eyes beamed around the room like lasers. Zak was struck with fear but showed a blank face as did most of the other men. Some simply turned their backs. Others made grim faces and stared back at that derrickhand, ready to fight if they had to but not willing to make a move that could possibly be construed as accepting his challenge.

Zak tried to gauge how many men it would take to subdue this man if they had to. If there were enough men in the room willing to try. He determined there were probably not enough.

The big man surveyed the bar and found it free of resistance. Almost disappointed, his eyes dimmed and he smiled warmly as he walked into the bar, throwing a nod at driller Rory, and another in the direction of Zak's table before taking a stool next to Frye.

While things returned to normal, Zak took a quick look around the room and noticed that while some of the men just shook their heads as they reached for the threads of their interrupted conversation, there were more than a few who sat staring fixedly at the mighty Samson as he ordered up a drink and began chatting pleasantly with Sam and the older worm.

LATE THAT NIGHT IN THE tent by the creek, Zak was having a devil of a time getting to sleep. He was thinking of throwing chain. Marty's suggestion had shocked him just about as much as Samson's Wild West entrance to the bar had, only more so. He thought of the chainhands he had met and come to know a little so far: Freddy Fifer, Smoke Denton, Chug Parker, and, of course, Jon.

Zak was comfortable at worm's corner and felt that was where he belonged until he became more familiar with the entire operation. But then again, worm's corner was the entry-level position, so to speak, and, come to think of it, he had to admit that on several occasions he had wanted to grab that chain from Freddy's hands and throw it himself, not simply out of frustration but because it looked like something he could do well. Also, having thrown chain at least once would come in handy if he found himself out looking for work as had nearly happened this weekend.

On the other hand, like Zak, Freddy had been on the job just a few weeks before his accident and though it was true that he hadn't been injured while actually throwing chain, he had, it seemed clear, become overconfident with his small successes, bitten off more than he could chew. Zak wondered if he wasn't making the same mistake by harboring illusions about his own potential abilities so early on. Anyway, after what had happened to Freddy, Jesse might not offer him the job. From what Zak could tell, he certainly wasn't obliged to.

If the decision were in Zak's hands, he would err on the side of caution. He wouldn't choose himself. He would go out of his way to find someone with experience. At least someone who had been a roughneck more than two weeks.

He tossed and turned in his sleeping bag, zipped up tight against the chill night air. He tried to regulate his breathing and relax. As he did this, his fit of confusion came completely untangled, and straightened out as quick and sure as chain whipping toward a cathead. The stillness of his tent filled with a compulsive burst of laughter.

"I wouldn't hire myself?" he asked the gods already laughing.

What kind of bullshit rationale is that? He had seen Jon throw that chain correctly and he had seen Freddy throw it incorrectly. As a matter of fact, one of the most frustrating things about watching poor miserable Freddy try to make up that pipe was that Zak felt he couldn't just walk over to Freddy and say, *Here, let me have at 'er*, and change places. Freddy had wanted to go back to worm's corner anyway, didn't he say so? Zak wondered what would have happened had he just taken the initiative. Perhaps if he had been around a little longer he would have. Maybe after his first few throws things would just have settled in that way. Maybe Jesse would have simply shrugged and said, *Hey, whatever works, works*. Of course, there was the question of pay to consider. Chainhand makes more than worm, motors more than chain, etc., the custom in the patch being to offer a job to the man in line for it. Worm to chain, chain to motors, motors to derrick, derrick to driller. Fair is fair. The roughnecks depended on it. It was well known that Jesse took that custom, and others, to heart. It went hand in hand with the way he built a crew that could then be called upon under extreme circumstances. *"We've been watching you Zak, that's why you haven't been hurt."* It was Jesse's call, and Jesse was considered a master at handling those delicate forces in the men who worked for him. It's why, apparently, he was able to demand so much. He could take these useless, wandering wastrels, ruffians, and renegades and turn them into roughnecks, real hands, thereby giving them something society wasn't about to—a chance.

So where did Freddy fit, and where did Zak fit into all of this? Freddy didn't fit, that was the problem. In hindsight, that painful fact had been obvious to everyone. And what about himself? Would that Widowmaker chew him up and spit him out as it had so many others? And what made him presume to be any different than Freddy? After all, what happened to Freddy really could have happened to anybody, and that type of thing had happened to a great many anybodys. On the other hand, who's to say that after a few weeks Freddy wouldn't have come around. At some point this had to have occurred to Jesse Lancaster too. Freddy was just wrong, that's all. That didn't mean that Zak was wrong. Jesse took a chance on Freddy, and Freddy had taken a chance on Freddy, and Freddy blew it.

Worst of all, what if Jesse had actually been right about himself on that awful night down there in Watford? What if he couldn't get it? Was what happened to Freddy Jesse's fault after all? Would it be Jesse's fault if it happened again to the man next in line? Was Zak next in line?

No, the truth of the matter is that everyone is responsible for their own level of commitment, to pull their share. And there's no rule out beyond the stars that says the allotted share one must pull be a fair one. It just is what it is.

Zak would know after his first throw of that chain whether or not he could get 'er. Everyone would know.

Everyone.

THERE. DO YOU HEAR IT? Right there.

It's so faint, more of a vibration than a sound. More of a change in the wind. Yes, that's definitely it now. Everyone on the tiny platform stopped talking in midsentence and listened. When the distant thunder of the locomotive was at last identifiable beyond doubt, a very pleased cheer went up from the crowd. They crept close to the edge of the railway platform expectantly, impulsively as a group, and stared down the empty tracks to where they turned out of sight. It must be moving very fast, they thought, for the reiterated bursts of steam could be heard making distant splashes in the air puffing many times per second. This, getting louder and louder as though someone was gently turning the volume on a stereo from zero to ten, was getting closer, closer, and closer. In another second, they heard the clanking gasping sounds of the gears themselves and the grating rush of huge iron wheels on cold iron tracks. Shouldn't it be slowing down? At the bend in the tracks the trees blew back, and from around the corner it roared into view. Full speed out of control and about to jump the tracks as it roared into the tiny station!

Everyone scattered. Zak turned and tripped over a screaming child hurting its little leg. As Zak went down he grabbed the child and handed it up to its frightened parent who then turned and ran. Zak attempted to get up and run after them but his bootlace had gotten stuck through a chink in the iron floor. The roaring in his ears told him it was too late. He turned to face the raging iron beast hurtling toward him so angry and loud as it exploded all around him. He whirled around in time to see Jesse, the engineer, at the brake handle, throwing in the clutch that sent the engine screaming into high-high. An air compressor kicked in, blowing scalding hot gas across his face. A terrific whipping sound sliced the air, and from out of nowhere a chain came flying, hitting Zak at the ankles, making tight wraps up to his knees, past his waist, pinning his arms, up to his neck. The cathead screamed. The rotary table whirled insanely. More chain fed in at his ankles as more chain played out at his neck. Just when he was sure his body would tear completely apart, mud and water began spurting up from under his feet, lubricating that chain as it spun faster and faster. Soon the mud was up to his nostrils and he bobbed and pitched through the muck to get air, gyrating like an inchworm in an oil slick. He gasped each time he broke the surface, the muddy water stinking of chemicals like sodium bichromate and caustic. In the pitch darkness he could again hear the puffing, chugging steam engine and then, by God, he could see it! A faint blur of light way off but getting closer. A boat? Oh please! A boat! "Over here!" Zak screamed, but his cries were drowned out by the downward pull of the heavy chain and he sank below the surface. He fought his way back up and for just a few seconds he could see in all directions. The boat was too far off. They'll never get here in time. He didn't have the strength to keep his head above the surface for two more breaths. Something broke the water just a short distance to his right, then again behind him, then to his left. God, something's in here with me!

The blur of light in the distance tightened into a beam that jerked one way then another, missing him each time. Something again broke water, this time just in front of him and was caught for a terrifying instant in the beam of light as it swished from side to side. It was a monster, a giant predator, a man-eating fish of some kind, but the face on it was fleshy, sickly, with a gaping mouth full of glistening teeth that bit at the filthy muddy water insanely. The side fins were big fat scaly human hands that slapped and splashed as it fought the current attempting to line itself up to strike. A wave pushed it beneath the surface. The searchlight hit Zak in the face. Jesse's voice pierced the gale. Zak attempted to answer, but his lips sank beneath the surface, his mouth filled with muck, and he was covered over sinking hopelessly downward. Something then hit him violently from behind, spinning him, turning him over and over. It hit him again hard from another angle with jaws that bit again and again trying to find a gap in the wraps of chain where the sharp teeth could break through. The jaws gripped him savagely and whipped him this way and that, but the wraps of the chain were too tight and the teeth that did pierce through went far enough to sting viciously but not enough to tear the flesh. It stopped without letting go. Zak's lungs were about to burst. Then they rushed upward through the filth together and broke the surface. They smacked into the fast-moving bow of the steamboat, the monster going one way, Zak the other, with the chugging engine loud in his ears. The steamboat crested a gigantic wave directly on top of him, exposing the boat's broad metal underbelly before it came crashing down. His chain-covered body clanged and bounced along the keel under the boat, and the staccato puffing of the engine roared in his ears as he was sucked with a violent yank directly into the propeller.

Zachary Harper burst from the sleeping bag, flinging away the covering with a desperate burst of energy to free his arms and legs. The cool night air whisked gently over him and he gulped for air in the blackness not knowing where he was. His heart was pounding like it would explode on the very next beat. He shuddered all over. It was Freddy's hideously pain-contorted face on the head of that beast. With a mouth all huge and crying and biting. The very image was nauseating.

Zak heard something. Was the dream not over?

A creepy feeling like something unfinished permeated his earth bound senses as though they had picked up a dream remnant that didn't fit this reality. The audio portion of his senses began to clear and differentiate.

Gurgling, snorting, huffing, breathing. Coyotes!

Sniffing, sniffing, sniffing with their long noses close to the ground at the base of his tent. Their flanks brushing the canvas ever so slightly as they moved. How many? Half a dozen? Surely they could smell him.

Can animals really smell fear?

Zak took several deep breaths and attempted to think his way clear of any panicky notions. What state had he left the bread bag in? Had he thrown a crust or two into the fire that morning? If they found a few morsels they would surely root around for more.

A coyote was sniffing around the flap of the tent. Had he zipped it up before turning in? He didn't think so. He reached up his pant leg and noiselessly withdrew the Ruana knife from its scabbard. Then he remembered the gun that Freddy had lent him. With his free hand, he felt through the pile of dirty clothes next to his sleeping bag and found the chamois. When he unrolled it, he could smell the scent of gun oil. Funny, he hadn't noticed that before. Just then all commotion outside the tent ceased. Zak took half a breath in the total silence. Would they attack? If he made a sudden loud and startling noise would they run off or stand and fight? In the blackness he abandoned trying to see with his eyes and let his ears and nose take over, pushing past the perimeter of the tent wall ready to detect the slightest changes. After three minutes, he decided, quite by instinct, to move. The gun in one hand, the blade in the other, he coiled the muscles in his legs and in one quick hop he popped through the flap into the moonlight. He turned in all directions as he moved to be clear of the tent so he could have room should they set upon him all at once. His eyes adjusted quickly. Nothing. He scouted around the entire tent. Nothing.

He stood up straight, holding the gun loosely at his side and looked around in every direction. "Where did you go?" The sound of his voice reverberated through the chill night air which iced his bones, sent a wrinkle up his back, and left him feeling untenanted, hollow, unknown. The coyotes were long gone and he had to ask himself if they had ever been there.

He put the knife away, rummaged through the tent, found his cigarettes, and, still hanging onto the gun, walked over to the creek. He was shaking from more than bad images and animals creeping in the night. While he smoked he held the gun in his hand. He leaned back against the rock and took in the night for what it was; beautiful, stark, embracing all he could see and all he couldn't, nearly accommodating his loneliness.

NEXT DAY, THE ROAR OF the engines as they sprang to life on the newly assembled floor ripped the peaceful air of a Montana afternoon. The burning number one diesel fuel spewing from the big Cats perfumed the air heavily and made the lungs work a little harder. The clarion scream of those engines joined with a clangorous screeching, creaking yawn as the tower was hauled up on its A-legs, ending with a long deep metallic groan as it settled into place overlooking this vast scene and the men who presumed to be masters of it.

Once that derrick was in place, they had a ninety-foot block and tackle at their disposal for hoisting up the rotary table, unloading the heavy stuff from the semis, and any other mammoth job that could be saved until that point.

The next couple of days involved tying all the loose pieces together. Wiring up the light plant. Tying up the big chain drive that ran through the Cats, through the drawworks to the rotary table. This chain was then housed in its own metal casing three feet off the floor, twenty-four inches across. For entertainment, and a few wows, the boys could watch Marty and Samson trying to outdo each other up in the derrick. Marty, into his small ape act, was swinging from beam to beam, putting in new light bulbs, while Samson looked a bit more like Kong scaling the Empire

State as he went about stringing up cable. The boys down below shook their heads. Some just grinned.

AT THE END OF TOWER that third afternoon the schedule for the hole was posted. They were due to spud-in that evening. Jesse's crew was on morning towers, eleven p.m. to seven a.m., relieved by Rory and his boys, seven a.m. to three p.m., followed by the Parker Brothers in the evening. The Cowboy Crew was down as relief. The past couple of nights, Zak had stayed in town at the hotel, and now, as the boys adjourned for a little shut-eye before returning that evening, he decided to stop at Sam's for a beer and a little quiet consideration of his next move.

The bar smelled of cinnamon and warm cider. The place was pretty dead but for a few locals who were scattered around the large room. Corey Nightingale was crouched over a box of tools inside the front window repairing the panes that Samson had cracked the night before. When Zak entered he gave Corey a fond hello, to which Corey responded with a curious face and then went back to work as though he'd never laid eyes on Zachary Harper in all his life.

Sam wasn't busy and she welcomed Zak with a warm smile and lifted brow as though she was genuinely delighted to see him, personally. She wore heavy-looking brass earrings that caught the light as it flickered through the ventilation fans overhead. Her billowy white crenelated dress seemed to spill all over her. Her long black hair was pulled loosely into a bun at the back of her head. Some of it tumbled down her neck. Her face was lightly powdered, her lips bright red and smiling. She sipped wine.

"That was some entrance Samson made last night," Zak said to Sam as he sat down, at the bar keeping one eye on Corey.

"Samson is all right," Sam said most forgivingly.

Zak pointed at the Miller tap; as he scootched to get comfortable on the barstool and she shook her head no and reached into the cooler for a cold bottle. Apparently the keg was dry.

"Well, he sure got everyone's attention."

"That was the point," she smiled as she plucked the top off the bottle with an opener that hung on a leather cord around her neck buried, when not in use, among bosom and beads. She thought for a second, and then decided to go ahead with a little more wine. The big green jug made a deep popping sound as she pulled the cork. "Actually, I was much more concerned about a couple of others who were in here last night. Samson's big entrance was more than likely for their benefit. Frankly, I was glad to see him."

Something like this hadn't occurred to Zak. "Well, he sure cut an impressive figure there in that doorway. I was reminded of learning in grade school about the barbarian invasions of Europe."

"Ah, Old Europe. Kurgans," she mused thoughtfully.

"Excuse me?"

"Another word for barbarians. Yes. I can see them very clearly now. Just like you say." She toyed thoughtfully with the big cumbersome rings on her long milk-white fingers. "A whole army of guys like Samson," she laughed and as she did so her smile lines deepened playfully and her face was transformed from looking tired and puffy to youthful and seductive. "On horseback, drunk, raping, pillaging, going wherever they want. Doing and taking whatever they want. Hmmm," she leaned on her side of the bar and one large breast came to rest on her braceleted arm. "And, of course, the stronger women they captured would come along with them to cook, and take care of them and tend to their wounds." They both watched Corey delicately remove a broken plane of glass.

Zak mentioned that Corey had given him the lowdown on the shack on Stitch Cronan's property, all of which was old news to Sam. She was much more interested in Zachary Harper. It was very flattering to have her full attention. She charmed and prodded him to talk about himself, without ever offering a slice from her own autobiography. You could tell her as much as you liked or you could tell her nothing. Most told her too much.

As he usually did when it was time to talk about himself, he mentioned Wall, South Dakota, and the names of famous people he had seen pass through there when he was a kid. Back when America had set out to discover its new Interstate Highway System. But he wasn't paying any more attention to it than she was. Her dark brown eyes searched his back and forth, dancing as they spoke. Remarkably, he was not self-conscious, though he was a little afraid of getting dizzy. She was assessing the way he talked, his colloquialisms, the changing hue in the color of his cheeks. What was she comparing him to? What events from her own life did she recall that, for a fleeting second, stirred a warm romantic mist into her eyes and a peculiar smile that vanished just as quickly as it came? Zak couldn't tear his gaze from hers, her dark eyes, her hefty form, and dumpling-like complexion. No wonder she gave Freddy the creeps. He asked himself what sights those knowing eyes had seen. How many places, how many lovers, how many dreams and delights had offered themselves up for her consumption and amusement? He wondered what kind of man it took to please her, or if any one man was enough. That's a lot of woman. He felt out of his league but, as in all things, eager to learn.

She withdrew, perhaps as a reaction to the undisguised glint of masculine curiosity that must have sparkled for a second in his bright blue eyes. She was too cool a customer to be given over to flights of fancy or to reveal herself without the proper solicitation. Somehow he got the feeling that a once-in-a-lifetime opportunity had just come and gone. To change the subject, she reached for a candle and lit it, pushing it away far enough so it wouldn't be distracting.

He mentioned that he hadn't actually seen Stitch Cronan's bunkhouse yet and when she understood that they were back to business, she turned her back on him and walked to the end of the bar, gracefully commanding every movable part of her body as she did so. How does a woman that big move so lightly on her feet? After a brief word with the man seated there, she beckoned Zak to walk over and join them.

"Zak, this is Bill Turner. He used to work over at Cronan's place." They shook hands and she discreetly left them alone to talk, but Zak followed her with the corner of his eye. Turner knew that Zak was a roughneck and Zak knew that he had once worked for Stitch; she had started them out even.

"That the same rig that was over there at Coster's?" Turner asked with a sly touch of cynicism, as though it was common knowledge that no oil had been found at Coster's and that the competence of the rig and its crews were somehow at fault, like there was some sort of conspiracy to keep them all from getting rich. Then again, there had probably been a lot of talk going on around town behind closed doors, in the bars and pickup trucks, as everyone watched and waited to see if Coster would strike it big and start the avalanche of profits that would come with a big oil boom. Or had their wishful thinking been inspired by out-of-town investors who were simply looking for a tax writeoff? It had happened before. Zak felt like it was one step short of saying, *And on top of it all, us decent folk have apparently been putting up with you assholes for no good reason.*

Zak decided not to ignore the implication, perhaps even to give the man some info he could then take back for the rest of them to chew on.

"That's exactly right, yeah, I'm workin' on that Bomac rig," he said, then added thoughtfully, "You know, it isn't my job to find oil. I just work on the rig that punches the hole. But we went down over six thousand feet at Coster's place."

Bill Turner responded to this with an appreciative grunt as he sipped his beer, acknowledging that it was a long way indeed.

But he wasn't too impressed. "It's funny though," Harper shook his head sympathetically, "two rigs side by side can drill, one find oil and the other come up dry."

"I do believe there's luck involved," Turner's hidden smile surfaced for just a second.

"I was talking to Corey over here about maybe finding a place to stay out on our next hole and he told me about Stitch Cronan's bunkhouse. Would you be familiar with that?"

"Yeah," Turner replied between long sips of beer. He tried to throw a meaningful look in Sam's direction but she was purposefully occupied at the other end of the bar and not paying them any attention. "Well, Corey ought to know," he said.

"I plan to find this Mr. Cronan and get his permission of course," Zak added.

"You're the same fella that was stayin' in a tent over at Coster's, right?"

"One and the same."

Turner looked Zachary Harper right in the eye for only the second time. Then he slapped some money down on the bar, bought a six-pack, and with a wink at Sam, he said to Zak, "Well, mister, I think the thing to do would be to head out there right now and see what kind of shape the old place is in."

When they hit the street, Bill saw Zak's Jeep and recommended Zak drive, muttering something about learning better how to find a spot if one is at the wheel, but Zak had the feeling this whole exercise was to satisfy curiosity rather than a gesture of kindness. There was little in the way of neighborly talk on the ride down. Zak was trying to construct in his mind the conversation Turner would have with his buddies the next time the subject of the oil rig down at Cronan's ranch came up. But what the hell, he appreciated the tour.

About three-quarters of the way to the new location, they turned, at Bill's direction, down a long straight dirt road. A mile or two later they turned again, left over a cattle barrier, and found themselves in a unique little gully that supported an abundance of life. To the right there was a high bluff of hills, to the left, a long thicket that led down a quarter of a mile to a gray shack that was flanked by half-dozen tall trees planted there many years before to serve as a wind break. Beyond that thicket was a field of growing wheat. At the rumbling sound of the Jeep, four horses looked up from where they had been grazing and lazily strolled off, swishing their tails behind them, stopping every few steps to nuzzle the ground with their soft fine noses. A little farther down a small cluster of cattle stood stock still. Pheasant lifted skyward from the tall grass, their sudden commotion drowned out by the low drone of the Jeep. A jackrabbit dashed heroically out in front of the Jeep, ran a short ways ahead, and then dashed back into the brush just as another darted out to take his place like in some relay race of hares. A tumbleweed rolled, and as they neared the house they startled a deer that bounded into a ravine at the back of the house showing the white underside of its tail. Zak took a deep breath as he shut 'er down, tasting the thick aromas that clung on the breeze as they drifted through this enchanting little pocket of life-enriched terrain.

Zak stepped down from the Jeep full of enthusiasm. "Y'know? Nature is so amazing. To think that Just this simple combination, a few hills, some trees, and a creek, and look how busy this little place is!"

"Yeah, one man and a gun could do all right back in here."

The shack was small and serviceable, if rundown to beat hell. One of the windowpanes was busted out at the front of the house. Through the broken window, Zak could see splotched and rotting linoleum floors and paint chipping off the walls. The front door was open and in the second that Zachary Harper hesitated, Turner pushed past him, stepping heavily into the front room. Zak was relieved that Turner had entered first; that Zak hadn't broken what he considered the unseen barrier of property. He realized that, had he been alone, he would have peeped in the window and then driven away to ask Cronan's permission to enter.

To the right through the empty front room, there was a living room with an old broken couch and an easy chair with the stuffing coming out of it. In the bedroom was a single bed with the springs busting through the right side, making the bed tilt uncomfortably. Zak remembered seeing a pair of heavy-duty cutters on location; with a snip here and there, he could cut the bad springs out so that he might at least lie evenly. Back through the front room was the kitchen. Bill Turner flicked a switch, and the lights came on.

"Well, you've got power," he chuckled, his voice sounded unnaturally loud as it bounced off the close-in walls. There was a 1950s-era kitchen set with a Formica table top and two chairs, one of which was missing a seat. A counter ran along two walls from the sink to a back door. The counter and sink were completely covered with an awful mung that had hardened into an evil-looking crust. Bill, noticing the question marks floating over Zak's head, explained, "Looks like ol' Stitch has been mixing his hot shots down here."

"What's in a hot shot?"

"A hot shot? I don't remember exactly what's in'm but it's generally speaking a bunch of magic potions you mix up and give to cattle when they need fixin'."

The fridge was filled with outdated chemicals that Bill advised he throw away at once. There was no bathroom in the place but the water was running, which meant that someone had dug a well at some point.

"You should do all right in here," Bill said with more genuine sincerity than Zak had yet heard from the man. "The only thing missing is Coster's outhouse!"

"I'll be just fine. It doesn't look like the roof leaks and this is about as close to location as I can get without moving in with Cronan himself."

"You might want to try Ben's Hardware back in town for one of those plug-in heaters when you have a little time. The nights are gonna start coolin' off pretty soon. Ever spend a winter in these parts?"

"No, never have."

"Well, you'll be okay here for the next coupla months but before too much longer you might want to start lookin' for a spot to rent in town if you're plannin' on winterin'. You'll freeze your ass to death here, that's fer sure. If you wait too long to get your name down on a spot, they'll all be gone by the time you decide you really need one. You can't always count on the hotel having spare rooms. That's too damn much money to be payin' day after day anyway."

"Thanks, I'll keep all that in mind," Zak said. They were walking between the trees along the rim of the ravine that dropped about twenty feet down to a small drainage creek. The roots of the trees jutted out nakedly in spots. From there the terrain opened wide and endless to the southeast. It was the only direction from the house that was open to the weather and by the looks of the vegetation and the permanent lean of the trees to the northwest, it appeared that weather from that direction was plentiful.

"Those would be yer summer storms," Bill Turner informed him. "Most of your winter storms come from the other side of those hills. But they aren't much protection. You're gonna want to be somewhere else."

"Well, I'll bet this little neck of the woods is mighty pretty in the fall," Zak put a happy ending on their visit as they climbed into the Jeep. The look on Bill Turner's face was a little envious and a little concerned. Zak wondered what kind of obligations Bill had taken on over the years to slow him down.

"That's true enough, 'ceptin' fall don't last too long in these parts."

They finished off the beer on the way back to town and Zak thanked Bill for his trouble which Bill assured him was no trouble at all. After dropping him at Sam's, Zak cruised back out to location. It was already dusk and Zak was afraid that if he went back to the tent he would fall asleep and be late for work. He parked a discreet distance from the rig, made himself a couple of sandwiches, curled up, and had a snooze. It was a quarter till eleven when he heard a car door slam. He sat up stiff and groggy as his door pulled open and there was Jon, bright eyed and full of it.

"Wake up chainhand! We're fast holin' tonight!"

XII

Jon threw his head back and let out a tremendous war whoop as Zak tumbled from the Jeep. All around them the rig was a frenzy of motion and excitement. The bright electric lamps on the tower seemed like huge spotlights; it was opening night and Zak was changing roles without a single rehearsal. As Zak grabbed his gear from the back of the Jeep, Jon clapped a heavy palm across his back, "Yes sir, good buddy, tonight you graduate to Roughneckin' 201, and I've got news for you."

"And what's that?" Zak turned, plunking his hard hat down on his head and tossing his gear over his shoulder. It was then that he noticed that his Scandinavian friend was dressed and ready to go. This was serious. They were off at a gallop for the bottom doghouse. Jon filled him in.

"Ol' Rusty finally got up the nerve to run off that friggin' Cowboy Crew!" Jon was triumphant. "Them dirtbags were so pissed I thought there was going to be a rumble right here on location. Jesse told Marty and me about it in town this evening just before it went down, and we went and rounded up Samson and the boys just in case George needed some help. We got here just as Carl and them were packin' up their gear. They were a-cussin' and a-bitchin' to beat hell. Really lookin' for it. When they seen us comin' they simmered down and split. This all just happened a little while ago and you, you silly bastard, you slept through the whole friggin' show!"

Zak laughed. That was one show he was glad to have missed.

"But that means that every day some crew or other is gonna have to double up or else nobody gets days off. There aren't exactly a lot of hungry roughnecks roamin' around these parts and we're still shorthanded, which means you're our newly elected chainhand. Congratulations!"

"Damn." Harper grunted and laughed nervously as he pulled on his overalls. "But wait a minute," he stopped in his tracks, "nobody's hired me out to be chainhand yet," he stated what he thought was the obvious.

"You need an invitation?" Jon laughed. "We're shorthanded there, Zakko! You'n me are gonna have to work motors, chain, and worm's corner once we've spud-in. We'll have Marty's help on the floor at first 'cause he won't be needed up top just yet. We can share worm's responsibilities after that, but there's no one left to throw chain 'ceptin' you big man!"

The thing that amazed Zak most was Jon's bedlamite enthusiasm. Instead of being morose over their apparent ill luck, Jon was elated. Feeding off the crisis of the moment, just ready and to get in there and fight like a tiger.

"Let's go chainhand, let's get it!" he roared and was off like a shot for the top doghouse as Zak hurriedly laced up his steel-toed boots.

Chainhand, Jesus!

And fast-holin', shee-it!

He assumed that drillin' must go real fast at first because the topsoil and then those first few formations are probably soft, but this having to double was a bigger worry, he fretted as he stumbled through the door. On the way up the ladder, he noticed his knees were weak. If they had to double tonight it would mean that instead of getting off work at seven a.m., they wouldn't see relief till three p.m. Tomorrow. Sixteen hours from now. His rubbery arms helped pull him up the stairs. Damn. If tonight was their turn to double, what kind of shape would he be in by then? Double-damn.

In the top doghouse things were quiet, earnest. Perhaps it was the final comeuppance and good riddance of that pain-in-the-ass Cowboy Crew, or the fact that their worst fears regarding Jesse had not come true, but there was none of the tension and stress Zak expected to find. Everyone knew this had to happen, that this was for the best. Now it was just a matter of getting it done. Heck, they had been shorthanded those first days too. Marty, Jon, and Jesse each had a different twinkle in their eye for Zak as his eyes met theirs. They were looking forward to this! The four men stood in the doorway for a brief moment watching the goings-on out on the floor and awaited their cue.

The Parker Brothers had gotten the ball rolling. They had finished unloading the pipe from the tractor-trailers and had laid it down in racks on the ground below. They had adjusted the counterweights for the tongs and strung up the boom line. In addition, they had even hooked up a rock bit for breaking soil and had run in the first dozen stands.

Jesse and the boys took over on the floor without missing a beat. The Parker Brothers disattached the kelly from the pipe in the hole and Marty, Jon, and Zak took hold of it from there and attached it to the pipe in the mousehole. They guided the ensemble, with Jesse stepping in for Andy Parker at that brake handle, over to the joint in the hole. The Parker Brothers then melted from the floor in the scant seconds it took Jon to dope the pipe and stab it down into the joint, but they congregated at the top doghouse door waiting and watching with a gleeful rough-neck curiosity to see what was about to happen next out on the floor. Zachary Harper meanwhile trotted over to the chainhand's position and picked up the end of the chain, determined to give them a good show, win, lose, or draw.

As soon as Jon was clear of that pipe, Zak let 'er fly with all his might! That chain just danced up to that top joint in crisp tight little wraps and though his follow-up move was a little unsure, he nevertheless stepped right up, face to face with that whirling pipe, trying as best he could to guide those wraps with the flat of one gloved hand while holding the loose end of the chain tight with the other fist, all the while keeping his feet free of the spinning rotary table. Marty and Jon whooped and hollered as they watched that pipe make up just fine. The Parker Brothers looked at one another as they stood there in the doorway and then moved on. And Jesse Lancaster grinned from ear to ear.

That first tower, things were happening all the time and that pipe just seemed to fall through the floor, things had just gone *Boom! Boom! Boom!* all night long. Jon, Marty, and Zak were in high-high and loving every minute of it. As quick as they could, they would finish a connection, drive another thirty-foot section up that beaver slide. As soon as Marty stabbed the pipe, Zak would fling that chain making up that pipe each and every time. Where Jesse really showed his finesse at that brake handle was making Zak look good throwing chain. If Zak's throw wasn't perfect, if those wraps were loose or his tension wasn't as sharp as it could be on his follow-up, Jesse would speed up or slow down to compensate and those six wraps would be right where they needed to be each and every time. The pace was so fantastic that not one of them noticed the night fly past. Or the glorious dawn.

Meanwhile, it was Marty's job to "mud-up." He spent every spare second down in the hopper dumping his mud sacks and mixing in saltwater. The deeper they went, the more mud they would need. When Zak asked him at the end of the tower how many sacks he had mixed, even he couldn't remember. Fifty? A hundred? Two hundred? One was as likely as another, things were happening so fast. It was a job to mix the right amount and keep it at the proper viscosity. Marty answered, "I mixed enough!"

IT JUST SEEMED TO HAPPEN that it wasn't dark anymore. Rory and his men showed up at 6:41 a.m. Jon, Zak, and Marty were almost disappointed. They could have doubled easy.

THAT AFTERNOON, ZAK DROVE INTO town. He parked the Jeep outside Ginger's Bar and sure enough, as he was stepping toward the door, down the street came a red Chevy TrailBlazer. The guy behind the wheel wearing a beat-up straw cowboy hat had to be Randy Hughes, just as Corey had described, and if that was Randy, then the big powerful-looking fella sitting next to him had to be none other than Stitch Cronan.

Stitch stepped down out of the TrailBlazer and adjusted his belt while squinting up into the setting sun. He had a great paunch that reached outward from his massive chest in a sweeping arc that curved downward and tucked into his new blue jeans along with his flannel shirt. He was a few years older than Zak had imagined, with an imposingly fierce countenance that grew more intense as he realized that the strange young man in the yellow baseball cap and the rimless glasses was approaching him with a purpose. Zak immediately felt like retreating and calling the whole thing off.

"Mr. Cronan?" Zak said, confidently sticking out his palm. Stitch just looked down at him like he was a bug on his boot. "I'm Zachary Harper, a worker on the oil rig over on your property. Mind if I chat with you for a minute?"

Stitch threw a what-have-we-here look over at Randy, then noticed Zak's hand which had been hanging in the air for the longest time collecting dust, swallowed it for a second in his giant paw, and then dropped it.

"What's on yer mind?"

"I've heard from a couple of fellas around town that you have an old bunkhouse down near where we're drillin' and I was wondering if you might see yourself clear to renting it to me for the next little spell while we're working over there." Then, dreading a lull, he decided to include his references, "Mr. Coster let me pitch a tent when we were over at his place. Well, we're done over there and what with fall settin' in, a fella could use a roof over his head."

Cronan smiled, then laughed, revealing a huge row of teeth, many of which were capped with shining gold. "Tell me something, mister. Have you ever seen that old shack of mine?"

"As a matter of fact, I have. Just yesterday Bill Turner was nice enough to ride out there with me and show me where it is."

"He was, was he?" Cronan winked from Zak to Randy who was now leaning against the blazing red TrailBlazer.

"Yeah, it looks like just the answer!" Zak had decided some time ago to take the ever-present inside joke, whatever it was, and meet it head on with optimistic naïveté. It was an honest approach and it had worked thus far.

Cronan paused, sizing up his new tenant, and with yet another sidelong snicker over to his buddy, tried to sound reluctant. "Well, I suppose if Old Man Coster'll let you use his favorite fishing hole, I can let you use my favorite hunting patch, just you don't go burnin' that little shack down though. Lord knows, I may have to move back in there myself one day!" Randy finally snickered out loud and spat on the sidewalk.

Zak reached for his wallet, but Stitch winced and put out a big hand. "Put that away, Jesus! I can't have people thinkin' I'd take money from someone to stay in that place!" Stitch looked right, then left, embarrassed should someone see Zak standing there with his wallet open and misunderstand.

"Thanks," Zak muttered as he hastily put the wallet away, but they had already turned their backs on him and disappeared through the door to the bar. Zak thought of following them, then stopped for an uneasy half second. He could visualize Stitch laughing and buying rounds and fielding questions about how things were getting along with his oil rig, and Stitch pointing out that one of 'em was using his old bunkhouse, you know, the same fella that was camping at Coster's fishing hole. Zak walked back to the Jeep instead and as he fired it up, he laughed. He was trying to see Stitch Cronan sitting on a bench in a big stadium wearing "someone else's name, someone else's number."

THAT WEEK THE WORK WAS unbelievably hard. On Thursday, Jesse's crew took the double, working straight through from eleven p.m. till three the following afternoon so that Rory's crew could have the day off. And they were back again eight hours later to work their regular shift. Because they were still fast-holin', Marty wasn't needed up in the tower and Jon and Zak were damn glad for the extra pair of arms and legs.

Amid all the hustle and bustle Zak had all but forgotten about his tent and the unfinished business of packing up his things and dismantling his old campsite. He had been staying at the Pioneer, and as soon as he had a little time he made the trek back out to Coster's Creek.

Zak arrived to find his tent collapsed and a big fat cow standing on it nonchalantly chewing her cud. She had taken an enormous shit right there, the big round pie still steaming behind her. More bovines had wandered about and claimed the spot as their own. Several had collected at the water's edge, or were standing in it up to their knees, drinking in gallons of fresh stream water in long slow draughts. Zak walked up to the cow standing on Freddy's tent, waving his baseball cap to shoo her off but she wouldn't budge. He hollered. He grabbed the cow by the ears and pulled, but the cow shook her head stubbornly. He stood to one side and pushed the beast with all his might. It barely shifted its weight. Finally Zak stood back and asked as pleasantly as he could, "All right dear, what is it you want? Hmm? Please get off my tent, please?" Just as it occurred to him to go to the Jeep and scavenge around for some food to lure it away, the cow gave a low rumbling sound and then plopped several pounds of manure leaving a second big cow pie before ambling off contentedly. He rolled the tent up like a taco and tied it up tight, scattered the campfire stones, and kissed that place goodbye.

Clearly, it was time to get to work on Cronan's shack.

The following Saturday it was the Parker Brothers turn to double for Jesse and the boys. Zak went back to the Pioneer after work but before going to bed he hit the hardware store soon after it was open, bought cleansers, plastic buckets, light bulbs, a heater as Turner had suggested, and after a long nap beat it out to his new abode. He spent most of the afternoon cleaning up the kitchen. He found storm boards under the house and nailed them over the broken windows. He clipped the broken springs from the chair in the living room and from the bed. He hit everything with Lysol. He unrolled Freddy's tent and scraped the cow shit from it with a shovel he borrowed from location, then set it to soak in the creek. A reasonable distance downwind from the house, he dug a deep hole for a latrine with the intention of pitching the tent over the hole as a makeshift outhouse, and covered the hole with another storm board.

Early that evening, feeling very good about himself and needing a few more supplies before the stores closed, he went back to town and, after picking up his things, stopped in at Sam's. He was disappointed not to find any roughnecks on hand but it stood to reason. The Parker Brothers were on the double and Rory's men were probably getting dinner somewhere. Zak would have liked to see Jon though, for a chat and a few whiskeys.

Then he remembered that Jon was probably off with Mary Ellen. Marty was most likely out at location with Cynthia, and Jesse had certainly shot back to Watford for the night. So Zak bought a case of beer and stopped on the way home for a bundle of hamburgers.

Zak dumped his gear in the front room. He put the beer in the fridge. As he sat down at the kitchen table with his bag of hamburgers he saw out the kitchen window the sun just over the top of a pointed hill overlooking the shack and was suddenly inspired to take his dinner and eat it there.

Climbing the hill to the west side of the shack, he laid out his supper, rolled a reefer, popped a beer, and slowly munched, facing east. The wind was from the west, the northwest; he turned his denim collar up, draped a woolen blanket over his shoulders, and sat Indian style on the rocky top of the hill looking almost directly down on the shack, the six treetops, and the rolling vista beyond.

For the first time in his life, he could really see the approaching terminator, the line between day and night; a wall of black as big as the land it was creeping across. The wind at his back was picking up, becoming colder, he imagined Boreas himself attempting to blow back or otherwise retard the progress of this marching wall of doom. The night was preceded by deepening blues and grays, overwhelming the golds and greens and browns in their path, swirling all shades into a deepening purple, then black. As the sun dipped down behind him, the last traces of light lapped at the gray wood of the shack, the brown and gravel path leading up to it, and tossed sparkles across the silver glinting of the creek below. When the line between night and day at last crept silently and painlessly over him, the temperature dropped just enough to be make him shiver.

The light he had left on in the kitchen below now sent a warm, beckoning yellow glow heavenward. Zak felt as though he could walk up to that door and hear a friendly voice welcoming him home.

"You've never lived without trying, right?" Corey Nightingale said. Zak whirled around, knocking over his beer while, in his embarrassment and confusion, he tried to formulate a "What are you doing here?" kind of sentence. But his mouth was full.

No one.

"Jesus, I'm cracking up!" he said aloud, with a half-hysterical ring of laughter to his voice. The sound of a true voice, if only his own, was reassuring. He righted his beer. He lit the joint. The silence, the serenity, plus the cathartic daily release of energy on the job, had wound him up tight but at the same time opened his senses too. As his tummy filled and the pleasing combination of beer and pot brought about a most pleasant buzz, he relaxed and saw himself sitting on the hill in the enveloping darkness. He was a manifestation of cosmic dust become cosmic fact, held together by cosmic fancy and by seeking, searching, needing, hungering, terrestrial necessity. His thoughts, once lost in the maniacal shivaree of the city, now came booming unimpeded from all quarters of his conscious and unconscious mind, making the recollection of Corey's voice seem like it had been shouted from some point just above his head. He wondered how his recent ancestors would have interpreted such intense perceptions. Without the distraction of technology or the underpinning philosophies of skepticism and science, or the interfering interpretations of politics, rationalism, and communal media, what conjectures, mysticism, and superstitions would evolve to explain and make such thoughts and emotions comprehensible, even serviceable? The very speculation called up images of native peoples, to whom these perceptions must have been part of their normal skill set, their interpretations then evolving quite naturally into human customs and norms. Bellowing gods, crafty goddesses, sprightly fairies, dragons, chimeras, and demons. Of hordes of men, hordes of beasts, migrations and frightened masses, moving in the night, moving in the day. As he listened for warning sounds at work on the rig, as he sniffed the air for changes, he was learning to use all his inarticulate senses.

But here and now, as he could see and feel without doubt, the geography was vast enough to accommodate his tempered yet expanding senses. And his imagination had a role to play in sparking curiosities that would lead to solving problems. He closed his eyes and breathed deeply through his nose and released the breath slowly through his mouth. He felt his spine, supple and strong, straighten as his chest expanded. He could draw a line from the top of his head, down his spine, and continue right through to the center of the earth. As he opened his eyes, he could feel himself reaching outward in all directions into the spectacle and the specter of this prairie night.

When he returned to earth, the shifts had changed. Things that moved quickly were hiding and things that moved cautiously were beginning to creep. All had a job to do. A job that meant nothing if not life and death.

He lay back against the bumpy ground, bunching a portion of the blanket behind his head as the last blue at the top of the dome faded, giving way, like a window opening, to the bright light of stars around which other dark planets roamed. He spotted his first satellite of the evening. It zipped along at a steady pace from northwest to southeast. He followed its progress, losing it momentarily among brighter star clusters, then picked it up again when it found a patch of dark sky background.

"JESUS CHRIST! WILL YA GET a load of this?" Zak heard Jon's voice echo through the walls of the shack and the walls of his brain. "Now here's one roughneck who knows how to live in style! Yes sir, you really are comin' up in the world there, daddy-o!"

Zak opened his gluey eyes for a half second and craned his neck to see where the voice was coming from. Nowhere. He felt the shack shake with thunder. In another blink he heard a loud

hiss, like the air condenser on the rig, and could feel a hand at the back of his head.

"C'mon old-timer, this'll fix ya up!" The smell that filled Zak's nostrils was unmistakably beer. Jon tilted a can, filling Zak's mouth and throat with a gush of freezing cold beer that sent carbonation bubbles exploding through his nose, and he sat up violently, coughing and choking, spitting most of it back all over himself and the blanket.

"I think he's going to live!" Jon announced to Marty and Cynthia, who were coming through the door, their arms loaded with supplies.

Zak looked dourly up at Jon and swung his feet off the couch and onto the floor. He ran his hands through his hair. It was longer than it had been in years and now, when he brushed his hands through it, it stayed back away from his face, the long greasy locks falling comfortably to each side.

With his thoughts beginning to sort themselves out and his rumpled feathers beginning to settle, he looked up into their three beaming faces and shook his head, "Good morning!" he smiled. "What's for breakfast?"

"You're drinkin' it!" Jon laughed and put the cold beer in Zak's hand. Zak shrugged, took a sip, and gasped as the cold bubbly beer went down.

"Mording hell!" Marty bellowed as he hobbled into the kitchen, "de day's dab dear ober!"

"That's right," Jon cracked a beer for himself, "in ten more hours we'll be back to work."

Zak stumbled past Jon into the kitchen. He said hello to Cynthia, who had seated herself at the little kitchen table. He leaned into the sink and splashed his face with cold water. Then he stepped outside and had a piss.

All that day the four of them cleaned, painted, scrubbed, scoured, and mended. By dinner time they had curtains up, windows patched, chairs that could support human bodies. Cynthia lined the shelves with paper and set Zak up with paper plates, plastic cutlery, and canned goods. They even erected Freddy's tent over the latrine hole Zak had dug so Cynthia could perform her toilette in privacy.

Cynthia cooked a chicken dinner. While she worked, Marty led the boys out to the Bronco and popped open the back.

"Now we're gonna hab sub fun!" he hissed and tossed aside a vinyl cover to reveal an impressive assortment of firearms and boxes of ammunition. The rifles were in soft leather cases and the handguns were in hard protective boxes. Zak whistled softly.

"Marty's got the finest gun collection around," Jon boasted for his friend.

"Yup," Marty deftly lifted a rifle. "Yushally I keep deze here locked up back in Watford." He opened the case, and the long black muzzle appeared, pointed at the sky. He studied it closely. He licked his thumb and rubbed the dust from the little sight at the end, making it glisten, then brought the weapon out of its case, hoisted it to his shoulder, and whirled away from them as though following a pheasant up from the ground. The rifle was slender and lightweight. The wood was fine and dark.

"Well, whadya tink?" Marty said with pride as he handed the rifle to Zak. Zak aimed at the hill.

"It reminds me of a doberman. You know those dogs are long and sleek and high-strung and powerful?"

Jon had gathered up their empty beer cans and set them up on the hillside over yonder. As supper cooked in the kitchen, the sun set to the sounds of exploding powder, clanging beer cans, screeching ricochets, and the kind of laughter that makes you want to run to the window to see what you are missing. Cynthia giggled as she worked. She hummed and whistled and talked to herself. She skipped to the window to watch Marty take his turn shooting and clapped her hands when he hit his target. With each report of a rifle outside she sang, "Pop! Pop! Chop! Chop!" Marty always told her that her cooking was like magic. He would arrive with bags full of stuff from the store, and she would turn it into supper when he wasn't looking. "Pop chop! Chop pop!"

Over dinner she watched the three of them eat every bite, reacting ecstatically with bulging eyes and stifled sighs to each finger-licking, lip-smacking, belching, reaching, clutching, tearing, face-stuffing mouthful. She was needed. She was a part of it all.

THAT NIGHT A VERY STRANGE character greeted the three rough-necks as their happy convoy wheeled onto location. As soon as they were out of their vehicles, the door to the toolpusher's shack swung open and a small, bow-legged man with messy hair and gray whiskers came limping out in a hurry to catch them before they disappeared into the bottom doghouse. At first, Zak didn't think twice, but it was Jon's ashen face upon stepping out of his car and seeing the old codger hobbling toward them that made Zak think again.

The old man called out in a voice that was practically a squeak, "Hey there! Howdy!"

Right away he gave Zak the creeps.

"I reckon you guys're Jesse's boys, eh?" the old fella stopped in his tracks, looking from one to another of them. Just when Zak was about to answer in as cordial a manner as possible, Jon exploded.

"Reckon shit! What the fuck are you doin' out here, Vernon!?" Jon yanked his hard hat off his head and drop-kicked it a good twenty yards across the muddy lot.

Vernon flinched, then craned his neck like a goose and squinted, "Jonny! That you?" and looking to Zak explained, "I wouldn't ah known him without the whiskers but that temper I'd recognize anywhere!" He hollered and spat and laughed and looked them all in the eye expecting they should laugh with him. Zak didn't laugh because he knew something was terribly wrong; Jon stalked off and Marty just stared in disbelief. There was a sickening mixture of panic, exasperation, and despair written all over their faces.

Vernon got down to business. "Now lookee here guys, I'm goin' t'be pushin' yer tools fer yuhs the next coupla weeks while Cleaver's on days off." He looked from one to the other and grinned as if he expected them to think Christmas had come early this year.

Marty put his hands on his hips and with a deep simian grunt said, "Oh Lord."

Jon stormed back. "I don't believe this shit! You know that we're shorthanded?"

"Sure I do," Vernon insisted, trying to sound soothing. "Look, Cleaver's got a new crew lined up and they'll be here in just a coupla days. You guys are doin' fine though, right? No big problems?"

"None till now," Jon spat, but the fight was going out of him. "Has Jesse seen you yet?"

"Sure has," Vernon answered with a sickly grin revealing more gum than teeth. "I think he's gone on a drunk, too."

In the bottom doghouse as the guys changed their clothes, Zak only wanted to know one thing, "Okay, so who is this guy?" Jon wouldn't answer. In fact, he wasn't going to utter another word until he saw Jesse Lancaster. So it was up to Marty to offer some sort of explanation.

"Dat, my friend, is de dumbest sum bitch ebber to step foot on an erl rig! 'Iz nambe is Vernon Orge!" Marty drew out the last name, *Oooorge*, and then stood there, all puffed up, looking Zak intently in the eye as though the name alone should explain everything. At last, Marty just turned, dropped his hard hat onto his head, and muttered, "And may de Lord hab bercy on our soulds."

Up in the top doghouse things looked bad. Jesse was leaning against the door to the floor watching the Parker Brothers make a connection. He was drunk as a skunk. *Great,* thought Zak, beginning to understand Jon's concern, *if something goes wrong we have a drunk and an idiot ready to leap into action.*

Jon produced a cup of coffee from a Thermos and handed it to the driller, who managed to slur, "Thanks," to his motorman before spilling most of it down his front. The steam rose off the material in little wisps. Jon refilled his cup and Jesse then took a long drink that must have singed every layer of skin off his inner lips and tongue, but he didn't even wince. He just blinked like he was having trouble staying awake.

When the Parker Brothers had finished the connection, Jesse's crew took the floor. As they passed each other, Paul Kimberly, their dark-eyed motorman, said to Zak, "You guys really gonna work with him like that?"

"Sure," Zak said as though nothing was unusual. Kimberly walked off, shaking his head, and Zak sidled up to Jon and with a nod in Jesse's direction said, "Is everything okay?"

When Jon realized Zak was asking about Jesse, he smirked and made a disgusted face as though Zak had asked the stupidest question in all the world. Then, seeing Zak's face fall, he grabbed Zak's arm, "Jesse? Shit! He'll be all right. It's that moron downstairs I'm worried about. Any damn thing is possible with him around! He was a lousy roughneck, a miserable driller, and it's inconceivable that he could be pushing tools! Bloody! Fucking! Inconceivable! I don't know what that fucking Rusty's got against us all of a sudden, but I'd sure like to know what we did to deserve this!"

The night passed with Jesse slowly sobering up in the top doghouse. Every time a new connection was needed, that driller would look a little shaky walking out onto the floor, his usually imperceptible limp a bit more pronounced, his steps a bit more cautious, but his performance at that brake handle was adequate. And those wraps would make up well enough to get the job done.

It was during those connections that Zak realized how ready Marty was to take that brake handle, and he lurked nearby each time Jesse stepped out onto the floor in case the old man faltered, which eased Zak's mind somewhat, but he kept an eye on his fellow crew members as well as his inebriated driller. From their example he too began to get a feel for the older man's moods, strengths, vulnerabilities, and distractions. Zak slipped into his roll as the third cog in an elaborate, though never mentioned, support system that had grown around the driller. It was their way of returning the many favors he did for them.

The following day, so certain was Vernon that a relief crew was on its way to them, to prove that he really believed relief was in sight, Vernon put everyone back onto their normal eight-hour shifts. His reason being that the relief crew would arrive any minute and when they did it would be best if everyone was on a normal routine.

"I'll believe it when I see it," Jon scoffed.

Naturally, the relief crew never arrived.

By the time a week had slowly, gruelingly passed, the situation had deteriorated. New shipments of bits were late. When that company hand came poking around the hopper checking the viscosity level of Marty's mud, he gave the derrickhand a balling out for not keeping it at the proper level. "Where's my filler!?" Marty bellowed when he had gone. And with no relief crew and the schedule still unchanged, everyone's days off were canceled. It got to a point where everyone was so pissed off that Vernon was afraid to poke his head out of that toolpusher's shack. Because of his hiding, the situation escalated—as every time the various drillers needed something done, their toolpusher was unavailable.

The roughnecks then took matters into their own hands, scouting around on their off hours, making calls, and trying to get a lead on a crew. At first they left notes with names and phone numbers on the knowledge box in the top doghouse. These messages would magically disappear when they were out making a connection, and nothing would come of them. They got the same frustrating results when they tried putting notes on the toolpusher's door with little bits of electrical tape. One evening when Jesse's boys arrived for work, they saw a note from Smoke Denton affixed to the toolpusher's door with a huge bowie knife that read simply, "I want to talk to you!" written in a jerky uneven scrawl on a torn piece of brown paper bag; a crudely drawn skull and crossbones delivered home the point. From that point on nobody clapped an eye on Vernon Orge for the remainder of Rusty Cleaver's days off.

A lot of crazy ideas were passed around the doghouse during those two weeks, as roughnecks, proud of their ability to spontaneously work through virtually any and all problems that might arise, groped for some solution to their current predicament.

"If we could find four able-bodied local boys, one of the drillers could double up with us and Jesse could break 'em out," Jon postulated. As eyebrows raised, he hurried on, "No shit, Marty and I could double a couple of times and give 'em some pointers. Jesse's worked with worm crews before, right?"

"Yeah, never will again either," Jesse shook his head but nobody believed him. "You really need someone up there with yer new derrickhand."

"I could do dat," Marty volunteered.

"That's beside the point though," Rory was pessimistic. "I ain't seen nothin' roamin' the streets of Scobey that comes close to resemblin' no roughneck."

"I've half a mind to twist off, gas up my outfit, and go find that fuckin' Cleaver and drag his drunken ass right the fuck back here," Denton wanted to cut to the chase.

"Don't take your outfit, take Frank's," Rory laughed and hocked up a loogie as he did so. Frank, the company hand, had been about as scarce as Vernon throughout their current ordeal. He had the biggest trailer on location and although there had been no complaints fired in his direction yet, as no one really wants to interfere with the man who cuts the checks, there were rumblings.

Zak could tell that this kind of talk could not only get out of hand, but could make matters worse. He said, "Well, if we weren't already shorthanded, I'd volunteer to shoot back to Watford and scare up some help. Maybe that could be a way to go. Someone could volunteer to go get help, like in the movies when the cavalry is pinned down, or the explorers are stuck in the ice."

Silence.

THE NEXT DAY ZAK SPOTTED a hitchhiker heading west out of town past the grain elevators and the rodeo grounds. The hitchhiker was wearing Redwing boots, beat-up jeans, a dirty AC/DC T-shirt under an unbuttoned flannel shirt and a hard hat. He had a duffel bag thrown over one shoulder, a six-pack of Pabst Blue Ribbon dangling from his free hand, and a can of beer in the hand he was using to try and hitch a ride with. Zak nearly went off the road attempting to U-turn back in the fella's direction. When he saw Zak turn around and pull over, the hitchhiker winked and grinned a wincing sort of hey-howdy grin, struck a bow-legged pose, and raised an a-okay thumb in the air. He walked bow-legged, too, with an extra bounce to his step like he was making minor yet tricky adjustments to his balance with every step he took. Zak realized, as the fella bounced and skipped toward the Jeep, that this was a man on his way to getting seriously shitfaced.

"Good t'go, eh?" the guy said as he leaped nimbly into the passenger seat, stowing his gear in the back with one easy flip. He reeked of beer, sweat, and cigs. He was slender and strong and agile with powerful shoulders and a tiny waist. He had beach-boy blond hair that jutted out in all directions from under his hard hat, which he wore cocked jauntily to one side. Mischievous blue eyes, a pug nose red with drink and sun, and a blazing blond mustache over a catch-me-if-you-can-come-and-get-me smile. "I knew it wouldn't be long before another roughneck come by!" he laughed. "Good t'go, eh?" he asked again with a blink and a nod as though he really was anxious to hear Zak's answer, he asked again, "Good t'go?"

"You bet," Zak replied with more amusement than gusto.

"Wanna beer?" asked the hitchhiker, ripping one from its plastic holder and handing it over before putting the six-pack down on the floor between his legs and taking a long hardy pull on his own.

"Oil field trash, eh? No better people in the world!" the man said through a boozy self-satisfied gasp. "You see a roughneck hikin' down the road, you know what t'do. 'Cause yer good t'go! No one else'll stop for'm that's fer sure, huh? Whatcher name partner?"

"Zak, Zak Harper," and they shook hands using the new world hand clasp.

"My name's Skidder, Skidder MacIntyre. Friends call me Skiddy."

"Well, where ya headin', Skiddy?"

"I don't know, out Highway 5 here a ways. I was kinda hopin' you'd know where that location is. Aren't you headin' out there?"

"Well, if I were this, would be the wrong direction. I'm south-east of town. I don't know of any other..." but as he was saying this, convinced that his passenger was fucked-up or crazy, or both, a procession of gin trucks turned west with them along with a water hauler or two, and it dawned on him that there was, indeed, another rig setting up in the Scobey area. This was big news.

"Nope. I'm sure it's out this way. I'm trying to catch up with a buddy of mine, Archer Hansom. You know Arch?"

"Can't say that I do."

"Well, he and I just twisted off from them crazy cunts down at Freeburn, back outside of Watford. You worked for them yet?"

"Nope."

"Well think twice about it before ya do. Them cheap bastards'll work ya blind then cheat ya out've yer bottom-hole. I got it out of'm one way or another though," he winked. "So who're you hired out with?"

"An outfit called Bomac."

"Bomac, don't know them."

"They're good."

"Well, this here one's called Blackhawk. Been with them yet?"

"Nope."

"Well, I have, they're all right. The toolpusher on this one's dumber'n a stump though. Jeezy-shit you wouldn't believe the crap we get away with. Ol' Arch is gonna go drillin' for us. Always saves me a spot on his crew. Arch is a good driller, knows how to fuck the dog like nobody I've ever seen, except myself of course. He's a mite rammy though, know what I mean?"

"Not exactly," Zak couldn't help but laugh. There was something of the put-on to everything this character had to say, and yet it wasn't like he was mocking or disrespectful. Welcome to my funhouse, he seemed to be saying, as though once Zak was hip to his perspective he could see the world for what it was, an amusement park of happy terrors.

Skiddy scrutinized Zak briefly and whatever question mark had suddenly appeared over Skiddy's head just as suddenly disappeared. "Well, ol' Arch is crazier'n a cunt at that brake handle," Skiddy laughed, "he gets a bit carried away when he's on a roll trippin' pipe so he's got this bad habit of yankin' that pipe out of the hole too fast and crown'n out."

"I've never seen anybody crown out," Zak admitted.

"You'll know it when ya do! And no one does it with more style than Archer Hansom. This last time I could just tell when we pulled away our slips and that ol' pipe just came flyin' out of the hole, I thought to myself, oh shit, here we go! There's just no fuckin' way he's gonna get 'er stopped before that kelly reaches the top and when he does that whole friggin' shebang is gonna come down right on our heads! So I just heaved them slips and took a flyin' leap over the railin's and landed twenty feet below right on top of that shale-shaker! Good thing I was about half piss drunk or I might've hurt myself! Sure enough though that kelly hit that crown so fuckin' hard you'd uh thought the whole damn rig was comin' down! As it was, that kelly hit the floor right where we'd been standin'! Bang! Same thing happened down in Wyoming last spring. Nearly shit-killed all of us! I was good and drunk that time too, thank God," and Skidder let out a laugh that rippled and rolled and swayed with the Jeep as they bounded over a rise, "'cause when I seen that big thing comin' loose I dove down the beaver slide and just rolled and rolled, din't even get a bruise. So Zak, that's what you got to say from now on, when you've just about had enough of their bullshit, eh? You just look 'em in the eye an' say, 'Feelin' a bit *rammy* tonight boys, yep, I'm feelin' a mite *rammy*, think I'll head 'em into town,' and that'll be good for about a two-day drunk, eh? Good t'go?" And Skiddy took a long, loud, wet drink, snorting and gurgling before pitching the empty can out the open door.

"Good t'go!" Zak fell in with the program and raised his beer in salutation.

"Good t'go!" Skidder laughed and popped another beer. "Anyway, I need to hook up with Arch, I know he'll be drillin' up here and if I get there soon enough, he'll put me in the derrick where I won't be any trouble. Nobody's comin' up there to give ya any shit either, know what I mean? I can hide beers up there, I can hide 'em in the mud shacks, too, but not unless I'm derrickhand," which reminded him of something unpleasant. His eyes stared straight ahead. "I got me into a bit of a fix back there in Watford."

"How so?"

"I'm waitin' on a case of universal joints for my pickup. It's eighteen years old, runs like a top but the universal joint keeps goin' out so I just up and ordered a case of 'em. Gonna take a couple of weeks so I thought I'd hike up here and make some dough. I'll work anywhere, I don't care. Derricks used to bother me until I learned not to look up. Once I learned not to look up I pretty much had 'er down, know what I mean?" And his little pun restored his good humor and he chugged some more beer, finishing with a loud gasp.

"I think I do, but I always thought the trick with heights was not to look down."

"Maybe. But derrickhand's gotta look down shit! I guess the idea is to not be too aware of the horizon, fucks with your equilibrium. But shit, you can sneak a few beers up there and while everyone down on the floor is standin' around tryin' to figure out what to do next you can suck one into ya. Hey, Zak, wanta smoke some pot?"

"Okay."

"Good t'go, eh?" he pulled out a bag and started rolling a number. "I worked down in Wyoming all summer and grew this behind the rig. There was this bluff and a bunch a pine trees in behind the rig and back behind those pines was a perfect patch of sunlight. That's moose country down there boy. You worked down there yet?"

"Nope."

"You will. It's nice down there. Prettier'n here, that's for sure." And Skidder paused briefly from sprinkling the dried leafy marijuana into his rolling paper to take a quick look out the open door at the fast-moving countryside to verify its barrenness. "It's perfect for poachin' down there. Deer, rabbit, all kinds of stuff." He licked the edges of the rolling paper. "You gotta watch out for the moose though. Holy shit are they ever mean. You don't ever want to get one pissed off. If you're ever growin' any reefer down there you got to be careful. They'll come and eat your pot plants sure as hell. Just love the stuff. So what ya do is you put some human hair on the plants. Y'know, just pluck it out of your hairbrush. They won't come near it then. So we used to fuck the dog and sneak in behind those trees, suck back some beers, and watch that pot grow. Jesus Christ those plants were this tall in no time. You gotta watch out for the male ones though. One male plant in with a bunch a females and everything turns to seed.

"So the thing to do is work your way down to Wyoming in the fall, save up some dough, and then roll on down to Steamboat, over in Colorado, for the winter months. Just lie low. You can stay drunk all the time! Before the season gets going, you can find a bartender or somebody to let you share their expenses on a room. Ask around. Then you can get to know some of the women that come up from Denver and from out West to go skiing. That's just great, huh? You're sitting there at the bar next to some sweet-smelling city girl wearing her new store-bought goin'-to-the-country outfit and sooner or later she can't help askin' what it is you do and you look her right in the eye and say 'I'm a roughneck,'" and Skidder threw an extra sneer into his delivery for authenticity, method acting, Zak believed, "and they don't know from roughneckin,' they just think you're the wildest, craziest, fuckin' outlaw they've ever seen—just what they came out here to get a taste of. Oh fuck it's a good time and it beats the shit out of roughneckin' in these parts in January and February." Skidder had a shudder just thinking about it.

"So then, what brings you up this way? Shouldn't you be headin' in the other direction?" Zak was doing some quick calculations to see what kind of money Skidder might be talking to make it all possible. Dividing how much he thought it was by how many weeks he would need to earn it.

"Well Zak, like I was sayin' before I got sidetracked, I was startin' t'get a little too well known down there. We was mixin' it up down at Fort Peck, the Sioux Reserve. Whoa shit," Skidder shook his head like he had just been hit in the face by a bucket of cold water. "And I thought I could drink! You don't wanna get caught fuckin' around with those bad boys, no sir-ee. I had to spend my last few paychecks gettin' some of my buddies from Tiger out of the slammer. Those Tiger rigs they're comin' out with these days are good though—big. Whoa shit!" Skiddy hollered again. "Nothing like the old-fashioned Tinkertoys they got runnin' out here in the boonies.

"So I fucked off up to Williston. I gotta put a new tranny in a buddy's Monte Carlo. That's another story. I owe a few guys back in Gillette. So by the time I get all that shit squared away I guess winter'll be here and I'll be fucked. I might be able to make it out to Steamboat before the season ends. It's good to get in there early though, it can be tough finding a cheap place to stay once the skiing season gets under way." Skidder mulled over his prospects for a frustrating moment and then, figuring what the hell, shrugged, and turned his attention to more immediate matters.

"Say, Arch is a hell of a guy. If he's still puttin' our crew together maybe you should jump ship and come along with us. It'd be a helluva note. I'll teach ya how to fuck the dog, Zak. I mean, no one can look busier while accomplishing absolutely nothing than yours truly. There's definitely a trick to it, and if anybody gives you any shit you just hit the ground runnin', smilin' all the while sayin' 'I hears ya!' just like them giving ya shit was doin' ya the biggest goddamned favor of your whole life. 'I hears ya!'" Skiddy said it again with a big broad smile, like he had cracked the secret code for living in the twenty-first century and was giving Zak a full demonstration. He then smiled the most shit-eating grin he could muster, struck a pose while raising his beer in the air, and said again, "I hears ya!"

"I hears ya!" answered Zachary Harper.

"I'm happy as a clam and don't give a damn!" yelled Skidder MacIntyre. He threw out a fist and a grimy thumb jutted up in the air, "Good t'go eh?"

"Good t'go!" Zachary Harper hollered back and the two roughnecks laughed and chugged their beers as the Jeep swerved and rumbled and bounced and frolicked down Highway 5, heading west from Scobey, Montana, bound for Blackhawk number seven.

The nipple-up process which Zak had recently experienced on Bomac 34 was just getting under way there at Blackhawk number seven and as he wheeled the Jeep, at Skiddy's direction, over to a cluster of pickups and motorcycles which had gathered off to one side of the central hubbub, Skidder waved and jeered and held his beer out the window like it was the official emblem of his berserker breed, the last of whom he represented with all the pride and good intentions the gods had chosen him for. When he wasn't flaunting his beer can he was giving people the finger, whether he knew them or not, and reeling with laughter as he did so, as if the mere recognition of a gin truck driver, or one of the guys in a car full of roughnecks, was a cause to be celebrated. They smiled and waved, or laughed and shook their heads. Skidder hopped out of the Jeep before Zak brought it to a halt.

Archer Hansom leaned against a rusted-out Chevy four-door with several other roughnecks gathered around him. He was tall and bony, had a serious face with a wiry goatee, like a roughneck musketeer, and straight black hair tied in a ponytail that hung halfway down his back over what was obviously a hand-made leather motorcycle jacket, worn, torn, and pockmarked, that clung to his frame like a second skin.

When Skidder tumbled from Zak's Jeep, Archer stepped quickly forward, ripped the unopened beers dangling from Skidder's right hand, and tossed them into Archer's car window in a motion so smooth and swift no one hardly even noticed.

Skidder, flaunting his attitude, stood back and chugged his remaining beer, putting the can to his lips and tilting his head all the way back in a classic pose, before backhanding the empty can into the window after the others.

Archer shook his head, looked down, and spat.

"I don't think we've ever been run off a location before we even started to work, Skiddy," Archer scolded.

"It'd be a first," someone else agreed.

Archer had a full crew dressed and ready to go now that MacIntyre had arrived, and they were just sitting on orders. It was several minutes before they got around to noticing Zak and, after a brief introduction, Archer tried to be helpful.

"I think all the crews are set, Zak, but you can go talk to Charlie over there, I'm sure someone can use ya while we're settin' up."

Zak explained that he was already throwing chain down on Bomac 34. As he spoke it occurred to him that it was the first time he ever heard himself described as chainhand to a group of strange roughnecks, and he tried to act like it was nothing.

"Yeah? Who's yer driller?" One of the men wanted to know.

"Jesse Lancaster."

"Shit, I know him," someone else said, "never seen 'im sober. Like Skidder here," and he kicked some dirt over Skiddy's boots.

"Must be one hell of a driller," Skiddy spoke up in mock seriousness.

"He is."

"He'd have t'be as long as he's been around," the man smiled. Everyone knew that some loyalties are not to be trifled with. No hard feelings.

There was some detailed discussion as to the exact whereabouts of that Bomac rig, and it was decided that sooner or later they'd all be runnin' into one another in town. Before Zak took his leave he explained that they were a shorthanded crew and if some latecomers happened along it would sure be appreciated if they'd send them Bomac's way.

"Will do," said Archer Hansom.

"See? If we get run off here we can roll on down to Bomac and pick up their empty tower there. So gimme one of them beers!" laughed Skidder MacIntyre.

BACK AT BOMAC 34 THE fact that a second drilling rig had moved into the area was old news. George Cleaver had already paid them a visit, as had Andy Parker and Rory, but they hadn't a hand to spare.

There was one consolation. At the end of two weeks those paychecks looked pretty good. Especially on Jesse's shorthanded crew. But it was still seen as sort of a miracle that when George at last pulled up on location he wasn't lynched immediately. George just greeted the angry mob with a scratch of his head. The days off had done him a world of good.

"Frankly, I'm surprised at you boys," he said feigning simple paternal bewilderment, "I thought you'd wrap old Vernon around your little fingers and run this rig yourselves!"

When it was argued that their schedules had been altered in such a way as to give them no days off, George looked at them like they were all crazy. He simply put them on twelve-hour shifts until relief arrived; that way no one would have to work sixteen hours to get a day off. Compared to what they had been going through, twelve hours on and twenty-four hours off with things running smooth would be a piece of cake. Next problem?

"Shit, George!" Rory was saying. "You're damn lucky one of these crews didn't sack 'em up!"

But George just wrinkled his brow as though this remark made him angry.

"What the hell for? I thought you boys would love to have someone like old Vernon to kick around for two weeks the way

I've been workin' your asses off around here." And by God, the way he said it, it was somehow indisputable, and not a man among them, including Smoke Denton, didn't walk away unable to explain what all the fuss had been about after all. But deep down, there were some who felt that George had abandoned them in their hour of need; they resented it and would never trust him as completely as they had before.

George gave Jesse's crew the first day off and though there were some grumblings, no one could argue with giving the short-handed crew the first break.

Jon was pissed anyway. Twelve hours on and twenty-four off meant that if you got off work at seven a.m. you didn't have to be back to work again till seven the next morning. Then you'd get off at seven p.m. and be back at seven the following evening. Get off at seven and be back at seven. Some people don't care when they sleep as long as they get their requisite number of hours, but those people are special. "He's going to turn us into zombies!" Jon groaned.

A DAY AND A HALF later Zak was sitting up on what he had come to call his lookout peak when he saw Marty's Bronco and Jon's Olds bustin' down the road toward his little shack. Everyone was all excited.

"Ol' Rusty's finally gone and done it! He's hired a crew and we're back on schedule. So we go in tonight at eleven instead of tomorrow morning."

When they arrived on location, Zak was not surprised when he stepped up onto the floor and found that he was relieving Archer Hansom's crew. Skiddy was climbing down out of the derrick and as he passed Zak on the floor he merely gave Harper a wink and a nod, barely letting on they knew each other. Zak could smell beer. When Jesse looked at the chart for the night's work he said "Shit!"

"What's the matter?" Zak asked.

"Them dumb fucks've been turnin' to the right and not gettin' any damn where all day. That bit's gotta come out. They fucked the dog on us is what they done. Some crews just sit and babysit the hole and let others do the work. They should have been halfway through a trip when we showed up." Jesse thought about it for a second and then threw up his hands.

"We can get 'er!" Zak smiled.

The next morning over breakfast Jesse's boys were feeling pretty good about themselves. They had tripped pipe the night before at record speed, shorthanded or not, and had plenty of time left over to powwow in the top doghouse. They decided to just let things slide for a while with the new crew. If this kind of thing got to be a habit they'd make a stink, naturally, but they had been without help for so long they were glad to even have babysitters. Besides, they felt that they were so damn good it just didn't matter. "Let'm give us all the hard work they can," Jon chortled. "Beats hell out of standin' around doin' nothin'."

"Dese guys're gonna shit on us every which-a-way," Marty laughed. "Maymbe we should just meet'm somewheres and teach'm what's what!" his eyes flamed and he brought a powerful fist into an open palm with a loud smack.

"I used to care about all that but after these past few weeks I couldn't care less," Jon said. "We're hot, man!" He was getting loud, and others in the restaurant looked around. "Did you see Jesse's face this mornin' when we came off the floor? This is the best damn crew I've ever been on! Go ahead and 'shit on us!' I don't care if they shit on us 'cause we can get 'er, damn it! What do we care? Leave us a bad drill bit? What do we care? We'll just trip that son of a bitch out of there, change that bit, and trip that son of a bitch back in! It ain't a problem! Man?" And Jon, now becoming ferocious, banged the table and confronted Zak as though Zak were the duly designated representative of the collective fates of the universe, "Man! What's the problem?"

"There ain't no fucking problem!"

"Fuckin' right there ain't!"

It was decided then and there that they would take every job that the other crews could leave for them. They'd do anything, without complaint or reservation. They were invincible!

Zak had great ideas.

They all had great ideas.

They would stick together forever.

They would see the world together! They would stay with Jesse as long as they could. They were the sons he never had. He was their father and mentor, their sage and guru. They'd go work up in Alaska with him, take him offshore in Texas. Then they'd save up their dough and head for the Middle East. They'd rough-neck the world over. There was no rig too big! The North Sea! Australia! Russia! Fuck! The possibilities were endless.

Those next few weeks flew by. Jesse would stand in the doorway smoking a cigarette and let each roughneck take a turn at that brake handle during connections. It meant a lot to Marty, who wanted to drill someday. But for Jon and Zak it was useful to just get the feel for what that driller's needs were in a crewman. If he was feeling frisky Jesse would actually go out on the floor and take one of the vacant positions while this was going on. They were the envy of the rig. They had the whole rig fired up! Rory's crew, those Parker Brothers, even Archer and his boys stood a little taller in their presence. From Jesse and the boys there were no secrets. Jesse's crew would know everything that had happened on that rig in their absence from the very moment they stepped foot on location. Other crews became dependent on them. "Save it for the wonder boys," they would laugh when a difficulty arose. And all the while Jesse's boys worked shorthanded and couldn't have cared less.

George held each member of Jesse's crew with a kind of awe and openly admitted that he had never seen a crew take over a rig quite the way Jesse's had. That company hand smiled and tipped his hat to them each and every time he saw one of them.

About four in the morning during one drilling tower, Zak entered the top doghouse to see Frank Kramer, that company hand, George Cleaver, and Jesse Lancaster all standing around drinking coffee. They had obviously been having a serious discussion and had just about exhausted whatever topic they were on. While Zak poured himself a cup, Jesse broke the silence.

"Shit Franklin, I've been doin' this all my life. If you've got the pipe, I can send 'er down the hole."

"I believe ya, Jess, but I don't know," Frank was leaning against a locker staring into his coffee cup which he swirled around in a gentle circle. "I got no problems with Jesse taking us deeper. If he says he knows how to rack the extra pipe, well, that I'd actually like to see. It's them other drillers I'm afraid of. That drill stem is mighty heavy as it is. I don't know how much more this ol' rig'll take."

"Well, she's built for ten thousand feet. We're pushin' that right now," George reminded them.

"Rory and Andy can get 'er," Jesse said quietly. "Hell, my trailer's right out front, I'm right here. I can keep an eye on it."

"Yeah, what's the story on this Archer Hansom?" Frank asked, using his official company hand voice.

"Hey, we needed a crew," George shrugged. "The other boys've had to cover for'm from time to time. But out here, well, shit."

"Jesse?" Frank asked.

"Handling all that extra weight is tricky but not impossible. We could try it for a couple of days."

"Maybe someone could switch days off with Hansom's crew," Zak jumped in, "that way they'd be out of our hair."

"That's a thought," Frank said, chewing on a thumbnail. "What I'd really like is a week though."

"I don't know," George shook his head. The politics of giving one crew early days off because they aren't up to snuff made him shudder. He could hear Smoke Denton already.

"Look," Jesse said at last, "let's give 'er a try one tower at a time. If anybody's going to make a trip, come and get me. I'll drop in on each of the drillers during their tower and if things look like they might go haywire, we'll just stop. We can take 'er slow and easy."

In the following days Zak would look up into that tower and listen to the structure groan every time Jesse picked up on that brake handle. They racked pipe where no one would believe pipe would go. Jesse and Marty would hold long strategy sessions on just where to set that extra pipe aside. And they got two thousand feet more than Bomac 34 was supposed to give.

Jesse was happiest of all. The night after they tore down the rig and loaded 'er up to be moved to the next location there was a party at Zak's shack. Nearly everyone was there and everyone got completely smashed. Jesse Lancaster put his arm around Smoke Denton and waved a glass at George, "Hey Rusty!"

George ambled over, smiling at the older driller and pretending not to have heard the name, "Yeah old-timer?"

"You see them three prick-a-lutes standin' over there all in a row having themselves a piss?"

"Yeah."

"Well them three sons ah bitches, them's the best fuckin' crew on this rig, them's the best fuckin' crew in this here patch, and them's the best fuckin' crew I ever had."

And it couldn't be argued.

That's why it hurt so bad several nights later, after they had nippled up northeast of town in the Medicine Basin, the day after bottom-hole checks were issued for the previous hole, when Zak and Jon tumbled into the bottom doghouse laughing and full of it and ready to go to work, to find Marty and Cynthia sitting expressionless, and George, wearing overalls, boots, work gloves, and a hard hat. Worst of all was his death-mask expression as he announced coldly, "Jesse's twisted off. This time for good. I'm yer driller tonight."

XIII

There was just no outward rhyme or reason for it. But his trailer was gone. His locker was empty. He had even taken his smokes and the bottle of Black Velvet everyone pretended not to notice from under the knowledge box.

Jon just exhaled softly and stepped out onto the floor. It was over. From now on it was just another job, just another rig. Just like that.

Zak bounced from Marty to George full of questions, as though some overlooked detail could be revealed that would prove that it wasn't true; that Jesse had just gone to town, that a simple explanation would put everything back the way it was. It was a mistake, that's all, but they only shrugged as if to say, *That's life in the patch, no big deal, we'll get by.* Only Cynthia had a mind to express what they were all feeling. It was in her eyes, her tone of voice.

"He come in this mornin' and asked me to get our things out from his trailer. Then he just drove away. Marty was in town. He left me standing in the mud with all our stuff."

She looked at Zak, who stood there stunned, deflated, without his happy noise. Instead of coming back to her with his usual encouraging words, he fell in line and followed the others as they trudged through the door and took their positions out on the floor. The men yelled a few angry yet necessary things back and forth to each other. Cold night air filled the top doghouse where Cynthia sat. She pulled her heavy sweater tight around herself and rubbed her arms to keep warm.

Out on the floor, bright overhead lights cast many tiny shadows at the feet of every object. The ringing engines pierced her ears like a fire alarm everyone pretended not to hear. The hard canvas weather walls, stretching up from the perimeter of the floor, created a box in which they all were placed. Those walls provided a neutral blue backdrop that made the space appear to shrink the more she watched. She wished they would roll them up as they sometimes did when it was hot out and the air was still.

They waited while Marty climbed the tower. Cynthia waited too. She waited right there in her chair. Tonight she would watch them work. She felt that there was nowhere else for her to be, even though Marty suggested she sleep in the Bronco with the radio on. She watched from her chair. She would know when her man was doing something important by the way those on the floor depended on movements from above. She watched George, at Jesse's station, his neck craned back, watching her man climb his mighty tower.

Marty would tell her stories at night to put her to sleep. He would tell her about climbing the ladder. Higher and higher until everything below got iddy-biddy. She would gasp in fear for him and he would assure her that the safety belt he wore on the way up made it impossible for him to get hurt. He would tell her about reaching the top. About standing at the top and taking a big drink of air. Shoulders back. Chest out. Looking out across the land and feeling like a giant. Like he could reach down and pick up Jesse's trailer and peep inside to see what she might be doing. Then he would lift the covers and peep inside and say devilishly, "And what are we doing?" She, however, would want him to finish the story. Her man, on top of the world. Then he would take another deep breath. He would walk along the perforated iron catwalk to his position, fasten his safety belt, and wave down to the driller below—he was ready. Ready to jam those long needles into the belly of the world and pump out its blood. "Like a big mosquito!" Blood for us to live on. Blood for us to dream on.

The rig rumbled and she jumped in her chair, startled. George had his right hand on the brake handle. His other hand grabbed one of the many levers of different length at his left and yanked it back and forth. The huge machine in which their fragile bodies worked and breathed began to move. For a crazy moment she closed her eyes and imagined George about to drive the rig out into the great big nowhere beyond the lights of the rig compound, slowly at first, until they could pick up the trail of Jesse Lancaster's escape and follow him home.

When those eight hours were over and relief was milling about the top doghouse, when George waved Marty down from the tower and the men exchanged places out on the floor, George's crew found Cynthia, sleepy but awake, still sitting in her chair, waiting.

THE MEN OUT ON THE loud loud floor worked in the silence of their independent thoughts. Together, those same thoughts occurred to each: that George was a good driller, that he lacked the fast clean touch that Jesse had. George also lacked the sense of mirth and playfulness that Jesse brought to his lively machinations. That pipe didn't talk to them the way it used to. It was just hard cold iron in a hurry. But George got it done.

Before very long the all-for-one-one-for-all-throw-us-your-worst-we-don't-care attitude on Jesse's crew evaporated.

Drudgery floated down on everyone like a soft smothering volcanic ash. Over the course of the coming weeks, if they arrived on location to find that Archer's boys had racked the pipe carelessly, or let the mud get too thin, or had perpetrated some other petty malfeasance, Zak and the rest would put it right before beginning their chores, but it was a nuisance. The work was hard, the extra work made it harder. The boys began to grumble. After tower, they went their separate ways.

Marty, who had had to take Cynthia back home to Watford and leave her there, was staying with Jon and Zak at the hotel and none too happy about it. Every time he called home there was some crisis or other that had Cynthia in hysterics. The thermostat was broke. The walk to and from the grocery store was too far for her to carry her bags. She was afraid to be alone. Little noises kept her up all night in terror. In one week, Marty had driven back to Watford after tower on three separate occasions only to learn that whatever crisis had brought him home had sprung entirely from Cynthia's head. As a result he got no sleep. And this had Marty edged. The boys began to worry that in his fatigue and crankiness, Marty might slip up during a trip, or make the kind of mistake that can cost a roughneck dearly. Marty was so intense and committed that the others said nothing to his face, but everyone had to be on their toes at all times. The added tension was something else they didn't need.

WHEN DAYS OFF ROLLED AROUND, Zak loaded up the Jeep and headed out for Watford City, North Dakota. He hoped to find a worm to take their shorthanded slot, maybe even a driller so George could get back to pushing tools. He also hoped to see Jesse Lancaster.

Before leaving Scobey he thought of recruiting Jon for the trip to Watford, but decided against it, and stopped in at Sam's for some breakfast instead.

"Will you try to bring him back?" she asked thoughtfully, considering Jesse, and Zak's mission, from a safe distance.

"No."

"That's smart," she said retaining her tone of passive interest. "It's important, I think, for you to step into Jesse's world for a brief time."

"What do you mean?"

"I mean from his world it may be useful for you to glimpse your own."

The more he thought about this last remark, the more it pissed him off. All the way down to Watford he turned it around in his brain. Neither Jon nor Marty were in a position to strike out and go exploring for the team. George had clearly failed. Jon was preoccupied with Mary Ellen and Marty would be spending all of his days off calming Cynthia's ruffled feathers Zak was sure.

But Jesse's world? Zak's world? What about'm? Business is business, after all, and right now business was a shambles. What about *our* world? What about *our* crew? What about the great thing we had going? Hadn't Jesse worked all his life to get a crew as fine as this? Jesse was the glue that held it all together. Not just on his own crew, but the entire complement of workers on Bomac 34 were, in one way or another, swept up in and beholden to the camaraderie and ethic that had been pouring off that floor at any given time. You could feel it. Even among Hansom's boys. Not only on the rig, but hell, you could feel it in town! Everyone, it seemed, was holding their head just a little higher. Other rigs were moving into the area and as the population of oil people grew, it was clear that those roughnecks on Bomac were the go-to guys in this corner of the oil patch. It appeared to be welcomed, too. Hell! People were happy. Jesse was happy, he couldn't deny that. Doesn't happiness count for something? That's why it made no sense. Zak then had to admit to himself that one reason he wanted to see Jesse was to make him feel guilty. To make Jesse look him in the eye and tell him he was twistin' off, tossing it all away for his own reasons which he hadn't shared with anyone. This wasn't just another rig, just another crew. Zak refused to believe that.

THE PRAIRIE STRETCHED OUT ENDLESSLY in all directions.

At first the eyes rejoice at the comprehension of such vast dimensions. It just feels so good to be able to take in so much; not only the mere physical pleasure of seeing so very far but the added realization that there is so much potential in a world. Before long, however, the soul aches for something to fill the void. Something beautiful, or something made beautiful because it functions so well within its proper space; something to fit together within this vast empty landscape in a harmony of fulfilled purposes. Something as magnificent as the open spaces themselves imply. Eventually each bump in the terrain is a call to celebration. Each distant weather pattern a welcomed, studied, yearned-for thing.

But those things can also seem so random, so rare. Before long they only serve to accent the loneliness. Without that some-thing, something that fits, a form of spiritual starvation sets in. Whose world is this anyway? Zak slammed a palm against the steering wheel. He pictured Jesse in a world in which no iron towers pierced the horizon and saw a frail, quiet, lame old man with a giant heart wearily pulling a long train of experience that stretched backwards into a distance that was only discernible in the movements and disturbances of the here and now. Was it fair to Jesse not to be allowed permission to stop the train? Was it fair for the train to insist he keep pulling?

No. It was all wrong.

Zak thought about Jon's world, shaping a life out of the bang and bustle of the oil patch, in spite of everything.

He thought of Marty's world. Standing alone atop the iron tower holding the slender threads of Cynthia's sanity in his crude, powerful, and yet unpredictable hands.

The fire that drove Zak onward in the direction of Watford City slowly burned out. The Jeep slowed to a crawl.

A question came creeping up on him like the unexpected betrayal of a friend. When his right tires nudged the gravel shoulder, he pulled over. He thought about turning back. There were, after all, immediate problems that needed solving. With another paycheck or two he could latch onto someone down in Watford. Hell, he could say fuck it right now and continue on to Watford and if he fell into something down there, well so be it. Why go back at all? Over is over. Through is through. If the others weren't concerned about keeping it together, why the hell should he? And shouldn't that tell him something?

He got out of the Jeep and leaned against the right fender. He wished he had a cigarette. The wind that whipped his face stung his eyes. Jon had Mary Ellen. Marty had Cynthia. Jesse had whatever demons possessed him. In the distance, dozens of miles off, a lone dull brown butte jutted up giving the horizon an uneven, jagged edge. In the giant sky, a single wisp of cloud looked like a smear of white paint on a pale blue canvas. And Zachary Harper had to face the facts.

There is no my world. He was moving between worlds. So it made sense that he found himself standing here, in the middle of nowhere, between not only the separate worlds of his fellows but amidst a constellation of worlds, each one nascent and unformed, each one needing only the seed of his intentions to alight for a world to congeal around him and make him, or claim him as its own. He had been resisting such a commitment lest he be swallowed up too soon, opting for the ephemeral over the telluric, to buy time, to gain experience, understanding, and the kind of self-knowledge these others seemed born with. How handicapped and insufficient was he? He had always relied on his instincts regarding when to move and with how much force, but he realized now he was not without his doubts. Those doubts were getting loud, impatient, and angry. Every time they paraded his insecurities out into the open for him to face in the cold aloneness of this place, his shame pushed them back into the dark corners where he felt they belonged.

The prairie does strange things to a man's mind. It calls upon him to fill this space with his own true self, and he would just have to wait and see what kind of creature that was. One thing he was coming to realize, however, was that someone not at peace with that self ought to take care how much time he or she spends alone with it.

He sighed and looked in both directions down the long empty highway. He took a piss, then hurried on in the direction of Watford City.

AS HE PASSED THE OLD Watford Cemetery northeast of town, as he passed the makeshift buildings of the various drilling companies and support businesses that lined the highway at the outskirts, as he rumbled and rolled past pickups loaded with crews some of whom nodded their heads when they saw him, as other Jeep drivers gave him the wave of friendly recognition from the oncoming lane, his spirits brightened. This is familiar. This place recognizes me. God, it felt good to be back.

Watford was rockin'.

Pickups, Broncos, and rugged four-wheels of every stripe jammed Main Street. It was midafternoon and all the bars were full. Not only the Sagebrush and the City Bar where the rough-necks hung out, but also Duffy's and Bitchin' Bob's across the street, where the local boys who did not care to mingle with the newcomers had retreated to, were overflowing as well. Every shop was filled with oilmen and locals. It was startling how the pace had picked up in just a few weeks. The contrast with peaceful little Scobey was remarkable. Watford, itself only five blocks long, seemed huge. On the south side of town the City Park had been turned into a trailer park that had the look of a small town all by itself. Dozens of trailers jammed in, practically touching one another. The busy pace that had marked the town before had by now ratcheted up a couple of notches to a full-blown frenzy. The excitement was breathable, electric, visible.

Zak pulled up in front of the City Bar and hesitated. There were no parking spaces and as he looked up and down the street, he realized he was directly across from the Watford City Post Office. Remembering that Calico had said he should check from time to time in case he needed to get in touch, Zak decided to park around the corner and have a look-see.

With so many roughnecks of no fixed address in town, the little old lady at the counter directed Zak to two large plastic bales in the back room marked General Delivery and told him he could go fish for himself. Neatly piled up in alphabetical order, he found the bundle marked *H* and right there on top he found two letters addressed to Zachary Harper, General Delivery, Watford City, North Dakota, 58854.

One was from Calico and the other from Jacqueline Loraine.

He had to think for a minute to place the name. He skipped, giggled, and danced out to the Jeep where he could read in private. Light on his feet he detoured into the pharmacy next door where he without a trace of conscience bought himself a pack of cigs. He tore it open like a starving man with a loaf of bread. Once in the Jeep, he tore open Jackie's letter the same way.

"A message in a bottle," she called it. He laughed. He lit up. She knew he was bound for Watford City, he had told her that much, and reason had it that he would at some point check his mail. Amazing. The letter was postmarked a month earlier but still, after reading just one line, he held the pages to his nose on the off chance that some of her might still linger there. He was sure it did. She was already sick of school, sick of her studies, sick of the boys who chased her around campus. She was sick of her lame-ass professors, well, that wasn't true, some of them were nice, anyway, the point was that if he wanted he could make the trek east to see her some weekend, that is, if he wasn't dead. But come to think of it, he couldn't be any deader than her social life in Morris, Minnesota, so even if he was dead, he should come see her anyway. Or maybe they could meet in the middle for a couple of days? In the bottom of the envelope he found two kernels of corn. One had a happy face drawn on it, the other sad.

The whole town was crawling with life. Supertramp was blaring on somebody's car stereo as they rocked down the street. He read the letter two or three times more and could feel his old self waking up, shaking off the horrors of the past weeks, especially of the past few days, as the blood flowed back into his vital organs.

Calico's letter was short and to the point. There was a guy named Lou Crawford, Crawdad to his friends, heading for Watford at Calico's recommendation. Lou was in a bit of a jam and needed some safe space and a place to work for a while till he could sort out his problems. He ought to make a good hand and he promised to behave himself. If Zak could find something for him it would be greatly appreciated. Zak could leave word for Lou at the PDQ Club in Arnegard. As far as school went he'd damn near twisted off several times, but figured he hadn't killed anybody yet so he might as well stick with it. One thing was sure though, them books were harder than any iron he'd ever seen. The first week there he hired someone to teach him how to study. He claimed it saved his life.

"I've taken some worm bites, but I'll be all right!" was how he closed, which made Zak smile from ear to ear.

Zak was ready for a drink. Instead of walking across to the City Bar as planned, he fired up the Jeep, turned right down Main and, as he passed a bunch of roughnecks coming the other way, he leaned out the window and screamed, "Yaaaaahoooo!" to which they answered with war whoops, hollers, and epithets of their own with a few choice horn blasts thrown in! Daylights must be just getting off, he thought. Before leaving town Zak jerked the wheel in the direction of Blackie's place, cruised by the house, but there were no signs of life. Damn. He scribbled a quick note saying he was in town looking for hands and stuck it in the door. He then turned right again off Main on the road to Arnegard. He passed the McKenzie Inn—No Vacancy—the Burger Ranch, and the Captain's Table, all of which he'd never noticed before, all jammed with roughnecks, chowing and boozing and raising hell.

Twenty miles or so down the road was Arnegard. There was no sign, and he didn't need one to tell him to turn right off the highway and cruise down the wide dead-end thoroughfare that led past several establishments and houses to a grain elevator at the end of the street. The PDQ Club, near the end of the boulevard on the left, had the look and feel of an old-fashioned cowboy saloon. It too was jammed. He created a parking space at the end of a row of pickups parked like horses tied to a railing. He hurried up the wooden ramp leading to the bar, his boots making a classic movie Western sound of leather on wood. Cowboys with barrel chests, thick necks, leathery faces with brilliant eyes and tall ten-gallon hats, farmers, rednecks, and roughnecks were three deep at the bar which was tended by the prettiest girl he had seen since hitting the Dakotas. She was average height with long blonde hair in a ponytail at the side of her head, wearing very tight blue jeans and a cowboy shirt tied in a knot at her belly button. This she wore over a halter top that did little more than push her very large bust up and out, creating what had to be the most spectacular cleavage within hundreds of miles. Zak plucked a five-dollar bill from the wad in his pocket and wormed his way to the bar. When at last he had her attention, he ordered a bottle of Miller High Life. She leaned forward reaching into the cooler, displaying those fabulous breasts with gusto and then standing took an opener which hung around her neck on a leather cord, popped the top, and slammed the bottle down on the bar, causing a foamy ejaculation rising at the top. "Ooops!" she giggled with a smile that was all dimples, "I think it likes me!" she said and swiping off the foam with a finger, stuck her finger in her mouth and gave Zachary Harper a wink that nearly knocked him off his feet. She ripped the bill from his grip and was gone.

"Holy shit!" Zak gasped.

"Best bar in town," said a guy sittin' on the stool next to him.

"I can see why," Zak agreed.

"Of course, it's the only bar in town," said his neighbor, deadpan, following the barkeep as she dashed to and fro.

Zak was thinking that if he didn't get laid right away he was going to have to break something. He looked around the bar and wondered if all these guys really thought they had a chance with her. Sure they did. It was the only thing keeping the peace. While he had this fella's attention, he figured he'd get down to business. "I know a rig that needs hands. Anyone around here lookin' for work?"

"Sure," the fella perked up, "where at?"

"Up in Scobey."

"Where?"

"Just over in Montana."

"Ferget it," the guy went back to studying the bartender.

When she returned with his change, Zak threw a dollar on the bar and asked, "You wouldn't have heard of a fella named Lou Crawford would ya?"

She stopped and struck a classic let-me-think-about-it pose, a hand on one hip, her eyes dancing up to the ceiling. She held the pose for about one-hundredth of a second, long enough to get four more at the bar to fall in love with her. "Nope! But my mom might. She's in the dining room," and she was off again twisting at the waist as she went, turning heads like at a tennis match.

Zak shook his head and he exhaled softly. The guy next to him was laughing quietly, his shoulders rocking under a leather vest, crows feet stretching all the way into his greasy hair.

Zak stepped away from the bar and his space was instantly filled by a fella who was downing his beer hurriedly so he could have the excuse to order another.

In the dining room, a line of people were at the salad bar, and older waitresses in black uniforms with white blouses were hurrying about with plates of steaks, potatoes, and watery vegetables. A handsome woman in her early fifties wearing a purple Old West gown that ballooned at the hips and reached all the way to the tops of her lace-up boots, with big satin roses in her reddish gray hair tied at the back, stepped in front of him and said with a smile, "Welcome to the PDQ Club, would you like some dinner?"

By the size of her bust and her very congenial manner this just had to be Mom. When Zak explained his mission, she was delighted to hear it.

"So you're the infamous Zak! I'm Lottie McCutcheon. What's taken you so long to find us? Yeah, that fella's been comin' in here all week. We were wondering if he hadn't made you up!" She laughed and gave Zak a pad and marker and suggested he leave his friend a note where he could be reached and pin it to the bulletin board in the hallway between bar and restaurant.

CRAWDAD! Go to Scobey Montana! There's a job for you on Bomac 34. Ask for it at the Pioneer Hotel, Zak wrote. He also included the toolpusher's phone number. As Zak was leaving, Mom called out. "Zak! There's a band here seven nights a week. Come back and have some fun!"

"I will!"

FROM THERE HE CONTINUED BACK to Watford and cruised about the little neighborhoods on either side of Main. On the western side of town, just a block or two from the police station and the courthouse, he passed a small gray house and there in the drive was Jesse's trailer.

Although the house was dark and Jesse's Merc was nowhere to be seen, someone was home. How did he know? He mulled this over as he walked to the door. Much the same way he had known there was no one home at Blackie's. He pushed the doorbell and, hearing nothing, he knocked three times.

"All right!" a voice spat from the other side of the door. It was a young male voice. Definitely irritated. Like some spoiled kid who has been told to turn off the TV and do his homework. Zak waited for the door to open. The voice spat out again, more irritated than before. "Well, what do you want?"

"Is Jesse around?"

Zak could hear hushed anxious voices; Jesse clearly wasn't here. Zak wanted to leave.

"What?"

"Look, my name is Zak, I'm a friend of Jesse's. Is he in? Could you open the door a second?"

There was more hushed conversation and then the door cracked open. A man in his early twenties with dark unkempt hair and a bad complexion stared out at him. He had Jesse's bushy black eyebrows, and a sullen unhappy look. *Lenny*, Zak thought. "Look, I've been workin' with Jesse up north, and we were all a bit worried…" Zak was interrupted by a voice that barked at the young man from behind the door.

"Open the fuckin' door, and let's get a look at the son of a bitch!"

The young man made a face, as if to say to Zak *Now look what you've done*, and pulled the door open.

Zak stepped inside.

As his eyes adjusted to the dark, it was the smell that assailed him first. Dirty laundry, old kitchen garbage, and urine. Cat urine, then human urine. The only light was that which forced itself through a shade on the living room window and a TV that flickered but with the sound turned off.

She sat in a wheelchair. Stringy black and gray hair clung to her pale face and fell over her soiled nightgown. She motioned with her head to the young man, who interpreted the command and dutifully, if grudgingly, moved around behind her and pushed her chair up close to where Zak was standing. Her black eyes considered him through a mocking sneer. Her teeth badly needed tending. Her body was inert though her head and neck held such a posture of excitement and loathing that Zak took a step backward and immediately tried to formulate an excuse to leave.

"No no, you get back here," she said. Her voice was wet and raspy, her wind strained. In spite of her afflictions, she spoke soothingly, as though coaxing some poor starving dog closer, so she could feed it poison. "Come, come here, that's right." He had to lean close to hear her and that proximity was truly unpleasant. "That's better. Let me look at you. Good. It's not every day I get to see a real, live, walking, talking piece of shit. Welcome."

"Ma'am," Zak was a bit more than startled, he straightened. "Look, I didn't mean to bother you, I think I'd better..."

"Sure you did," she said in a voice dripping with false empathy, a tone that she slipped in and out of with such dizzying weirdness it was chilling. "Since when did any of you pricks give a rat's ass about bothering anyone? Hmm? Any time of the day, or night? No no, no. You stay where you are, and you listen here. Jesse's finally got hisself a real fuckin' job, for the first time in his life, what's left of it, poor dear, and neither you or any of yer prick-a-lute friends are gonna come around to fuck it up. Hear?"

"We were just concerned, that's all, I..."

"We? Who's we?" She craned her head left and right to see if maybe there were some others just outside. "Oh, you must have brought a turd in yer pocket. Hmm? Now, was it you was concerned? Well, fuck you! The only concern, any of you arse-holes have is where yer next piece of tail and yer next drunk is comin' from! Huh? Now isn't that right? Of course it is. Where was yer goddamned concern when Jesse was out whorin' and boozin' and callin' it work, all them years, while I was raisin' a fuckin' kid and tryin' to scrape by on the table scraps he sent home, what he hadn't already drunk up? Huh? Answer me that, now. Concerned. Please kiss my ass. Concerned. You probably got a little girlie stashed away somewhere's yerself, an' yer no more concerned about her than you are some stupid, half-lame old man. Hmmm? Fuck you. Please?"

"Ma'am," Zak couldn't think. As he leaned in all he could see was her feet, which were bare, bone white, her toenails yellow and long. He wanted to say something in defense of the old man. He couldn't believe how miserable and wrong about him she was. "Jesse's one of the most respected…"

"Respected? Jesse? You shut yer lyin', fuckin' mouth! And you show a little respect for those who know better'n you. Nothin' any of you cocksuckers sez is worth a fuck. Do you know that? Hmmm? Who really, I ask you, has any respect, for a dried-up old man who's pissed his life away? Huh? *You?* Well, now, there's an accomplishment. Did Jesse earn *your* respect? My, how lucky we all are. An' you came all the way here from shitville to tell us? My, my. Listen here. If he really worked all them years, where's 'is pension? Hmmm? Where's 'is savings? Look at us. Look at this piece of shit hole we live in. This is what you and yer goddamned bullshit comes to!" *She was getting to him, she could tell and with this realization she gained confidence, momentum, and strength. She wanted to twist the knife. Yes. What she was saying was reaching this one. It felt too good. His face had fallen. Yes. He was listening. Really listening. To the truth. Her truth. The only truth allowed in this house!*

Zak took a cautionary step backward, and Lenny inched the chair closer.

Her loose limbs suddenly found life, strength, and a bony arm reached out and her long fingers gripped his shirt collar and pulled him down till his ear was at her lips.

"Tell me somethin', arsehole, what kind of a job calls itself roughneck? Have you ever given that a thought? Hmmm?" He could feel the Moisture from her rotten lungs spraying his inner ear. "Huh? Answer me that!" she hissed. And here she slipped back into that matronly sympathetic tone one might save for a sick child. Releasing her grip on his collar, her slippery hand slinking back under her filthy blanket. "It'd be like having a job callin' itself loser, or hooligan, whoremaster, or grave robber. Fuck you," she said sweetly, as though saying "there, there." "Roughneck!" she suddenly spat, full venom returning. "That's a laugh'n a half!"

Then she wagged her head in a mock impersonation of a youthful, prideful man, "'Lookit me, honey, *I'm a roughneck!*'" A youthful prideful man turned inside out. "'Yes sir-ee. No one can tell *me* where t'go or what t'do! *I'm a roughneck*. We're goin' places, *sugar!* We're makin' *money!!* So's we can git *outta* here!!! You'n *me, baaaby!!!!*'" This last she hissed so loudly it sent her into a full-tilt blue-faced coughing fit.

"Mom," Lenny broke in, sounding truly frightened.

"Shut up! You goddamned useless tit! Yer as bad or worse'n any of'm," and returning her attention to Zak, she cut to the chase. "Listen, mister, you get yer fuckin' ass outta here and down the road, and you tell yer worthless roughneck friends that Jesse Lancaster has twisted off, once and for all, an' he ain't never comin' back, understand? Now fuck off! And don't you, nor any of yer kind, ever come around here no more." She coughed several times more right in Zak's face, her black eyes locked on his, her face turning red and her eyes filling with water. She spat whatever it was she coughed up at Zak's feet, hitting his steel toe with a thwack. And then she looked up at him with a yearning doleful pitiable expression, as though she expected him, or wanted him, to hit her. And when he didn't, she smiled.

Zak staggered from the house. He gulped fresh air as he dragged the toe of his boot on the grass. He was disgusted and angry with himself for listening to her for so long. When he got to the Jeep, he rummaged through the back for a paper towel and, holding his breath, wiped the bloody mucus off his shoe and tossed the paper onto the drive. When he backed out of the drive, he nearly hit a car coming down the street, stomping on the brakes just in time.

Lenny's sullen face peered after him through the living room shade as Zak roared away.

More than her words, her image and the stench of that place, that corner of hell, kept coming back quick as he could chase it away. He parked around the corner from the City Bar and tried to get a grip. He checked himself in the mirror. His glasses were crooked. His hair was dirty. His eyes had a strange off-center look. Like he was insane. He gripped the steering wheel with both hands until his knuckles turned white. He closed his eyes and put his forehead to the steering wheel. He desperately tried to think of something else, faraway places where people either didn't care or actually believed that the oil and gas they burned in their cute little cars and cozy little houses arrived by magic in the middle of the night, requiring only sufficient funds in one's account at the end of the month to keep it coming. He wanted to be anywhere they might have done away with or surpassed this ugly stage of human development. He wanted to be anywhere but Watford City, North Dakota. He wanted to wear nice clothes. To see people meet and greet. He wanted to listen in on conversations about books, or art, or money, or sporting events. But even if he could transport himself to a place like that he wouldn't, he couldn't. Not with these clothes, this hair, this face, these eyes.

IT WAS LATE AFTERNOON. A warm beam of sunlight passed down the street chased by a cold dark cloud. Pickup trucks and cars jerked and nudged impatiently by. Engines revved. Voices mingled. A din was rising all around him not unlike the constant harangue of a drilling platform. And everyone looked just like him. Worn, dirty, tired, and more than a little crazy.

An elderly woman walked slowly up the street. She had a pleasant face and new blue beauty parlor hair. She wore a well-cared-for beige winter coat. In one hand she carried a small handbag. In her other hand she carried her mail. She stopped at the curb and, tucking her letters under her arm, she opened her purse and, as she waited for the traffic to clear, she touched up her lipstick. She did it perfectly, without having to see herself in a mirror. She put her lipstick back in her purse and crossed the street with a measured, confident step. A pickup truck glided to a stop a respectful distance from her, allowing her to pass without having to break her proprietary stride. At the other side of the street another woman stepped out of a shop door and they had a brief and amiable chat.

Once at home she would put on a pot of tea and sit at an old family coffee table and read her mail. Her house would be clean and quiet with finely polished oak and cedar furnishings. A miniature Big Ben on the mantle over the fireplace would chime on the quarter hour while its smooth swinging brass pendulum counted off the seconds. Handmade lace doilies would rest on the worn arms of comfy chairs in the living room. On a bureau or a wall would be a framed black-and-white photograph of a middle-aged man wearing a benign smile. Somewhere else, Jesus, brown-skinned with long hair and fine gentle features, staring up toward heaven. In her backyard, the soil from her summer garden would be turned. In the pantry would be jars of tomatoes and delicious things for winter broths and stews. In just a little while it would be time for her to start supper.

"MARTY!" CYNTHIA SHRIEKED WHEN SHE saw Zak through the window in the door. He could hear her footsteps hurrying off to find her husband. Zak shook his head. Why, he wondered, did she have to get Marty to open the door instead of opening it herself? He still felt shaky over his encounter with Mrs. Lancaster and in this hypersensitive state wasn't in the mood for any more weirdness. He suddenly wished he had gone somewhere else.

"Hey." Marty pulled open the door, turned and humped back into the kitchen where he had a bunch of tools spread out on the floor. He lay down on his back and resumed fixing something under the sink, grunting and huffing. He was doing a job. Cynthia stood there clutching her hands in front of her, blushing and smiling. "I'll be dun wit dis in a sec," Marty said, and went back to wrenching on a pipe. "Git yerself a beer."

For an awkward few moments Zak sat with Cynthia in the living room. There was a velvet landscape on the paneled wall over a velvet-covered couch. The TV was on so loud you couldn't hear yourself think.

"Nice to have Marty home, huh?" Zak shouted.

"Yes, but I hate it when he works. He's gone so long. It's scary here. Things get broke."

"Yeah," Zak sympathized. "Has the sink been broke long?" He heard himself starting to talk like her and shuddered quietly.

"And the phone rings. I don't answer."

He nodded matter-of-factly. Well, of course not.

"'Less I knowed it's Marty. We got a special signal." She frowned, wondering if she hadn't just betrayed her man by telling Zak their secret. "He gets so upset when things go wrong. The sink got broke too."

Zak shook his head, unable to think of a thing to say. He drank his beer.

Mercifully, Marty strolled in with a beer and plopped himself down in his La-Z-Boy recliner. He grabbed the remote from its place on the arm of the chair and turned down the sound. "So Zak, what're you up to?"

"I don't know. I had nothing to do up there in Scobey so I thought I'd come down here and see if maybe I could scare up a hand or two for George."

"Yeah? What for? Dat's Rusty's fuckin' job. You should be pushin' tools on dat fuckin' rig," Marty rocked back and forth, agitated, edged. "Dat's Rusty's gottdamned job!" he shook his head.

"Well," Zak shrugged, "I just came from Jesse's place, whew, have you ever met that wife of his?"

"Nope. He always told us to stay away. I hear she's fuckin' nuts or somethin'."

"Well, I wish someone had warned me. Goddamn, that's the scariest thing I've ever seen." They were unimpressed, and Zak didn't feel up to doing an impression sufficient to make them understand what had just happened to him. He wasn't sure himself.

They walked into town and stopped at the diner. Four things were on the menu: Fried chicken, fried liver and onions, fried steak, and fried fish. All entrées came with French fried potatoes and canned or frozen vegetables. Zak ordered the liver, just because it was nasty, and he felt nasty. It occurred to him that back East he always ordered at a restaurant things he wouldn't have at home. He'd go out to eat for something special. Here, in the heart of cattle and produce land, this is what there was to eat. No wonder everybody's having heart attacks, he grumbled. The liver was delicious. It was appalling.

All evening, Marty talked on and on about who was who and what was what, but all Zak could see and hear was Mrs. Jesse Lancaster. He tried to see her as a young beautiful woman. As a lonely wife with a man who worked away from home. As a mother. And every path, each scenario, led her to this, a wounded soul, a bitter vindictive heap of decaying flesh. And yet, still, with the end so clearly near, with all her resources either gone or broken or spoiled, the battle was still mightily engaged. There would be no surrender, not to the bitter end. He could see the scars she inflicted on Jesse and Lenny as tribute for the pain she felt they had inflicted on her. Lenny, tethered to his mother's disappointment, distrust, and loathing, fulfilling her prophesies by his subconscious incapacity to live up to his father's expectations. Her revenge.

There is no justice here. Zak wondered to himself if the very idea of justice wasn't a masculine thing—if men invented justice, a twisted rational with which they skewered the inequities of existence in their favor, and if women invented revenge, a quid pro quo where at least each doggie got its day. A masculine/feminine point/counterpoint built right into the spiral double helix, DNA, the law of opposites, the Way of the World.

Or maybe not.

Zak listened to the beefy beef-eaters all around him and this grotesque surrealism of American frontier images began to paint themselves in distorted lines and blending colors. A frontier that had never represented itself as anything but a bleak, barren, and dangerous place. And yet, somehow capable of containing and sustaining a fantastic illusion, superimposed over a more permanent landscape, the sole purpose of which is to mask the fact that all we, mankind, have done is channel our savageries in varying degrees of intensity and purpose. But through that painful effort, savagery becomes civil, and that is a process which can uplift a semiconscious being to a more perfect sentience. It was a lesson of the frontier. Any frontier. That things begin somewhere. But what an effort, and what pain. So much sacrifice for so little gain. And it didn't sit any better with Zachary Harper than the greasy meal he packed away there in the Watford City Diner, Watford City, North Dakota, United States of America, AD 1979.

THE TOWN WAS FULL TO overflowing, there would be no place to stay tonight. Zak accepted Marty's offer of hospitality, although he would have preferred heading for the PDQ Club, hearing a band, raising hell, and taking his chances. Instead, he stretched out on the couch in his sleeping bag.

Cynthia went to the back of the house to the laundry room and selected a stuffed animal from her collection to sleep with her and Marty that night. She giggled and laughed like a child as Marty held the nose of the big blue elephant around the corner to wish Zak a goodnight.

As the darkness enveloped him, as the sounds of the house died down, Zak lay awake thinking of the lady with the blue hair he had seen crossing the street that day and fantasized about being an ex-roughneck, older, her gardener and handyman, sleeping on a cot in a warm space, in a room she had fixed up just for him, out by the garage.

XIV

The next morning Zak awoke before dawn. The room was stuffy and dark. A clock somewhere ticked loudly. He was restless and most definitely wanted off that couch and out of that house. He sat up, pulled on his boots and, in the kitchen, found a paper towel and a pen and wrote a makeshift thank you note before letting himself out the kitchen door. Frost had settled on the lawns of Watford City. The Jeep roared to life, echoing through the quiet neighborhood, and Zak smiled devilishly as he escaped into town, wondering how many dreams he was interrupting and how many had merely incorporated his loud roar and rumble into their predawn vagaries.

In town all was quiet as well. Morning towers hadn't gotten off work yet, and as he drove down Main he chuckled to think that this was probably the only quiet time of day, those hours when the evening tower crews had had their fill of food and booze and before morning tower crews came roaring through town looking for the same thing. His sense of relief at leaving Marty's was suddenly upon him and, instead of going to the City Park, which had taken on the character of a gypsy camp, he found a dirt road west of town, past the little hospital and the schoolyard, and drove up onto a hilly overlook and sat there waiting for the sun to come up. He slept deeply, if for only forty-five minutes, but long enough to wake up feeling fresh.

"Zakko!" Freddy Fifer hollered when he saw Zak approaching through the trailer park, bottle of whiskey in a brown bag he rested on his shoulder like a musket.

Freddy was camped out in a big lawnchair under an awning that stretched out from his trailer door. It was an Indian summer day, probably the last day of the year that would be comfortable outside, and everyone was busy either partying or getting ready for the harsh weather that was just around the bend. Freddy was already juiced. He had a big box of beer at his side and his cast, which extended from above the knee to his toes, rested on a neatly folded blanket.

"Zakko and Franzetti! Zachary Dackary Dickary Doo! Haa ha haa!" Freddy bellowed in a great big voice. As Zak approached, laughing, Freddy dug into the beer box with a big chubby mitt and tossed a beer out to Zak, which he caught with his left hand. "Better get with it there, partner!" Freddy laughed. Zak sat down Indian style next to Freddy and popped the beer. Before they spoke another word, Freddy tilted his can back and, after chugging the rest of its contents, smacked his lips with a satisfied gasp and then gracefully tossed it up, basketball style, onto the canopy where it landed with a clang among several dozen others. "Skyhook!" he smiled and dove into the box to fetch another. Once they were on equal terms with fresh new beers, they were ready for a visit. Freddy was clearly something of a hero with the hundreds of roughnecks coming and going and they moved around him like some kind of monument.

"Christ! I think I know who you mean!" Freddy said in genuine horror, interrupting Zak's account of what had taken place at Jesse's the day before. "I've seen that spooky bitch at the clinic! She sets there and waits and gives ya the hairy eyeball like she's got a big ol' butcher knife under that blanket an' any second she's gonna get up outta that chair and start hackin' 'er way in to see the doctor. Scary shit! Not good. Uhhuhuhuh," he shuddered, his fat jowls rippling comedically. "You shoulda walloped that crazy ol' cunt when you had the chance!" In seconds he had Zak laughing so hard he wondered why in the world he hadn't stopped to see Freddy the first minute he hit town.

"I'm okay now, Zak," Freddy suddenly became serious when it was time to fill Zak in on the status of his leg. His big fat smile fell, and the flesh around his mouth got loose and watery like a frightened child. "But brother, this has been rough. All sorts of problems. The docs in Williston sent me down to the hospital in Rapid City and they said not only did I have all them breaks but there's what they call a spiral fracture running all the way up. The nerves are nuts. One day she's numb all over, the next there's like burning everywhere. Most days she just aches like hell. Then, shit, I'll be feeling like a million bucks and suddenly Whhooosh! I'll get a pain that's sharper'n a razor blade that sends me clear through the roof! I'm goin' in again in a few days so they can check on the new knee. Then after months of healing, I get months of some kind of therapy. They rebuilt the knee, reset the breaks, put pins in, pikes, screwplates, a total reconstruction job. I'm gonna be down and out quite some time and not looking forward to it. But hey!" he brightened, and from under his lawnchair he pulled a big plastic bag half full of urine with a tube that hung down and disappeared under the blanket on his lap. "Ain't this the greatest fuckin' thing you've ever seen? I never have to get up to piss! I can just drink beer all day! A nurse over at Rapid rigged it up for me. Said astronauts and drivers use'm on long hauls. It's like a rubber.

Fuckin' great!" Then lowering his voice, his eyebrows dashing upward, he said, "she put it right on my dick for me!"

Zak shook his head.

"Y'know what?" Freddy asked with a delighted smile. "Jesse comes t'see me every day. We play checkers. The ol' fuck is good too. Kicks my ass."

"I'd like to see'm."

WAY IN THE BACK OF the shop at Zeke's Auto Parts, sitting on a bench contentedly filing down a rusty bolt, sat a smallish man with dark hair and bushy black eyebrows. Jesse Lancaster held it up to the light which hung from a hook over his left shoulder. His fingers looked like ginger roots, the creases in which seemed permanently stained with grease and mud. His brown eyes grew wide as he assessed his progress, his eyebrows lifted, his square jaw dropped slightly, and he returned the bolt to his lap and filed some more. The sound of footsteps cautiously approaching made him lift his head in time to see Zachary Harper winding his way through the hulks of old cars and bulky machinery that lay strewn about everywhere. Jesse nodded his head and went back to his filing.

"Good mornin'," Zak said quietly, and sat down beside him.

Jesse nodded.

"How ya doin'?"

"Not bad. I guess you're wonderin' what I'm doin' settin' here filing down this old bolt?"

"Actually, I was just thinkin' that looks like just the thing you should be doin'."

"Oh?"

"I thought I'd come down here on days off to help George look for some hands. Have you seen Blackie?"

"Ah, so, figure you'll go pushin' tools now, eh?" Jesse gave one of his signature silent laughs, his shoulders bounced, his squinting eyes remained focused on the bolt in his lap. He considered Zak's request. "Blackie? Nope. Ain't seen'm. He's out West. Drillin' in Wyomin' somewheres." There was a silence, then Jesse asked, "How's old George like drillin' again?"

"He's crankier'n ever. He's good though. Not as good as you."

Jesse laughed silently once more, tickled at the thought of George at the brake handle, ready to get pissed at anyone or anything at anytime. "The boys?"

"They're grumblin'. Hansom's crew's still givin' us fits, but we're okay."

"Yeah, I figured you'd be all right, yer good hands. Hansom and them bunch'll only hang around for a paycheck or two, then they'll be out of yer hair." They sat for a few awkward seconds and then Jesse said, "Look Zak. My wife's real sick. Lenny, well, he won't hang around much longer and there won't be much I can do for him once he's gone. I kinda figure this is a time when I should be home."

"That makes sense."

"Just don't no one go over to the house no more, okay?"

"No problem there," Zak shook his head.

Jesse gave a wry smile, "So I gotta get this done, eh? Tell the boys to look me up when they come to town, I'll be here, or over at the City Bar. Oh, and one more thing. You tell ol' George to give Marty a shot at that brake handle when he gets a chance. Tell'm I said."

"Will do," Zak promised.

With that he went back to filing his bolt. He squinted his eyes and concentrated, his jaw set hard, gettin' 'er done, as though Zak had already gone.

And that was that, that was goodbye.

XV

Mary Ellen put on her favorite dress. A gold form-fitting affair with a textured weave that matched her wheat-colored hair and gave her figure a more rounded, more voluptuous look. The shoulder straps broadened, then cut strikingly down, and gathered up her breasts in snug, tantalizing bunches, leaving her collarbone and neck exposed.

She tried on a slender gold necklace, then decided against it. Tonight she was in the mood to feel a little naked.

She bought the dress at a second-hand store in Minneapolis two years ago and had worn it exactly once. Certainly nowhere in Scobey, Montana. It was perfect for a candlelight dinner date at home. She curled her hair to give it some bounce. She put on makeup. From a bag of shoes at the back of her closet, she dug out a pair of gold, black-soled sandals with just half a heel.

She was self-conscious about her imperfect skin. Every bump and blemish screamed out at her. And her daily ablutions of creams and oils softened but did not alter the fact that she tended to be pale and a little pockmarked here and there. But she was tanned and muscular from long summer walks, and the heavy lifting she sometimes had to do at the bar. Her color was good, she concluded, and after shaving her legs and trying on the dress, she decided to let her legs go bare as well. The stockings she had bought went unopened. Besides, what if he showed up looking like a roughneck?

She moved the small table her father had cut from the center of an old barn door from under the bedroom window and made of it a dinner table for two using her grandmother's handmade lace tablecloth. The old cloth had lain in a trunk so long it needed to hang over the railing of her apartment balcony all day so as to lose its musty smell. The stitching had come undone here and there, but it was still pretty, partly because it looked as old as it was. She left an unused pack of matches she had saved from a nightclub in Minneapolis next to the candle on the dinner table.

The chicken was almost ready. The vegetables just needed steaming. The wine was open and rather than have a glass without him, she drank a beer and absently thumbed a women's magazine.

When she heard his car, she hurried to the window and watched him get out. He was wearing a windbreaker, a new T-shirt with the factory fold clearly showing over his abdomen, clean Levi's, and his best dress boots. He looked different. Older. He had a bottle of something with a ribbon tied around the neck under his arm. In the same hand he held flowers.

Flowers, all right!

With his free hand he reached into the backseat and picked up a box which he handled by a string that tied around it.

"I've got a date!" she laughed out loud.

She guessed that his next move would be to close the car door and then straighten and look up at her window before proceeding up the steps. Her apartment was in the back of an old house owned by an elderly couple who were never there, off visiting grandchildren scattered throughout the Dakotas and Wyoming. She stood anxiously back from the window, hoping that the bright orange of the setting sun would obscure her form in its reflection.

He did look up and appeared to linger. Was he staring right at her? Her heart quickened. Her fingers touched her lips.

Lipstick. Oh shit.

She dashed to the bathroom, her sandals clicking on the hardwood floor, touched up her lipstick, and then scurried to the door just as it knocked twice, then once again. She put a pleasant glad-to-see-ya smile on her face and pulled the door open just enough to frame herself perfectly in the doorway.

He had cut his hair. It now parted on the side but not too far off center and fell over his ears. She liked the look. A little turn of hair lifted then fell across his forehead rakishly. Yes, she liked that a lot. And right then, noticing his hair combed that new way, she had an unexpected moment of clarity. She suddenly saw the future so vividly her knees went weak. Like she had opened a present she had waited a long time for and at last knew what it was. She remembered thinking at that moment the words, *Ready or not.* In his eyes, in that lock of hair, in that new look which would remain his look from now until the grave, she could see down the entire highway. It was a nice place. She felt comfortable there. Secure. That was worth a lot.

Thereafter, on evenings like this, when the sun was skirting the horizon and the last colors of the day were bright and glowing, when the seasons were in midchange and the world didn't know if it was warm or cold, she could conjure up this feeling by looking away and then back at him. Her sense of relief lifted her off her feet. *I'm going with it!* she thought, and would remember thinking that too, with a certainty bordering on glee. In the doorway, seeing that his hands were full and that, physically, he was momentarily helpless, she reached her arms delicately around his neck and kissed him warmly on the mouth, taking the time to enjoy the newness of his lips, the smell of his skin, and his inability to resist or even speak. When she opened her eyes, she laughed at the preposterousness of it all and said, "Hi."

"Hi," he said, his face warmed by a dash of embarrassment, overcome by surprise and delight.

He brought her a bottle of cognac, because she had said that she liked it, and flowers, which she placed in an empty wine carafe he recognized from the hotel.

She opened the box and when she looked inside, all ready to say something nice, she stopped, and looked at him questioningly as he lit a cigarette.

"Here, you lift it out by this," he said, reaching in and lifting up what looked like a hook from a clothes hanger.

She lifted out a jangle of fishing line, polished bolts, and bits of broken glass, their jagged edges ground smooth, an old spring, and a hunk of copper wire. From the center of it was tied a beautiful polished multicolored stone about the size and shape of a shot glass.

It was an awkward contraption that didn't make any sense. She was sure she had ruined it somehow, whatever it was, in the act of just lifting it from the box. He held his cigarette between his teeth and squinted from the smoke burning his eyes as he gave one arm of the thing a delicate push and gently lifted one tangled wire over another arm and presto, the whole thing fell into place, the stone's weight acting to balance the piece. The mobile tinkled and turned as she held it up.

"Oh! Now I get it!" she turned it this way and that, her eyes darting from point to point. She turned to him and beamed, "Thank you!"

"The rock is a core sample from about a mile down. It's tens of thousands of years old."

A fern which hung from a hook by the balcony window found a new home in an empty corner on the floor, and the mobile went up immediately. She opened the sliding balcony window slightly to let whatever breeze could find its way in to play with it, causing a giddy, chiming, clattering sound. The sun had just dipped blow the horizon, and the sudden drop in temperature caused goosebumps to ripple across her arms and up her thighs beneath her skirt. She blushed but thought he didn't notice. She closed the window.

Over dinner her eyes studied his jaw line. He chewed slowly and swallowed before saying a word, sometimes pausing for long moments in midthought to complete the process so as not to talk with food in his mouth. She wondered if that could get to be annoying. Is he on his best behavior, or does he really eat like this? Then she realized she'd have to be pretty far gone to be concerning herself with issues such as that.

"Do you miss Jesse?"

"Yeah."

"Bad?"

"Well, it wasn't just Jesse. Everybody watched everybody, and was ready to lend a hand?" Jon realized that he was unaccustomed to discussing his work with anyone other than a roughneck, and finding the right words was a challenge. "Like, if somebody needed help, you went right over and helped'm. I don't care who it was, chainhand, worm, or whoever, you changed oil, everybody was there, you packed up oil in a five-gallon bucket, you have to go down on the ground, they have an oil pump there, fill your five-gallon bucket and carry it up the steps. That's how we change our oil, everyone carries two five-gallon buckets up those steps..." And Jon relaxed, he could talk to her about work, he smiled. ·

"Wouldn't it make more sense for whoever is in charge to write down the names of all the guys on all the crews and then perhaps rearrange the names to fit each crew more specifically together?"

He smiled again. "That would make *too much* sense. Out here, anyway, each crew is its own independent unit. They can either get it or they can't. They work as one, sharing the load and protecting each other. The stakes, of course, are life and death, so we count on the driller to lead the way."

She didn't want to think about danger on the rig right that moment, so she changed the subject and told him about her two years of college in Minneapolis, about growing up on a cattle ranch with five older brothers. That she had thought of joining the military just to get out and see something else of the world but was glad she hadn't. Not that she was a gender snob, but living with that many men was something she never wanted to do again.

It takes five men to run an oil rig, Jon thought.

They listened to Bonnie Raitt records while they ate. After dinner she found a scratchy old copy of Beethoven's "Appassionata," and as the needle hissed and popped its way across the vinyl surface and the first notes filled the room, he took her in his arms and they danced in the candlelight. She closed her eyes. She had worried he might react negatively to classical music, and had some Charlie Rich standing by just in case, but no, he was happy, it was like a movie score. Perfect.

He buried his nose in her hair above her ear. Her smell filled his senses. Their bodies fit perfectly, causing them both to relax and melt into the rhythm of the music, of the air, and of the gentle energy all around them. His big hands roamed.

"I love the way you move your hips," he breathed in her ear. His hands found the top of her hips and moved slowly down each side where her hips squared slightly. He didn't grope. He studied her shape. Her sigh told him that was a good thing to do. Her arms reached up around his neck, leaving her body available should his hands choose to roam further. She drank in his swimming blue eyes then closed hers and luxuriated in the feel of those big rough hands on her body. He pulled her hips to him and she could feel him there in front of her, pressing against her pelvis across to her hip. She felt herself turning liquid beneath her short dress. There was a lot of raw power there, she could feel it. She felt weightless. His cheek rested briefly on the top of her head. And she felt him kiss her there, a gesture of such warm affection she sighed. When she pulled away, her hands descended down his chest. She took his hand and led him to her bedroom.

In the bedroom it was dark, and before turning on the light she pulled a royal blue veil from the closet door and draped it over the lampshade beside the bed. She had tested this gesture the night before and was certain that this light would hide her imperfections. Imperfections he would never have noticed until, in more familiar moments, months later, she pointed them out to him. They kissed long and hard standing there. His hands moved gently up her thighs, lifting her skirt. She was naked underneath. She studied his reaction which was to simply sweeten his eyes and pull the dress completely over her head. Oh yes, he knew what he was doing. The cool air in the room swirled around her naked body and the feel of his clothes against her skin made her feel more naked still. She reached between his legs and pressed her soft palm over that part of his slacks that was showing signs of life and squeezed him gently. As she did this, her other hand yanked his shirt out of his trousers. He pulled the shirt over his head without unbuttoning it further and it fell to the floor. She sat down on the bed, and a sound escaped his lips as she pulled down his zipper. She unbuckled his pants and pulled them down, and his sex swung forward, climbing steadily with each pounding beat of his heart. She squeezed it, then kissed the tip, then put it in her mouth. He shifted his weight to make it easier for her. After a long moment he stepped out of his remaining clothes and then pulled her to her feet. They embraced in the blue light for a long moment, lingering in the first feel of each other's warm flesh. They lay down slowly, lying on their sides facing each other, their hands exploring, their eyes searching each other's eyes.

"I love the way you smell."

"Your hands feel good."

"That's very nice," he said, indicating the curve of her hip as his hand traced its outline up and over from her waist to her buttocks.

"Mmm, your chest is beautiful," she moistened a finger in her mouth and traced a nipple.

His hand found her wet between her legs and she smiled, almost laughed at how aroused she was and a little self-conscious that her trembling body betrayed how long it had been since someone had touched her like that.

They relaxed and got into it. She took hold of him and squeezed gently, feeling his stiffness and tugged ever so slightly on it as they breathed in each other's sweet exhalations.

"That dinner was so nice," he said while gently sliding his hand over her cunt and reaching between her legs, which she opened for him as he went. He softly squeezed her ass, feeling her moist pubic hair on his thick wrist. She bore down on him there and squeezed her thighs tight for a second, shuddering sweetly. Then she had to part her legs further to accommodate his roaming hand. He squeezed her inner thigh hard. She squeezed him back. He moaned.

"Did you like it? I thought I would keep it simple. The dinner I mean," she whispered, her voice trembling slightly.

"It was perfect," he said, "and so is this," he kissed her again.

She purred happily and kissed him back.

Neither of them had a condom.

Years later they would tease each other. "You bonehead," she would laugh, "a beautiful young woman invites you over for dinner and you don't have the sense to bring a condom?"

"Me? I'm a nice guy I am. How was I to know you were lying in wait for me with your gold slippers and no underpants? If you had planned to take such advantage of my poor youthful and naïve self one would think *you* would have bought one. Shit, you thought of everything else!"

"Oh right! I'm going to go into the Scobey Pharmacy, with Big Alfie, whose eyes nearly pop out of his head and whose tongue practically hits the floor every time I go in there, and buy condoms? Tell him and the rest of the world, I'm safe, ready, and waiting? Really, some roughneck!"

Instead of intercourse, they explored. They talked and laughed and chased each other around the bed like squirrels on a tree trunk. They rolled around for hours. Alternately laughing and talking and teasing and then growing silent and allowing their bodies to do the talking. They pulled the covers around them and breathed in happily the sweetness of their first night.

ZAK OPENED HIS LOCKER DOOR and noticed right away that his gloves were missing. No one had ever borrowed his last pair before. But then again, with Hansom's crew hanging around, anything was possible. "Shit," he fussed and slammed his locker shut. From now on he would have to go back to locking up, which meant a long frustrating rummage through the Jeep to find his combination lock. Once found, he then had to remember the combination. He didn't. He tried to bring it back as he stomped up the stairs. No dice. He pitched the lock into the trash as he stepped into the top doghouse. It hit the metal can hard and loud. Everyone looked up momentarily, then resumed what they were doing.

Frank Kramer, that company hand, George Cleaver, and Archer Hansom were in the top doghouse along with a new guy who was standing off to one side. The guy was a densely packed powerhouse with thick shoulders. He had rocky features which stretched his skin tight over his skull and thin blond hair combed back on the sides with a flip over his forehead Elvis Presley style. He clearly had been wearing it that way so long he no longer required grease to hold it in place, but he greased it anyway. He was standing in a corner facing into the room, like a man accustomed to worrying about his back, smoking a cigarette and eyeing everyone suspiciously. Right away Zak noticed his missing gloves dangling through the son of a bitch's belt.

Frank Kramer was standing next to the knowledge box, going over a chart from the previous tower with George and Archer.

"Jesus Christ, Archer!" George slammed the door of the knowledge box down in disgust. "It took you a whole tower to trip some pipe? What kinda bullshit are you guys pullin' around here?"

Hansom shrugged.

"Glory be!" Marty howled as he entered from the floor. "Congratulations Georgie boy! You go out and find a new hand at last?"

"This is Lou Crawford," George nodded in the direction of the new hand standing in the corner. "And Frank here is goin' drillin' with you boys for a spell," George said casual-like. Frank was clearly there to take George's place at that brake handle.

Zak walked over to Crawford and gestured to the gloves. "We always ask one another before we go borrowing things," he said.

"Then make sure you do," Crawford said and looked at Zak with a want-to-make-something-of-it? face. He had a large disturbing gap between his two tobacco-stained front teeth.

Great, Zak thought. *So this is how it is? We finally get some help and he turns out to be a prick, introducing himself as a bad-ass by starting shit before he's even met anyone.* Should Zak bother to mention that it was he who put the notice up at the PDQ Club? Or that O'Mally and he were related? Perhaps not. Maybe no one was doing anyone else a favor in this situation after all. Asshole or not, having a full crew should be an improvement and ease everyone's load. Still, Zak couldn't help but wonder what Calico could have been thinking of when he sent this guy their way.

Marty, who had witnessed this exchange, hobbled over to Crawford, snatched the gloves from his belt, handed them to Zak and, before anyone could speak, threw open the cupboard and, fetching some new pairs, tossed them at everyone declaring, "Today, glubbs are on de new guy!" Crawford said nothing. "Dey cost two bucks fifty a pair, four times," he said to Frank, and to Frank and George said, "Better to keep dat closet locked up too from now on." He hit Jon in the chest with his new pair just as the motorman was coming through the door. Frank marked it down.

George sighed, with not a little disgust. Well, that's one way to get introduced to your new crew.

An hour earlier, Archer Hansom had been sitting in the top doghouse going over the charts from his tower before relief was due to show. He smoked a cigarette and shook his head. It had taken eight hours, an entire tower, to round-trip only nine hundred feet pipe. Jesus, what a nightmare.

And that fuckin' Skidder up in the derrick was piss drunk when he arrived, and had been drinking steadily since he got up to the crow's nest.

Each time they disconnected that pipe and pushed it over to bank and Archer set it down, it took several seconds for derrick-hand to yank in back into those fingers returning it to an upright position. In the meantime that pipe swung and swayed like he might lose it altogether, and if that happened, the three of them would have to climb that derrick and walk it like a jungle gym, around to the far side to push it back. After about a dozen or so stands like that they were ready to climb that tower and toss Skidder over the side. Twice Arch had to send motorman Scotty up the ladder to straighten Skidder out. Each time Scotty been up there about half an hour and came back down smelling like beer. It must have been quite a party up in the tower, bombing the boys down below with empties; Skidder and Scotty standing up there having a piss over the side, one arm over the other's shoulders, singing "Remember the Alamo." But down on the floor it had been nasty, and Arch was planning on a fight when Skidder came down, if he didn't fall down first. Either way, he was running that son of a bitch off. Enough was enough. Friends or no.

To make matters worse, George had come up to the floor and chewed him out for moving so slow and Archer hadn't had a leg to stand on. "Goddamnit! If you can't whip a crew inta shape any better'n this then you have no business at that brake handle!"

While George and Archer had been standing there, Archer had seen over the toolpusher's shoulder the glimmer of a beer can sailing toward the reserve pits; another fluttered down over the pump shack. If Cleaver had seen or had any idea what was going on, they would have been run off right then, and George would have dedicated his life to seeing these jerks had a hard time latching on anywhere ever again. But then Archer wondered, just what could George do? Run the rig by himself? Everybody loved to boast that Jesse could do it, but Archer knew he couldn't. Maybe if George got mad enough he might. But not for long. Or maybe George could patch together some volunteers from the other crews to keep things going for a day or two. Either way, Archer didn't want to find out. It was time for Skidder to dry up or clear out. And Scotty was in shit with him as well.

At the end of tower, everyone was waiting for Skidder to climb down and get what was comin'. Johnny Bailey, Archer's chainhand, was coiled up, ready to explode. Archer was debating with himself how to get everyone off location before the fireworks began. Johnny was blameless and Archer thought he might deserve better than to get run off with the rest of them. Archer Hansom sighed, looked up, and muttered, "What a bunch of crap."

Just when he was thinking Skidder might have passed out up there, or was just too plain scared to climb down and face the music, they saw something moving up above.

There he was. Out on the diving board waving his hard hat like the Lone Ranger, whoopin' and a-hollerin'! He was holding the inverted T-bar of the Geronimo line between his legs. The Geronimo line—a cable that served as an emergency escape line for the derrickhand, stretched tight from the derrickhand's station to the ground below hundreds of feet away from the rig.

"Hey Scotty."

"Yeah Arch?"

"Who was it installed that Geronimo line?"

"Why, it was Skidder. Well, Skidder'n me."

"Yeah, and is that Skidder's pickup parked way the fuck out there where that line touches down?"

Scotty gave a squint in that general direction.

"Yes, I do believe it is, Archer."

"Aw shit," Johnny Bailey spat as his eyes followed that line from the ground back up to the crow's nest.

And Skidder MacIntyre waved his hard hat in the air above his bright blond head and hollered "Hi! Ho! Silver!" as he leaped gracefully into the night air, landing in a sitting position on the T-bar, and, keeping one hand on the squeeze brake over his head, sailed swiftly but gently to earth as that T-bar rolled down the line like an alpine amusement park ride. Skidder hit the ground with a single somersault, hopping to his feet and, after a sweeping bow Sir Walter Raleigh style, hard hat in hand, he jumped into his pickup and was gone with a roar down rig road, his red taillights weaving this way and that as they disappeared into the night.

"I'm starting to hate that son of a bitch," said Archer Hansom.

"Bastard," spat Johnny Bailey.

"Well fuck a duck!" laughed Scotty. And they turned on Scotty menacingly just as George and Frank and the new guy arrived up in the top doghouse.

FRANK KRAMER WAS FROM SOUTHERN California. He had earned his oil field stripes in Bakersfield. His dad had been in the oil patch, too. Frank drove a beat-up Chevy Chevelle with bald tires and a heater that didn't work. He was the type of guy the average rough-neck would take one look at and say *No way, I ain't workin' for him.* He looked like a city boy. But he let his men go about their jobs, and only butted in when he thought it might do some good. Most times he was right on. Jon, skeptical as always, withheld judgment for a couple of weeks. Frank proved to be a cool customer, if a bit tenuous at that brake handle, and, like Jesse, had the diplomatic skills and rare common sense when dealing with his men to ask, rather than give orders, when difficult tasks or unpleasant chores needed doing. This was a most appreciated trait.

One day, as all were gathered in the top doghouse, Jon strolled in with a present for their new driller. It was in a burlap sack with a piece of twine tied at the top. Frank untied the string and pulled out a twelve-inch crescent wrench. Written on the shaft in thick black ink was: "Property of F.K. Driller, BOMAC 34." On the other side was printed the simple legend, "Widowmaker."

"Good thing I ain't married," he laughed as he thanked them. It was exactly the type of wrench that had jutted out of Jesse's hip pocket at all times for thirty-odd years. His only true and trusted companion, and the right hand of a thousand and one Indian tricks.

"Dat dere som bitch will save all our lives somb ob deze dayz." Marty clapped his big palms on Frank's shoulders. "If you lose it, I'll hab to kill you."

"Um, thanks," Frank said.

"You keep 'er here," Jon explained, taking the wrench and jabbing it down into Frank's back pocket. "Don't ever let any one of us ever see you without it."

WITH CRAWDAD IN WORM'S CORNER and Frank at the brake handle, new rhythm set in among the crew. Although Frank agreed with Zak and the rest that Crawdad was a "surly and unpredictable bastard, personally," everyone had to agree that their new worm showed up for work on time, was strong with the slips, and never faltered during trips. "That's all I care about," Jon concluded, and with this mutual agreement, the Crawdad issue was settled. But no one liked him. He was a habitual kleptomaniac. No roll of tape, clipboard, or set of bootlaces was safe. Everyone had battened down the hatches good and tight ever since he arrived.

If the boys had their work caught up during a drillin' tower, they'd disappear. Crawdad would wander up to the top doghouse and ask, "Where's Jon and them at?" And Frank would shrug, "Must be down in the mud shack sleeping." What few awkward attempts Crawdad made at being buddy-buddy with his crew-mates went ignored and an uneasy truce settled in.

It was while Zak and Jon were crawling about the rig with Freddy's old Zurt gun that Zak wondered aloud how in the world he could approach George about letting Marty go drillin'. Zak shared Jesse's last wish, so to speak, with Jon, and the motorman took a good long think on the subject. They would need another derrickhand, Jon observed, and they both agreed Jon loved his motors, and Zak had taken a genuine shine to throwing chain. Neither of them wanted to graduate to derrickhand.

"Besides," Jon said, "it's really frickin' cold up there."

Before long both roughnecks began eyeing Crawdad with curiosity, as if he might be a likely candidate for derrickhand. He was built for the work, and certainly, he was crazy enough. But as in all things, the solution to one problem most always presented new difficulties. If Marty went drillin', and Crawdad could be trained to work derricks and manage the mud, assuming he could be talked into it, then they would need another worm. Ideas began to germinate.

One or the other of the co-conspirators would sidle up to Crawdad after a trip and say something like, "Hey, you're pretty good at racking pipe, ever racked pipe up there?"

Or another might casually let drop something subtle like, "You know, Marty sure knows a lot about that mud, I'm sure he'd tell you all about it if you asked."

One thing Jon and Zak swore was crucial was that Marty get nary a whiff of what they were up to until the time was right.

MARY ELLEN BROUGHT THE DRINKS as Jesse's old crew, minus Jesse, congregated at the hotel bar one afternoon on days off. Marty had brought Cynthia up from Watford because she missed Scobey, meaning she missed everyone's company, and she was rosy cheeked and happy as she sipped her Sprite and listened to the men talk freely and openly about work again, for the first time really, since Jesse twisted off. She and Marty got an extra room. And all were reunited, like old times.

"The work is harder now, isn't it," Zak observed once they were settled in.

"Eben wid dat rough tough worm you got down dere?" Marty was twinkling, half-serious, half-not, expecting an avalanche of bitching about Crawdad in response.

"Well, what I'm sayin' is," Zak went on, not taking the bait, "I find I have to watch Frank a lot more than Jesse. I mean watch him, not necessarily to learn from him either. I always think, or anticipate, that he's going to do something that Jesse would do, and then he doesn't. Then I have to look out, or wait for him to get it. To catch on. Sometimes he does, sometimes he doesn't."

"That's because now we're working through problems, solving things on the run," Jon said. "Instead of having someone who's seen it all before, like Jesse. Now we've got a worm driller and I don't think our little California Dreamer has too many Indian tricks up his sleeve."

"Dat car's a hoot!" Marty kept it light-hearted.

"Yeah, that three fifty engine will last a lot longer than that little go-cart they put 'er in."

"That little sardine can scoots pretty good though."

"As long as there's five roughnecks packed in tight weighing her down."

"Until he gets that heater fixed, packed in tight is the only way to stay warm."

"We smell like sardines in dat little junk bucket too!" Marty laughed and snuggled Cynthia close, making her frown with pleasure.

"Well, driller gets a gas allowance for drivin' us to work each day," Jon chimed in, implying that a ride to work was a perk he approved of.

"Well, dat sure, and bedder da Frankie Mobile den dat new Bronco get all fulla muddy stinky old roughneck sardines!" He squeezed Cynthia again and she giggled.

They got quiet for a moment, each one thinking about the brink of winter, knowing Marty's Bronco and Zak's Jeep would get called into service one way or another, sooner than later.

"Marty," Jon lit a cigarette, "remember last year when Jesse's Merc beat out all them four-wheels gettin' to the rig in the snow?"

"Heh heh," Marty gave a raspy chortle, "I got out to open dat gate. I looks up'n sees ol' Jesse backin' dat bastart up da hill an' he come barrallin' down trew d'snow just a-bouncin' and a-flyin'! Tought ol' Jonny't have hisself a hart tack!" Marty laughed hard.

"We had passed all these good ol' boys in their four-wheel pickups'n such," Jon laughed as he added some details for Zak and Cynthia's benefit. "They were stuck, and diggin' like hell to get themselves out, and that ol' Merc of Jesse's, rear-wheel drive, bald tires and all—just like Frankie's outfit, 'cept bigger and heavier of course..."

"Ant a heater dat werked don' forget!"

"...was passin' 'm right an' left. Well, we could see the problem up ahead from the side of this other hill. There at the bottom was a ravine and up the other side of it was a cattle barrier that also had a gate. We knew we'd never make it if we had to stop comin' up the other side, so Marty hops out and jogs down there to open the gate, and Jesse starts backin' 'er up. Jeez, must've been a couple hundred yards up this hill."

"I seen dat ol' blue bastart comin' down dat hill and I know'd dere weren't a single tire touchin' da grount when you cleared dat cattle barrier. Best damnt snow drivin' I ebber did see!" Marty laughed.

"We said to the other roughnecks, 'You boys need a pull?' They were so pissed!"

"When I got back into da car ol' Jonny's face was white like a ghost!"

"I had three or four knots on the top of my head from hittin' the roof each time. I swear we left the ground completely four or five times. My hard hat was in with my gear. I swore I would only drive with Jesse ever again wearin' that hard hat. We never got stuck though."

"Yeah, but ebbry-buddy else did. Dey'd be stuck in da snow and we'd be stuck at work and we'd have to double!"

IT WAS LATER THAT EVENING when Marty and Cynthia, Jon and Mary Ellen, had melted away, that Archer Hansom walked into the Pioneer Hotel bar. And Zachary Harper was the man he wanted to see.

XVI

Archer Hansom's plan was a simple one, and coming out of the blue the way it did, quite a welcome surprise.

"Zak, I think it's time there was a truce between your crew and mine. What I mean is, I think old Skidder may have given you boys the wrong idea about us."

Zak was startled.

"It's just that we've watched the way you boys work through things, and we realize we've got a good thing going here on this rig and would like to ride it on as far as we can. You're the best crew of roughnecks I've seen in the patch. We've got an experienced toolpusher and good iron. Let's pull our resources together and make this work for everybody."

They got some beers and sat at a table.

The amazing thing was that what Archer proposed was something akin to what had been brewing in all their minds but no one had threaded the beads together yet. Archer's crew needed someone to work derricks. Up until now, he had been working shorthanded and needed a derrickhand. That couldn't go on much longer. Now he had been doing some asking around and figured that if he could trade a worm's corner man from his crew, even-steven for Crawdad, Archer could teach Crawdad derricks. He also knew a good man who could work all positions except driller and was an especially good derrickhand. The new man could work derricks for Zak's crew and then Marty could go drillin'. Marty drillin' for Zak's crew would have the added benefit of getting Frankie Boy off that brake handle.

Of course there was a catch.

"His name is OK Wellman. The OK is for Oklahoma City, where he's from. Anyway, he's getting into the Rapid City airport at eight tomorrow morning and we need someone to drive down there tonight, pick him up, and bring him back. Now you boys are on days off, so we were thinking maybe one of you could go get him."

"I'm ready to go right now," Zak said, but then grew suddenly ponderous. Should he bother Marty and Cynthia with this? Jon and Mary Ellen? George Cleaver?

"I was discussing this with Cleaver this morning," Hansom read his mind. "He said he didn't care, but that out here, well, special situations require special solutions, and that if it was all right with you boys he didn't have a problem. Also, he's been a little concerned that Frank is having a little too much fun drilling again, and wants him back in that trailer of his doing his job. I think old Rusty is helping out with company hand's chores that rightfully aren't his to do, and that could and will lead to any number of problems. Rusty said he'd keep an eye on Marty those first few towers but was a little surprised he didn't think of that himself, Marty's perfect! And besides, don't take this wrong, but you guys, without a driller, aren't really a crew, company hand could hire you guys out to do anything.

"Why not just let Wellman work derricks for you guys?"

Archer sat back in his chair, smiled a weary kind of smile, and said, "It's complicated. Besides we have no way of getting him up here, and there's still the Frank issue. No, we think this works out better. I'll tell you something though, and this is the truth, not that we all haven't had our problems, but after what you guys went through with Lenny, and then fat boy Freddy, and then Lancaster, a good strong hand like Wellman will be a breath of fresh air. That and the fact that I've broke out several derrickhands, I'm an old mudman myself. I spoke with Crawdad the other day, and to be honest, he sounded real happy to join our crew and get a fresh start. Has he been a problem?"

"Only at first. He's a bit of a pest, and lock up your stuff."

"Well, up in the derricks is where he belongs, as long as he can get 'er. You know, Zak, Jesse always had the best crews. You're Jesse Lancaster's chainhand. And don't worry, OK'll fit in better with you boys. Fuck, the guy reads books. And Crawdad will be a better fit with us. Almost anyone would be an upgrade after Skidder."

Zak looked at his watch. It was almost ten o'clock.

"It's about four hundred fifty miles down to Rapid, so figure about seven or eight hours."

"Well I should leave right now," Zak said.

"I'll leave a note for Marty here at the hotel and fill him in tomorrow," Archer said. "Now look, if you're not back in time for any reason, the boys will gladly double for you guys, we're good t'go on this. Whaddya say Zak?"

"How will I know this guy?"

"How?" Archer drained the last of his beer. "Look for the roughneck getting off the friggin' plane. Oh, and another thing, don't no one ever call him Okie."

ZAK GRABBED A SIX-PACK FOR the trip and filled his water jug from a tap at the bar, made some peanut butter and jelly sandwiches, and was on the road in less than an hour.

THE JEEP THUNDERED DOWN EMPTY highways and through the chill black night. As the hours ticked by Zak had many doubts. What would happen when Marty and Jon got wind of this? Would Frank, the company hand, go for it? Did Marty consider himself ready? What if Archer is fuckin' nuts and everybody but Zak knows it? And what if Marty and Jon would rather twist off and take their chances back in Watford? Would either of *them* have gone on this mission? Maybe Marty would have appreciated making his own decision as to when he would break out drillin'.

"Why am I doing this?" he asked himself out loud. The simple answer was getting company hand back in his trailer hiring roust-abouts and water haulers was needed. He's the freakin' boss after all. And nobody wants to put Cleaver in charge as de facto company hand, that's for sure. Wasn't it anomalous situations like this, when routines and protocols are broken or disturbed, that unpredictable shit happens, people get hurt? And if the end result was giving Marty his big chance drillin', well you can't beat that. Things had been happening, changing so fast, Zak hadn't really considered what it all meant. And by the way, what was that bit about being Jesse Lancaster's chainhand, being good crew and all that horseshit? Flattery? Buttering him up to take the deal? Hardly. Without a driller to lead them and protect them, like Archer said, they aren't even a crew. Having Marty for a driller would be great. With Marty, Jon, Zak, and maybe Johnny Bailey on the floor, OK up in the derrick. Yes, that would be worth the drive to Rapid for. On the other hand, if the others twisted off, he could hardly blame them. On the other hand again, if they did twist, being Jesse Lancaster's chainhand would go a long way down in Watford.

Oh what the fuck, too late now, thought Zachary Harper as the sun came up over the eastern horizon on his left, tossing gold all over the roiling rolling grasslands with just a glinting of frost over the endless distance in all directions. If Archer was full of it, or the boys didn't go for it, if this OK character turned out to be a shitwheel, well, so be it. And Zak laughed out loud and had to admit, getting rid of that fuck-stick Crawdad would make going to work a pleasure again all by itself.

He rolled up to the Rapid City airport an hour early, parked, and walked in, sat down at a little food counter, and ordered up an omelet. The airport was small and cozy with a decent-sized lobby/rotunda-like main area with plenty of Native American art, and welcoming images everywhere. *Civilized*, he thought. When OK's flight landed, Zak strolled down the concourse and smoked a cigarette while he waited at the gate.

OK Wellman was a head and a half taller than the tallest folks to emerge from the jetway. He had broad shoulders, a broad forehead and high cheekbones, and black hair evenly cut just above the collar. He carried two duffel bags, one large, one smaller.

They spotted each other immediately.

"OK," Zak approached and stuck out his hand. "I'm Zak, a friend of Archer's." OK had a huge hand that swallowed Zak's whole.

"Hey Zak, nice to meet you, just down from Scobey?" He had a deep gravelly voice that matched his size but not his complexion.

"Got here an hour ago," Zak reached for one of the duffel bags and OK handed him the smaller one.

The average citizens coming and going there at the airport all took notice of OK Wellman. Zak remembered a bible passage about a time when giants roamed the earth. If true, this Wellman character might just be a long-lost strain.

On their way out to the parking lot, Zak filled him in on his version of the Archer plan.

"But goddamn, ain't it like that?" Wellman seemed to be on familiar ground. "You never know in the oil field, man. One day you show up on location and your crew is run off, and another's hired on. Or a buncha roughnecks have put their own heads together and solved a problem that was right there for the solving all along. But hey, Archer says it's a sweet setup you boys have. It means a lot to me to be able to just dive right in and get to work without all the bullshit, politics, searching around, having to yak it up all the time. That can get on a guy's last nerve."

Zak couldn't help but think, *Well sure, I guess we are making it easier for you.* He didn't care. Corporal Acts of Mercy, he said to himself. Now where did that come from?

"And sometimes I just need to get back out to big country. You know what I mean."

"Oh yeah," said Zachary Harper.

"We're all just a buncha bulls trying to escape our own private china closets." The bright morning sun made their eyes squint. "Seriously dude, sometimes just walkin' down a city street, I get the temptation to reach out and smack every horse's ass I see right across the face. And they're fuckin' everywhere. I want to swat every pretty girl I see right on her beautiful fat ass, and go take a joyride in the most expensive car in town. Trust me, when I start itchin' like that, it's time to get back to the oil field, or at least back out here, to someplace like this, where I'm not liable to break anything. The farther away from civilization the better. Scobey sounds perfect."

As they reached the Jeep and Zak fished his keys out of his denim jacket pocket, OK stopped in his tracks. "Wahoa, what the fuck?" he gasped with disbelief. "Is this your outfit?"

"The Jeep? Yeah," Zak was nonplussed.

"Well, this may sound a little crazy, but I've seen this Jeep about twenty times in my dreams lately, no shit. What do you call it?"

"Déjà vu."

"No, what do you call the Jeep?"

"Uh, well, I guess I just call it 'The Jeep.'" Zak laughed as they tossed OK's duffel bags in the back and climbed inside.

"No, you were callin' it something else. It'll come to me. Damn."

As Zak fired 'er up OK suggested they continue into town and pick up a few things.

"Yeah, I was born in Oklahoma City, but I was raised just north of here in Belle Fourche," OK volunteered on their way into Rapid. "But my great-great-grandmother was either a Cheyenne or a pure-bred Lakota. My great-great-grandfather was a white man, an Indian trader. They say he specialized in hoops and hats. Would make'm for food, pelts, and peaceful passage. I kinda gotta love the idea of all those Indians ridin' around buffalo country wearin' Wellman Hats!"

"Hey, maybe you should learn the trade? Every man is always on the lookout for the perfect lid," Zak enthused. "Wellman's Black Hills Chapeaus!" They both laughed.

"Well anyway, I was just back to Kansas City to visit my old grandma, she gave me a pouch of tobacco and personal trinkets to take up to Bear Butte. So once we're under way, if you don't mind, we'll take a little jog up that way. You'll probably dig it."

In town, they pulled into an Army Navy store and Wellman got himself a big heavy winter coat and a sleeping bag, a knife, a canteen, gloves, a Zippo lighter and the fluid to fuel it, among other things.

By now, hunger and fatigue were beginning to rear their ugly heads. Both men had been up all night, in OK's case, two nights, and a few hours' sleep, a shower, and a good meal might come in handy for the long haul. At the Hotel Alex Johnson they sweet-talked the pretty clerk at the desk for an early check-in. Separate rooms. They paid cash.

When Zak descended to the lobby midafternoon, beneath the giant wooden beams, taxidermy, and native and cowboy art, he found OK Wellman sitting in the restaurant enjoying a big, delicious bison burger.

He had a plan.

"Look, I spoke with Archer and he says everything is a go with your boys and his. My old man up in Belle Fourche is a transmission specialist. He's got an old Buick I can have, but it may need a little work. Won't take long, it's on the way, his shop is pretty well stocked. Then I'll have some wheels and can follow you north. He says we can stay the night at his place, then roll north first thing tomorrow."

"Works for me," Zak laughed. This mission was getting longer and more complicated by the hour, but hey, if Archer and them were cool, so was he. Besides, OK Wellman was good company, and this little sojourn was doing wonders for Zak's frame of mind. They'd ride into Scobey like the freakin' cavalry!

"By the way, that was a nice turn you did for grumpy ol' Crawdad. We all owe you one," OK was saying as Zak's bison burger arrived.

"You know Crawdad?"

"Well enough. Jesus, the caliber of people you can meet out in the patch sometimes," he shook his head and mowed down on the last of his burger. "I mean, some of these folks are, you know, like on the verge of being socially retarded. Cripes!"

The waitress delivered a couple of pints.

"Crawdad and I broke out at nearly the same time in nearly the same place, in the early seventies during the overthrust boom. But hey, I know Calico too, you know him right?"

"Sure I do."

"Well his real name is Terry, Calico was a name some sweet girl gave him way back when 'cause of the color of his hair. He hated it at first, but once we heard about it, that was it. We made sure it stuck. Blackie started callin' him that, if I remember correctly. Suits him though, even if he hates it. I was workin' motors for Blackie up on the slopes when Calico was Blackie's chainhand. Diesels are my thing. I can tear down and put back together just about anything that runs on diesel. That's another reason I'm okay with comin' back to the patch. We're all just one big happy family, eh pardner?" he laughed and slapped Zak on the shoulder with a hand the size of a baseball glove.

"Crawdad and me worked together for a spell. I was building roads up there when I wasn't roughneckin', so we didn't see each other much. He and I never came to blows, but that attitude of his gets his ass kicked every now and again. He's great at startin' fights, I understand; I don't think anyone's ever seen him win one though. You can only put up with so much of Crawdad's shit."

Once out of the hotel, they stepped across the street to Tally's Café for some takeout sandwiches and bottles of pop for later, and it occurred to Zachary Harper that OK Wellman was used to running on a lot of fuel himself.

BEAR BUTTE, SOUTH DAKOTA, IS a mountain, not a butte, that rises up more than four thousand feet out of the surrounding prairie floor, a huge hump in the flat endless wilderness. They say that if you look at it from a distance and squint your eyes just right, it looks like a bear lying down to sleep. In the autumn, the leaves on the surrounding cottonwoods and elms all turn yellow before they fall. Cattle sprinkle the vast prairie like little black dots, fleas on a giant carpet.

As they passed through Sturgis, Zak saw Halloween cobwebs and spiders and paper witches festooned on picket fences and real jack-o-lanterns on front porches. He realized he had utterly lost track of the calendar, his sole attention in that regard focusing on days on, days off, and marking the slow descent of the mercury as each day got a little colder, and a whole lot shorter.

"Some assholes are always trying to build something at the base of the mountain," OK said with disgust as they approached from afar. "White men have always been willing to destroy anything for a short-term commercial interest. A giant parking lot, how does the song go? Now they want an amusement park or some shit to draw even more bikers and spectators. They'd spoil this for everyone year round, just to sell a little more booze and bullshit for a long weekend in the summer. The folks who actually give a shit can only win those battles every so often. The developers will get their way eventually. Don't ever take anything for granted," OK sighed. They wound their way up the drive to a small parking area partway up the mountain.

"So do you consider yourself native?" Zak asked.

"Not at all, would never presume to be. No, I'm a white man," OK said thoughtfully, as his black eyes scanned the familiar horizon. "But you know, I feel the blood, I really do. It boils up in me sometimes where I can't contain it. So it doesn't matter to me, Cheyenne or Lakota. I think it's stronger in me than in most of my kin, almost all of whom are fair. Granny says I'm the first man in the clan to come out with anything like Indian features. She had an aunt they say whose hair was dark as a crow. What draws me is the spirit, the oneness to nature, the being a part of everything. That's what I feel, really strong at times." They got out of the Jeep and walked to the edge of the first hill.

"Look out there," OK pointed. People were moving slowly, reverently, over the face of the mountain. Some were stooped over, fixing small colorful ribbons to the low branches of scrublike plants, or little bags, or what looked like broken mirror glass and colorful beads, affixing them to spindly trees.

"It's a religious thing. They come here to this holy place, like Mecca, to pray, to give or to add their own artifacts or gifts, to commune with the Great Mystery. Are you a religious man, Zak?"

"Not really. I was raised Catholic."

"And twisted off a while back?"

"Pretty much, although I think that opened my soul to greater possibilities, if that makes any sense."

"Well, sure it does, you're no stranger to ritual then at least."

"No stranger at all." Zak was watching as the Indians moved about the mountain.

OK dropped a heavy arm about Zak's shoulder. And he gave him a friendly jerk to his massive body, hugging him close for a moment. It was an oddly familial gesture.

"So what we call the Great Spirit is really a Christian translation, because Christians have to turn their gods into people, rich feudal lords and such. But a more accurate translation of what these folks call Wakan Tanka isn't Great Spirit, but Great Mystery. Doesn't that make more sense?"

"Certainly. If you let it, you can get this territory in your blood, I'm sure of that."

"Well a lot of blood ran hot and spilled freely here. There's no way you couldn't sense it one way or another." OK's arm returned to Zak's shoulder as he pointed with the other. "Okay, do you see that little bald mound at the top of that little hill about fifty yards off?"

"Yes."

"Well, that's a famous place called Teaching Hill. It's where Crazy Horse and many other wise men stood and spoke to the many nations that would gather here for prayer and for council. You could say that to the Indians, it's kinda like seeing where Jesus gave his sermon on the mount. The ancestors of the Kiowas, Mandan, Erikara, Sioux, Cheyenne, and who knows how many others, came here seeking visions and to pray. It's where they all decided that the White Man's incursion into their territory would stop at the Black Hills, live or die. Little Big Horn wasn't long after.

"So anyway Zak, I'm going to climb this mountain and I'm going to tie Grandma's pouch up at the top. It might take a while. You can roll back into town for a spell and come get me later, if you prefer, but I'd be honored if you'd join me."

And Zachary Harper looked into OK Wellman's dark black eyes and said, "The honor would be mine."

"You're cool, Zak, I see now why Archer picked you. Okay, let's grab some stuff from the Jeep. The Park Service rangers don't come up here much, they let the worshippers be, but just in case," with a thick long finger OK wrote the word "Tatonka" in big letters in the dirt on the hood of the Jeep.

"I christen this Jeep Tatonka! Zak's mighty buffalo spirit! That's the word I was looking for, man!" OK Wellman laughed. "That's what it was, in the dreams we were callin' your rig Tatonka! Hot damn!"

OK grabbed the bag of sandwiches and his leather bag, Zak grabbed the water jug, and OK unrolled his new sleeping bag and draped it over his shoulders saying, "It can get cold up there." Zak grabbed his and did the same.

It took more than an hour for the two men to follow the narrow winding path up the mountain, but when they reached the top, it was easy to see why such a place might be described in mystical terms. The view was astonishing, in that the land below was flat as a table top extending out in all directions.

"How far can the human eye see? A hundred miles before the natural curve of the earth creates a true horizon?"

"From up here I'd say two or three hundred miles," OK guessed. "But think about this, there was a time, not terribly long ago, where a buffalo herd might fill that entire space you see before you."

"That is hard to picture, and bloody frightening."

"So after thousands of years of roaming gigantic herds, imagine how deep in buffalo shit this whole country is? Now, some believe it was the policy of the United States to kill off the buffalo to make way for cattle, and also to rob the Indians of their major source of sustenance."

"Look," Zachary pointed east, "you can already see night approaching." It was as though very far off a heavy black line was drawn precisely across the land, and behind it a blackness that was all encompassing.

They stood and watched for several minutes.

OK then set about picking up rocks and strolling about the top of the mountain, placing them here and there.

"We must keep facing east as we pray," Wellman said, while placing one rock, then another, and it appeared he was making a rather loosely defined circle around them both.

"And what type of prayers are we into here?"

"For me, prayers are always of thanks. Thanks for the gifts of air, water, land and sky, food, drink, companionship. Here we have six stones, one for each direction. We will face east, where the light comes from. We'll feel the wind from the west, the cold from the north, the warmth from the south." Wellman sat down and draped his sleeping bag around him. Zak did the same.

From his leather bag OK pulled a jug of wine, a tobacco pouch, and what looked like a hand-knitted child's sock, bright red, green, and yellow, with blue threads interlaced throughout. He took a peek inside, then tied it shut with one of several ribbons he had.

"In there are a few strands of Granny's hair, my own, maybe some of her grandmother's, a tiny picture, I'm not sure of who. Old tobacco, beads, a broken crayon, personal things."

He set the little pouch aside and then fetched a stone from his bag. "Granny says this stone is actually from a fossilized buffalo bone, made into a pipe. I don't know if it's true, but then again, I don't think it matters, it's a good pipe."

He dipped his giant fingers down into the leather tobacco pouch and took out a pinch of something and placed it in the bowl.

"Kinnikinnick, that's the name the Indians gave their ritual smoke. The breath of life," OK smiled and lit up, handing the pipe, the blue musky smoke swirling about, to Zak, who took a deep long toke, then coughed loud and hard. His face turned bright red and his eyes watered.

"A ritual tobacco, some sacred tree bark, herbs, and a little extra," OK took it back and smoked a little more. "Smoke this and you can never lie, because the breath of life can never be false."

"It's delicious."

"It goes better with this," OK took a long pull on the wine and handed that over as well. The wine had a crisp spicy blackberry flavor, and yes, complemented the smoke very well.

The wall of night fast approached, much as Zak had observed from the hill above Stitch Cronan's shack, except here it was much more fantastic, pronounced, leaving a deep blue sky blanket besparkled with flickering stars as it passed overhead.

"Some say that the Milky Way is the Spirit Path the souls of the dead take south when they are released into the heavens. Somewhere at the end is a little old woman who decides which way the spirit is to go, and gives them a nudge in that direction."

"I hope she's not anyone I know," said Zak. "You know what I always think when I see the Milky Way...I feel like a lone wolf, or some wise old elk, sitting in a forest, on the other side of the Hudson River, say, and looking at all those lights, at Manhattan, and I don't know what it is. That I would never guess it was twelve million people, going about their lives."

"Wow, so you think the Milky Way is like a big teeming city," Wellman considered the idea, "and we're just dumb fuckin' animals who can't tell that's what it is. You know you mayn't be too far off there. I like that a lot. Damn...I like the old version too. I imagine those I've known who died, swimming down that highway of light. And that old woman, shoving the assholes one way, everybody else going the other."

"I like that version too," said Zachary Harper.

OK refilled the pipe. Then he held it up to the sky, "To Wakan Tanka, The Great Mystery."

"The Great Mystery," repeated Zachary Harper and took another slug of wine, then traded the jug for the pipe. The thick blue smoke swirled about them both.

OK held up his granny's knitted pouch and blew the smoke from the pipe through it.

"I always felt that we become manifest, corporeal, I mean, from spirithood to personhood, that is, for a reason. On purpose I mean," Zak said as he sat back, feeling very whimsical.

"And why is that?"

"Well, it could only be, to my way of thinking, that we can do things here that we can't do there. As corporeal entities, flesh and blood and bone, we can make decisions of consequence. Decisions that define us. Decisions that inform our spirit self as to who we really are. Our actions then becoming evidence as to how much we've learned, or evolved."

"Like give me an example."

"Well, like deciding to come up here with you this evening rather than just find a bar in town for a steak and a beer while you got your chore accomplished. Maybe in that other world, where we come from, where we aren't necessarily physical beings, perhaps we can't make those decisions of consequence. But here, because we're flesh and bone in the here and now, those decisions, perhaps all decisions, are in one way or another irrevocable."

"Hmm, and the decisions we make in the other world?"

"Perhaps there you just are what you are."

"Yeah, I think I get it, like decisions that also involve life and death maybe."

"Any decisions about anything. How late to sleep, what to eat."

"Some tribes believed they needed to pray to the goddess of the hunt to allow the animals that would sustain them to offer themselves for sacrifice, that's where prayers of thanks come in. It would be a decision of consequence to go against a code like that, wouldn't it, it would define you differently."

"I hadn't thought of it in a context like that one, but yes, that fits for me." They sat in silence and exchanged the wine and the pipe some more.

OK gathered himself up and strolled over to a low bush and fixed Grandma's pouch to an inner branch, muttering and speaking and humming and praying. He took other ribbons and affixed them to branches near and far.

Zak leaned back against a rock, pulled his sleeping bag about his shoulders, and watched as a fog crept up the mountain. He could hear his own voice humming, and groaning, and singing the medicine song he had made night after night by Coster's Creek. As the mist enveloped them, the air turned very cold, and snowflakes whirled and danced.

In the distance down the mountain, he thought he saw something move. It disappeared, then reappeared, first behind a short tree, then behind a cluster of rocks. He got up and moved toward it. OK was with him, talking and muttering and praying all the while.

"The sacred tobacco is the Totality, the fire we light it with, the Great Spirit, and we are smoke, without identity, without ego…"

The figure in the smoke was a small animal. No, it was just a form moving in fog and falling snow. They moved closer.

"The smoke is the life breath of Wakan Tanka, it is the life within you and the spirit and the breath of your Wakan being. The rocks, the plants, the stars, the beings with feathers, the beings with four legs, the beings with two, all are Wakan Tanka." OK's face was long, his eyes big, he blew smoke from the pipe into Zak's face. He put his mouth over the burning bowl and blew the smoke directly into Zak's mouth. Zak sucked it in, it was refreshing, fulfilling, and he exhaled a plume that swirled and fell and rose all about them.

The form moved again in the fog. It caught Zak's eye, now here, now over there. It was a woman, so young, so beautiful. She stepped out from behind a rock. She wanted to speak, she was reaching, holding something out to Zak, her sacred smoke dissipating. The snow and the fog reformed into many shapes.

"Purification, expansion, union…" Wellman was muttering.

Zachary turned to the sound of OK's voice. He handed Zak the pipe, he smoked, blew the smoke into Wellman's face. They were sitting side by side wrapped in their sleeping bags. The fog swirled, the snow fell, she appeared in front of Zak once more and stepped close, and he handed her OK's pipe, he wanted it back, she was gone.

He wandered the fog-draped mountaintop in search of her. Coming up the lonely path toward him, he saw a large animal. A buffalo? It stopped and sat back on his haunches the way a large dog might, blocking his way. The snow and fog turned it slowly white, until all was white, until it was covered over, until it too was gone.

When Zak awoke, he was laying on his side wrapped in his sleeping bag. OK Wellman was sleeping behind him, wrapped in his sleeping bag, huddled together for warmth, and protection. Zak was small in Wellman's powerful arms.

I lost his pipe, Zak thought in a panic. He pulled free and reached about looking for it, looking for her.

"Hey partner! What are you doing?" Wellman said into his ear.

"I lost your pipe, I'm so sorry!"

The air was clear. The night was cold. There was no fog, no snow.

Wellman dug around and found the pipe. "It's right here."

They picked up their gear and made it down the mountain path. They took a long, circuitous route that came to many endings, overlooking a cliff, or a stony precipice, each with its own new perspective on the surrounding scene, a different position beneath the stars. Zak thought he saw her again but no, it was just another wisp of smoke. They sat and watched and breathed

in and out. Eventually they found themselves looking once again at Teaching Hill, everything painted a dark brilliant silver and blue under the late-rising moon.

"Okay, so, there was 'a little something extra' in that pipe?" Zak said, as he realized he was drenched in sweat. "I could swear I'm tripping right now."

"You are."

Their boots rang loud on the gravel leading back to the Jeep.

"Just a little gift from the southern tribes…a little peyote… in the smoke, in the wine, good for cleansing the soul and freeing the mind, don't you think?"

They popped a couple of beers as they drove down the mountain. The night was electric and singing; the Jeep, Tatonka, was singing too.

"She was beautiful, I know I've seen her before, but I don't know who or where. I think I'm in love with her."

"You've met the Wakan Maiden," OK laughed. "Of course you're in love with her. And you always will be. Did she bring you anything? Did she bring you a pipe?"

"No, as a matter of fact, she wanted yours, and I gave it to her. She wouldn't give it back."

"I hate to think what might have happened had you refused! Man, a decision of consequence, wouldn't you say? Yes sir, all that and a white buffalo too!"

"Well, it was covered with snow."

"Was it now?" Wellman laughed.

THEY REACHED BELLE FOURCHE BEFORE dawn. Wellman's dad had left a light on.

XVII

They slept late.

It was early afternoon when they found sausages, scrambled eggs, and chopped-up potatoes, tomatoes, and onions, all in the same skillet down in OK's dad's kitchen. They just needed a little flame under them and some bread in the toaster. *Some Old Bay seasoning would be too much to ask for,* Zak thought, but he did find a bottle of Tabasco in the fridge to give the whole concoction a little jump. A note informed them that the coffee maker was good to go as well. Just push the button. They were starving.

Arthur Wellman, or Arty, was a quiet man, slow, thoughtful. He didn't wear jeans, he wore dungarees with suspenders, a small pipe constantly between his teeth, a straw hat shaped like a small fedora, all coming apart here and there. He was tall and lanky, a little stooped at the shoulders, and walked with a pronounced limp. His big hands were soft leather, marked by plenty of scars, gouges, and gashes, with long crooked fingers that looked like each one of them had been broken at one time or another. He had one squashed old yellow thumbnail.

Zak could smell his flannel shirt.

When he entered the kitchen, OK got to his feet so father and son could have a quick embrace, an old-fashioned hug, some kind of hey-howdy-hello just under their breaths.

"Now I know you boys are in a terrific hurry," Dad said as he got himself a cup of coffee.

"As a matter of fact we are," OK replied.

"Well, c'mon out here, I've got something to show you."

They followed him out the kitchen door into the crisp air and afternoon sunshine. They passed the open garage where a coral green 1971 Buick Electra with a half-vinyl roof was sitting in a state of deconstruction. Big as a boat, it looked like an old mare, sway-backed and rusting badly. The vinyl roof was peeling. Parts of the body had been sanded down and patched. The engine was in many pieces large and small. The tranny was missing. *So much for OK's new ride*, Zak thought, but he said nothing, wait and see, and followed the others around back.

"Well, whaddya think?" OK's dad made a grand gesture with a long arm, pointing to a fat red trailer, big and round at both ends. It had what looked like new tires and was all spiffed up.

"It's a 1957 Flying Cloud, Airstream, whaddya think, boys?"

Both roughnecks scratched their heads and approached it with caution, trying the door, peeping inside. It was clean and tidy, big and roomy, with lots of heavy-duty modifications. Around back, a bank of propane tanks were stacked neatly behind a thick steel cage with a big nasty lock on it.

"I thought Airstreams were silver," Zak said.

"They are, and this here's a classic. But its last owner was nervous someone might want to steal her, so he painted it red and removed all the identifying brand names and the like. But she's a good old girl, eh?"

OK was awestruck. "This is fuckin' genius! Where did you get it?"

"You remember old Jim Brand down at the Harley dealership? Well, he's had it a long time. I think he used to sell'm even, back when, I mean. Jim and his wife used to take it on vacations every year up into the Rockies and out to the Pacific Northwest. They've been letting his boys use it for road trips, hunting and the like, but they don't need it anymore. Well, I told him you were goin' roughneckin' again, and knowing what housing is like out in the patch, we thought it might come in handy, if I could fix 'er up, that is. It needed a lot of TLC, new flooring, all new waterworks, winterizing insulation top to bottom'n such. If nothing else, it'll make a good guest house."

"No shit?"

"No shit," his dad said with a mirthful quizzical twinkle in his eye, like it was so unusual for him to do anything for his son. Those little sarcasms aside, Zak could tell they were very close, almost brotherly. "If worse comes to worse you can drag 'er back and ride out the winter here. I was hopin' to have that old Buick ready for you too, but she's not there yet. Give me another coupla weeks. You got a hitch on the back of that outfit of yours, Zak? If not, there's one lyin' around here somewheres."

An hour later they were on the road, pulling a 1957 Airstream Flying Cloud, fire engine red, up Highway 79, headed north. At Castle Rock they turned on 168, then north again on Highway 85. By the time they reached Buffalo, South Dakota, they were hungry and needed gas.

One intersection of whitewashed buildings didn't show much promise. OK volunteered to fill the gas tank and Zak hit the small grocery and convenience store and grabbed some bread, a big jar of pepper jelly, and a fat pack of baloney, ketchup, mustard, and more peanut butter.

The clerk, a local pimple-faced boy, gave Zak an odd look, then seemed to figure out the reason for his customer's eccentricity.

"Oh, you here to find some bones?" he asked as he placed the items in a paper sack.

"Pardon me?"

"Dinosaur bones. The country around here is chock full of'm. T-Rex's especially, you know, the big mean ones. They tell me there's only one other place in the world where you can find'm."

"No, I had no idea."

"Oh, I thought you were part of the team across the street." He pointed to another whitewashed building with a mirrored glass door. There was no sign, nothing. "Go knock on the door. It's okay, they don't mind. They've got'm just lying on the floor, giant claws, and teeth, and leg bones, hip bones, ribs, a jawbone you could practically walk in and out of. They've got buckets and trays full of the stuff. It's super cool. Apparently you can't swing a dead cat in these parts without finding some."

Zak emerged into the sunlight with his goodies and was two steps toward the white nondescript building across the way when a giant paw landed on his shoulder.

"Change of plans dude," OK was a little breathless. "Just got off the phone with Archer, seems his chainhand beat the shit out of Crawdad. Everyone's twisted off. We're all supposed to regroup back in Watford. Archer, some guy named Marty, and Blackie are forming crews for some new Tiger rigs comin' in. If Tiger Mike is movin' in, you can bet there'll be plenty of work and roughnecks crawling all over the place!"

They jumped back in the Jeep, and they were Watford City bound.

"So much for the Archer Hansom plan, eh?" Zak said as they motored north.

"Probably wouldn't've worked anyway," OK was keeping an eye on Zak's driving because he had a tendency to jerk the wheel this way and that once he was passionate about whatever he was saying. They both had to yell to be heard over the Jeep's mighty roar, the tape deck, and the wind rattling through the ragtop. "But on the other hand, if the plan was a basic reshuffling of crews, well, this accomplishes that for sure."

Zak was keeping an eye on that big heavy Airstream but, as far as he was concerned, they were gliding along just fine as long as they took it slow and easy.

"Besides, bringing everybody down to Watford and getting on with Tiger Mike is a step up as I see it. I hear those rigs out here in this country are gettin' a little age on'm."

"Dinosaurs."

"Yeah."

On the way up to Watford, Zak instructed OK in the fine art of making baloney and pepper jelly sandwiches, with a dash of ketchup. And goddamn if OK didn't think they were "Splendiferous!"

All the way up to town they discussed and debated every combination of crew they could come up with, like hockey coaches arguing forward line combinations, and the endless possibilities thereof.

They talked about the Airstream, how practical it was going to be once Watford was overbooked and winter set in hard.

"It's big enough for two, that's for sure," OK thought out loud. "Having an extra hand taking care of things might be a good idea, we'll both be workin' our asses off. Why don't we just make a deal right now to share it: care and maintenance, keepin' it stocked and warm. At least until we twist off, or kill each other. I mean the way you say you've been livin', this oughta seem like the Waldorf Astoria."

"Yeah," Zak was pensive. "Everyone's been warnin' me to get my name on a place soon. And I've been meanin' to, but I didn't want to tie myself to owing anybody any money for any length of time, or to being up in Scobey. Now it seems that was a good choice."

"Well, you're welcome to bunk with me."

"Well thanks, thanks a ton, I appreciate it, I really do," and Zak's look of surprise and gratitude was sincere. Their handshake sealed the deal.

"And honestly," OK chortled, like he had just outfoxed the fox, for some reason. "As soon as Arch and the rest see me in this thing, they'll set upon me like a blizzard of rabid dogs. Seriously, I'll have five of them shitbags livin' in here in no time, and there'll be no way of gettin' rid of them. And that's the hideous evil truth."

"The hideous evil truth!" Zak fired up a cig. "We'll need to beef up security first thing. If it's half the madhouse up there in Watford that I think it is, we'll definitely need to lock up tight."

They hooted and hollered at the extra oil patch traffic that was already in evidence as they got closer and closer to town. Indeed, it seemed like a lot of guys had the same idea, hauling their own living quarters with them. One thing was certain, everybody was gassed up and ready to get 'er!

Zak pulled into the City Park which was already more than half-filled to capacity with RVs, trailers, and vehicles of all kinds modified to be lived in.

"Over here," OK pointed to an open area around a big square concrete patch. Zak pulled up and they hopped out. "This is where water and electrical comes into the park. There's probably another like it over there somewhere. Anyway, stay close to this and perhaps we can figure out how to get it all turned on."

They unhitched the Airstream in a spot they assumed would form a lane, perhaps a main thoroughfare, should that many vehicles arrive soon after, and Zak suggested they get some dinner. He had just the spot in mind.

The PDQ Club over in Arnegard was packed. Rows of pickups, bikes, hot rods, and shitboxes galore lined both sides of the street out front.

"Zak! You made it back! How lovely to see you again, and who is this?"

Lottie McCutcheon, the pretty barkeep's mother Zak had met on his previous visit, greeted them at the door wearing an Old West hoop skirt, a very busty lace-up top, and a beehive hairdo wig with flowing reddish blonde curls tumbling in ringlets around her neck. Her makeup was outrageous.

Zak introduced her to OK and she looped her arm through his and ushered them in as though they had been best friends and customers for many many years. And OK looked at Zak with quizzical eyes that very nearly said *Help me!* as they entered the joint.

To the left was the bar, three deep with customers. There were booths and small tables as well, all filled with roughnecks, farmhands, local gals out for dinner, with a loud hubbub and cigarette smoke. In the back, the band was setting up for later.

A "Make Love Not War" poster was in a prominent position over the bar alongside a framed and glassed poster of three people standing at a men's room urinal; the person in the middle was a foxy gal wearing a miniskirt, cowboy hat, and boots. Another large sign read "Subsidy Hell! It's Our Money!"

To the right was the dining room. That was filled to capacity as well.

"I'll put you boys down for a table, it'll only be a few minutes, and what can I get you to drink?" Lottie led them to the bar.

They gave her their order and followed her to the waitress station where the bouncy little blonde bartender came right over. "Hey Zak!" she called out as she handed over their drinks and she had a big warm smile for OK as well. Lottie drifted off to other duties, and Zak and OK sipped their beers, watching the bartender do her thing.

"Boy, that's nothin' but trouble," OK said with a happy growl only Zak could hear. "I bet nobody's gettin' close to that."

Suddenly a gust of hot wet beer breath hit Zak in the back of his head.

"If you fuck her I'll kill you!" A squeaky grizzled whisper assailed his ear.

Zak turned to see Skidder's beaming face bearing down on him grinning ear to ear.

"And if you don't fuck her, I'll never speak to you again!"

They laughed, slapped hands, and gripped each other's fists, and bumped shoulders in a powerful embrace.

Zak introduced OK and the three of them fell in to chatting while watching the bartender bend way over to scoop some ice, then stretch up on tippy-toes for the glasses which were just a little too high over her head.

Over steak and fries, Skidder gave them the lowdown.

"Crawdaddy 'borrowed' somethin' from Arch's chainhand, Johnny Bailey, and ol' Johnny decided to put the boot to'm! Christ he was givin' it to'm somethin' awful, but holy smokes, just when it looked like he was finished, ol' Smoke Denton shows up and he wanted some of Crawdaddy too! Crawdaddy came to life then boy, and they really went at it—for about fifteen seconds— him and Denton, but old Denton just shot out his boot and fuckin' kicked that sombitch right upside his face. He was out cold standing up! Hearin' nothin' but the fuckin' birdies singin'! Oh fuck, so he's lyin' there all passed out and they says, this won't do, so they turned on the hoses and gave it to'm good! He was up'n outta there in a flash! Or in a splash, eh?"

"Were you there?"

"Fuck no, but I heard the story so many times already I may as wella bin! Anyway, them crazy cunts all shook hands here in Watford yesterday. Crawdaddy's still gonna be on one of the new crews with yooz all, so fuck a duck, eh?" Skidder raised his beer, "Good t'go?"

"Good t'go!" they clinked bottles.

"You never know in the oil field," OK shook his head.

Zak and OK stayed for the band, who played a bunch of Waylon & Willie covers, some country swing for the older folks, and some outlaw country for the younger ones. OK and Skidder danced with some of the gals at the club, and Zak talked shop with some of the good ol' boys at the bar.

At one point Zak was telling Lottie about the newly acquired Airstream and how great it was going to be having a roof over their heads with winter coming on. She suggested he join her at their next chamber of commerce meeting and ask the mayor about getting the City Park's power and water turned on. *All right*, thought Zachary Harper, *now we're getting somewhere!* He also wondered about getting the town's medical preparedness a makeover too, if that was even possible.

Later that night the two roughnecks made it back to Watford and crashed in the Airstream. They fell asleep in their sleeping bags, making plans to customize the beast the next day.

They woke early to the sound of loud hard banging on the Airstream's door.

"Fuckin' open up!" they heard Skidder yell.

When Zak unlatched the door, Skidder's furry blond head poked inside.

"Which one of you is Ricky and which one is Lucy?" he hollered into the trailer. "We seen the Jeep!" He had Archer Hansom in tow and within minutes they were off to the Sagebrush, all, that is, except for Skidder, who said he had some other place to be.

When Archer and Zak stepped into the bar, there they all were. Crews from Bomac up in Scobey, as well as a couple of dozen other early birds from down in Deerfield who had been working on those Cardinal rigs, and a few more grizzled fellas who could only have come from over in Gillette, sniffing the air in anticipation of Tiger Mike moving into the area.

As soon as they were in the door, Zak saw arms waving from a table in the back and there with a couple of other fellas were Marty and Jon.

Zak shook hands with everyone, giving Jon and Marty each a strong arm yank toward himself in a kind of smashing-into-each-other gesture of brotherhood. He introduced OK, and within minutes Wellman fit right in.

"You weren't gettin' rid of us that easy," Jon laughed as they sat down.

"We thought you twisted off!" Marty lied. "Beer for bregg-fast?" He poured from a pitcher of Old Milwaukee into an empty ten-ounce glass and handed it to Zak.

Blackie had been working with Tiger down in Gillette for just a couple of months, and when he heard the company was moving soon into the Watford City area he twisted off and sacked'm up. He beat it for home, bringing several hand-picked men with him. Then he quietly spread the word to the better hands he knew that it would be first come, first served for the choicest spots on the newest rigs. Blackie's crew would be made up of hands from Gillette but had also hired out Smoke Denton from Rory's crew to throw chain.

Archer and his chainhand, Johnny Bailey, had picked up Samson, or Ogre, the giant derrickhand from Rory's crew as well as Billy Knott, motorman, and Rory's worm, old man Frye, as well. What had happened to Rory was anyone's guess.

Marty's crew was already set. Jon would be motors, Zak chain, OK in derricks, and a new guy, Tommy Tomlinson, working worm's corner.

"So, everybody says these new Tiger rigs are sharp, but I can tell you first hand, the ones he had down in Colorado were junk," Tommy said as he delivered a fresh pitcher of beer. "I mean, I've heard what out-of-date iron horses those Bomac and Republic rigs can be. Shit, some of them rigs are so much work just to keep'm drillin', months can go by with out'm gettin' properly scrubbed. So now they're not just huge trouble to work on, but they're filthy dangerous too."

Overhearing this, Blackie joined in.

"Oh no no, these new ones are state-of-the-art triples, still three pipes to a stand. Much bigger than we've seen around here, that's for sure. Vic Earlman, you all know Vic, well he and some other drillers got hired out to go down to Louisiana and consult with them puttin' these ones together. The notion being that the men who're gonna work on'm ought to have a hand in buildin' 'm. That's pretty smart."

"Smart? That's unusual," someone said.

"Unheard of," Jon agreed.

In the middle of all this, the Parker Bothers walked in. Crawdad was with them. The left side of his face was purple and swollen up to beat hell.

WHEN ZAK AND OK MADE it back to the Airstream everyone had already taken to calling Big Red, they found quite a surprise waiting for them.

Parked alongside the trailer was a late-model navy blue Chevy Suburban, and Lottie McCutcheon and her daughter Julie were unloading things.

"We just thought you boys could use a feminine touch, seeing as how you appear to be moving in for the season," Lottie smiled, holding a gaggle of cooking implements in one hand and a stack of dish towels in the other. Pretty Julie was all smiles, wearing a pink down vest, tight red jeans, and workboots, her hair down on one side and pinned back on the other.

Without the beehive wig and the hoop skirt, Lottie looked much smaller and younger than Zak remembered. They had brought a bunch of plates, bowls, cutlery, towels, and cleaning products from the PDQ Club.

"Stuff we replaced a while ago and hadn't gotten rid of yet," they explained. Before long there were curtains up, fresh sheets and heavy blankets, pillows in pillowcases all in place, and the four of them were sitting down to a roast chicken dinner with peas, mashed potatoes, gravy, and white wine. Not long after that, the place was cleaned up, dishes stacked in their appropriate cabinets, etc., then both women kissed both men sweetly on the lips and left, promising to return soon.

"What just happened?" OK Wellman asked Zachary Harper.

"I'm not sure," answered Zachary Harper. "But I hope it happens again."

It never did.

THAT EVENING, MARTY'S CREW MET at the City Bar and Zak got the story of the great Crawdaddy Smackdown several more times. Most versions were pretty much in agreement with Skidder's regarding the facts, but somehow, depending on the teller, each rendering was funnier than the last.

"So, this Tiger Mike everybody talks about…" Zak said, opening the floor to anyone with the particulars. The new guy, Tommy, started in.

"He's a rich guy big shot, really flamboyant. He dresses up in these crazy suits, drives big expensive cars, always has a buncha broads on his arm. Will fire ya for spittin' on the sidewalk, or lookin' at'm sideways, or wearing orange or some such shit. But he ain't cheap, passes the dough around pretty good, pays better'n anybody else out here."

Jon, on the other hand, had been doing his homework.

"Tiger Mike was a cab driver. No kidding. He married an heiress, a newspaper heiress maybe. These new rigs he's got cost about four million apiece. And they're big. Triples, like Blackie said. How far can they go down, Marty, twelve, fourteen thousand feet?"

"If they can git down twelb-fourteen, you can bet ol' Blackie can take'm down fifteen 'r twenty."

"Christ, that's almost three miles," Jon sighed. "And them rigs are new? Never nippled up before? So we're the guinea pigs."

"Guinea pigs?" Zak asked.

"It's new iron," Jon scratched his chin. "Well we're the ones who're gonna have to make all those pieces fit together."

When all this was going to happen was a matter of great conjecture and concern, as there were other wildcatters moving into the area as well, and holding out for a spot on Tiger that might or might not happen could cause them to miss a good job with one of those outfits. Everyone promised to keep their ears to the rail, their noses in the wind, and to give a shout when there was news. The boys bought a case of beer and followed OK and Zak back to Big Red for a nightcap.

Late that night, as OK was stepping over Archer, Skidder, and Jon, either stretched out on the floor or huddled in a ball under a blanket, snoring peacefully, Zak head him chortle as he passed Zak on his bench, "How's that new security system of ours workin' out?"

Zak joined him out in the fresh cold night air, and as they emptied their bladders in tandem streams, they looked up into the night, and it started to snow.

XVIII

By dawn the next day roughnecks were poking their heads out of RVs, pickups, windows, and doors. The ones who hadn't thought or cared about the arrival of winter cared now and got busy. Although the snowfall had been light, the temperature was dropping steadily, as it would a little more each day for the foreseeable future.

Zak and OK motored over to Williston for heavy-duty winter work clothes, Carhartt thermals, the works. Zak got himself a pair of black heavily oiled waterproof, steel-toed logging boots, the kind with the cowboy boot heel for a little extra height and traction.

That evening Marty found Zak at the City Bar. Zak was just settling in for the evening after a hearty meal at the Burger Ranch, when Marty came in and joined him. He was all business.

"Jon's gone back up to Scobey to see Barry Ellen, and I neet a chainhand right dow!"

Blackie, he said, was out drilling for a Challenger rig an hour southwest of town, and was going to be shorthanded for at least one night starting tonight.

"He wants me to go drillin'," Marty fussed behind the wheel as they hurried south.

"So what's the deal?"

"Imb not sure, sometink about sumb dumb wormb driller stalling de number one engine, den fuckin' up n stalling number two!"

"Fuck!"

"D'whole fookin' rig's shut down, lights are out, sez it's quiet like a ghost rig out dere. Dey're worried about de damn hole cavin' in, de whole works!" Then after a moment of deep thought he said, "De mud might gel…"

Zak wondered how it was possible.

"Dat company hand got so pissed he run dat toolpusher right off and pulled Blackie off dat brake handle and said, 'Yer pushin' tools!' So Blackie banged on my door after he run off that wormb driller and he sez, Marty, you're drillin' and we gotta go now! So I sez, well lemme have my own freakin' chainhand at least, and he sez who and I sez Jon, but fuck! Jon's not here, so I sez Zak an he sez okay!"

When they arrived at that Challenger rig, there were a lot of roughnecks and other hands milling about down on the ground and sure enough, things were just as quiet as can be. It was spooky—with the sun almost down and no lights on—anyone who knew what that rig should have looked and sounded like would have had a shiver, like a devil's fingernail running up their spine. But just as Zak and Marty were running for the stairs they heard a roar of thunder, the entire rig shuddered, and the number one giant Universal engine up on the floor sprang to life!

The two men dashed up the stairs and stopped halfway when an ear-piercing shriek and a long metallic wail told them the light plant was starting up too, and the big bright lights in the tower aiming down at the floor and others around the rig suddenly came on.

From all over the rig and the surrounding location there arose a human cheer!

Marty and Zak landed in the top doghouse where several roughnecks were watching the doings out on the floor and trying their best to stay out of the way.

Blackie and a couple of motormen were pulling open that number two Universal; another man, the company hand, was standing and pointing at this and that, handing tools to one or the other, and screaming to be heard.

Marty pulled Frank Kramer's crescent wrench marked "Bomac 34" from his back pocket and waved it at the driller as he muscled through the gang of guys at the door. And when he saw Marty, Blackie signaled him to come right out onto the floor.

Zak and the other boys watched as Blackie put Marty at the brake handle and gave him some quick instructions regarding some signals they were going to use. Marty nodded yes, understanding all. Then Blackie returned to that number two Universal.

"How much throttle?" someone yelled.

"How much choke?"

Blackie and the others were banging and cursing, and signaled to Marty who hit that throttle, then the brake, and that rig shuddered again. After a few encouraging attempts, they got that bastard jump-started with a mighty roar.

Blackie then relieved Marty and pointed—*You, and you, and you, off the floor! Then—you, you, and you, out onto the floor!* The men being called into action took their stations, and Zak realized it was chainhand's call too, and he took his place without hesitation.

The big compressors hissed, and that rotary table turned, and the pipe in the hole began circulating, nice and slow, a little rough at first, but within a few minutes she was turning smoothly, almost like nothing had ever happened.

When Blackie was certain they were in the clear, with fresh mud flowing, he motioned to Marty, who stepped right in and the driller stepped away, and Marty smiled as his foot rested on the throttle and his strong right arm grabbed that brake handle. Zak realized that this was going to be a moment that small ape, that derrickhand from Jesse Lancaster's crew, his friend, would remember. He looked like such a natural at that brake handle too, it was kind of beautiful. And Zachary Harper was grateful for the joy of being witness to Marty's first tower as a driller.

The rest of that tower and all of the next Marty and Zak went about their business. Blackie's motorman and worm were strong, efficient, and a pleasure to work with. All those years in the derrick with Jesse Lancaster down below at the brake handle had given Marty that same silky feel with brake and throttle, and that pipe moved swiftly and glided to a stop so smoothly the boys could really pick up the pace making those connections. Between connections, and to familiarize themselves with the rig and its crew, Zak followed Marty down to the hopper. Marty declared the mud operation up to snuff. Marty checked on motorman's motors, making sure there wasn't any damage from the power shutdown that might have gone undetected before. At seven a.m., relief arrived and had to be brought up to date on what had happened in the intervening towers. Blackie took Marty and Zak aside and let them know that this could go on another week if they wanted the work. They said sure.

On their way back to Watford that morning in the Bronco, Marty was in a mood to remember.

"I was motorman, ob course, before I went up in de derrick. Der's somb good motormen out dere today, we were a liddle bit good and a whole lot lucky!" When Zak asked Marty if he was going to miss being up in the derrick, Marty said, well yeah, but one never knows, he thought he'd be back up there one way or another from time to time at least. But to be honest, he had always wanted to drill, he knew he was ready. Then Zak mentioned how nimble Marty appeared when ascending or climbing down that tower, and Marty gave a wry smile Zak hadn't seen before.

"Dat was de acksident," he said.

"Oh?"

"I was a kidt," Marty explained in that strange accent no one could place. "Ya, I hat jist turned sixt-teen. My daddy got me a job at a sawmill, loggin', out West. Ob course he wouldn't buy me no boots. I had ta wait till payday to get'm, so I wore only my Chucks. So sure enuf, on my second day I wanted to show ebbrybody how strong I was, tossin dem giant logs about. But I drobbed a giant one on bote my feet. I didn't say nuttin' but I broke bote my big toes. Anyways, so I went and hid, I tucked each broke toe under my udder toes, den tied dem Chucks on real tite. Hat to walk on de sides ob my feet dat way I do. So dey just healed up dat way, bin dere ebber since!"

"Good Christ, Marty!"

"Ya, but what could I do? My fadder woulda kilt me for losing work as soon as I started. Woulda said I did it on purpose, woulda throwd me out. Boy dem doggys hert, boy, cried myself to sleep many a night at that ol' loggin camp, for a year or two dat's for sure."

"Marty!" Zak scolded.

"Ya ya, I know, Cyn says I should go get'm broke and put right. But, well, fuck! Fix one and hobble around for six months, then fix de udder one'n hobble about some more? I nebber told anyone about doze toes, but Cyn, it's a kinda secret."

"It's safe with me," Zak promised, but for the rest of the ride back it was all he could think about, staring at Marty's boots, turned in a bit, and he shuddered.

OF COURSE ONE WEEK TURNED into two, then an open engagement. No one was sure when those Tiger rigs were going to show up and some, like Jon, wondered if they would at all. Jon was now commuting every few days from up in Scobey, and Blackie eventually hired him out with another crew on Challenger as well. Some nights Jon stayed with Marty and Cynthia, other nights he spent on the floor in Big Red.

Every day Zak would wander over to Freddy's trailer, but there were no signs of life. Every day it snowed a little more and every day it got colder.

ONE MORNING ZAK HAD JUST stepped quietly out of the cramped tubelike shower on the Airstream, pulled on his long johns, and was about to hit the rack, when there was a polite little rapping at the Airstream's door. He eased it open, and there was Lottie McCutcheon, wearing her Sunday best.

"The chamber meets this morning, Zak. Hurry and get dressed so you can get a good seat!" Zak found a clean white cotton button-down shirt, wrinkled to beat hell, in the bottom of his duffel bag, and clean jeans and boots, splashed on a little Lilac Vegetal, let the sleeping dogs lie there in the trailer, and they were on their way.

The Burger Ranch was open early and the lot outside was filling up. Inside, the well-scrubbed, fresh-faced Best of Watford City were loading up on free coffee and cakes, stacks of bacon and egg sandwiches, and a big bowl of canned fruit.

Zak looked around the room and took a standing spot along a far wall near an exit, but close enough to hear and see what was going on. Several other rancher types lined up alongside him so they could duck out early and quietly if they wanted to.

Checking out the crowd, Zak recognized many faces he had seen about town and was able to identify local bankers and real estate folks, shop owners, farm supply and hardware dealers, a doctor and dentist type, a couple of dozen very solid citizens, probably the ranch and landowners currently hosting wildcat drilling operations, all looking for information. Scattered about these were several of the very disgruntled.

The atmosphere was loud and tense. Many were meeting and greeting cordially as always, but their pleasantries were drowned out by the hubbub and commotion throughout the room as everyone got their coffee and breakfast and took their places, moving chairs, tossing coats, settling in. One grizzled farmer inching his way to a seat in the middle of the room was calling people out, pointing at them and cursing. Others just shouted out agenda items. Sitting along a makeshift row facing into the room with a portable podium with a microphone and built-in speaker were the chamber officials, Lottie among them, and the morning's guest speakers.

The secretary read the minutes from the last meeting. The treasurer reminded everyone that their dues were overdue, which got a group chortle and a couple of *So whats* from the crowd.

"Where's Partridge?" the grizzled farmer in the middle of the room called out. There was a grumbling from those who thought he was rude and out of order as well as from those who wanted an answer to his question.

"Mayor Partridge was kind enough to let himself be our guest two meetings ago, but he is not obliged to come to chamber meetings, Mr. Kryder," Lottie broke in.

"I want to know if these oil people are using up all our water?" a deep voice called out from in the back.

"Now Bill, we have our schedule for the meeting right here," Lottie scolded and held up a sheet of paper that everyone had on their chair when they came in. Few had studied it.

"We'll get to water, Bill, but that's more of an issue for the legislative council, and as you know, those meetings are open to the public, so please, let's stay on course here," one of the panel said calmingly.

It was Lottie who took the podium first.

"First we'll hear from Cecil Pumphrey. Cecil is from the Salisbury Trucking Group, a proud North Dakota company by the way, and Cecil is also a member of the Greater McKenzie County Chamber of Commerce. He has degrees in geology, works closely with wildcat companies, and has worked with the North Dakota Geological Survey to keep track of doings in the Williston Basin at large, but more importantly, Cecil helps us anticipate changes in the patch before they happen. Thanks for getting up early and joining us this morning, Cecil," she said and sat down.

There was polite applause.

"Thanks Lottie, hi everyone. I've been going around, when I can, to some of the local chambers, because I know a lot of you don't like having your lives disrupted the way we have lately, and I know others of you are happy to have the oil boom back in a way we haven't seen since the late sixties.

"We're in the position we're in because the good people over at OPEC raised the price of oil, and also because of the Red Wing Creek discovery.

"As you know, when OPEC raised the price of oil, risk capital that had gotten all cozy collecting interest in savings accounts suddenly wanted a sniff at that higher oil price. That plus the fact that when oil was too cheap, there was a big decline in production at about the same time that oil consumption was really taking off. So here we are, a few years after the latest finds at Little Knife and Mondak, the price of oil is still going up, consumption is still on the rise, and so, consequently, there's an exploratory drilling boom going on that will necessitate a prolonged developmental period after that."

"So the fuckin' Ah-rabs did us a favor!" someone shouted, and everyone laughed hard.

The hubbub increased.

A member of the panel raised a hand.

"Yes Adam?" Lottie encouraged the man to get up and take the podium.

"Who is that guy?" Zak asked the man next to him.

"I think he's from the mayor's office, name is Nossiter. He's the number-cruncher guy everybody has to go through to get their leases submitted and approved."

"I was just going to say," Nossiter was tall, severe, and utterly humorless. He was a tenuous public speaker. "That the upside here is that with an exploratory boom going on, there's also a lease rush under way."

"Tell us something we don't know!" someone called out, and everyone laughed. From there, Nossiter began to fumble through his notes. He mentioned that in 1970 there were less than three hundred thousand dollars in lease bonuses handed out, compared to last year when the number had skyrocketed to twenty million; this year was closer to thirty million dollars.

Somebody called out that no one had come to him wanting to lease *his* land. Someone else told that guy to shut up.

Cecil Pumphrey added to Nossiter's stats. "There's between a hundred and twenty to two hundred rigs in the area now, and if the Canadians are serious about nationalizing their oil industry, we'll inherit another couple hundred rigs from up there."

"They ain't waitin'!" Kryder called out. "They're leavin' now before the government takes'm!"

"I doubt that'll really happen," Cecil Pumphrey answered, but nobody heard him.

Pumphrey and Nossiter then began to have a cordial conversation, comparing notes out loud for everyone's benefit. Amoco was nearing completion of a ten-inch, forty-thousand-barrel-a-day pipeline from Billings Nose to its main line, while Koch Industries was doing the same with a natural gas pipeline. All in all, by the end of next year North Dakota should be putting out forty million barrels. The state's usage this year was projected to be in the twenty- to twenty-five-million-barrel range. By the end of next year North Dakota, at full capacity, would be contributing one percent of the nation's needs, or enough oil to run the entire country—for four days.

Zak decided to duck out for a smoke.

"They done in there yet? I want one of those bacon and egg sandwiches before they're all gone," a middle-aged gentleman in clean jeans and a suede jacket over a checkered shirt asked Zak, as he motioned with a cigarette that he'd like a light. Zak hit him up. He blew out the smoke and looked back toward the Burger Ranch side door where loud garbled conversation could be heard, then a roar of laughter, then a round of applause. "These meetings used to be civilized, no speakers really, free food, everybody would just schmooze and bitch about business. Now they're like mayor's council meetings, same folks, yakking and squawking the same old shit."

"Zak Harper," the roughneck introduced himself.

"Scott Becker." They shook hands. "I'm on the Planning Commission and a half-dozen other boards. You must be the roughneck Lottie was telling us about. The City Park guy?"

"Lottie mentioned me?"

"Don't be so surprised. Lottie's turned the Hospitality Committee she chairs into her own personal marching society. You know, like in the French or Russian Revolution when some guy who's only in charge of hockey pucks ends up runnin' the whole show?"

"Hockey pucks?"

"She started out in charge of coffee and donuts and floral arrangements and now she's chair of meetings, organizing committee functions, keeping everybody focused. She can get more done over a couple of sodas, two ounces of whiskey, and a handful of bar nuts than any three in there. But the City Park has us all scratching our heads. What'd you have in mind?"

"Well I'm not sure, but at least during this next stretch it sure might be nice to get the power turned on over there."

"Yeah, you know there's a city ordinance says you can't stay more than three nights consecutive in the City Park. Of course, that was when the only people passing through were the odd motorcycle gangs and what have you. We've changed it to three weeks. But that won't hold up either. Clearly we've got nowhere to put you guys. We've tried to get the drilling companies to put up a camp outside of town, but they don't wanna spend the money, and the ranchers don't want any part of it. Plus there's just too many different drilling outfits comin' in and outta here, each with its own troubles, for any of that to come together. You fellas sure seem to be makin' the best of it, no matter what we do. Maybe we could get the power turned on for ya. Think you could pass the hat over there and see what kind of donation those boys could make to Parks and Recreation? Trash pickup alone is already a problem."

"You got a card?"

"Sure. Tell you what, Zak, let's go get a couple of those bacon and egg sandwiches."

Back inside, the meeting was breaking up and everyone was standing about eating, sipping coffee, and talking loudly when Becker led Zak over to Lottie's hospitality table. There was a giant bowl into which people had tossed their business cards, some handmade. He fished out several and said, "Take these with you. These are the folks who can make your lives a lot easier over there."

Back outside, Zak leaned against Lottie's Suburban, smoked a cig, and flipped through the cards. Barber shop, refuse hauling, game butcher, police, clinic, power and electric, propane, sewage, savings and loan, and several members of the mayor's council.

"Watford is run by the mayor and the mayor's council," Lottie explained, as she gave him a ride back to the park. "They have equal authority so no one person can just make decisions without the others. I was hoping to introduce you to Adam Nossiter, but actually Scotty Becker is perfect. He's low key, gets things done, never quarrels. Best of all, he's always around but never a pest. I mean, had you not told me, I wouldn't have known he was there, but he's always about."

When they arrived back at the Airstream, Jon and OK were gone, and as Lottie dropped him off, her eyes were twinkling.

"Your buddy OK has been a regular at the club lately, Zak. He and my Julie seem to have hit it off, but we haven't seen you around."

"Oh I've been workin' nights, it'll only last another few days. Yeah, I've been missin' the club, don't worry, I'll be in. By the way, I hope OK is behaving himself."

"He's smarter than the average bear around here, that's for sure," she winked.

About six hours of blissful dreamless sleep later, the door to the Airstream opened and OK, Jon, and Marty came in.

"We're run off," Jon said as he handed the sleepy man lifting his head from the pillow a beer. "Blackie's back to drillin', they got themselves another toolpusher. Tiger's comin' in next week, it's official. Blackie's gonna twist off from Challenger to go work for Tiger and says we all got jobs! So this'll be our last chance to head'm back to Scobey and pick up our checks from Bomac! But we can leave that till morning. C'mon sleepy head, we're on days off, let's go get drunk!"

XIX

Zak didn't drive directly to Scobey, Montana. He left Watford City early and he drove directly to Bomac 34 instead. It was a late autumn, early winter's day. A light snow had fallen in the night, and gave the entire scene a bright, glowing contrast to the gray overcast sky that reached far and wide blurring the horizon. On the drive up, light flurries animated his views and gave him a warm memory of childhood excitement and possibilities of adventure that made him smile.

When he got near to location, the Jeep, Tatonka, had a slow slippery climb up to the hole on the hill.

To his amazement, there was a giant roadwork Caterpillar, a quarter-of-a-million-dollar piece of machinery, perched at the top of rig road with a long industrial cable attached, pulling a thirty-thousand-gallon water hauler the last leg up the hill in the snow. Zak four-wheeled around the giant water truck and pulled up next to that big Cat, put his hard hat on his head and got out, lit a cig, and just watched those boys get it!

"Hey Zak!" he heard a familiar voice rising above the racket to see George Cleaver crunching his way through two inches of snow toward him, a walkie-talkie barking in his hand. They shook hands warmly.

"George!" Zak gestured to the Cat pulling that water hauler up the hill. "This has got to be your finest hour!"

"Yeah, that Caterpillar foreman overheard us on the CB radio having trouble, and before we knew it there comes this big rig up the hill, like the cavalry. Frank hired 'em out for the remainder of the hole. He talked that foreman into plucking a bunch of guys with roughneckin' experience from a few other outfits too, and we were back up'n running in no time!"

They chatted amiably for some minutes, both discreetly avoiding the Crawdad Incident. Zak filled him in on the situation back in Watford, and George shook his head with a grin when he heard about Tiger Mike rolling into the area.

"Driller Rory is still here, Hale Parker, and some of the others. Those boys don't have much faith that Tiger's gonna come through, and Rory, stubborn old cuss that he is, says he don't wanna work on no new iron. Shit," George spat into the snow, "what're ya gonna do."

In a drawer in that toolpusher's trailer, where George said it would be, was an envelope marked, "Jesse's Crew." Zak plucked his check from the bunch as well as Freddy's and Marty's.

As he was turning to leave, Zak noticed a shoebox full of Bomac Drilling Co. stickers sitting on a file cabinet. He rubbed the dust from his hard hat with the sleeve of his coat and ever so carefully stuck one on the back. After admiring his work, and proud of what it took to earn it, he grabbed a few more stickers for Jon, Marty, and Freddy before stepping outside.

He then took one last look around. He saw Samson up in the derrick, but no one else he knew, so he decided not to linger. He wheeled down off the hill and continued on to Scobey, Montana.

A hot shower and a shave, a good meal, a real bed, and a night away from the Watford City circus suddenly had great appeal and so he checked in at the Pioneer Hotel.

An hour later, he was scrubbed and clean of face, and settled in at Simone's. Stragglers from lunch were just finishing up. Others were burrowed in at the bar for the long haul.

Zak was finishing his first beer and thinking of just chilling for the rest of the day, hoping maybe to see Jon and Mary Ellen, when in walked Sam.

She breezed in through the kitchen, as usual, and was all smiles and pretty as can be. Her long black hair with a new tinsel-like streak of silver hung over her left shoulder, curling down in a silken coil gathered at the top of her breast by a piece of purple yarn that matched the stitching in her lacy billowing blouse. She wore deep blue stretch pants and tall furry boots and she seemed very pleased to see Zachary Harper. She pulled up a stool beside Zak, her perfume washing over him in a euphoric rosy-vanilla haze, her beads and bracelets clattering musically.

"It's my day off, sweet man," she smiled flirtatiously, and tossed a look at Hal, the barkeep, who reached not for her usual jug of house red but for a rich ruby port, and poured her a small glass.

She was full of questions, her voice deep and sonorous, her accent, which Zak always presumed was French, or French Canadian, now had a deeper, more sultry tone; sardonic, world weary. There was an extra something going on in the back of her throat. He thought she even rolled an R. Eastern European?

"And how is poor Freddy?"

"I'm not sure, he's been gone for a while."

"You must make him understand that we miss him. What about Jesse?"

"Jesse's okay, I think he's on the verge of retirement."

"Well, it's been hard for him, but he will find his way. And what about Skidder, Archer, and their crazy crew? The Parkers? The cowboys?"

"Everyone is scrambling for winter quarters."

She really did lose a pile of customers when everyone twisted off. Zak sympathized.

"So let me get this straight," she tapped his wrist with her long purple talons. "There's a big fight out at the rig, so everybody gets angry and quits. Then you go, and abandon your friends here in Scobey," she made a little pout, "and everyone follows you like the Pied Piper down to Watford City. All of you heroes get jobs on the same rig so you can continue your arguments down there, instead of here?"

Her brow wrinkled with displeasure but the twinkle in her eyes told him she was playing.

"No, no, no," Zak was embarrassed nonetheless. "You see, initially, I went down to Rapid City to pick up a derrickha…"

"Let's not quarrel, dear," Simone said soothingly, gently play acting. She placed her hand on his wrist. She brightened as their eyes met.

This foolishness is nice, thought Zachary Harper. He noticed she wasn't wearing as much makeup as he remembered. Still pretty, younger than he thought, maybe forty-two? She had crow's feet that made her big black eyes soft and mirthful. The lines on her face weren't angry ones, they were smiles, and those smiles were alluring in all their different aspects. Only her tone of voice said it might be, and was in some ways, a mask.

"When I heard that you were gone I was actually a bit fearful we might not see each other again," she said so offhandedly he thought it might be true. "It would make sense, after all," she shrugged, as if conversing with herself.

"That would have been *my* loss," Zak replied, "but I would never have left without saying goodbye, you've been a terrific help to me."

"Well," she sighed with relief, "you are here now, and it is, after all, my day off, and I must hurry home. I'm going to cook a big lamb stew, and promised Corey to give him some tomorrow. Now, won't you be a dear and help me carry some groceries out to my car?"

"Well sure," Zak followed her through the kitchen. Yes, the accent was definitely French, he reassured himself.

"My house is about ten minutes from here," she explained as he carried a big box and followed her with some groceries to her truck parked out back. It was a Dodge Ramcharger that had clearly died and come back to life somehow. Yes, there were men in her life a-plenty.

She shifted a grocery bag from one arm to the other as she unlocked the gate at the back of her outfit. She then leaned in to place her bag inside and Zak admired her hips. *Someone, not saying who, could become rather devoted to that*, he thought.

"Zak, if you're free today," she said as she shut the back gate and, moving toward the passenger door, pulled it open, "why not ride out with me? You can help make the stew. Wouldn't a home-cooked meal be nice? I'll bring you back later. Hop in!"

He did and off they went.

Simple as that.

Yes she had rooms and an office above the bar and she stayed there most nights, but the house was a lifesaver when she needed to get the bar out of her system for a spell.

"It is just a cottage, but I love it," she explained as she operated the vehicle's standard transmission with both hands and feet, and she looked quite youthful doing it, almost giddy. Zak breathed a happy sigh as he watched the rolling landscape pass and he cracked his window, felt the cold prairie air in his face, scented with gasoline, carbon dioxide, and her perfume and port. About ten miles west of town they pulled off the road, snaking up a long winding drive that led to a small house with a blue roof halfway up a hill that could be seen from quite a distance.

Simone's cabin was a small one-bedroom affair, nestled into the side of the hill. They grabbed the box and bags from the back and she opened up the house, turned up the heat, and lit a couple of coal-oil lamps.

Zak set down his box as she got settled, and he went and stood before the large living room window. The endless view from up on that hill was spare of trees or much variation but impressive in its depth and distances.

In a corner there was a sewing station, and Zak noticed quilts of all shapes and sizes, made of all manner of remnants, tossed over chairs, spread across the bed, over the back of the couch. The sleeping area was one step up with a curtain pulled back. The décor was spare, which was a bit of a surprise considering the ornate style in which she had decorated her bar.

"I've come to love this view, you can see so far," she appeared at his side and handed him a goblet of homemade plum-red wine. "Look," she pointed to a big gray weather pattern off to the left that appeared as though the sky was falling, then she pointed to the right where clouds were parting and rays of sunshine were beaming down. "I can watch the clouds for hours."

The wine had a sweet, velvety texture, with a peppery finish. It was delicious.

Her arm slid around his waist, his around hers. Their personal contact was even more intoxicating.

"A great place to sit and read," Zak said.

"Yes, or to sit and let your mind go empty, like the view. Do you like the wine?"

"Pure ambrosia," he smiled.

When Zak admired the small paintings at either side of the window, primitive but pleasant renderings of woolly evergreen mountains and deep blue-green lakes, she smiled.

"My mother painted those from memory of where she grew up in the province of Quebec. When the view of all that nothing starts to get to me, these can chase away a dreary feeling, give me peace."

They melted into each other's arms for a long, sensuous embrace. He buried his nose in her neck, her hair, and he squeezed her. He took a delicious, deep breath, and he made a growling, purring sound of pleasure that she responded to innately, squeezed him back, and gave him a little nip on his neck.

Then she put down her glass and took his face in her hands and smiled warmly, her deep dark eyes happy as they drank in his. Whatever she had been looking for, whatever question was in those eyes, had been answered affirmatively he could tell. They embraced again, her sumptuous body now fitting the contours of his own, and she kissed his neck, then she smiled, and kissed his lips with a short quick peck.

She took his hand and led him to the kitchen area where he helped her unload the groceries and they laid out the ingredients for their dinner.

"One thing I love about living here, yes, the people can be crude, but they each have a skill, and each skill when joined with the others becomes a skill for the survival of all. One can fix your car, another can build a front step, others can keep the cold from getting in or the heat from getting out. Most of the men are good with their hands, and the women are too. Yes, I have a lot to be thankful for."

"Well, they have a lot to thank you for, Simone. I mean, think about how dreary this town would be without your generosity, the way you take care of us roughnecks, your cooking, and well, without your beautiful self, my dear."

"Well, everyone works hard." She smiled over her shoulder, thanking him for the compliment as she set up a cutting board and started placing vegetables and knives on it. "And unlike in some small towns, I like the fact that everyone knows each other's business, it keeps us safe."

"Safe? From who?"

"From each other I suppose. Or mysterious strangers," she winked. "Oh, there always is a dark river beneath the surface of human doings, but you mustn't let it get too deep, too dark, or too fast running. So you must have contact, there must be empathy, there must be mutual need and respect, so that the rumors will die as soon as they fly."

"Is your mother still with us?" Zak asked with a look toward the paintings by the window.

"She is always with me, but no, she passed on several years ago. That's when I left Quebec and came here. Lilly and Hal joined me shortly after I took over the bar. I don't think I could have managed early on without them."

"Why here?"

"I want to ask you that question."

"I suspect our motivations aren't too very different," he answered cryptically, which seemed to satisfy her.

He was chopping onions and she was mashing spices with a mortar and pestle. She set Zak to work carving a slab of lamb into little square chunks.

"Mother and I owned a small bistro in Montreal. One night a very pleasant Yankee couple, elderly, came in and sat down. Graham and Nora Cheetle were their names. We had the most delightful conversation. They had never tasted real French food, French wine. They wanted some of our recipes. They said they were from a small town in Montana. Showed me a picture of the saloon they owned. The Corkscrew Gulch Saloon. I don't know of a Corkscrew Gulch. But it looked so far away, so small and peaceful. So, after Mama was gone, I sold the bistro and I got in the car and drove straight here.

"They hired me without question, to cook and tend bar at first. Then they retired and put me in charge. First Mrs. Cheetle died, then he not too long after. They left me the bar, the truck, this little house."

"What a change that must have been."

"A welcome change. At home the Quebec separatists had come out of the hills, out of the woodwork. They loved our little bistro, it was out of the way, small tables, dark booths, jazz on Thursdays and Sundays. They had been stirring up trouble for a decade or more, but now they whipped themselves into such a frenzy there was a real crisis, an uprising it was called. Living in their own angry little world, they thought they could usurp the mighty colossus the state had made. Idiots they were, to be sure, but beautiful idiots. Beautiful, talented idiots.

"Then some people were kidnapped, a British consulate, a labor minister or councilman or some priests, or whoever it was they hated. Others killed and were killed. I don't think any of the real criminals were at our bistro, but they sympathized. So the military took over and roamed the streets for a while, searching homes, making arrests. Many of my people are from the old country, Zak. Soldiers in the street are something we don't like to see."

"How did you manage to stay out of it?"

"I didn't! The police came to talk to me several times. Then the soldiers came too. They would say 'What do you know about your customers?' I would say 'I know that they all hate you.' 'Why?' they would ask, and I would say, 'Why does anyone hate anyone? Because they are not like them!'

"Then Mama died so suddenly. There is so much pain in the world Zak, it seems foolish, but one wonders why it isn't just natural for people to spend every waking moment easing the pain of others."

"Well you sure take a lot of the pain out of living in a place like Scobey, I mean, if not for you what would happen to Corey..."

"Corey is a very special case. I suppose I inherited Corey from Graham and Nora, along with the bar and the house and the car. Cheetle was a colonel in the war. Corey was a gunner, the kind who shoots at airplanes. It was in Sicily I think they said. The Americans were attacking with planes full of paratroopers in the middle of the night. They simply forgot to tell their gunners on the ground that they would be passing overhead. Idiots. Corey knew by the sound of their engines that they were ours. But the rest of the gunners did their job and they unknowingly murdered thousands of their own men that night. They found Corey the next day wandering about the wreckage of those planes, chattering and babbling. Colonel Cheetle took him under his wing, but he was broken."

Zak sat back and stared at the ceiling as though seeing the entire battle. Corey losing his mind, pleading with the others to stop, and when he couldn't stop them, dashing out into the night of fire and death.

"They said that Tommy Coster was on one of those planes. He died a year later from his wounds. Corey believed he had shot Tommy down, but everyone knew Corey didn't fire a shot that night, they were going to court martial him for disobeying the orders to shoot, when Colonel Cheetle stepped in. Strange is the mind is it not, to carry such guilt for something you didn't really do?"

"Strange indeed," Zak said in a tiny voice. "Corey showed me a medal."

"A Canadian boy in the sanitarium took the medal off his own chest and gave it to Corey for trying to stop the shooting of the planes. He was a hero to the shell-shocked lunatics."

"There is something noble still about the man."

"Yes, I am glad you can see that, Zak. It is part of what I love about you."

"Tell me Simone, whatever became of your beautiful idiots?"

"They scattered, some were arrested, locked up, and the keys to their cells thrown away. Some were killed. I don't know about the rest, perhaps they got on with their lives.

"And what about you, Zak, where were you in October 1970 while my Québécois were losing their minds?"

"I was at a small college in Colorado taking theology, comparative religions, with minors in theosophy…and banking."

Simone threw her head back and laughed, "So you were going to be a priest!"

"No, far from it. But this was a Jesuit school and I wanted to learn philosophy, and they teach it pretty good. But you're right, 1970 was a crazy year."

They were letting the stew simmer, sipping plum wine. She took his hands in hers and turned them palms up.

"May I look?"

"Of course."

"Your left hand shows the life you were born to lead. The right one, the actual life you are leading. They appear to be two remarkably different stories. Would you like to hear them?"

He nodded yes.

"Look at the left hand, all the lines are strong and bold, long life, deep in head and heart, the fate line intersects the head and heart lines with meaning and purpose. Now look at the right. The head line is strong, but not as much, the life line is weak here, here, early, and here, earlier still, and the heart line is broken, here, and again here, and further along the heart line seems coming apart, again and again, it even disappears here and here. Tell me Zak, has love been so indifferent to you?"

Zak's face was open, his eyes transfixed on his open palms, two different lives passing before his eyes.

"The fate line," Simone traced the line bisecting his head and heart lines, the fate line running south from between his first two fingers down and down. "Look, on the left, there is no doubt that this is a man who has every intention of fulfilling his purpose, whatever that may be. But here on the right, it has split in the middle, until now we find there are actually two faint lines where once there was one, running side by side. This, I have not seen.

"So, Zak," she poured more wine, "You apparently decided *not* to be a priest…"

Zak sat back, pensive and serious.

"The last time someone read my palm I was a little boy. My father and I were traveling. The palm reader introduced himself as a magi or magus, from Somalia. The magi took my left hand and after just a glance he gave it back to me and said, 'You trust the ones you love too much.' You know, I thought he was stupid or crazy. It made me angry, I mean, who else *should* I trust? But what he said lingered in my mind. Later on that same trip, a woman read my tea leaves, and she said, 'You give your love as freely as you give your trust, you should learn the difference.' I was stunned, how in the world can two such things tell the same story? One clarifying the other! All I could think was, there's a lot more here than meets the eye."

"I can explain it simply." Simone sat back, considering him, her eyes twinkling; she sipped her wine. "You know, Zak, the scientists and mathematicians, the alchemists are correct when they suggest that you alter a thing when you touch it, which can only mean that you too will be altered when something touches you. So then, is it so hard to believe that a mere cup of tea, once you have consumed its contents, or the lines on your face or hand, cannot be read for the stories that they tell about you?"

"It makes sense to me now."

"Does it *yes* Zak? Then tell me. Tell me about your own beautiful idiots."

"I was the idiot, and not so beautiful it turned out. The youngest vice president the bank had ever recruited. One of the top bankers on the East Coast took me under his wing. I was so proud. I loved him the way you might love a surrogate father. Together we started piling up international accounts. Until one day I saw in the back of the newspaper a small AP report about a series of massacres carried out in small mountain villages. You see, it was at that moment I realized I had been recruited for my youth and naïveté. The loans purportedly were for schools. Books. Farm equipment. Food. But the money went to soldiers, guns, and the merciless liquidation of those whose only crime was to want to organize, to save their families. One little paragraph. I looked around those offices and I was suddenly—other."

"And," she held his right hand in her hands, studying that broken line of fate, "and that is when you stepped off the path?"

"At each turn, each step I take outside, my heart breaks again, and again."

"And the pain of it, of those heartbreaks, is the badge of courage, or honor, that you carry."

"I can do it," he said quietly.

"You know you don't have to, you can let it all go, yet you carry it anyway."

"I know."

"Look at me, Zak."

Their eyes met.

"Are you aware that you are weeping?"

He reached his fingers to his face and felt the tears running down.

"No," he laughed in embarrassment. "I never cry."

"Boys and little girls cry, Zak, men and women weep, and always for good reason."

THE NIGHT COVERED THE LITTLE cabin on the side of the hill like one of Simone's quilts, and they made love, and sampled the stew, on and off, clear through till dawn. The candles burned down to flickering wicks. The early light reflected off the snow and brought that glow into their bed as they lay dozing, talking, and making love some more. Then, together, they plunged into a deep and satisfying sleep.

Zak awoke to eggs, ham, paprika, tomatoes, onions, peas, and sausage all baking in the oven, filling the little cabin with the most welcoming flavors. Wearing just a smock that fell to her thighs, Simone ladled her breakfast casserole out onto grilled homemade bread. He grabbed her long floral silk robe from the back of a chair and put it on.

She poured some cognac into their coffee, and before they got cleaned up they made love again, long and lazy and slow.

HE HELPED HER PACKAGE THE stew, sausage, and eggs for Corey, and before they got into her Dodge to return to town she took him in her arms.

"Better to do this here," she smiled, and kissed him long and hard. For several minutes they lingered over that kiss outside, she leaning against the door of her truck, the cold air in their lungs, snowflakes gently falling, their wet mouths still exploring, their final embrace trembling with want, a kiss to last forever, a kiss for remembering.

She dropped him at the hotel, but before they parted she said, "You know Zak, you and Corey have something in common."

"Yes?"

"Neither of you are guilty, Zak."

She blew him a kiss before leaving him there and continuing on to Corey Nightingale's, and then to Simone's Bar, formerly the Corkscrew Gulch Saloon, Scobey, Montana.

ZAK DROVE SLOWLY OUT OF town. From the comfortable old Pioneer Hotel, past the gray peculiar rectangles of the grain elevators by the ballfield and rodeo grounds, under the many shades of purple and blue that painted the early afternoon sky, and Zak took it all in.

Her perfume lingered on his clothes, her taste on his lips. If she had asked him to stay he would have, forever.

And Zachary Harper wept, quietly, happily almost, all the way back to Watford City, North Dakota.

XX

Hunting Season!" read the hand-scrawled sign, hoisted between two dinged-up thirty-foot drilling pipes that now straddled the entrance to the Watford City Park.

Where Zak and OK had parked Big Red had indeed formed a lane, like a major thoroughfare through the encampment as at least a dozen more RVs had established residence on either side.

When Zak and Tatonka pulled up alongside Big Red he saw Archer and OK just across the way standing in front of a beat-up old blue Mallard Goldeneye.

"Hey Zak, come meet the new neighbors!" Wellman called out.

"Me'n Skidder picked 'er up for next to nothing and hauled 'er down yesterday," Archer said. "She's a bit primitive compared to Big Red, but she'll do."

Archer pushed back the door and Zak poked his head inside. Old towels were pinned over the windows, muddy boots, dirty socks and underwear were strewn about, and the little sink was full of empties.

"Might get pretty ripe in there come spring," OK said, and with a nod of his head directed Zak's attention just a shade to his right.

"Hey, who's got a new truck?" Zak strolled over to a big dusty black Chevy half-ton snuggled up to the Mallard, the words "Up North Auto Parts," emblazoned on the sides.

"That's Skidder's," Archer explained. "Seems he ordered a case of universal joints for his outfit a while back, and the distributer wanted to meet the man in person who made such an order. Now get this, he hires Skiddy to be his regional distributer and he has this new truck. So Skiddy, on about his third day making deliveries, goes and pokes a hole in the rad of his old beast, I mean, on purpose. The truck literally caught fire while we were having beers over in New Town. So he just phones his boss up and says, my fuckin' truck is dead, you gotta send me down another right away! So his boss says, well what the fuck, here take this one!"

"Well, good for Skidder...I think!" Zak laughed.

Archer, Zak, and OK strolled back over to the Airstream.

Inside Big Red, Skidder was sitting at the table sipping a coffee and copying the names and numbers from all the business cards Zak had hauled in at the chamber meeting a week before onto a pad attached to a clipboard. Skidder had changed. He was wearing a fresh clean work shirt with the name "Skiddy" stitched in red on a white oval patch on his left breast. His huge mop of yellow hair had been cut back, like trimming a hedge, still only somewhat under control. He was wearing glasses.

"Here's one we should call right now," Skidder said, holding up a card. "'Selwyn Clerk's Handy Dandy Propane Service. They could start making the rounds tomorrow." And then he whistled, "Whoa nelly! Lookee here! Let's get this fucker dialed up right now!" he held up the next card. "'Jeffrey Bowles, Field Butcher, All Season Long!'"

"Christ, there must be twenty trucks' full of guys out huntin' as we speak!" Archer said.

"Yeah," OK said, catching on. "Jesus, there's probably an army of gun-totin' sons a bitches on their way here right now with enough game to feed and probably clothe the whole tribe!"

"Wow!" Zak jumped in. "Do you think that field dress butcher will know how to turn those pelts into anything useful?"

"Absolutely not, city boy," Skidder laughed, "but, well, lemme think…"

"Indians," OK said pensively.

"Indians?"

"Well, they've been into the tanning of hides for, oh, twenty thousand years?"

"Well good t'go, eh?" Skidder clinked his coffee cup to beer cans all around. "Leave Butcher Bowles to me and you go find some hide-tanning Apaches!"

"No Apaches around here, Skidder," OK said to laughs all around.

"No? Shit, I love the name Apache, just sounds bad-ass as all fuck."

Without realizing it, the men gathered that afternoon became the unspoken, unelected, committee of roughneck due diligence. And shit started getting done.

The next day, following Scott Becker's suggestion, Zak tapped on every door, window, and pickup truck, politely interrupted every conversation and, in just a few hours, had collected seventeen hundred dollars in cash that he then took to the bank. He walked out with a cashier's check for that amount that he then took to the Parks and Recreation Department at City Hall. They were stunned.

Before noon, Jeffrey Bowles was setting up a butcher shop in a big open space yet to be claimed by incoming roughnecks, and already had a few deer hanging upside-down. It seemed like every half hour another vehicle came rumbling into camp with antlers and hooves sticking up from the back and roughnecks hootin' and a-hollerin'. There were deer strapped across the hood or across the roof of every kind of jalopy; ring-necked pheasants, sharp-tailed grouse, Hungarian partridges, and prong-horn sheep galore. Bowles had some boys rig up an even bigger structure to hang the larger beasts on, and still they kept comin.' An eighteen-point elk, easily a thousand pounds of meat, was the prize of the lot.

Along about dawn OK shook Zak awake. He was off to meet some guys over at the Fort Berthold Indian Reserve, but needed a ride. Zak had a full day planned, so tossed OK the keys and went back to sleep.

That was the day Zak found Freddy Fifer back at his trailer. During the course of their visit, Zak returned his pistol and coffee pot.

"Jeezey Christey! I'd forgotten all about'm!"

During those precious weeks before winter's all hell broke loose, good old Freddy could be seen in a lawn chair by the small bonfire that sprang up then, or hobbling about on one crutch looking for folks to pass the time with. That bonfire was tended by squads of roughnecks on a twenty-four-hour basis, and became the center of social life for a while. If you wanted to find someone who wasn't in his trailer, that was a good place to look for him.

JON AND MARY ELLEN ARRIVED with what Mary Ellen called their Can of Ham; a small round two-wheel Mallard that did, indeed resemble a can of ham. Jon had rigged it up for winter and they pulled it into camp behind a new used '75 Chevy Caprice. Zak and OK guided them through the camp to a discreet little cubby-like elbow around behind a thicket of trailers to set up in. It took Mary Ellen one afternoon to find a job at the McKenzie Inn doing everything from making the beds to manning the office. She also took a lunch shift over at the PDQ Club three times a week, and they were good to go.

The countdown to Tiger Mike was under way, winter had yet to set in, but you could sure feel it, and taste it, on the wind. The temperature was now constantly below freezing with the mercury slowly going down and down.

"Ass-biting cold!" Skidder was already saying.

OK returned with Zak's Jeep and several Indians who cut a deal with Bowles and the rest of the committee. The Indians would take whatever hides the hunters didn't want and return with half of them turned into usable blankets of leather and fur. The other half they could keep and sell on their own. They even got Bowles making winter pemmican: thin strips of meat scored and put on tall handmade cottonwood racks, tall enough that critters, bugs, and roughnecks wouldn't disturb them, just down-wind from the bonfire, to dry. Within a week they had a ton of the stuff, enough for the Indians to take a third and everyone else to nibble on all winter long.

TWO NIGHTS BEFORE TIGER ARRIVED and everyone went back to work, a bunch of boys attached another handmade sign to the hunting season banner over the park's entrance:

"Ruff Neck Jam Bo Ree!"

As the meat was packaged up and doled out to their rightful claimants, those unclaimed goods would go toward a giant cook-off. When most roughneck hunters heard this, they gladly turned over a portion, if not all, of their kill to the cause.

Late that afternoon, two half-ton pickups were placed on either side of the little bonfire, their back gates open and facing in. Big speakers were hooked up to cassette decks blasting country music that could be heard throughout the town.

"Too bad we can't set up a rig platform right here and have a chain-throwin' contest, eh?" Skidder joked as he sipped his beer and reveled in the near pandemonium of the place. "Listen?"

One truck was blasting Johnny Paycheck's "Take This Job and Shove It!" while the other blared Waylon & Willie's "Good Hearted Woman." It was madness.

Archer had an idea. He went scouting around and came up with two cassettes of Merle Haggard's *Mama Tried* album, and using CB radios for ship-to-ship communication, counted down "Three, two, one, *push play!*"

When the music started they were still almost two seconds apart, which only whipped everyone into an even more berserker frenzy, one music system echoing the other. Soon there was a pile of cassettes in a box with people rummaging through them searching for duplicates. They roasted piles of sausage, fowl of many different varieties, and a whole deer, with some of the men from Fort Berthold hanging around to help out and enjoy the party.

Just as things were getting under way, Zak took the opportunity to pass the hard hat and collect enough for Bowles and even some more for the Parks and Recreation Department.

At one point, members of the executive roughneck committee of due diligence were standing several paces removed from the action when Scotty Becker strolled up and joined them.

"This is starting to take on a life of its own," he said, as everyone danced, and drank, and howled. There were a couple of fights.

Freddy, meanwhile, all hopped up on booze and painkillers, took a spill. A bunch of fellas picked him up and hauled him back to his trailer, and put him on his bunkbed where he pissed himself and passed out. They left him to sleep it off.

Meanwhile, roughnecks had formed a giant circle and took turns dancing drunkenly into the open space, each doing his own hilarious roughneck boogie. Zak even took a turn doing a

Mr. Natural truckin' swayback stuttering two-step from one side of the ring to the other.

"Some of the town folk have called the police," Scotty quipped as he and the boys sipped their beers and enjoyed the show. "Our one cop is over in Killdeer having his supper, he called me. Said I should call him back if we really need him. I suppose he could drive over when he's through and throw all you boys in a jail we don't have. I'm sure you're breaking a couple of hundred ordinances no one's bothered to look up before," he said as someone handed him a joint. "The church ladies want the National Guard called out," he laughed. "I wonder when they'll show up?"

"They better bring their own beer," Skidder replied.

"Not to worry, Scotty," Archer said, one long arm draped about Scotty's neck. "By supper time tomorrow you'll never know any of this ever happened."

The last time Zak saw Scotty Becker that night, he was dancing a drunken can-can with several other roughnecks in the center of the circle. Their arms over each other's shoulders, they turned left and kicked, then right and kicked, horribly out of sync with one another, kicking each other in the ass, in the shins. At this point, Smoke Denton cannonballed into the chorus line, knocking them all down like bowling pins. An enormous rumbling wrestling match ensued. As the body pile moved about the circle, Skidder pointed with a beer and a cig in the same hand and said, "Them's the Dallas Cowpies!"

By two p.m. the next day, those roughnecks had their little camp cleaned up like nothing ever happened.

TIGER MIKE DRILLING RIG NUMBER one was east of town. Turning north at Johnson's Corner, past the Four Bears Lodge on the Fort Berthold Reservation, then over the Missouri River Bridge, seven miles down the first dirt road on the right after the bridge, then a left where the road ended, then three more miles and bearing

right for another four miles, until they found an old abandoned farm. Up that road another couple of miles, there it was.

Jon Sandlak had been right. That new iron on Tiger Mike was raw, and rather than the usual two or three days to nipple up, it took three grueling weeks. The challenge, of course, was to get all the pieces to fit just right. They had to cut a hole here, refit a piece of pipe there, readjust a drop hole, and reroute the entire water system around. The wiring had to be invented almost from scratch.

Zak found it tremendously exciting to piece a giant rig together that had never drilled a hole. No one really knew how to put it together. Every rig, after all, has its own way to take it apart and put it back together. The way those two doghouses line up, for example. Until you try you don't know for sure if you do this one first, or the mud house, then you realize you forgot to prop up the canteen. All the while those gin trucks keep unloading new pieces of the puzzle.

Jesse knew Bomac inside and out, could do it in his sleep. But no one knew this rig, and no one would know if they had got 'er right until they fired 'er up and gave 'er a go.

It was Marty's crew now, with Jon working motors, Zak throwing chain, Tomlinson at worm's corner, and OK as derrickhand. The bottom line in the oil patch is that everyone wants to make as much money as they possibly can. So those crews on Tiger were the envy of everyone because Tiger Mike paid more than anyone else.

OK Wellman really excelled. He could handle a cutting torch and a welding machine, and could get any engine to start, skills that really came in handy. He had learned all that stuff farming as a teenager. Zak didn't even know where the dipstick was on those big diesels. He was a fast learner, though, and didn't need to be shown more than once what went where. But this was the rig of rigs. It was new and it was huge and clean and packed with power. Two giant Caterpillar engines, the biggest anyone had yet to see, which didn't leak twenty gallons of oil a day, as those Superiors did on Bomac 34. It sang and growled and purred sweet screaming loud music to roughneck ears.

On top of it all, everything wanted to freeze, and freeze hard. So they spent their time welding and hammering, cursing and filing, and after each tower the boys were dead on their feet.

The rig also had giant heaters capable of blasting four hundred degrees Fahrenheit. It was enough for now.

Once they spudded-in and those elevators swept upwards into the tower, they would glide back down already coated with hard thick ice, and the boys had to grab their blowtorches—six-foot propane wands that they kept running all the time—to blow the ice away long enough to get 'er done, each and every time.

A COUPLE OF WEEKS AFTER the Ruff Neck Jam Bo Ree, those Indians returned, and soon there were several roughnecks trodding through the ever-falling snow wrapped in heavy deerskin or elkskin hides, noshing on pemmican, which everyone called jerky. A padlocked box behind many a trailer was full of naturally frozen meats of many kinds. Archer and Skidder lined the inside of Baby Blue with pelts. OK and Zak used them on their beds and wore them about their shoulders, lined the walls, and lay them on the floors.

It was about then that Mary Ellen dropped in to bring Freddy a tub of soup she had made. She found him in shocking condition. The trailer stank of rotten flesh. Freddy was half out cold, stupid with painkillers and booze, with what looked like puss oozing out of his cast near his toes. When the docs came, they whisked him off to Williston, and as Zak and OK helped load him into the ambulance, the doc explained.

"He must have reinjured the leg and not known it, or decided not to do anything about it. The leg wanted to swell up in that cast and got badly infected. It seems like he might have, well, urinated or something. I can tell you though, they'll have to take the leg to save his life. He owes you one, little lady," he said, turning to Mary Ellen, who was in tears.

AND THEN IT TURNED *REALLY* cold.

Along about Thanksgiving, Rory and Hale Parker and the last of the old Bomac 34 crews pulled into camp, having TD'd, or touched down at last. They had a present for their old pals. Bomac had given everyone a turkey for the holiday. They must have had thirty of them in the back of Rory's pickup. Zak and OK took a half dozen to work, and all they had to do was set them in the open mouth of those giant four-hundred-degree heaters and those birds cooked up just fine. They ate them with their hands.

Between Thanksgiving and New Year's, six of the region's roughnecks were killed on the job. Two more got drunk, got lost in the mazelike labyrinths, where everything was snowy white and all landmarks were obliterated by the snow. They passed out and froze to death in their trucks. There were a hundred and ten serious injuries.

One roughneck at another location got caught up in the chain and the drawworks tore him in half.

On another rig, a driller crowned out. That kelly flew up to the top of the rig, hit the top so hard it busted free, and on the way down knocked the derrickhand from his perch, sending him a hundred and fifty feet to his death. Then the kelly, the blocks, the elevators, and the whole shebang crashed down to the floor and squashed big Danny Waller like a bug. They said he stood there watching it come down and just couldn't move.

"I guess that driller was feelin' 'quite rammy' that day," Skidder sighed when he heard the news.

A lot of guys had at least a touch of frostbite. OK, working up in the derricks exposed as he was, had it on the tip of his nose, a couple of his fingers, a couple of toes, and one of his ears.

"Jesus, that wind is evil as sin. You know up there the tower; she just sways. Doesn't look like it from down below but up there in that tower you can really feel it, how she sways. It's like you're a flea atop a giant flagpole."

"Ya," Marty sympathized, "it's like you gotta get your tower legs. Den when you get back down, you can still feel 'er swayin' when yer standin' still!"

As it got colder and colder, Zak and OK kept a big white paint bucket in the Airstream for middle-of-the-night pissing. They would use it, then open the back door, and toss it out. A yellow ice splash formed each night, but was soon hidden under the next layer of snow.

Across the way in Baby Blue, Archer and Skidder just cracked the front door long enough to relieve themselves through the opening. Consequently, there grew an enormous yellow mound of ice just to the left outside the door. It was waist high by Christmas. The inside of their camper looked like a cave-man's dwelling. Archer had taken to painting elaborate little stick figures on the deerskin; here one throwing chain, there one falling from a tower. Each time he heard of another casualty, it went up on the wall.

Skidder and Josh Corban, his boss, rented a tiny warehouse space west of town for shipping and receiving. They hired Jesse Lancaster to man the phone and keep the heaters blasting. It became a roughneck refugee parlor from the cold. There was one rule only—no beer—but Jesse had his ever-present Black Velvet handy under his desk for keeping his coffee the way he liked it.

At the Sagebrush between towers, OK and a new guy, Cowboy Bob, had a regular table. Bob had been chief ramrod at the Campbell Soup Ranch down in Wyoming, the largest ranch

in the state, or so he said. Bob had been riding the range on horseback all his life and had lost his pickup in a poker game. Guys remembered seeing him hitchhiking into Watford City with a saddle over his shoulder and a duffel bag under his arm. And now, even in the harsh winter, he would ride out into the snow checking on and servicing cricket wells. Religion and politics were all he cared about. Most steered clear of them both. Zak couldn't get enough. "The Cowboy Preacher," they called him.

"Look," OK would say under his breath to any newcomers to their round table, "If ol' Bob asks you if you ever heard of a feller named Rosmini, or the constitution of social justice, do us all a favor, and just say sure, and get up and go have yourself a trip to the bar."

"Enjoy the boom while it lasts," Bob would snicker when he had a few belts in him. "Down in Florida, President Carter has a test program where the government will write off a hundred percent of your costs switching to solar power, and they have a ninety-eight-percent success ratio of people asked to participate. Yes sir, your days are numbered in the oil patch, boys!"

The snow fell, and then it fell some more. The constant white was blinding. Wind chill was reaching twenty below and still sinking.

On Tiger they were working twelve and twenty-four. Marty was drillin' for Zak's crew, Archer had another, and Blackie had his. Twelve hours on and twenty-four off, and although it made more sense as the commute was becoming a genuinely life-threatening pain in the ass, it was also turning the men into zombies. Getting to work at seven p.m., off at seven a.m., then back at seven a.m. and off at seven p.m., the day/night schedule had some just dizzy and confused, and cranky as hell.

Tiger number one was the rig of rigs and on that first hole they went down 12,411 feet. Adam Nossiter over at the mayor's office said it might be the deepest well ever dug in North Dakota.

THE WEEK BEFORE CHRISTMAS, ZAK had just awoken from a nap. OK had been spending a lot of his off hours over in Arnegard with Julie and her mom, so Zak blissfully had Big Red to himself a lot of the time. As he stepped out of the Airstream with a mind to hit the Sagebrush for a bowl of chilli, he could hear the low rumble of a GM motor with a bad exhaust pipe. And there coming toward him down camp road in the snow was a big old 1967 deep purple Cadillac Eldorado that had seen better days.

The car came skidding to a stop right in front of him and from inside he could hear a female voice shrieking, "There he is!"

The door flew open and out leapt Jacqueline Loraine.

"Zachary Harper! You big beautiful bastard! There you are! I can't believe I found you!" she shouted with triumph, and flung herself into his arms and laid a kiss on him that was cold, wet, and sweet as corn.

Before he could speak she introduced her companion plump, adorably bedimpled gal pal, Erica Simpson.

Astonished, Zak invited them into the trailer. As they warmed up, they explained that they'd decided to spend at least part of Christmas break roaming around roughneck land looking for him. Their first stop had been the Sagebrush Bar and they were directed straight here!

"I kinda figured from your postcards that this would be the first place to look and if you were around someone would know where you were."

It was just a few moments before Archer Hansom, alerted by his nose for adventure, tapped on the door. When he saw Zak's company, his face brightened, "Well hello there!"

"Let's get some chilli!" Zak suggested and the four of them trooped off toward the bar. When Jacqueline took Zak's hand, Archer took Erica's.

After a quick bite and a round of delirious conversation and several beers, Zak and Jackie left Archer and Erica at the bar, and he gave Jackie the cook's tour of Watford City.

Of course she got straight As that semester, had written an anthropological paper on the people who worked the road crew with her that previous summer, which had gotten published in some rag that publishes that stuff, and had pinned his postcards to the wall over her homework bench, and talked herself out of breath getting him caught up.

When they passed an eyeglass store, she pulled him inside.

"Really, you must do something about these poor crooked frames," she mothered him, just a little. The saleswoman recommended FDA-approved safety glasses. They had thick black frames and were just ugly as hell. "We call those 'birth control' frames," she winked at Jackie as Zak tried them on. He ordered a pair of those for work, as well as a pair of brown square durable Z87s that weren't quite as ugly, then a pair of horn rims that actually looked good on him.

He explained that he had to be up for work at five thirty the next morning, so he had to turn in around eight or nine p.m. at the latest. They were back in the trailer by five, and rolled around in deerskin blankets on and off all night, talking, playing, laughing, and loving. Since Zak and Archer were working opposite shifts, it must have been eight or so in the morning when they heard Archer and Erica creep in and take OK's bed in the back, but Jackie and Zak barely noticed them, giggling like schoolkids under the skins.

The next eight days went by in a dream. Twenty-four hours between work towers gave them a few hours each day to talk and get to know one another. They hung out at the PDQ Club with OK and Julie and Lottie, and palled around a bit with Archer and Erica.

At one point Zak and Archer heard Erica say into Jackie's ear, "You were right! This place is just crawling with nothing but great guys!" The girls were treated like celebrities, and were flirted with outrageously.

Skidder plopped himself down in their midst. "Hey Jackie," Skidder asked with that wild good t'go twinkle in his eyes, "Do you know why Zakko there loves it so much here in the patch?"

"Why, Skiddy?"

"Because dope comes in five-gallon buckets, joints are thirty feet long, and there's a pusher on every rig!"

The boys groaned.

They ate fried chicken, liver and onions, and burgers at the Burger Ranch. Zak even made Jackie one his patented sandwiches for which he was becoming a bit of a legend: cheese, peanut butter, jelly, relish, A.1. sauce, baloney and, because she was special, he added a dash of Heinz 57.

"What in the world do you call this?" she asked, afraid to take that first bite.

"Condiment Surprise!" he smiled.

And just like everyone else, she loved it.

On days off Zak and Jackie drove Tatonka over to Minot to get away from everyone and be truly alone together, if only for a day and a night. They stayed at the cozy Riverside Lodge, heard some music at the Covered Wagon, and ate at the Dutch Mill. They told everyone they were married and that their rings had got lost in the mail.

WHEN JACKIE AND ERICA DROVE away, off to see the Crazy Horse Memorial going up near Mt. Rushmore, in the snow, Archer and Zak stood there in the morning gloom, and Archer Hansom turned to Zachary Harper and asked, "How did you meet her again?"

"None of your business," replied Zachary Harper.

But that night, the pitch black enveloped him and the wicked cold returned, and as he went through the motions out on the rig, even with, as Jesse used to say, that chain a-crackin' and those tongs a-breakin', the absence he felt brought him some of the longest and loneliest moments he had known in quite some time.

I want to see what she sees, I want her to see what I see, he thought. And the beat went on.

DAYLIGHTS TOWERS WERE PUNISHING, BUT the night towers were truly a struggle for survival.

Just getting from the Airstream to Marty's Bronco was hard to endure. Then from the Bronco into the bottom doghouse, then back outside and up those stairs, took a herculean effort. And those four-hundred-degree blasting furnaces only ensured they wouldn't die on the job.

Seventy below, someone said of the wind chill. No one wanted to hear it. With only the eyeballs and nostrils exposed, Zak could feel the sweat under his arms and in his crotch growing ice pellets on his flesh as he worked.

As the weeks wore on, it began to dawn on the roughnecks in the City Park that there might not be any but the one Tiger rig coming their way after all. Sure, there was plenty of work with other wildcatters in the area, but Tiger was the rig of choice, the carrot everyone wanted at the end of the stick, with its big new iron and high wages. The excitement and happy rumors had stopped. As a consequence, the population of the camp began to dwindle.

Day after day, night after night, Zak began to feel that the earth had slipped out of orbit, that it was turning and twirling so slowly, so randomly, dropping away from the sun. He thought that Gaia had lost her sense of purpose, was drifting aimlessly through space, that she no longer cared, that she had willfully fallen out of sequence and communion with the other planets. That she was twisting off.

At seven a.m. when he got off work, it was still dark. Nighttime arrived, impatiently, in the late afternoon. The night sky was so black and hostile and cold it wasn't hard to imagine that one of these rigs could actually puncture the heart of the world, and bleed her to death.

The cold can do strange things to a man.

IT WAS MID-FEBRUARY, THE WIND it was howlin' and the snow was outrageous, as the old song went, and as Marty and the boys were beating a path in the dark down rig road, Marty suddenly stopped the Bronco.

The rig was gone.

"Did you take a wrong turn?" OK asked. They all craned their necks in every direction, but the lights, the sound, weren't there, nothing!

Marty crept forward.

"De path in de snow is fresh," he said.

When they rounded a bend at the top of a small incline, his headlights picked up the rig in the distance, dark and silent as a tomb.

"Omigod," Tommy said quietly.

"Dere's deth here," Marty said just as quiet.

"Gas?" Zak thought out loud.

"Can't be sure," Jon answered.

They crept forward.

The giant rig looked like a huge ship sitting peacefully on the bottom of the ocean. They could hear the wind whistle through the girders.

"Dere's cars still here," Marty observed as they got close.

"Look!" Zak pointed up to the floor where flickering flashlights were whipping about.

"Well, it ain't gas!" Tommy said.

The five roughnecks leapt out of the Bronco and ran through the blistering cold to the bottom doghouse door and used their cigarette lighters to find their way in the dark.

They got dressed in shivering silence, firing their lighters every couple of seconds to see what they were doing.

"Marty, what the fuck is going on up there?" Zak asked as he hauled on his thermal overalls.

"Doze engines are all down, dat's alls I know! But I have a good idea."

They tumbled out of the doghouse door and made tracks to the stairs. They found a roughneck sitting on the bottom steps, not moving. Marty gave him a shake, he groaned.

"Grab dis guy and carry him up!" Marty gave the command. "He'll freeze to deth down here if we don't!"

It was Billy Knott, Rory's old motorman from Bomac 34, working on Archer Hansom's crew, who greeted them inside the doghouse.

"The diesel fuel has jelled and the engines are dead. The boys are out there trying to bleed the lines right now!"

"Fuck dat!" Marty said as he pulled his crescent wrench from his back pocket. "Wellm'n, Jonny, Billy, come witt me, Zak stay close, we'll need dose strong arms." And Marty grabbed a roll of duct tape as they marched out the door.

There were six or seven roughnecks all holding flashlights for the men crouched down dealing with those clogged fuel lines, and Marty said "Gimme three flashlights and tape'm together and make me a torch. You guys keep doin' what yer doin'!"

Marty hobbled past that big number one Cat, past the boys trying desperately to bleed the lines, and down a short flight of stairs to another motor house on its own skid just behind and below. They burst inside. Marty grabbed the new torch and, after a quick look around, said, "Dere it is!" and grabbed a thirty-pound iron bar with points at the end. He looked around again and found its extension and quickly fitted them together. He stood by the engine.

"Okay, we gotta do dis or we all gonna die in here! Listen! Dis is de rig's second trottle. Number one trottle is up at driller's station. We gonna start diss back up like an old Model T, by crankin' it with all the torque we can get. Dis ten feet of pipe will give us what we need, but it's gonna take a bunch a tries. We gonna use Jesse's system! To stay strong we get two guys try and crank it, after dey try two or tree times den two more guys tap'm on de back and take obber, diss is gonna work but we don't have long! Ready?"

"Yeah!"

Marty jammed that cheater bar into its rightful spot, then told OK and Jon to grab that bar as he went and manned the starter.

"Now!" Marty screamed, and the two men gave it everything. It moved, but not much.

"We gotta hear it click! Again!" They hit it again. Nothing. After two more times, Zak and Billy took a turn, then Tommy and Jon, then OK and Zak. A little panic was setting in and the boys got mad, and when they got mad the adrenaline gave them extra strength. Jon and Billy took over, and as soon as Marty heard that life-saving click, he hit the starter, hit the gas, the engine roared then died, and the torque kicked back, sending Jon and Billy flying!

Zak aimed the flashlight, and OK and Zak found the cheater bar, put it back in, and the two roughnecks cranked that son of a bitch with all their might.

Click!

Starter! Throttle! Boom! That big engine growled, then sputtered, then caught, and roared back to life!

The boys up on the floor cheered.

Diesel went pumping through those freshly bled lines and Tiger Mike rig number one thundered out in the black frozen prairie night. Soon the lights were back, and heat was pouring out onto the floor and into the doghouses.

It was Archer's crew they were there to relieve, and Archer was exhausted.

"The rig shut down in stages and we couldn't tell what the hell it was," he said over smokes in the top doghouse after he and Marty worked together to get 'er turning to the right again, circulating to maintain the hole.

"That was some Indian trick, Marty," Jon said with admiration.

"I nebber seen diesel fuel gel like dat before. But I heard about it," Marty said.

"I didn't think it was possible," Zak said.

"Normbally it ain't," Marty said. "But, well, you seen anyting resemblin' normbal out here, Zakko?"

Zachary Harper just shook his head.

"You never know in the oil patch," smiled OK Wellman.

Marty led his men back out onto the floor and the roughnecks took their stations.

And the cold, and the night, and the tower continued.

ONE YEAR LATER

EPILOGUE

What was it Skidder MacIntyre had said? Something like, *Save up your pay and when that brutal Dakota/ Montana winter hits, head'm on down to Steamboat Springs, Colorado, and stake out a place to burrow in for the season.* Zak thought he might even have seen good old Skiddy thunder past him on the highway riding one of those newfangled Harley-Davidsons, the one everybody loved to hate, with a belt drive instead of a chain. *I bet old Skidder got it for nothin',* he chuckled to himself.

William Zachary Harper settled onto a barstool at the Calliope Saloon and surveyed the bottles on the top shelf. Irish whiskey. Good Irish whiskey. Damn. He ordered a glass, neat.

The ride down from oil patch country had been pleasant, but for the cast on his left foot where Tommy Tomlinson had dropped a collar sub that busted the steel toe out of his boot, cracked the bone in the top of his foot, and broke his big toe. Boy it hurt. He shuddered to imagine young Marty, tucking those broken toes under the rest and pulling on those socks and shoes. Zak had made it through the rest of the round trip though, before twisting off for the season.

Once in Steamboat, he had found a group house full of bartenders and other food-service types, ski slope operators. He bought himself some new clothes. The guys back at the house even told him they could find work for him. He said he would wait until he got his cast off, but really, he just wanted to rest, to think, to crawl back into his own skin, to be left alone, to think on his next move.

The whiskey didn't burn much after the first couple of sips, and warmed his blood. All around him sat tourists, city types, locals, and a few cowboys. Skidder had been right, it was a pretty cool spot. Everyone was laid back, not too showy, not as many stuck-ups here as you might find in the more resort-like towns built only for millionaires and their wealthy brats.

A year or more after starting out, good old Skidder had himself quite a business, four trucks and ten guys scouring the region emanating from Watford. Yes, he and Josh Corban made quite a team. Josh let Skidder do his thing, and he said Skiddy saved his business.

Tiger Mike Davis went broke, and sold that big beautiful rig right out from under everyone for scrap metal, just when they had all the kinks ironed, hammered, and welded out of 'er.

Freddy Fifer shot himself through the heart with a Colt .45 long-barrel revolver. It was a classic. They called it the "peace-maker." It was the gun that won the West.

Before leaving the patch, Zak and Marty stood witness to the marriage of Jonathan T. Sandlak and the lovely Mary Ellen Swayzee, with OK Wellman, minister by mail of the Universal Church of Man, presiding.

As William Zachary Harper sat at the Calliope Bar, Steamboat Springs, Colorado, lost in reflection, odd familiar voices broke in.

"Oh Cy, those people at the Bison Gallery loved your work! I'm so happy for you!" a tall, blue-eyed blonde said enthusiastically as the two entered the restaurant bar. The other person was an even taller, handsome man who held her gently by the arm as they kicked the snow off their boots and removed their gloves, their cheeks rosy with the sun and the wet and the cold.

Zak froze in his seat.

Samantha Pennington, or Penny as she liked to be called, and Charles Winston Young, or Cy, also known as The Mad Painter, took barstools just a few seats down from where Zachary Harper was sitting and ordered Irish coffees.

"Well," Cy rubbed some snowflakes out of his hair. "We never found Willy, but at least I got a gallery showing out of this trip."

Zak had had a small media company on the side along with his banking job in his pre-roughnecking days, and these two were daily fixtures in his Georgetown rowhouse. Penny, among others, even rented rooms from him for a while. What would he say when they saw him? They had been such great and close friends. How could he even open his mouth to begin to tell them who he was, what he had become?

"Oh Cy, I can't believe I dragged you all the way out here for this. I'm so sorry. Thank God for the Bison Gallery!"

"Don't be hard on yourself, Penny, it was kind of a fools' errand, I'll admit, thinking we could just drive out here, walk into a bar, and expect someone to just say, oh here he is. But hey, Penny, stranger things have happened."

"Oh I know. But I was so sure. Gillette gave me the creeps, and Williston? It was like slipping back in time."

"Well, hey, we got to see Devil's Tower, Mt. Rushmore, I thought Rapid City was the real deal."

"Yeah, I guess. But damn, I was so sure," she sighed.

The lump in Zak's throat was growing with each familiar inflection in their voices. He wanted to leap out of his seat, scream, *Here I am! You won't believe where I've been!* But then what would he say?

They finished their drinks and paid up. As they got off their barstools and zipped up their brightly colored down jackets, Zak took a chance and briefly looked them both in the eye. Penny smiled. He smiled. Cy gave him a friendly nod, and then they turned and walked out the door.

In the mirror behind the bar, William Zachary Harper saw a man with longish salt and pepper hair, wearing a bandana and horn-rimmed glasses, with weathered skin, and a bit of a beard.

They smiled at one another.

ACKNOWLEDGMENTS

The writing of *Roughnecks* took place over a thirty-three-year span. In the course of all that time there have been scores of readers, editors, researchers, roughnecks from all walks of life, storytellers, doctors, park rangers, wildcatters, and many more very dear and patient friends; people whose largest contribution was simple encouragement, which, at times, you must know, is the greatest contribution of all.

Here are but a few:

Rose Solari, Joanna Biggar, Lisa Grey, Ken Butcher, John Freeburn, William Lawrence, Coleman Brewer, George Sterling, Kelly and Janice Kulseth, Darrel Fortner, Ted Husted, the forest rangers at the Theodore Roosevelt National Park, James E. Fox of the South Dakota School of Mines and Technology, J.B. Hoffman, Alan Sonneman, Nita Congress, Steve Caporaletti, Loraine Vahey, Vincent S. Dicks, Robert E. Kibler, Russ Hanson, ShaunAnne Tangney, Mary Von Drehle, Ron Baker, John F. Patterson, Richard Peabody, Miles David Moore, Doug Hale, Murray Freeburn, Zachary Patterson, Patty Hankins, Joe and

Betty Tate, the Watford City Chamber of Commerce, Steven Waxman, Randy Stanard, and Ron Kidd.

An excerpt of *Roughnecks* appeared in *Gargoyle* 58.